Getting to the Hart of It

A Complicated Romance

Stephanie Price Buchanan

Getting to the Hart of It

Edited by Stanley O. Williford

Cover Design by Jabb Productions, Inc, Los Angeles, CA

ISBN 9780692024805

To all those with a Dream...Take a chance, reach for the sky,
You can make it happen!

Acknowledgments

Along this book writing journey, I've encountered many people who have helped me with their advice, comments and love. Two readers were with me from the beginning sentence, my sister Cheryl Price, who cheered me along the way and who has always said, I had a book in me. Also, to one of my best girlfriends, Barbara Byndon, who demanded her chapters if I took too long to finish them. Many thanks to them both for keeping me motivated and focused, for the time it took me to complete this story. Thanks for your support girls, love you!

A special thank you to my mom, Dr. Betty Price for reading it quickly and loving it. I could not have finished this process without your love, help and support of me always. My mom passed the book on to her spiritual daughter, Kimberla Lawson Roby who read it and gave me feedback. It didn't hurt that Kimberla is a New York Times Bestselling author and she allowed me to pick her brain on every possible writing topic. Your help was amazing and incredible, thank you so much!

Lots of love and hugs to my husband Danon for his support. Once he realized I was really writing this novel, he shared his vast knowledge of publishing and marketing, which was awesome. Thanks for all your love & encouragement!

To Stanley Williford, the coolest and most awesome editor. Thanks for working with me through this process to make the book read smoothly and flow perfectly. In addition, he was a fan of the story which was simply icing on the cake. You rock Stan!

A shout out to my friend and fellow author Angela Yarborough, who was incredibly encouraging along the way and shared all of her knowledge, as well as emailing me articles and buying me magazines that would help me. To Barbara and James Byndon of JABB Productions, Inc., for my book cover design and my postcards, which I love...a million thanks for your support and love.

The support of my family, The Price family was amazing as I prepared for my release and launch date. Thank you for sharing my book with friends, tweeting, facebooking and instagraming it, you are the best – my brother Frederick, sister-in-law Angel, brother-in-law Mike, and nieces Adrian, Nicole and Carrie. Love to my sister Angela who plans on single handedly getting me a book deal in the near future. And to my dad, Frederick K.C. Price, a great teacher, author and most of all, father.

To my in-laws, Winford and Bernadine who are huge supporters and my writing twin cousin Dawn Buchanan...you've got next! To my BFF Tamara Taylor for making me do my first book reading to her and then reading the rest of it in light speed! And to Rebecca Lynch, your excitement and encouragement has been overwhelming on every level! Shout outs to Raquel Watts, Kim Smith and Nina Tunzi for cheering me on!

To my encouraging friends, my readers who have shared with me their love for the story and my FB followers, thank you sooo much! You know who you are and I appreciate you.

Additional love & appreciation to my Maryland, Louisiana and Texas sister friends & fam; Dr. Dee Dee Freeman, Brelyn Freeman, Carol Rowe and Kermeshea Hilliard Evans. To the women of CCC, especially Women Who Care, thank you for being a part of my life. You're the best!

Finally, to my best work to date, Tyler, Justin and Sydney…mommy loves you!

1 The Beginning

When I first saw Josh Hart I was rushing back to my car. With my low trust factor for men, I rarely date and, really, hardly ever take the time to notice them. But in my rush to leave the Roosevelt Elementary and Middle School, where I had just dropped off my 10-year-old son Chris, I did a double-take at the man I had never seen before. He was talking animatedly to a group of moms by the school's front entrance.

He appeared to be in great shape, with toned legs and arms, and a natural body language that exuded confidence. He wore light blue Nike shorts with a white Nike tee, which set off his mocha-colored skin perfectly. The moms surrounding him were in deep-listen, or more properly, deep-looking, as he held center stage. One lone dad was clearly not impressed and stood a ways off, listening with his arms folded.

I chuckled at the scene and smiled as I walked away. I figured Mr. Personal Trainer must be the new gym teacher and sooner or later Chris would encounter him in class. It was only the second week of school and there were several new teachers, so I knew I would get a better look at him later. For now, I shrug it off. He was probably married or already attached, and who knew what kind of person he was. Besides I'm not looking. Well, I am looking, but only in the visual sense.

As I make my way to work at the Sunset Park Community Center, I try to quickly apply some light makeup and lip gloss at each stoplight. I don't want to be late. The new soccer coach for kids, ages 8 to 14, is joining the staff this morning and I want to get in early already made up, with a pot of coffee brewing.

Usually my co-worker and best girlfriend Sharon brews the coffee while hanging over my desk, as I finish applying my eye shadow. On this day, we decide to look ultra professional and basically be waiting with a pot of coffee, with his schedule printed and on his desk and five dollars each just in case he prefers Starbucks.

As I whip into my park at the community center, I notice a black Audi pull in the parking lot. The car comes to a crawl to look at the community center sign, something that happens frequently. Lots of people get us mixed up with the YMCA, which is about three blocks over so hurriedly, I grab all my stuff – purse, briefcase, heels and sweater – and hustle into the Center. I notice the Audi is parked directly across from me facing the street. I wonder whether it is the new coach and make a mad dash for my cubicle before he shows up.

"Well it's about time, Alicia." It's Sharon coming up behind me.

"I know, I know, Chris forgot to bring his handbook home last week so I had to get out the car. . . ."

"You poor thing," she interrupts

"I know, right? . . . my face was not finished and my dress wasn't zipped!"

Sharon chuckles at the image. "I had Chris zip me up and then ran into that office to ask the horrible new school secretary for a handbook. Took her 15 minutes just to find it and I had to pay $10!"

"The tough life of a mommy," she says, teasing, and I agree. I tell her I believe the new coach may have pulled in the parking lot behind me but I was unsure and didn't stop to look.

"No worries," she says, "I have printed out the schedule for you and laid it on his desk so we are good to go."

"Thank you so much!" I say, giving her a little hug. Sharon and I are co-managers. We take care of the coaches, instructors and teachers. She takes care of toddlers to 7-year-olds and I cover the 8 to 14-year-olds. We work Tuesday through Friday and then there's a weekend staff that works Saturday to Monday. Our Community Center has classes and programs for soccer, softball and basketball in our wing of the facility and each of us has various coaches we report to.

It is really a fun job, and a great environment to work in. We have both been at the center for almost six years and have become the best of friends. Sharon is already a grandma at the young age of 45. Because of this, she thinks she's the boss of me since I'm only 37 with a 10 year old. She does have a lot of wisdom though, so sometimes I actually do let her mother me.

"So did you get a chance to Google Mr. Joshua Hart this morning?" I ask.

"Yes I did, Alicia. He is from the San Diego area, born and raised. He has been teaching soccer since right out of college. Mostly elementary school P.E. coaching, one high school job and some summer camp programs. There was no image, but he is just in his early 30s, kind of a baby."

"Well, yeah compared to 70-year-old Coach Dennis, everyone is a baby," I say, stifling a laugh, but Sharon actually laughs, remembering Coach Dennis and all the naps he took.

"Well he sounds very nice to me. I also checked his incoming paperwork and he has a son that's 10 just like Chris, who will be joining the team. It also says he is single" – and she raises her eyebrows – "and he will be living close by in Culver City, just like you and Chris."

"Wow, you didn't miss much did you, detective?"

"Nope, I didn't miss much at all. I had to get the four-one-one for you because although you wanted to know how he sized up as a boss, I wanted to know how he sized up as a potential suitor for you."

"Seriously, Sharon?"

"Umm, yeah."

Sarah the receptionist let out a whistle. She is the funniest 65-year-old grandmother of fifteen you could ever meet. Sarah has not grayed so she doesn't look her age, and with her red hair and pale skin she is a mature beauty who loves a compliment.

"Real looker at 12 o'clock, ladies," Sarah announces.

Myself, Sharon, Harvey the janitor, Jill the part-time clerk and Lance the seniors coordinator all jam close to the window by my desk.

"People, back away from my desk! This is my new boss coming in and I wanna make a good impression," I jest.

"Well, he's already made an impression on me," Jill says.

"If I was 30 years younger I would totally go for him," says Sarah.

But Sharon sounds the voice of authority, saying: "I've already earmarked him for Alicia so back off everybody!"

"Omg, really?" I say.

Harvey and Lance both nod their heads in agreement with Sharon and Lance adds: "Younger guys do like older women, Alicia."

"Lance, I'm not that much older than him! Besides I'm no cougar searching for younger men."

"The point is, you could be, Alicia."

I giggle. "Wow, what are you 20, young man? I'm calling your mother," I say, and everyone laughs.

"I think you should totally go for him, Alicia. He and his legs look really nice," Jill says. Then she says words in her language that we do not understand.

"Can I be professional, you guys? You are really making this hard for me," I say.

"I bet he has rock-hard abs, too," says Jill. She is a 38-year-old Cuban wife and mother who clerks three days a week at the center. Her lawyer husband takes care of everything so she basically works for fun.

"I bet you're right, Jill," comments Sarah.

"Quiet you guys," I say in nervous laughter. And then I make everyone go back to their stations.

I look closer, and realize I've already seen Joshua Hart. He's the nice-looking man the moms were ogling over at Roosevelt this morning. And Jill's probably right – rock-hard abs. He has on sexy sunglasses and carries a backpack, as well as an old rolling briefcase. I figure they must contain his files and contacts. Nike running shoes top off his outfit as he stops to check his cell before getting to the front door.

I get a closer look at why the moms in the parking lot were hanging on his every word. As he starts to open the door to the

center, I take a deep breath. In mere seconds I have to greet him
and introduce myself. I am going to be spending many hours a
day with him.

I start to break out in a cold mini sweat. How am I going to
work with this guy? I really have to get it together. *Breathe, Alicia*,
I tell myself.

"Good morning, sir," chimes Sarah at the front desk.
Everyone else has gone back to their areas, although they are all
in position to sneak looks at the new coach.

"Good morning. My name is Josh Hart and I'm the new
soccer coach."

"Yes, Mr. Hart, we've been expecting you. Welcome to
Sunset Park Community Center. My name is Sarah Davis and let
me introduce you to our staff."

She starts to introduce him to everyone and as she turns
toward us we stand. Sharon looks at me from her cubicle and
whispers, "He is soooo cute! Turn up the charm, Missy."

Why is my heart starting to beat fast? I inhale and start to feel
myself calm down.

"And this is your personal assistant as well as our office
manager, Alicia Parsons. I will leave you in her capable hands."
Then Sarah winks at me. My co-workers are too much.

"Good morning, Ms. Parsons, very nice to meet you," he
says, as he reaches out to shake my hand.

"Thank you. It's nice to meet you, too, Mr. Hart." *Man, it
really is nice.* But I keep that thought to myself.

"Okay, let me stop you there. Please call me Josh or Coach.
Mr. Hart is my father."

I smile. "Will do, Coach. And please call me Alicia, all my friends do." Then he smiles.

"Well let's get you settled. Your office is right over here and we can dive right in."

"Sounds good." Then he turns around and says to everyone, "So nice to meet you all. Thank you for the warm welcome and I am really looking forward to being a part of the team here."

Everyone says you're welcome and then he goes into the office. I sneak a look at Sharon and she gives me thumbs ups and fist pumps. I shoo her off and turn back to his office with my most professional face.

I melt on the inside. *How in the world am I going to work with this man?*

Stephanie Price Buchanan

2 Miniature Golf

Life at the Center took on a whole new meaning with Josh Hart in the building. The energy was a bit higher and my need to thoroughly check out my clothes the night before became a must. The staff was extra bubbly around him, which was hilarious to watch, and he of course had a way with everyone. Sarah was extra friendly when he would arrive in the mornings. He would stop by and talk to her about her hair.

"Oh Sarah, I love your hairstyle today," he'd say.

Sarah would touch her hair and say "really," as she batted her eyelashes.

"Absolutely," he'd say and she would smile this megawatt smile at him and he'd give her a bigger smile right back.

He and Harvey would talk cars. Harvey has repaired several Chevys in his garage, and it appears Josh collected model Chevys as a child as well as built replicas of them as a teen. He seemed to bond with everyone, including Sharon. They would discuss the issues of the day – current events, past events and even gardening.

"My mom kept a beautiful garden," he told her. "No kidding." And then he proceeded to pull out his phone and show her photos. I would be standing by my cubicle giggling, while noting his wow factor: so likable, so charming. There's got to be a catch to this Josh Hart, I thought.

I finally cleared my throat on this day in early September for the third time. I had team charts, statistics from last year and the boys' schedule all ready to discuss.

"Okay, Sharon, I need to see the coach now," I say to both of them.

"Oh, sorry, Alicia, it was my fault," Coach apologized. "Sharon was telling me how much her garden looks like my mom's."

"Oh really," I say.

"Alicia, it is beautiful! His parents have lived in Paris for the past eight years and her rose garden . . . no words," she says, super excited, so I grin.

"Well that sounds just peachy keen, you two, but the season starts in just one more week and we've got to be ready. Let's go, Coach."

"Yes ma'am. Guess that's why she's in charge," he says to Sharon.

"You better believe it. Don't let that innocent face fool ya, she is no joke," Sharon adds.

"Umm hello, I'm standing right here," I say, trying not to laugh because this is quite comical to me.

"Josh Hart reporting for duty," he says, as he passes me to go in his office.

Sharon raises her eyebrows and mouths "go get 'em, girl" to me.

I shake my head "no" while giving her raised eyebrows and a little laugh as I walk into his office.

"Sorry about all that," he says. "It's just that everyone here is so friendly. Like family, and in San Diego I had a boss that would shut us down at the first sign of anyone having an enjoyable conversation."

"Really? Sorry to hear that. But glad things are going well for you here."

"Well you're a great boss to us all."

"Well, you're actually *my* boss," I say smiling. "When I worked my business full-time I wanted to treat my staff as I would want to be treated. You spend half of the hours you're awake with your co-workers, sometimes more. It should be a place you like to be. So when I joined the Center I started treating this staff the same. We really are like family." I paused and then go on, "and speaking of family, did you also live in Paris for a while?"

"Oh no, my parents went there on a 40th anniversary trip, and my mom fell in love with the place. Somehow she convinced my dad to move there upon retirement and they've been there about eight years.

"Wow," I say, "that's my dream trip. Have you been?"

"I have. I helped them move and then I try to visit at least once a year. It really is beautiful. You should come with us one time," he says nonchalantly as he signs on his computer. You and Chris. Derek would love that."

And would you love it too? I wonder.

"Well maybe one time we will," I say instead.

As we move on to the business at hand I keep replaying his statement in my head and wondering if he would say that to anyone else. Am I special? Or would I just be a tag-along so I could watch the boys while he hangs out with his French friends?

Later at lunch I tell Sharon what he said to me.

"Oh my gosh, he wants to take you to Paris! How romantic is that?"

"I did not say he wants to take me to Paris, he just threw it out there like it was Phoenix or something. I was thinking would he say this to any friend. He is such a character."

"Yeah, a cute single character with no girlfriend in sight!"

"Can you dial down the matchmaking for one conversation, please?"

"Not really, Miss-invited-to-Paris!" We both crack up.

In the evening, I think about our conversation and go online to look at the sights in Paris. Oh how I want to see the Eiffel Tower, wearing my beret, and sit at a cafe eating a croissant and drinking an espresso, even though I don't care for the taste of them. Just then Chris pulls me out of my dream sequence.

"Mom. Mom. Mom!"

"Oh sorry, yes, Chris," I say yelling over the banister to him.

"I called you a million times." *Guess I was really daydreaming.* "Derek wants to know if I can go to the miniature golf place this weekend. He said his dad said maybe the four of us can go if it's okay with you." I find myself smiling like crazy. Is this a date? Does my boss, the hot coach want to go on a double-play date? I find myself a little giddy. Here we are just barely a month into his job and we are going to hang out. I don't think the Center has rules about these kinds of things. It's more like a parent chaperone thing anyway.

"Mom!! He's on the phone. Can I say yes, please?"

"Yes, we can go. Tell him I'll talk to his dad about it tomorrow," I yell downstairs.

The next day Josh somehow beats me to the office. I bring in the Starbucks and say, "Give me a minute and we can continue on with our scheduling."

"Sure, by the way, I heard the boys made a plan for this weekend and we are the chaperones," he says smiling.

"Uh, yes, I heard that as well. I was going to confirm with you that it's definite. Miniature golf right?"

"Yes, we'll meet you for golf first and then Johnny Rockets. Friday night at 7 sound okay?"

"Yes, sounds fun."

"Great," he says, sounding genuinely excited.

I go back to put away my purse and turn on my computer and my heart is beating a mile a minute. *It's for the kids, Alicia, calm down, this is not about you. At least, we're driving separately so we won't have that car ride talk to worry about. Then again I could talk team stats or averages. Yes, I could and bore the crap outta him.*

After lunch I call my sister Trina to tell her about my weekend. She already knows about Josh and has been telling me to ask him out, as if I would make a first move. I tell her it's a play date for the kids. She says it *is* a date, and that I should dress as such.

"But it's really for the kids" I say again.

"Well, the kids are big, sis. He could have taken the boys himself to do these activities. Including you in the plan is about him. So doubt it all you want. He is interested and so are you. So what are you wearing?"

"Well, I was thinking jeans and my black boots. Casual but not too casual. What do you think?"

"Sounds like a good plan. And what top? I think cleavage is in order for this outing. Not a lot since the kids are there, but just enough so when you bend down to look at the top of your golf club he can see down your blouse."

"Trina! You sound just like Sharon. You two are outta control," I say laughing. "I am wearing a moderately cut blouse, thank you very much."

"We're just trying to help you out," she says, and we both laugh.

"Just remember," she says seriously. "It is an opportunity to connect with a really great guy who's a really great dad."

"Okay, I agree it is an opportunity. And maybe I can get the scoop on the mom."

"Please do. I don't know what she was thinking, but I wouldn't have let a good man like that outta my sight." I agree with her and we chat some more before I get back to work.

As the week drudged ahead it seems it took a year for Friday to arrive. As I prepared to leave for the day, Sharon came over.

"Alicia, I hope you have a fantastic time tonight," she says. "The fact that your first date is with your kids makes it even more sweet as far as I'm concerned," and she reaches out to hug me. I hug her back.

"Thanks, Sharon. I will. Chris is so excited so I get to appear calm, although I'm excited too."

"Glad you're excited, doll. Call me," and she walks away waving.

I pack up and dial into Josh's office. "Hey boss, I'm heading out."

"You beat me," he says. "I'm packing up now. See you at 7 then."

"Yes, at 7."

I drive home grinning and throw on some old Mariah Carey, blasting her classic hit "Fantasy," to pick up Chris so we can get ready for our double date.

Chris and I arrive at the Bridge about 6:45 p.m. We park and walk to the miniature golf course. As we get closer, Chris takes off running as he spots Derek.

"Hey, Derek! Hey, Coach Josh!" He yells and waves to announce we have arrived.

I did look cute-casual in my black jeans, my H&M scoop neck top, a light jacket and my black flat Kenneth Cole boots. I wore my hair in a side ponytail with soft bangs. But Josh was a vision. Maybe it's the megawatt perfect teeth and smile, or maybe it's the hot body. And must he wear shorts all the time? He had on a plain black tee with his shorts and a black cap, but he was perfect. Now granted I don't get out much, and I certainly don't have many dates. But this guy is just nice, and nice to be around. Chris is usually my date, or I don't take one if he's not old enough to go to wherever I'm invited. I like to flirt a little and meet guys, but dating not so much. So maybe he looks extra good to me because this is not something I normally do, but either way I decided he's *fine,* as in the old-school word for hot.

"Hey, Derek," Chris says and they high-five each other.

"Hey, Alicia."

"Hey Coach," I say.

"Okay. For tonight, I'm just Josh to you."

"Okay, I say," with this giant grin I can't quite get rid of. *Cut it out, Alicia. Just act natural.*

"You guys been waiting long?" I ask Derek.

"No, Ms. Parsons, just a few minutes. Thank you for meeting us tonight. My dad said it would be more fun if we all came out, so let's go have fun!"

"Yeah!" Chris exclaims. I smile and try not to blush. Basically, Derek just told me his dad suggested I come.

Maybe Trina and Sharon are right. He may really like me.

I look at Josh and wonder if I see him blushing as he says, "Okay guys, let's get in here and see who's gonna win." The boys cheer and off we go.

We have a blast. The boys are having so much fun, and I am enjoying being with them as much as being with Josh.

What an awesome little team we make!

We are laughing and having a ball and at the end of the course we decide to get something to drink. While Josh is ordering, we are standing off to the side and the cashier says, "What a beautiful family you have." He turns to look at me to see if I've heard her, and since I did I raise my eyebrows as if to say "She could be right." He says to the lady, "Well thank you very much," and then looks back at me and gives me a smile that has my heart doing a double flip.

Geesh, does this guy have a spell over me or what!

"Well guys, should we pack it in and go over to Johnny Rockets for burgers?" Josh asks. The boys do not agree.

"Ahh, Dad, can we play one more round, please?" Derek pleads. And then Chris joins him. "Yeah, please, Coach."

He looks over at me again, "Well, Mom, what do you think?" and I smile, "Okay, one more game, but you guys go ahead. I'm going to sit here and cheer."

"Okay, thanks, Mom. Let's go, Derek!" And they head over to the start of the course.

"You're just going to abandon me like this?" Josh asks.

"Boys-only round," I say.

"Ahhh!" he mock-complains and heads over to pay for the game. I pull out my phone to see who's played me in Words With Friends and Scramble With Friends as I am addicted to both. A few minutes later I look up and he's headed my way. I almost panic. Why isn't he starting the game? I see the boys looking happy and playing around, but Josh is heading toward me. I feel the heat in my face and I'm so glad I'm more Caramel than Vanilla latte, because the red would be rushing to my face. It was bad enough there was a small sweat starting at my hairline. Nervous energy! It gets me every time, and it's so embarrassing.

"Well what's going on?" I ask, trying to distract him from the growing line of sweat I wasn't quite able to pat down.

"I told the boys to play. I told 'em parents like to sit sometimes."

"Oh I see," and I reach down to close out my phone game.

"Is that Words?"

"Yes, it is. I was just about to look for a space so I can finish my sister off. I'm winning big," I say.

"Oh, well then you probably can't handle me. I come with the wins every time!"

"Oh really, is that a challenge?"

"It certainly is," he says laughing. So we exchange gamer names.

We sit in the quiet for a moment and I take it all in.

I'm feeling happy, Josh seems happy and the boys are very happy. The lady said we were a beautiful family. I could be a mom to two boys. It would be Chris times two and I could do that easily.

"What are you thinking about, Alicia?" Josh asks, interrupting my thoughts. I try not to blush because I am after all thinking of him and me and our boys.

"Just about how much fun this is . . . I've never even been to this place."

"How have you managed that? It seems Derek has dragged me here every weekend since we've been in town," he says, and I give a slight laugh.

"So are you enjoying the beautiful city of Los Angeles?" I ask, so I'm not just staring into his eyes.

"I really do like it here – the school, the parents, my neighborhood, the Center and working with you."

I feel the heat rise to my cheeks from his warm and toasty comment.

"Well, I'm glad you're finding our lovely city, school and Center welcoming," I say. Then I decide to venture out . . . "so what made you leave San Diego after all these years?"

He looks at me, trying to decide, it seems, if he wants to divulge the information.

"Well, it's kind of a long story, but I'll condense it." He shifts a bit in his seat and for the first time he seems a tad uncomfortable.

About 11 years ago I met Derek's mother, Eleanor, at San Diego State. I was always very focused on school and higher learning so I dated casually only, nothing serious. Then one day I met her at the track. She was on the girls long distance team and I was training with my physical education program. Instantly, we made a connection and I invited her out to lunch that next day. I know this sounds weird coming from a guy, but literally it was love at first sight." I look at him like ahhh and I guess he notices.

He says: "Kind of corny I know."

"I like corny," I say with a dreamy look in my eyes.

Who falls in love at first sight? He's so cute, but I need to hear the rest of this story.

He half laughs at my comment.

"Okay, so from then on we were a serious item. My parents were concerned because they thought I was losing focus, especially my mom. I didn't lose focus, I just fell in love and couldn't do anything without her," he says and chuckles. "I guess this happens to us guys who fall in love for the first time at 22."

Funny, his story is similar to mine, I was just younger when the love bug hit me.

"So we started seeing each other less in front of my parents, but more away from them. I was spending all my time at her place and after about a year or so she tells me she's pregnant. Of course, I'm shocked because I'm thinking we used protection. But I was stupid, just a stupid kid doing grown-up things. Didn't know anything and we had a baby on the way. We were both about to graduate so at least we got our degrees."

I nod that I agreed that was a good thing.

"So we ended up getting an apartment to prepare for the baby and I asked her to marry me. She said she wasn't ready and a baby wasn't going to change her mind."

Hmmm. She should've hooked up with Rick, my ex.

"But then the best day of my life happened, he continued. "Derek was born and since then he has been the very best thing."

I smile and say, "I know how you feel."

"When he turned 2 my parents moved to Paris. Of course, they had since forgiven me for altering my life plan, as they were madly in love with Derek. My mom asked if Derek and I wanted to come with them, but I told her I couldn't leave Eleanor. I thought that although she wasn't taking to being a mother, that she loved me. Disappointed, they moved."

He sighs and then asks, "Are you sure I'm not boring you?"

"Not even close," I say.

He sighs again. "Okay, another year passes and finally we make a plan to get married, something small on the bay with a few friends. The morning of the wedding I find a note she left me saying, she's just not ready to be a mother and wife. She had packed everything and flown home to her parents in New Orleans. I thought it was an overnight bachelorette party, but she was making her escape."

Again he looks uncomfortable. All I can do is try to close my mouth because not only did she leave this wonderful man at the altar, she left that fine boy. I look over at him and Chris and could never imagine walking away. Maybe taking my child and running, but never leaving my child.

"What about Derek? Did she eventually send for him?" I ask.

Josh sighs again.

"No, Alicia. When she finally returned my call she said he was better off with me since she was never much of a mother and I was an incredible father. I don't think her mother was very good to her growing up. She had no example to follow."

Wow, he's taking up for this woman. He is some kind of man.

"So," he goes on, "I had to explain to Derek what had happened as gently as I could, and he was very sad, always looking for her."

"I told him when she felt better I was certain she would be back to see us and, of course, he really didn't understand. After a couple of years she seemed happy and I thought she would return to San Diego, but she said she was feeling like herself again and that she'd met someone. I was devastated and made up a story Derek would understand, but it was hard because *I* didn't understand. I still don't. She basically broke both of our hearts. She married the guy a few years ago and that's when I started making plans to move down here. My first coach connected me with the Center. I interviewed last year and they said a spot would be open soon and that's when we moved down this summer."

"Wow," I say for loss of a better word. "You've been through a lot. But you are an awesome dad and for that you have to be proud of yourself."

"He's my boy," he says, looking over with genuine love at Derek. "I still hope Eleanor realizes what she's done to her relationship with him and makes amends. Obviously, it's too late for me."

He says this and looks away. And I know then he really loved her and probably still does.

"Well I'm sorry to hear how you ended up at the Center, but I'm glad you're both here. The kids, the parents, the Center are all so blessed to have you."

"And what about you?" he asks, looking directly into my eyes.

"Me?" I say, looking down at my feet. "I'm blessed, too." My heart starts beating at a very high pace and when I look up into his eyes he's staring at me, smiling as if he really likes me.

Just then the boys break up the intense stare.

"Dad," Derek screams, "Mom," Chris screams. "It was so much fun, it was so awesome, we both won," they are so happy and excited we laugh hearing about their stories from the course.

"Well, okay, guys, are we ready for some burgers and shakes?" Josh asks.

"Yes!" They both scream enthusiastically.

"Then let's go," Josh say, but he squeezes my hand and says, "You're a good listener; I like talking to you."

Stunned, I swallow and say "thank you." The boys pull us out of the place and towards Johnny Rockets. We have fun-filled conversation about their teacher, the latest Spiderman movie and what other flavors would make good shakes. Throughout the night I'm almost certain I can see Josh staring at me. I guess I see him because I keep trying to steal glances at him.

The night ends at the escalators. The boys high-five, and I reach out to shake Josh's hand and he reaches over for a hug.

"Thanks for a great night, Alicia."

"No, thank you."

"Let's do it again soon."

"YES"!! The boys chime in together. We both laugh and say goodnight.

As soon as we get in the car Chris says, "Mom, that was the best night ever. Derek is the coolest friend!"

"Aww, Chris, I'm so glad you have a new friend. You have so much in common. Derek is a great kid like you."

"Yeah, and Coach Josh is great, too."

"Yes he is" I agree, and I'm so happy it's dark in the car so Chris can't see the blush spreading across my face.

3 Pizza & A Movie

The next two weeks were crazy busy and kind of a blur. There were new parents, tons of paperwork, uniforms to order and supplies to locate. It's always exciting when the season is about to begin because at the Center we have lots of foot traffic and energy going on.

Since our double-date with the kids, Josh and I have chatted away from work twice – once, to get Starbucks for everyone in the office, and another time when he picked up Derek from our house after a sleepover. It's been very sweet between us during these exchanges. It's the getting-to-know-each-other stage. When we went to Starbucks I heard about all his different coaching jobs – from the girls' volleyball team at a middle school to a high school soccer squad that didn't listen, never became a team and lost every game. He had me in tears sharing about the constant hilarious fights he broke up in and out of the locker room. Then he said he went to quit the job and before he could make his way to administration he had a letter relieving him of his duties.

I shared about being the teacher's pet in my sophomore year of college. I told him it wasn't my fault the teacher took a liking to me, and how scared I was when a group of girls in the class confronted me about it. My knees were literally knocking as they approached me at the sink in the girl's restroom, but all they wanted was to know how they could get in better with him. Then he was laughing as I made up a routine for them to try, including smiling, keeping the same sweet tone in their voice and turning their heads to the side to listen intently. One of the girls even took notes.

Then Josh randomly blurted out, "So you were stealing hearts back then, too, I see." He caught me off-guard with that comment and I smiled because whether he knew it or not he basically had just said that I was in the process of stealing his.

When he came to the house we talked about my condo and what a great deal I got on it. He asked how often Chris' dad visited, and I told him whenever he felt like it. I told him how I knew Chris needed his father in his life so I told him he could visit, see Chris and take him places whenever he wanted. Sadly, though, I told him, Rick is a ladies' man and goes from woman to woman looking for something his tragic life is missing.

Josh pondered that one for a moment and then said, "He's looking for you, but since none of them are you, he will never be satisfied."

I wanted to ask him then if he was a psychologist as well as a sports major, because in my heart of hearts I knew that was what was going on with Rick also.

"Well, if he had stepped up as a husband and father he wouldn't have to be out there looking," I said. "But that's another story for another time."

In between these shared moments we would text, sometimes to just say hi, sometimes to share a joke, and often we would use a work question issue, which would give us the opportunity to chat. We would also see each other at work, but there we were all business. Of course, there were the stolen glances and my skipped heartbeats, but we were completely professional. At the

Center everyone would know your business if you didn't protect it.

Sharon was thrilled. She was excited about the date with the boys, about the texting and about us getting to know one another. She wanted to know when there would be a real date between us.

"I don't know, Sharon. We often text about upcoming movies, what activities we like such as bowling, but so far no invite. I think he's still getting to know me."

"That's all well and good. But I'm waiting for him to get to know you at the movies in the dark. Sharing the same popcorn and feeding each other Raisinets! When's that date coming?"

I hollered. "It's coming later, you nut! We're taking things slow to protect the boys and probably his heart. You know he's still in love with Eleanor deep down."

"Yeah, but she's gone. If he focuses on you at the movies, he will forget her. Besides, I see the way he looks at you and love is not far from his heart. I just know it!"

"Really hopeless romantic?" I say smiling.

"Yes. I know these things. So if he doesn't do something soon I'm going to offer to keep the boys at my house for a pizza and a movie night and tell him to take you out."

"Wow, well okay! Can I counter that with a sleep-over at Auntie Sharon's?" I say and chuckle.

"Now that's going a bit far. My kids are out the house and I only want to see my grandkids overnight, not those grown-ups that are their parents."

"Yeah right, you talk more trash," I say, laughing.

As the week comes to a close, we spend Thursday and Friday prepping for the following Monday, when practice will begin for the fall season. The volunteer dads come in to speak with Josh to learn about their duties. Sharon and I work on the Center's newsletter, which features a story on our new coach, important dates, game dates and updates on Sharon's coach, Coach Barnes, and his entire program. When Friday ends we are all pooped.

As I close out, Sharon comes over to give me a quick hug goodbye. "So no plans for the weekend with Mr. Wonderful?"

"Nope, he didn't say a word, but I'm fine. Chris and I are on for our weekly movie and pizza night. Tonight we are watching *Star Wars* and *The Empire Strikes Back*."

"Sounds fun, super mom. I'm glad you are the way you are. No worries about dating anyone, just you and your son making your own happy."

"Got that right. He's not leaving me for another woman and he has to listen to me. He's the perfect man," I say smiling. She chuckles.

"Okay, well have fun with Chewbaca and Luke Skywalker, and we'll talk later. Love ya, sweetie."

"Love you, too, Sharon," I say and then Josh steps out of his office.

"Oh great. Alicia. I caught you. I know you're leaving, but do you have one minute."

"Oh sure. I'll be right in."

"Goodnight, Coach," yells Sharon.

"Ahh, goodnight, Sharon. Enjoy your weekend"

"Thank you, you too," she says, and then he disappears back into his office.

"Opportunity knocks, girlfriend," Sharon whispers as she waves on her way out.

"Goodnight, Sharon," I yell, shaking my head amused.

I grab my pad and pen and hurry to go back in his office. Chris does not like to be the last one picked up from the after-school program so I gotta hustle.

"Yes, Coach," I say, as I stand by the door.

"Umm yeah, thanks for staying. Just really quick, did you get the email sent to the parents about the opening practice and pizza welcome party?"

"I sent it out yesterday. Is there anything else you wanted to add?"

"Oh no. I was just making sure they got it before the weekend." *Now he knew as well as I that when we met Tuesday we decided the parents needed to have the email by Thursday at the latest. Did he just want to see me before I left?*

"Well, great. I should've known my highly efficient assistant and office manager would have that small detail covered." *Am I detecting nervousness in him?*

I smile and say, "Okay, well then if there's nothing else ... and he interrupts me.

"Well actually, Derek and Chris were talking on the phone about the *Star Wars* double feature going on at your house tonight and . . . " I start to smile, because he is so cute trying to beat around the bush. I decide to take him out of his misery.

"Did Chris invite Derek over for tonight?"

"Actually, he invited us both over. But I told Derek when I let him out this morning that nothing was set because you didn't know so I guess I'm letting you know, but of course no pressure. We were going to do pizza and surf Netflix tonight."

I was already smiling because the boys were so cute, but now I realize the boys and the father are all cute. Of course, this means pizza movie night will be a look-cuter-than-usual pizza night for me, but I'm up for it.

"No need to surf when I have the anniversary DVD collection of *Star Wars,*" I say smiling. "We would love to have you join us."

"Really? Oh the boys are going to be hyped. And *Star Wars* is one of my favorite movies of all time so I may be more excited than them."

"Well, wanna make it for 7? Text me your pizza toppings and I'll order for us so we can start the movies right away."

"I've got one better. We'll pick up the pizza and bring it. Tell me what you guys like. My treat for barging in."

And then we talk pizza toppings and the fact that he has to go to Round Table, because it's our favorite. I leave his office on a cloud, grab my things and go pick up Chris. When I arrive he and Derek don't know anything so they are talking about playing video games online together tomorrow. I let them know we are having pizza movie night at our house and they cheer and discuss what DSi games they also want to play each other on that night. Then, out of nowhere, Derek runs over and hugs me and says, "Thank you so much, Ms. Parsons."

I am so touched by how sweet and well mannered this young man is.

"Oh you're welcome, Derek. It's going to be a lot of fun. See you in a little while okay?"

"Okay," he says again, so happy, and then tells Chris goodbye. On the way home I hear about how awesome I am, that he's sorry he shared our plans but so glad I'm so cool and let them come over.

When we get to the house I tell him to hurry and take a quick shower and pick up his room. I walk through the living room collecting magazines, video games and mail, and then throw the few dirty dishes in the dishwasher. It's a perfect condo for Chris and me to entertain company, I think. I hang up my jacket on the hooks next to the door across from the tiny guest bathroom.

As you walk by the staircase you turn right into the living room/den where I have a brown couch with gold and burgundy flecks and throws, because we love to watch TV with blankets. Then we have our recliner and two brown storage-style ottomans. The kitchen has a counter that looks into the small living room. Next to it is our dining table for four, which sits next to the sliding glass doors overlooking the pool from our balcony.

I love our place. I run upstairs to change and freshen up. I have brand-new grey sweats from Victoria's Secret, so I throw those on. They do have the word "Pink" printed across the butt, but the letters are black and not so noticeable, plus they're the boyfriend cut so they're a bit baggy. I decide on a black v-neck tee from Old Navy, and my black super comfy footsies. It's an around-the-house look that's cute without trying too hard.

The next thing I know it's 6:55 and the guard is calling to let me know they've arrived. I feel a little flicker of butterflies in my stomach about being with him for a double feature in my house. Where will we sit I wonder, on the couch together? Or, no, the boys will sit with me on the couch and Josh will sit on the recliner. Men love recliners. So in my mind that's the plan and I exhale knowing this is going to be a fun night.

They come in with the pizza and the chatter begins. The boys are loud and excited. We discuss their favorite and not-so-favorite teachers and who is going to be on the soccer team this year before they resort to their favorite topic of video games. Josh and I are left to chat about the parents that came in this week, the ones who made us laugh, the pushy ones and his volunteer dads. It's much harder than I thought to sit this close to this really handsome, really sexy man with his navy Nike tee and shorts on.

When the kids break off into their own conversation I find my heartbeat speed up and a cold sweat coming on. I really need to get it together.

"Are you warm?" he asks nonchalantly, "because it is a bit hot in here." I feel relieved that at least my house is actually hot and it's not just me.

"You know it's so small it does get heated up quite quickly," I say. "I'll just open up the sliding glass door for a bit."

I try to walk over to the door without tripping, looking like a dork or hyperventilating. I feel his eyes staring at me and wonder if he had a fast pulse too.

Is this is a crush? If it is, aren't I too old for one? Apparently not, because this is exactly what this feels like.

We finish dinner and start the first movie. I'm sitting next to Josh on my not-so-big brown sofa. As I put the movie in the DVD player, the boys move over the ottomans with Josh's help, and they claim the floor space. Josh then sits on the couch to wait for me. I was wondering through the first 30 minutes of the film whether Josh set this plan up with the boys. If so, I applaud his skills. We all enjoy *Star Wars*. The boys had never seen it, and they loved it. They asked questions, which I eagerly answered and they talked out about what they like. I explained to Josh before we started that we could talk at our home theater.

It was after 10 p.m. when the movie ended, and I saw some yawns from the boys. I asked them if they wanted to call it a night. No way, they said, no way! So I offered up ice cream sundae's and that woke them up. Josh closed the sliding glass door while I made the desserts, complete with sprinkles and whip cream. Derek helped me in the kitchen while Chris sat with Coach and discussed soccer.

"Ms. Parsons, thank you so much again," Derek said when we were alone. "This is what dad and I do on Friday nights and it's always fun. But being with you and Chris is super-extra fun."

I love this kid and I think it's because he reminds me of mine.

"You are so welcome. This is really fun for us too since it's usually just Chris and me."

He smiles. "Do you think we could do it again really soon?" he asks.

"I don't see why not," I say.

"Cool!"

We take the ice cream in and I start *The Empire Strikes Back*. Everyone is happily enjoying their dessert. I am done quickly, as I only made a small scoop for myself. I need to watch the carbs. They do not look good in the sweats or the tee.

About midway through the boys start yawning and I guess in a desperate ploy to stay awake they ask if they can go to Chris' room while we watch the rest of the movie. Josh and I look at each other knowing they are being jivey.

"Okay," Josh says, "but when the movie is over Derek we are going home."

"Okay, Dad, thanks." They run up the stairs and then we are suddenly alone. Besides the movie, we are completely quiet. My heart is actually racing, but I'm trying to be cool. Then it seems for some reason I get a whiff of his cologne.

Surely he didn't just spritz himself. I'm thinking with all this quiet my senses are heightened and he smells terrific. The girl in me is feeling shy and unsure of herself. *Should I say something? Should I try to figure out how to sit closer to him? Should I try and hold his hand? Oh my gosh, I am rusty and old at this. What if it's all in my head and he doesn't actually like me!* Then I panic that I'm a bore. As I'm in deep thought I guess I sigh out loud.

"You okay" Josh asks. "If we're wearing out our welcome, we can go." And he's serious like he's really concerned I'm tired of them.

"Oh no, that's not it. Already thinking about all the things I have to do next week. I have a bad habit of doing that – over-thinking."

"Yeah, I noticed," he says, and I widen my eyes and he breaks into laughter. "I'm sorry, Alicia, but it's kinda funny. I know it's because you're so organized," he says smiling, trying to stifle a laugh.

"Well thanks for laughing," I say, and hit him with one of the throw pillows, "I've done it my whole life, but I'm always hoping people don't notice." He's still trying not to laugh, so I smile.

"Well, just know it's what helps make you, you. I find it....." and he's thinking, thinking. "Refreshing," he finally says.

I say, "something about that sounds sincere yet laughable at the same time," and glare over at him. Next thing I know we are downright laughing, and I realize it's after midnight, so we have got into the sillies, you know, where you over-laugh at everything. Finally, after we both stop cracking up, I push him on the arm and say: "This is all your fault! We missed the entire second half of the movie laughing."

"I know, and I'm sorry," he says. "Oh yeah, I can tell," and I push him lightly again on his arm – his firm-toned arm.

I realize I just lost focus and I need to pull it together. Although I am madly "in like" with Josh I gotta keep my emotions in check. Rick spoiled it for all other guys. I don't give anyone a chance because I can't afford to have my heart broken that way again. So I date occasionally and then disappear from their lives. The last guy I saw was almost a year ago. I figure I have a son to raise. If there's still some guys ticking when he's graduated from high school I'll go on a manhunt then. But for now, I love 'em, or rather date 'em, and leave 'em.

We're both quiet now and even though the credits are running on the TV, we don't move from the couch. I turn toward him a bit and say, "Thanks for coming to our pizza movie night."

"No, thank you. We kinda invited ourselves, but I'm glad we did," and then he turns in toward me and says, "Maybe we could do it again, like next Friday."

He's looking in my eyes and I notice his are a warm brown and I don't see anything behind them, just a guy who may really like me. Then he reaches over and takes my hand.

"I do like you Alicia and I hope it's okay if I try to get to know you on a deeper level."

Yep, you know it: my heart is beating and I'm pretty sure I got a small electric jolt when he took my hand. I'm speechless.

"Well, what do you think?" he says in anticipation. And I find myself smiling shyly.

"Yes, it would be great if you guys come over again next weekend." He smiles and reaches to move my swooped bang out of my eye. *Second jolt!* "And yes, I would like to get to know you better, too." Then he moves closer. *Heartbeat is in my throat and it's so loud I know he can hear it.*

In an unsure voice, he asks, "So does that mean you like me, too?"

OMG! Like him! I could probably love him, but I can't allow myself to just yet. I look down at the blanket where the boys were just a little while ago and then I shake my head yes and look towards him.

"Yes, I like you too." And then it happens. He kisses me. Really sweetly, really softly and really short, because we hear feet on the stairs so he pulls away and we're staring at each other. I'm thinking: Best Friday night ever!

I don't know if the boys said anything, but we looked up and they were standing in front of us. I let go of Josh's hand, but not before I saw Derek see me do it. He didn't say anything to Chris or either of us, but he grinned as if he had just found out the blind date he set up went well. I'm thinking, Did Sharon recruit a 12-year-old? I'll have to ask her later.

"Mom, can Derek spend the night?" But before I could say anything Josh said, "Not tonight, buddy. He has to help me with laundry and house cleaning tomorrow."

"Aw Dad! Our house isn't that dirty." We both laugh, but the boys are not amused.

"Okay, I tell you what guys. If you both do your chores really good tomorrow we can come by to get Chris for ice cream and lasertag in the afternoon, if it's okay with your mom."

I see the excitement on the boys' faces, "Okay, I can go with that plan." "Yay," they say, and start yelling and cheering.

The boys pack up Derek's stuff and Josh turns to me and says, "I had a really great time tonight," and he reaches over to hug me. *Final electric jolt of the evening.*

"Me too" I say smiling, "see you guys tomorrow then?"

"Yes," says Josh, "I'll call when I'm on the way." And then they are gone and I find myself smiling on the inside too.

What just happened? I let someone get to know the real me. The goofy-sweat-pants-wearing me, and it felt good.

I turned off the light then and went upstairs with thoughts of our first kiss on my mind.

4 Family Matters

The next morning I wake up wide-eyed and bushy-tailed. *Did one of the most awesome evenings of my life happen last night? Yes, it did.* I lay back in the bed replaying the entire evening over in my mind. I look over at the clock and it's only 8 a.m., so I decide to relax a bit and give myself a break. At 8:15 the phone rings. I knew it could only be one person – my mom.

"Good morning, Mom," I say bright and cheery.

"Good morning, Alicia. I thought I might wake you, it being Saturday morning and all."

"Nope. I was just relaxing before I get started with cleaning up."

"Well, you know dear, this is a very good time to pray and read your Bible." My parents live by the Word and raised us on the Word. So I know that she is right, but sometimes I just get downright lazy.

"You're right, Mom. And I think I will this morning. It's so beautiful and I have so many things to be thankful for."

"Well amen to that!" She loves it when her kids go spiritual. I think it fills her heart with joy.

"I'm calling because Trina is really going through it with Michael and I thought maybe you could call her and show her some sister love."

Michael is Trina's ex. They were divorced just six months ago, and he is miserable. Of course, when he married her he made her miserable, so they're actually kind of even now.

"Oh wow, Mom, I'm sorry to hear that. I sure will call her later on today. Can't let Lil sister go through these things alone. Thanks for letting me know because she always says things are just fine when I ask her."

"I'm sure she does. You know Trina doesn't believe in letting things get her down, but he is way over the top with the calling and even stopping by. I know you have been through this and you can offer her some advice and sisterly love. By the way, how is Rick? Is he coming to see my grandson like he should?"

"Well, Mom, not so much. He came through last month and took him for a movie and pizza. But you know how smart Chris is. He said Mom, does he really think one movie makes him a good dad?"

"My goodness! That Chris is smart as a whip! I miss him and I miss you. I cannot wait to see you both at Thanksgiving."

"Me too, Mom. I can't wait to see you either."

"Okay, baby girl, thanks for looking out for your sister and I'll talk to you soon. Give Chris my love"

"I sure will. Love you Mom and give Dad my love, too."

"All right I will. Love you too, sweetie. Goodbye."

I tell her bye and hang up. I absolutely love my Mom. That is the only thing hard about living away from home. But I had enough of the Bay Area growing up. Now I just get to visit and it's great for that, but I am always ready to come back to the best city in the world.

I do, in fact, pull out my Bible and read through several chapters of Proverbs and then I pray. I pray for my blessed life, for Christopher, my family, my home, my job, my friends, for Rick that he'll be a better dad and then I pray for Josh and

Derek. As I finish, Chris runs in and jumps on my bed. I say "Good morning, son," and he says it back, but then wacks me with a pillow. We commence with a full on pillow fight until we are laughing and passed out on the floor.

"Let's go get breakfast, Munchkin. Then we will clean up and you can finish your homework," and before I can finish he adds, "and then get dressed for hanging out with Derek and Coach."

Smiling I say, "Yes, get dressed to hang out." Then he bounds out of my room and downstairs toward the kitchen. I grab my robe to follow, knowing I will see the future love of my life in a few hours.

By about 3 p.m., the house is clean, homework done and we're both in the living room dressed. Chris plays video games while I make out a grocery list and then Josh calls to say they are five minutes away. I check my hair in the hall mirror and tell Chris to wrap up his game so I can walk him down once the front booth calls us. I take Chris down and Josh jumps out of the car and says, "I would've come up to get him."

"No worries, this way you guys can just go. He's asked me for the last two hours when were you coming."

He nods his head, "Derek too. Well," and he pauses for a moment, "You know you are welcome to come with us."

Then Derek pipes up: "Yes, you can sit in the front seat." Too cute, I think.

"She has grocery shopping to do," Chris adds.

"Yes, my boss is right. I have to run a few errands, but thanks for the invite." Josh looks a bit disappointed. *Score for me,*

I have him missing me already! "Well, okay then. I'll text you when we're on the way back."

"Sounds good," I say and stoop to look in the car window. "Have fun guys."

"We will," they say, and then they are off. I watch them drive away and then head back up to the house. Shopping and the cleaners await.

About 5:30 I'm back home, groceries put away and I sit down on the couch to call my sister.

"SISTER!"

"Hey Trina Beena. How's my favorite little sis?"

"Good. I miss you, though. How are you, big sis?"

"I'm good. Just missing you, too, and wanted to check on you and my handsome nephew."

"So Mom got you to call me, huh?" She chuckles as she says it.

"Umm, can I not call my little sister to check on her? Geesh!"

"Yes you can, but I know Mom is worried about me, but really, I'm fine. Michael is just acting a fool for no good reason. He acts like he forgot he wanted the divorce! We were having issues as you know, but I was willing to work through them. I wanted my son to be with his dad living in the same house, but I dealt with the break-up. Now he wants to just about have full custody, and you know that's not gonna work."

"Yes, I do know that. He's got a lot of nerve considering he was the one who was never home when Matthew was in his house. Men are always missing what they had in the first place. You know I don't get their point!"

"Exactly! I've been very fair, but he has started picking him up from school on my days and keeping him an extra night when he knows he's supposed to come home. Just rude stuff like that. I don't want to take him to court but, Sis, if he keeps this up, I will."

"I am so sorry, Trina. This is the last thing you need with you starting your new job at the law firm."

"It really is. And I love the job! Being a legal assistant is so perfect for me and I work for one of the partners. So having a fool for an ex is unacceptable, as I'm on call just about 24 hours."

We continue on with our conversation and cover Mom's latest shopping spree, Jackie's twin girls who just started high school, and Dad's recent infatuation with golf. After it seemed we covered everything I told her I would let her go.

"Wait just a minute, Miss Thang! I need the latest update on the coach. What's going on with Mr. Cutie-pie? And most of all how was the date?"

I smile just thinking about Josh, but I coolly try to take the smile out of my voice. Otherwise, my intense like will be a dead giveaway.

"We had a blast. His son and Chris are best friends and so we took them miniature golfing, as you know, and out to dinner. We had so much fun just talking and getting to know each other. He ended up telling me about Derek's mom."

"So what's the word on her?"

"She left him at the altar, or rather left on the day of their wedding. She left Derek with his dad and hasn't been back from Louisiana since. He told me all about the baby asking for her and how he tried to cover for her. It was kinda sad, but seeing Josh with his son lets you know that maybe he really was the better parent."

"Well, obviously! Who leaves their own child? Oh my gosh! That's horrible" she shrieks.

"I know!"

"But I cannot wait to meet this interesting, dedicated, got-my-sister-smiling-in- the-phone, cute hot guy who dates you and your son, and his son!"

"I know," I agree with her as I laugh at her comment. "Come down one weekend and we can all hang out."

"That sounds good, and Matthew would love it! I'll see if I can get any time from the firm. Otherwise, I can always do a weekend getaway."

"Okay, let me know."

"Will do, Sis. Now that we've got that all cleared up, has he tried to make a move yet?" Internally, I smile at this question.

"Dang, Trina. We've only been on one double-date with the boys!" I say, laughing.

"Yeah, but you guys work together. How about hooking up behind the vending machines or closing his door. Hello? Must I tell you everything, Miss Goody Two-Shoes!"

"I'm not a goody two-shoes, I just wanna take things slow and not rush fast thing!"

"Okay, okay," she says laughing.

"However, for your nosey information he did kiss me last night and I let him."

"YES!! Finally, a guy you don't push away, or are through with him after one date? Ohhh, I like him already! "Well, is he a good kisser?"

"Absolutely," I say with emphasis, and we both break into girly giggles.

Just then the front gate calls me so I switch over to tell her it's him and the boys.

"Okay, Sis, tell Mr. Dreamy I said hey and give him a high-five for me," she says excitedly.

"Okay, I sure will."

"And kiss my nephew,"

"I will. And I assume you'll give Jackie the scoop, and Mom the clean version?"

"You know it!" and we both roar with laughter because Trina is the official information hub of our family.

"I love you, Lil' Sis,"

"I love you too, Alicia."

And then we say goodbye. As I am musing over the phone call I think about both of my sisters, as we had a ball growing up. Great parents and a wonderful home life. I love them all so very much.

The knock at the door alerts me to the boys.

"Hey guys," I say after swinging open the front door.

"Hey Mom, Hey Ms. Parsons, Hey Alicia," they all say in a row.

"Did you guys have fun?" I say excitedly.

"It was so cool," and great and fun is all I hear from the boys.

"How about you, Dad? Did you have fun too?" I say.

"Yes, I did. Even though they ganged up on me at laser tag I still had fun," he says teasing. The boys think this is hilarious so they tell me everything that happened.

"Well come on, Derek, let's get home." The boys complain, but he tells them to calm down because they can play XBox online once they're both home and ready for bed, which calms them down. Then he turns to me and speaks lower.

"I didn't want to assume you wanted to hang out, so I fed the boys. Chris ate plenty so I hope that gives you the night off. I would love to hang out with you again tonight, but I can't have you getting tired of me that soon." He says this while staring in my eyes, in my personal space with his lips mere inches from mine.

I nod my head slowly in shock that he fed my child dinner and would love to spend this evening with me, too.

"Thank you, Josh. That's one of the nicest things you could have ever done for me," I say as I'm looking in his eyes.

"I figure you work hard, you're a great mom so you deserve a break."

And then we are just looking at each other all goo-goo. The kids come to interrupt us. He hugs me goodbye and says he'll text me later. I close the door staring at them through the window as they walk away. *Is this guy for real?* I watch them get in their car. He has got my interest piqued.

On Sunday, Chris and I relax after a huge breakfast I made for us. He started playing video games and I pulled up church online. My mom talked about me so bad about not having a church home so I made one of the local churches in L.A. my online church. I'm never late, pay my tithes and do this all in my

PJs. Call it laziness, but I call it being connected to God. I used to go with Jackie to church in Riverside when I lived with her and, of course, when I was at home with my parents, but since being on my own I have not. Sharon invites me all the time and I've been a few times with her. What I like is that she doesn't push, and if I say, "You think I could go with you on Sunday?" she says, "Most definitely. I'll pick you up." Her no-pressure approach makes it easy.

In the afternoon, I get a text from Josh and then it turns into a complete conversation, a textathon really. We talk about our mornings, about practice tomorrow, about my family, about Trina coming down and about his feelings for me. *Is it possible to feel shy over a text?* Well, I do! He's saying I am the sweetest, nicest, most beautiful person he has had the pleasure to cross paths with in a long time. He wants to let me know he will take it slow but that he is pursuing me and hopes that is okay. I told him it was. All I could think was I cannot wait to tell Sharon about this weekend. I think we went back and forth for at least an hour and a half. It was too much fun. His last text said: "Until tomorrow…I'll miss u…your face…your eyes…your lips"

I feel an electric jolt again, and he wasn't even here. I tell him he's making me blush and I will see him tomorrow.

Since Chris was online playing games with Derek, and they were communicating via earpiece I snuck upstairs to call Sharon.

"Hey girl, how's your weekend been going?"

"It's been great, Alicia, just relaxing. We are sitting here now watching *Die Hard 2*."

"I'm sorry. Want me to call back?"

"Not even. Tony is over here snoring," and I laugh. "Tell me, is there an exciting reason for your call? Usually you text me. What's up, little lady?"

"Well, pizza movie night turned into double-date pizza movie night with Josh and Derek."

"What?!!" she shouts. "Woo hoo! I knew when he called you in his office it wasn't about work?"

"Oh really?"

"Yes, there was nothing left to discuss. Ohhh, I am so happy. Was it a great time?"

"Was it ever," I say and then elaborate on every detail of the evening, from him buying the pizza and bringing it over to the ice cream sundaes. And then I tell her the boys went upstairs to play.

"OMG! Did he kiss you?" I start to giggle. "He did kiss you! I knew it. He doesn't waste time. I like him so much!" I can't stop laughing because she's hilarious.

"Okay, so tell me everything! Where was he sitting, where were you in comparison to him? Did he hold your hand? Grab your face? Push you back on the couch...."

"Sharon!" I say to stop her. Of course, I am laughing because she is so dramatic about it.

"It was perfect," I say, and then go on to explain him grabbing my hand, moving my bangs and saying he liked me as if we were in junior high. She was totally enthralled in my detailed account.

"He's such a gentleman," she says, exhaling. "I just know he is the one for you!"

"Well, that remains to be seen, but for now he is sort of wonderful. This afternoon he took the boys out for Lasertag and then took them to dinner. He told me he did it so I could have a night off, because I deserved it. Who does that?"

"Nobody does. But I knew something was special about him the first time I met him. He's a keeper so please give him a chance."

"This time I think I really will. I do like him and I like Derek. I could be a mom to two boys," I say smiling.

"Aww, you considered you guys like a family. I love this. You so deserve to be happy."

"Thanks, Sharon. I probably need to sit down with him soon and tell him about my no sex-before-marriage rule. No matter how much I like him I'm not going back on that rule. Sex changes everything!"

"And that can be a good thing," Sharon says, chuckling, "but I'm with you and do understand. Letting him know early is a good idea in case he doesn't want this kind of relationship. That's so smart, Alicia, because you do need to protect your heart."

"I'm going to do it soon," I tell her.

After we hang up the phone I prepare for the long day tomorrow, and as I went to sleep I thought about how I will broach this touchy subject with Josh. I'm hoping it won't be a deal breaker.

5 Soccer Practice

Monday finally arrived and Chris was excited about practice. In just two weeks their season would start, and just thinking about spending all that time with the team had him up early and very talkative.

When I dropped him off at school I told him that I would swing around right at 5 and pick him and Derek up for practice. "Okay, Mom, we'll be waiting. Thanks." I watch him run over to his friends and I smile at the easiness of life at 10 years old. Not a care in the world and that's how it should be.

As I pull out of the drop-off zone I see Josh waving to Derek from their parked car. Then I see Jessica Waters appear to stop him before he got in his car. She is smiley and giggly and it annoys me. I find myself wondering if Josh might find her interesting or attractive. Just because he was never a ladies' man before doesn't mean he couldn't start now. Maybe he was already bored with me. Maybe he found her hour-glass shape more appealing than my two-hour-glass shape. But then I remember that I'm not his and he isn't mine so I speed up to pass them quickly, but he yells out, "Wait up, Alicia!" I hear him although the windows are up, but I act like I don't. Best for me to get to work and start on the ballet weekend schedule. Mrs. Gordon had emailed me her entire program so I needed to get it on our website and up on the bulletin board.

I decide on oatmeal and a Pumpkin Spice latte for breakfast. I had a long day ahead of me and I was thrilled the new fall

flavors had just come out. As I parked my car I saw Joshs' black
Audi out of the corner of my eye. Then a text came in from him,
I wanted to know if you wanted Starbucks... Then another...Oh,
I see you're here. Save me a space in line. I did save him a space
but I had to talk to myself, because for a minute I didn't want to
see him at all.

"Hey you, I was trying to catch you at the school."

"Oh, really. Well, I saw Jessica over by your car so I certainly
didn't want to interrupt," I say, more tartly than I meant too. He
stared at me in confusion but then it's as if he got it.

"Oh, this is a great moment in our relationship" he said half
smiling.

"What is?" I asked, clearly still annoyed.

"Your first moment of jealousy. You're so cute with your
little attitude and snappy remark." He says this in a sweet gooey
voice and with a smile on his face. I try not to be amused, but I
can't help it.

"Be quiet," I say and push him out of line, trying not to
smile.

Then he comes over and puts his arm around me, and
whispers, "I'm not interested in Jessica. Only you." And he
kisses me on the cheek.

So wow, now I'm blushing in Starbucks with electric shocks
running up my legs, and I say "Well, I wasn't really jealous, you
know."

He replies serious, but smiling, "I know you really weren't."

We order, take our drinks back to the office and kick
into high gear. I get working on the ballet schedule and Sharon
starts working on the salsa schedule. The evening clerical staff

will post everything and be armed with all the info needed to answer questions.

It's a busy day and at 5 p.m. it just gets busier. Sharon leaves at her regular time and tells me to have fun. Officially, I become soccer mom at 5 so I close out, go pick up the boys and take them to get a bite to eat. Josh and I made this plan earlier in the day, so he would be onsite in case any of the parents arrived early or they had any questions before practice begins.

When we got back the parking lot was full. Parents were out on the field, the assistant coaches were in place and Josh was talking to a group of parents. After we were all assembled he went over the schedule of practices, discussed what was expected of the boys, the parents and what would happen on game days. He told parents they were free to watch practice, or otherwise be back at 6:45 to retrieve their kids. Practice started about 6:10 that night and most parents stayed in the bleachers. I was able to meet a lot of the moms and dads. That night there were more moms than dads, but I knew it would even out as the weeks went on.

That first night the boys shared in detail with me about how fun it was and how excited they were. Josh asked how I thought it went and I said great.

As Friday's practice rolled around the kids all started to call me Ms. Alicia, and that's when one of the volunteer fathers told another dad I was the team mom, so if he needed anything to ask me. Josh overheard him and thought it was a great idea.

Then he rounded up the parents and told them, "Coach Rob nominated Alicia Parsons to be the team mom, and I think it's a great idea. She manages the office at the Center and already does our paperwork anyway, so it makes sense. Everybody okay with that?"

I thought Jessica Waters would disagree, but even she didn't. I was the official Soccer Team mom. All the parents clapped and I was pretty happy.

After that night's practice, we went out for pizza. At first it was just the four of us but then Coach Rob, Jessica and a few other parents and their kids joined us. It was a great time getting to know each other. Afterwards, it was still early so Josh asked if we were still on for a movie and I said of course. They went home to clean up and we went home to do the same and wait for them.

As Chris and I pull into the complex chatting and laughing I stop when I notice the brown BMW parked in the visitor parking area. My heart sinks. It's Rick.

"Isn't that Dad's car?" Chris asks. And before I can answer he gets out of the driver's seat. "Mom, it is dad. I wonder what he's doing here." And my baby boy sounds as annoyed as I feel. I guess we both knew unless he said hello and then left, that he was infringing not only on Friday night movie time, but also on Josh and Derek's time.

I leave the garage door up so he walks in and says "Hello, Alicia."

"Hey, Rick," I say, trying my best not to sound too super annoyed.

"Chris, how's my big man?"

Chris slowly gets out of the car, "Hey dad. I'm fine."

"You look great, son. How's everything been going? Isn't the big game tomorrow?"

Chris looks at me and then back to his dad and says, "It's next Saturday, Dad." "Oh, okay. I guess I got my weekends mixed up."

I tell him to come in so I can close the garage and then I roll my eyes as I use the key to open the back door.

"Well dad, I have to take a shower cause my new best friend is coming over tonight for movies." Rick looks perplexed. "Oh okay, it does seem like you had something else on your mind."

I've never seen Chris like this. He is so impatient with his dad tonight.

"Mom, may I go upstairs now?"

"Sure Chris, go on ahead and get clean." He then looks over at Rick, "see you later, Dad."

"I'll be here when you come back down, son." Chris stops in his tracks, "You will?" I am sure Chris thinks his night of fun is ending and he could be right.

"Go on up, Babe," I say almost urgently. I don't want his dad to get enraged because Chris is definitely annoyed.

Then Rick turns to me. "Alicia, I really thought the email said the game was tomorrow." I sigh, "No, I definitely said the weekend of the thirteenth. Besides, Rick, it's Friday night and the games are on Saturday."

He shrugs, "Well yeah, I know but I thought he and I could hang out a little before the game and I could catch up with him. But he seems like he doesn't want to be bothered with me. Have you been saying anything to him?"

Now I know this fool is not asking if I told our 10-year-old anything negative about him. Doesn't he know I don't have to?

Chris gets disappointed without me doing a thing. So I tell Rick this and he starts to get loud with me.

"Are you kidding me, Alicia! You are talking to him about me, and you're out of line!"

OOHH! I'm going to blow.

"No, you're out of line for showing up tonight pretending to be a dad on the wrong weekend of your son's first soccer game!"

"See, this is why I can't talk to you. You're one of the reasons why I don't see Chris more."

"Excuse me" I yell, "*you're* the reason you don't see Chris more!" Now we are glaring at each other across the room because we know better than to be up close. I never think it's smart to talk to a man like he's crazy, but tonight this man has shown me he's totally crazy! In addition he is messing up my plans with Mr. Wonderful. This almost makes me as angry as him being a raggedy dad.

"It sounds like you want me to leave?"

I sigh again. "It's not that I want you to leave, Rick, I just want you to be here for Chris. He needs his dad. I am doing the best I can as a single parent, but you've got to meet me halfway. And now that's he's becoming a young man he needs you even more. He's probably frustrated tonight because you got the weekend of the game wrong. That shows him you don't pay enough attention to care!"

I'm half screaming and Rick looks kind of wounded. He takes a seat and puts his head in his hands. I have no feeling of wanting to console him or rub his back or tell him it will be okay. I just want him to agree to do better and get out. Come back tomorrow and take his son for burgers. But not tonight.

Just then the phone rings. It's the guard booth. Josh is here. I start to panic internally as I realize in mere seconds my ex would be meeting my future. I know it was far off in the future but I certainly didn't want Rick spoiling anything.

"So I guess that's Chris' little friend."

"Yes that would be him."

I could hear Chris run across the landing and start making his way downstairs. I had no way to stop whatever was going to happen.

"Mom, I heard the phone so I think Derek and Coach are here." I smile sweetly and nod my head yes.

"So the soccer coach brought him over?" Rick asks, still in his funky tone.

"Yeah, Dad, Coach is Derek's dad. We had movie night last Friday too." Explosion one just hit the living room couch. I so wish I could run for cover.

"What the...!" Rick exclaims. I glare at him from across the room, but I'm also glad he remembered to watch his mouth in front of Chris. I don't play bad language around my boy.

There's a knock at the door and the inevitable is about to enter the living room.

"I'll get it," Chris yells. Anxiety is looming over me like a huge cloud.

Be calm, Alicia. You can handle this.

"Hey, Derek! Hey, Coach, come on in" I can hear Chris' happy voice saying. "My dad stopped by, come on and meet him." So innocent, I think. Let's see if Rick can keep from showing out.

"Dad, meet my best friend Derek Hart and his dad Coach Josh."

"Very nice to meet you, Derek," he says ever so charming. He can really turn it on when he wants, I think.

Then Josh extends his hand. "Nice to meet you, man. Joshua Hart." He's so gracious, but I am sure he wishes I would have warned him. Technically he doesn't know enough about Rick to dislike him like I do but still, this cannot be a pleasant surprise I'm sure.

"Rick Parsons." And I see a small bit of the funk still left in his body language. He does a quick once-over of Josh in that guy way they do it. More than likely he is trying to figure out why he's here.

Josh turns to me then. "We brought ice cream…to celebrate the first week of practice," he says searching my eyes. As if to ask, *Should I leave because this is a bad time* or *should I stay because you look so tense.*

"Thanks, you guys," I say smiling and looking directly at Josh and then turning my attention to Derek. "We really appreciate it. I guess I better get it in the freezer."

"Well this is really cozy, isn't it? The coach and my wife playing house." Okay, well World War II has officially just erupted in my living room, which tonight seems extra small.

My super sensitive ears hear Derek whisper to Chris, "Are they still married?" Chris whispers back, "not in forever."

"Boys," I say, "why don't you go up and play some video games. We'll call you down later for the movie."

"Okay, Mom, thanks," Chris says, and then they run upstairs to his room.

When I turn around I see that Josh has taken a seat on the couch. He is not leaving and I am loving him for that right now.

I glare at Rick who is standing in front of the kitchen bar stools with his hands balled in fists. He beats one of them on the bar.

"First of all, Rick, I am not *your* wife! Second of all we already had movie plans with Josh and his son, and thirdly, it's just really none of your business!" I kinda half scream that last part. Mind you, I am mild-mannered and although things can annoy me I rarely raise my voice to a scream and I'm never outright angry. But tonight I am.

"Really, Alicia? I come over here to see my son but get surprised when some man shows up. Then I find out the man is my son's soccer coach! What did you expect me to be other than upset," he fires back at me.

Leaning against the living room wall, I rub my hand across my forehead and try to find peace within myself, so I don't scream at this sad excuse for a father I see standing across my living room.

"Look, you showed up unannounced on the wrong weekend. We already had plans and I'm sorry if this makes you feel irritated or uncomfortable but a simple text would have saved you driving over here," I say more calmly.

He breathes in loudly, obviously still annoyed. Josh is looking straight ahead on the couch, almost like he's my bodyguard. In the midst of this mess he is happiness. And that's 6-feet-1 of happiness.

"Well, sorry," Rick sort of mutters like he's 12. "Next time I'll make sure to text first, I guess," he says with an attitude.

Then he walks across the room past Josh and me and calls upstairs, "Chris!"

Chris comes running down the stairs, "Yes, Dad."

"I'm leaving, big man. Give me a hug." He hugs his dad. Not lovingly like he hugs me but just enough to suffice his dad. "See you at the game, okay?"

Okay, Dad," he says in a tone that suggests he will believe his dad when he sees him in the stands. I know Rick picks up on it, but to save face he stays quiet.

"Bye," Chris says while running back up the stairs.

Rick then turns to me. "Make sure you aren't talking down about me when I'm not here, Alicia," he half barks at me. "I'm his dad, not some soccer coach boyfriend of yours!"

My stress level is through the roof! Who does he think he is? I'm so mad I could use profanity. But before I can think of a quick retort, I see Josh rising out of the corner of my eye. I've gotta get Rick out of here – now.

"I'm not trying to be his dad," Josh says evenly.

Oh man, the crap is about to hit the fan now.

"Excuse me, Coach, I was talking to my wife…." but before he could say another word Josh spoke again.

"She's not your wife, man. I wouldn't be trying to date another man's woman."

"You know what, I think I've had enough of your smart mouth," Rick says turning as if he's going to head back into my living room. But I step in front of him.

"Let me walk you out," I say, looking up intently into his face. With Rick standing almost 5-feet-11 it appears I'm a tall guy magnet. Funny, since I'm only 5' feet 4 in my bare feet.

Rick is so mad. His breathing is uneven and he is seething. I see Josh move again and am grateful he sits back down. This is when Rick starts calming down and finally looks at me.

"I'll call you this week," he says and then turns and storms out slamming the front door.

I stand there for a few minutes shocked at the exchange that just took place in my normally mellow household. I feel tears stinging the corners of my eyes and I stand there still facing the door trying to compose myself.

And then I feel Josh place his hand softly on my shoulder. "Are you all right?"

I try to swipe at my tears and turn around to face him. I see the concern in his eyes and I know he really cares. I open my mouth, but nothing comes so I shake my head no. And I lean into him and he hugs me. We just stand there in the dimly lit hall as I sob softly.

"I'm here," he says, "let it out." In the midst of all my turmoil I feel peace. *Who is this man that has come into my life? Is he for real? I don't know, but for right now I am going to believe he's meant to be here.*

We sit with his arm around my shoulder and I let myself forget about the drama of the evening. I enjoy the movie without us saying one word. His presence is more than enough to comfort me and eventually I fall asleep. Right before I do he kisses me on the side of my forehead.

We have never talked about what happened that night with Rick, but I will never forget the kindness he showed me. He rescued me and I knew I would never forget it.

6 The Conversation

The next week went by pretty fast. Chris seemed pretty much unfazed by his dad's unannounced Friday night visit. I had no idea if he would try and show up again, but I was certainly hoping he wouldn't. To the game would be fine, but not to my house the night before.

On Tuesday I text Trina about Rick showing up at my house and that Josh showed up. When she texted back about 45 minutes later, she responded: "What?! I'm callin yu in 5." I should have known she was not letting that get by on a text.

"Hey Trina," I say pleasantly. This is going to be one animated conversation, I think.

"Alicia Renee, I know I did not read that deadbeat dad Rick showed up at your house. Say it ain't so!"

I start to actually laugh at this point.

"And she was in such disbelief she added me to the call," comes another sisterly voice

"Jackie?!" I yell.

"Yes, little sis, it's me. Trina texted me just before I left the office to take a family on the hospital tour. The father's surgery isn't for another week, so I got my assistant to do it. I could not believe what Rick did in the midst of your boyfriend showing up."

Now I'm really laughing because she's not only made Josh my official boyfriend, but she stopped the patient's hospital tour. She is an administrator for the Riverside Medical Center. It's demanding, but she's the best at her job. She promoted right up to her current position.

"How are you, Jacks?"

"I am doing well, Licia."

"And the girls?"

"Oh your nieces are just fine."

Trina clears her throat, "Umm, this little reunion is just warming my heart, but can you two talk later? I wanna know about Rick at your door while Josh was in your house." We both kinda giggle at her impatience and say we're sorry.

"Well, girls, in getting back to the original question, oh yes he did. He was waiting for me to pull in my garage."

"WHAAAT!" they scream in unison. "Were Josh and his son with you?" Trina asks.

"No. Gratefully they had gone home to clean up after the practice."

I then break it down for them detail by detail. This was my second time retelling the story as I had told Sharon yesterday at lunch.

"Oh my gosh, for real? I am so loving this Josh," Jackie says.

"And I need to find out if he has a brother for me because that whole calm military, stand-up-for-you-and-himself-and-then-protect-you vibe is on point, and I am totally feelin' him," Trina adds.

"I know, right ,Trina? I didn't expect it at all. Talking about a man having your back…I was peaceful because of him in the midst of all that turmoil."

"I can see how, Sis. And I am just so happy and excited that you have a man that cares so much for you. Hang in there and you'll see that all men aren't bad."

I knew Trina was right and I agreed with her.

Then Jackie had to put her two cents in since she thinks she's the boss of us. "Trina, you don't need to say that to her. She knows all men aren't bad by looking at our daddy and my John".

"I do agree on those two," I reply, "but it makes me wonder if you and Mom got the last two good men sometimes."

"I often think that as well," Trina adds.

"Oh my little sisters, there is someone out there perfect for the both of you. And Alicia, this Josh sounds like a great possibility."

"Yes, he is pretty wonderful. I guess I'll keep him around a bit longer," I say as they both agree. Deep down, though, I just wonder if he really is too good to be true. But I won't voice this to my sisters. I don't want to sound too cynical about men.

"Well loves, I better go check on Mr. Arthur's tour, but thanks for including me on this call. It was way better than a text." Jackie says, and I agree.

"I'm going to try to get down to a game to see my nephew soon and then I can meet Josh."

"Okay, that sounds great, Jacks. Just let me know which weekend."

"Me too! I don't want to be left out!" Trina says, as we hear her pouting through the phone.

"I'll let you know what weekend, Sis, and then maybe we can meet Josh at the same time and double up on the intimidation, Johnson-style," and then we all crack up.

"Talk to you soon. Love you guys," Jackie says.

"Love you, too, Jacks," we both say.

Before Trina and I get off I say, "Oh, and by the way, I'm sorry to say Josh is an only child."

"Darn it," she says, "then find me a single dad that wants to move to the Bay Area." We laugh and chat some more before getting off.

"Thanks for calling," I say, and I really mean it.

"Of course. You helped liven up my Tuesday afternoon."

Then we both say I love you and hang up.

They had responded just as Sharon did. She could not believe Rick showed up unannounced one week early for the game, and on the wrong day.

"You should have told him he was a month early! You sent him all the info for the first game and the schedule in an attachment. He makes me so mad! And you are too nice to him!" she says fuming.

"I know, he is so over the top. I'm just glad Chris was distracted with Derek so that he didn't actually have to soak in how ridiculous his dad acted."

"You think he'll actually come out to the game Saturday?"

"Oh trust me, he'll be there. Knowing the coach is, I quote, "my boyfriend," he will definitely want to make sure everyone in the stands knows he is Chris' dad."

"Well at least he brought out one good point, Josh *is* like a boyfriend."

66

"How funny, I said the same thing to myself," I say laughing.

So now that everyone had the four-one-one on the meeting of Rick and Josh, they could all see how serious it appears Josh is about being in my life. I guess I realized this, too, and that's why on Friday at lunch I asked if he wanted to go to CPK. I had been craving a pepperoni, sausage, mushroom pizza and driving there together, would prove a perfect time to share a bit about myself with him. With the game being tomorrow I wanted a little one-on-one time with him before the weekend officially started.

We drove to the CPK in the Marina to get our takeout. On the way I brought up the subject of dating.

"I've been wanting to talk to you before things get too serious between us," I said, looking over at Josh as he drove up the freeway.

"Uh oh, am I going to like this conversation?" he asks.

"Yes, it's going to be fine. It's just something I feel you should know about me."

"Okay" he says, "shoot."

"Well, I've been a single mom most of Chris' life. Occasionally, I have had dates because someone wanted to set me up with someone. I have rarely sought out anyone on my own because I've always been too busy with Chris, his homework, activities and my floral business. I did, however, date a client one time. He thought he could get lower-priced arrangements for his boutique hotel since we were dating. I can't tell you how fast I sent him packing!" I sort of laugh at the thought.

"I bet. I'm starting to see you don't go for any kind of mess in your life."

"Got that right, and that's why I have to be mindful of my lifestyle, especially in front of my son." I then clear my throat. "So I wanted to let you know that I have lived a celibate life since I've been divorced from Rick. It's just something I feel is important to me as a woman and a mother. I want to show respect for myself by sticking to this vow and so far so good."

I breathe in again and sneak a look over at him. He is listening intently. "With all that said I felt I needed to let you know this as our relationship seems to be blossoming, so to speak."

He pulls into the parking lot, finds a space and turns the car off. I'm starting to wonder if he's upset or annoyed with me for my candor. My heart is beating as he turns to look at me with a serious face. Cute face, mind you, but serious.

"Well, Ms. Parsons, you consistently amaze me."

"I do," I say timidly. "Is that a good thing?"

"Are you kidding me? It's a great thing! At some point I figured you were going to ask me why I move so slow. I am totally subscribed to living the celibate life. I don't want Derek getting attached to someone I'm not going to be with for the rest of my life." Then he opens the door and gets out. Before he closes it he says, "so far, he's pretty attached to you," and then he winks.

What the heck just happened? He listened to my spiel, agreed with it and then points out that he feels the same way. There must be something wrong with him because he's too much like a dream come true.

As he pays for lunch at the counter I am in awe of how he took my news and of the statement that Derek is getting attached to me. *Wow, how sweet is that?*

We leave and we're getting back in the car and he asks, "Everything cool?" And I say "yeah, really cool."

"Good," he says. And we get in the car heading back to work without another word being said about it.

I sneak a look over at him. He is h-o-t hot. He's got a handsome face with great legs, obviously from all the coaching. Then he wears shorts everyday and makes all us girls swoon. Maybe I should just buy him sweat pants as a gift and tell him I don't want him to be cold. *Pure thoughts, Alicia. Do other people talk to themselves in their mind this much?*

I then wonder how committed I am to the vow I made to myself and the Bayside Christian Center at 15 years old. Of course, three years later I broke it, but I've started over. And I will stay pure, for my second time around, until marriage because I want to. And now with Josh on board, we can stay focused on this goal together.

That evening we did hang out. We only watched one movie, though, and then called it a night. The boys were a little upset, but with the game the next day we all needed our rest. We all hugged and said good night at the door.

After they left, Chris asked: "Do you really think Dad will come to my game?" I felt an ache in my heart because how could I be sure, but I told him, "I am sure he wouldn't miss it for the world." He smiled, and I had to believe Rick will be there as he said he would.

In the morning I made a full breakfast with eggs, toast and bacon and got my little athlete to the field on time. Actually early, since I had to get all the coaches' paperwork out of my desk, and get the stat sheets for Tina Ramos, Eddie's mom. She is really helping me out by taking the stats. Then on Monday I can individually input everyone's stats into the computer.

The game start time is 10 a.m., so about 9:30 parents and families start arriving. And at 9:50, I see Rick at the top of the stands. I am so happy for Chris, because he sees him also and waves. Then Rick sees me and smiles and I smile back. So happy he didn't burst my son's bubble.

The game was awesome, mainly because of our big win. We were all so excited and the team was happy, hugging and high-fiving each other. Sharon and her husband Antonio came, as well, so afterward they came down to see me on the field.

"Hey, team mom! Great game!"

"Aww thanks for coming guys," I say, and hug them both.

"Chris is getting so big. I could barely recognize him. And he's got talent," Antonio notes in his heavy accent.

"Yes, I am so proud of him!" I say, gushing. As I look over at him I see his dad approach him and I can tell by Chris's animated movements that he is sharing his excitement with his Dad. And I am happy for him. I wish Rick would be there for him all the time.

"I see dad showed up today."

"Yes, Sharon, and you cannot know the relief I felt when I looked up in the stands and saw him! Or no, on second hand you do know," and we both look at each other because we've already discussed it so many times.

Coach Josh comes over to hug me and Sharon. We are laughing because he is yelling, "We did it! We won!" Then he stops to acknowledge Sharon's husband. He introduces himself and thanks him for coming out to the game. "Also, thank you for allowing your wonderful wife to work at the Center," he says. "It wouldn't be the same without her."

"Well thank you, Coach," says Antonio. "She loves it there. I tried to tell her to come home, but she says it's not just work at the Center it's family. So I gave up." Both men find that funny.

"She and Alicia keep that place running smoothly so I'm glad to have the chance to work with her," says Josh. And then he winks at Sharon as he continues chatting with Antonio.

"Alicia, if I was single you would be in trouble, and that's all I'm saying" she says flipping her long bangs back in a sassy way.

"Well, thank goodness you're not then. Besides you have your Latin lover, Antonio! Back off already," and that really makes us laugh and make corny remarks as Rick approaches.

He speaks to Sharon who says hello really sweetly back to him and then he introduces himself to Antonio. He turns to Josh and says "What's up, Coach? Good game."

"Thanks, Rick. Good to see you again."

"Likewise," Rick says and then he turns to me. "So I was thinking I could take Chris over to Shakey's to celebrate. Did you have any plans?"

"Well, I think the team is all planning on going there so that's perfect."

"Oh well, I may want to take him somewhere else then so we can have some bonding time."

Now, I really want to slap him so he can get some sense in his bald head. He should have been bonding for the last 11 years. But I breathe in as I choose my words carefully.

"The thing is, I know Chris will want to be with the team, considering this is the first game and win. So why don't we all go to Shakey's and then you and him can go miniature golfing or catch a movie after?" Sharon is completely engrossed and nodding her head as if I made a really great suggestion.

"Here's the thing, Alicia, I have some business about 3 p.m. so that won't really work." Now I'm glaring at him. *Just come to Shakey's then, dummy!* This is what I really want to yell, but Chris comes over just in time.

"Auntie Sharon, hi!" She tells him hi and gives him a hug and Antonio congratulates him and pats him on the back.

"We can go to Shakey's, right mom?" And of course I say yes and then he turns to his dad. "Can you come with us, too? All the parents are bringing their sons." And that's it. Ricks face actually softens and he says, "Yeah son, I can come for a little while."

"Yay!! Let's go! May I ride with Coach and Derek?" He says looking at me, but then he remembers his dad. "No, that's okay, Mom, I wanna ride with Dad." I say okay and almost for one half of a second feel sorry for Rick. He looked so defeated when Chris mentioned Coach and Derek.

"Come on, big man, let's go. Alicia, we'll see you over there?"

"Yes, of course," I reply.

I then check with Sharon and Antonio, who decide why not spend the whole day with the team. I'm thinking Sharon is going for emotional support and I thank her with my eyes. Everyone had already left or were almost to their cars. Derek had decided to ride with his other friend Joey, so Josh asks if I want to leave my car at the lot so we can ride over to Shakey's together. Of course, I say yes. He thanks Bill, the Center's weekend worker for gathering up the equipment and then grabs his duffle bag with one hand and my hand with the other. I am pleasantly surprised and, I think, a bit shocked. We weren't really "out there" with our relationship yet and even though only a few parents hovered they could be taking note of the coach and the team mom.

There I was over-thinking again. Just go with it, Alicia! So I proudly walk with my hot guy, who I can probably consider my boyfriend, to his car.

We small-talk about the game on the way – how great the kids did, how great our sons did and the amount of support we garnered for our first game. We are both very excited.

Then we get to Shakey's and everyone is having fun. Coach Rob is ordering all the pizza and a few of the parents have taken seats to hold one long table in the middle of the room. I'm mingling and chatting it up with various parents when Rick approaches me.

"Uh, Alicia, this isn't really my scene. I'm not getting to spend time with Chris at all. That's the main reason I wanted to take him somewhere else."

Oh my gosh, I want to reach up and sock him in the face so bad, because he's so selfish!

"I'm gonna get out of here. Tell big man I love him and I'll call him next week."

I stand there stunned and don't say a word to him. I just let him step aside me to leave. And this is the same guy who just said last week not to talk about him in front of his son. When is he going to realize I don't have to? I think I'm still in shock when Sharon comes over to snap me out of it and we sit down at the end of the table. She already knows what happened without me saying a word. She pats my hand from across the table and says, "I'm sorry."

Chris is so disappointed when I tell him his dad had to leave. I see his little face crumble. But Josh walked up to us right at that moment and Chris says "I'm glad Coach Josh is here at least." Josh smiles down at him and Chris gives Josh a half hug before running back over to his friends. After Chris walks away, Josh says "What's up? You look sad, Beautiful."

Did he just call me beautiful? I almost forgot what was wrong with me.

I then explain the entire scenario to him and he shakes his head as he listens. When I tell him Rick left without saying goodbye he even looks sad for Chris.

"Was he always like this?" I think for a moment and say, "not in the beginning. But then fatherhood changed him. For the worse."

"I'm sorry to hear that," Josh says, placing his arm around me.

He does know all the parents are here doesn't he? If he's not worried about it, I won't be either.

"Remind me to tell you the story of Rick next time we have an extra minute," I say.

"Sure thing," he says. Then he goes off to play in the arcade with the kids as I sit down to a slice of pizza with Sharon and Antonio.

7 How I Met Rick

Rick and I met in high school. We were both very young and very stupid. I wish I had listened to my mother when she told me to stay a pure and chaste young woman. Instead, I listened to my friends who swore losing my virginity was no big deal and to Rick when he said if I loved him I would "go all the way" with him. I did make him wait over a year because I was into fairy-tale love and happily ever after. Besides that, up until that time I had no time for boys, as I was busy with sports and drama club. But when I turned 16 and was on the track team, I spotted Rick. He ran the 100 and was a newly transferred junior. I kindly told the coach I could give him a school tour and offered to show him the ropes around school and introduce him to everyone. We became fast friends and I developed a healthy teenage crush. By the time we were leaving junior year, though, everyone had scoped him out and not being very aggressive, I literally watched all the girls fall over themselves getting to him from the sidelines.

He had hair back then and with his mixed heritage of black and Spanish it was dark and wavy. He was quite the catch. I remember hearing over summer he had hooked up with Chanel Blake, the head cheerleader, but later he would tell me that was only a rumor. I never did find out the truth, but I did have my suspicions. And not just about her, about other girls also. When we returned to school in September I was so excited to be a senior and my friends and I vowed to have all the fun we could along with keeping our grades up. I had applied to UCLA, and nothing was stopping me from moving down to Los Angeles. Rick ended up taking the same elective course I did. It covered office management and secretarial training. I worked in the main office, answering phones, doing mailings, assisting the secretarial staff and even running errands. He was also an intern and we hit it off immediately, for the second time. First things were slow between us but then we got each other's phone numbers and I started picking him up for school in the morning and dropping him off in the evenings. We studied together and his mom liked me and my family liked him. He was hoping to go to UCLA, as well, and hopefully on a track scholarship. I was trying to get into their business school so I could get my degree in business management. I hadn't decided what kind of business, but I knew I wanted to work for myself.

Friday nights were spent making out in my small black Ford Escort with the sun roof. We would drive over to the Cal Berkeley area, see a movie and grab pizza. We were trying to get a feel of college life and what it would be like to be on our own. My parents wanted me to stay near home and go to college close by, but it was my dream to be on my own. Besides, with my sister Jackie living in West L.A., I had someone who would look out for me. I didn't want to leave my little sister Trina, but I needed to go "find myself," I thought, and moving away would afford me a chance to grow up without being babied.

As prom time rolled around Rick was set to go to UCLA. He had gotten his scholarship and I had been accepted with financial aid. I felt like my whole life was coming together perfectly. I had the perfect guy who had told me I was his one and only and that we would be getting married after college. Plus my school of choice had accepted me. Jackie and her husband said I could stay in their refurbished garage so I was all set.

When prom night came I was feeling giddy and in love. I wore this awesome pink taffeta gown with dainty silver sandals. Rick got us a limo and unbeknownst to me a room at the Fairmont in San Francisco where the prom was being held. Although I had mixed emotions, I knew I loved him so toward the end of prom I went to the room with him. My first time was nothing I expected, quicker than it looked in the movies and there was no romantic soundtrack playing. It was uncomfortable and I found myself in the bathroom afterwards crying. I was disappointed in myself and guilty because "no sex" before marriage was regularly brought up in our home and I had just made the vow of purity at church the year before. Now more than ever I knew Rick and I would eventually marry. After breaking my vow with him, at least that would somewhat make it right. At least that's what I thought in my recently-turned-18-year-old head. He told me he loved me more than ever and we would be together forever. And I believed him.

After high school we bummed around until August, and then we packed up and our families moved us. Rick had a dorm room on campus and with Jackie living only about 20 minutes (without traffic) from UCLA, we were excited about our future. The week before school started we were both given the "don't-act-a-fool-out-there-by-yourself talk."

We were very focused on our studies and both did very well throughout our college years. We always made time for our relationship, though. Eventually he got a place off campus and I spent hours studying there, even though he had two annoying roommates. We were happy, though. He also took a business management course because he knew track was not his career and saw himself in real estate. We both graduated and our families came down to celebrate with us. I was so happy with how life was going.

To wrap up the next five years, Rick got his real estate license and started out at Remax Real Estate Santa Monica on Wilshire. I started out with a law firm in Century City and then found my way to a medical practice as an office manager in Culver City. Jackie was finally going to move out of her house in West L.A. as my twenty-fifth birthday was approaching. I realized I needed a place and mentioned it to Rick. He still had one roommate in his apartment in Westwood. First he had the nerve to suggest moving in together when he already knew I was not living with him without being married. So I started looking for my own place as my sister prepared to move out to Riverside.

Well, for my birthday that year he suggested we go to Las Vegas. He said his roommate had a time-share and we could come and even my best friend was welcome. While in Vegas he proposed in front of the Paris hotel on Las Vegas Boulevard! Very exciting and very romantic. He made our closest friends were there because he told them his plan of proposing and eloping with me all in one weekend. I knew it was a horrible idea because my mom and sisters would literally kill me! But because I was really stupid and young, his plan of us being able to live together immediately meant I wouldn't have to look for a place because we would be legally married. So I weighed the options in a split second and the answer was easy because I knew I wanted to marry him. Remember, I was a fairy-tale girl and he was the one I had lost my virginity to. Plus we had planned to be together since the 12th grade anyway, so I said yes. For someone so smart I was making the dumbest decisions.

Fast forward one year. We are living in his apartment in Westwood, without his roommate, of course, and I am pregnant and miserable in this small space with no air conditioning. Rick seems moody and unhappy while I am pregnant, but I chalk it up to him having pregnancy symptoms with me. But then Chris is born and everything wrong in the world is right again. Upon meeting their grandson my parents were immediately in love and all my wrongs were immediately righted. Rick and I were totally in love with Chris, too. But over about six months he changed. He was still in love with Chris, but me not so much.

He felt trapped, I think. Too much responsibility too soon. He started hanging out with the fellas, coming home from work late or sometimes not at all. I asked him if he was cheating or just not in love with me anymore. He said neither of those were true, but that *this* life was so different and he just wasn't ready to settle down. When we were in high school, he told me his dad left his mom and never returned. I knew he didn't have a good example to follow, but he told me at 18 years old that he was going to be the complete opposite of his father. So when he started "acting out," so to speak, I didn't understand since he had asked *me* to marry him. Plus he had wanted to have kids right away, so he could enjoy them while he was young, he said. I didn't understand how he could turn on me like that, so I was confused, frustrated and hurt.

For about two years I went through this with him and eventually the numbers on the phone bill were other women and the texts buzzing through after midnight were saying, "I thought you were coming by?" So one day when Chris was 2 ½ I packed our stuff while Rick was at work and moved out to Riverside with my older sister Jackie and her family. She took us in and cared for us while I went through my recovery process of anger, sadness and grief. I had long since ended my job at the medical office, but I was good at saving my money. I kept my separate account entitled "mad money" even while I was married. I got my life together, moved back to West L.A. and went into business with my girlfriend Stacy from high school. It was a flower business and I really loved it. The business flourished, and I made a very comfortable salary, so comfy that we moved to a nice condo in Culver City by the time Chris was 5.

So I was back on my feet and felt it was the right time to file divorce papers from Rick. He had begged me to come back over and over, but by then almost three more years had passed, and I realized I couldn't do it anymore. I had stayed separated all this time so Rick's feelings wouldn't be so hurt, but I knew it was time to move on. He wasn't ever going to change. We were together a long time, but if the pressure of a family was too much then he needed to go somewhere away from me. I had a son to raise, and that's exactly what I intended to do. He still lived in Westwood, and of course I let him see his son, but it was pretty random. We were cordial, most of the time, but only because of Chris. I knew I would never love him again because I could never trust him again.

As I looked at Josh, his face said it all and I realized I must have said too much. But then his solemn stare turned into a mild grin and he said, "You're a rock star, Alicia. You handled your business, raised your son and still managed not to block Rick out of his son's life." He took another sip of his iced coffee before continuing.

"I'm sorry Chris has had to grow up without his dad in the home, but you did what was right for you and your son and you should be proud of yourself. I know I'm proud of you."

I smile as I look out over the ocean, "Well, thank you and I appreciate you for saying so. I guess I have done all right for us. When I left the flower shop I decided I didn't want to do a formal business so I started working out of my home. I still have a young lady that does arrangements and I provide them for hospital gift shops. When I brought Chris to the Center five years ago for baseball I saw the opening for office manager and thought I could do this job and still keep my account with the hospital. I finally take a sip of my Coffee Frap. I realize then that I must've run my mouth all the way from Starbucks to the park.

"Very innovative," he says.

I turn toward him. "You think so?"

"Are you kidding me, I can't believe Rick let you walk away." Gee, I think, he always knows the right thing to say and I smile at him and he smiles back.

Why is his smile making me weak in the knees?

"Well, thanks for meeting me." I say. "I just needed to clear my head from the drama of the last two weeks."

I had called Josh the night before to see if he wanted to meet for coffee once we dropped off the boys. I know Monday is his intense workout day at the gym, but he said he could do a half day for me. After we parked on Ocean Avenue right across from Palisades Park, we made our way to the Starbucks at the third street promenade. After ordering we walked back to the park and walked along the path overlooking the ocean, until we found the right bench for me to finish my story. It was a beautiful day at the beach in late October. Although it was a bit cool, it was totally clear and you could see all the way up the coast to Palos Verdes.

"This is why I love living here," I tell him. "Don't get me wrong, the Bay Area is beautiful, too, but it gets really cold."

"I've never been but always wanted to go and see the Golden Gate Bridge."

"Really?" I say, surprised. "Well then you should come up for Thanksgiving with us. I can show you the bridge, we can get clam chowder at Fisherman's Wharf and we can take the boys on the cable cars."

It all came tumbling out so fast I scared myself. I didn't wait to hear if he even had other plans for Thanksgiving. I felt really stupid.

"What I meant to say was, if you don't have any plans for Thanksgiving maybe you might like to come up with Chris and me to my parents' house," I corrected.

He stands up and reaches for my hand and so I take his and stand up. He starts to walk down the path again as he states, "My best friend Davis and his wife Skye had invited us to San Diego for the holiday already."

"Oh of course, you already have plans. So no worries, it was just a spur-of-the- moment thought," I say, stumbling over my words. He stops and turns towards me then.

"No way, Parsons. Your invite trumps his. I'm texting him right now to tell him thanks, but no thanks." He really stops walking and takes out his phone to start texting.

"Well, are you sure? You might hurt their feelings."

"Trust me, they are going to be thrilled. They've tried to hook me up for years now. If anything they are going to be begging me to bring you to meet them."

I smile at the thought. He is telling his friends that he will be spending Thanksgiving with me because I'm special to him.

Just then he puts his arm around my shoulder, puts his iPhone above our heads and says "smile."

"Josh! I don't look cute enough today for you to show your friends. Don't text that!"

"Sorry. It just sent."

"Seriously. I'm gonna kill you!" And he starts laughing. "Oh yeah, it's really funny," I say pouting.

He reaches over to hug me and I act like I'm gonna pull away. He doesn't let me and when I go ahead and hug him back he says in my ear, "You're always cute and they need to see the woman who has my heart."

He releases me a bit and we are standing face to face. "They do," I say in that squeaky gooey voice us girls use when we're flattered.

"Yes, they do." And then he kisses me.

We finish our walk holding hands, discussing our holiday plans and enjoying the day. After he drives off I realize how much I really care about him. I never invite a man to anything that has to do with my family. I have to admit it to myself, I am really starting to imagine him in my future and it makes me happy. I pull away headed home, smiling all the way.

8 Candy Fall

I was super excited the next two weeks thinking about our trip up to my parents for Thanksgiving. I was also grateful my parents did not include the whole extended family at these holiday events. It would be my sisters, nieces and nephew, brother-in-law, my grandma Georgia, Uncle Bobby and his wife Aunt Tee. I had already told Jackie and Trina, who were thrilled they were finally going to meet the famous Josh. Their trip to one of Chris' games hadn't worked so far, so now they could meet him on our home turf. He just doesn't realize how in for it he really is.

Derek and Chris were making big plans for their three-day trip and considering what games and systems they will be taking with them. I've been thinking about what I will wear and plan on dragging Sharon over to Century City for shopping one Monday. She was so impressed with me for asking him and, of course, reminded me that a man willing to meet my family probably wants to be part of the family. I like her point. I have never taken a guy to meet my parents since they met Rick when I was 16. Better to wait until I was serious about someone. I guess I'm serious about Josh.

Until then, the coming weekend is going to be a party. It is the official "Candy Fall" party for the Center. Everyone who takes a class regularly or plays on a team like the boys do, are invited to attend. They just need to sign up, tell us how many are in their party and pay $5 per person. It's usually about 100 to 150 people on the gym floor. We decorate in orange and brown to represent the fall colors and then we have Candy everywhere. In bowls for free, big bags of it for winning prizes and then we put

items like candy apples and candy corn on sale for 50 cents and $1. Sharon and I love hosting the party because the kids have so much fun. All paid staff chaperone and the volunteers assist with the games and prize giving.

We do it the last Friday of every October and this way even if kids don't celebrate Halloween or their parents don't let them go trick-or-treating they still get a chance to have some fun around the same time of year. The name "Candy Fall" represents lots of candy falling like leaves – kinda corny but it was chosen by the community staff at that time. It was my suggestion, and I was thrilled when it made it on the ballot and ecstatic when it won since I had just started working for the Center. It's a perfect event because Chris has never been out trick-or-treating door to door, just as I was not allowed to go.

This year I came as Tinkerbell, although I was a completely modest fairy with a white cardigan over my shoulders.

"Alicia, I hope you know Tinkerbell did not wear a sweater over her leaf dress, Chica."

"I know, Jill," I say, laughing since she is looking at me quite intently. "It's cold in here, brrrr." I say walking past her. I had already been through this with Trina, who said I was the biggest dud she ever knew. I told her it was either Tinkerbell and a cardigan or a medical assistant in scrubs.

"Okay, go as Tinkerbell with a coat then. At least your pretty track star legs will be showing. But seriously, Alicia, you are such a prude. Get free, girl!"

"I don't need to be, Trina, you are free enough for both of us. Tinkerbell would have her belly out and a deep V-neck if you were wearing this outfit." She giggled at that.

"Shut up and get it right, I would've done the V in the back," and we both thought that was hilarious.

I go looking for Josh, who is in charge of the door. The event runs from 6 to 10 p.m. and it was now 5:45 and almost show time. Josh is Robin, Derek is Batman and Chris is Spiderman. I take some great shots of the three of them out in front of the Community Center, and then we have Sharon take photos of the four of us once we get inside.

"Uh, Tinkerbell, can we lose the sweater?" says Sharon, sounding like Trina. And of course I tell her no. Again I repeat that it was the only thing I could find last minute other than the boring medical scrubs. I had texted Josh to ask him if he wanted to go as a doctor, but he said he was going as Robin to Derek's Batman. Then I said I would be stuck getting the Tinkerbell outfit. He texted back "as in the fairy chick with the wings and tiny dress? YES buy that one" and then added a smiley face. I smiled in the store but I already knew I would be wearing a sweater over it and shorts underneath this mini dress. So okay, maybe Trina was right when she called me a dud.

I find him talking with Sarah near the entrance as she is helping with ticket sales for the night. I just want to remind them to check the list before letting people in. Sticking to the RSVP list is a must when it comes to food and candy. We don't want to run out like we did in 2008. There was almost a riot when everyone that evening didn't get a candy bag. As I am on my way back to the gym, Josh waves me back over.

"What can I do for you, Robin?"

"Well, Tink, did I hear there would be dancing a little later?"

"As a matter of fact there will be dancing," I say and bat my eyes with the extra long lashes at him, "Want me to save one for you?"

"Heart be still," he says as he dramatically grabs his chest. "Please do."

"Aww, you kids are too cute," Sarah said adoringly.

As I walk away, he yells out "I can't believe you pinned those wings to your sweater!" I turned around and gave him a look.

"Tink is cold, okay people," and the two of them crack up.

Back in the gym I make a beeline over to the snack tables. "Sharon are you ready on your end?" I ask.

"Yep." She's wearing a Diana Ross off-the-shoulder dress, white faux fur and huge wig, which she keeps flipping behind her shoulders. "Punch, candy and food stations are ready to go, Ms. overdressed Tinkerbell."

I cut my eyes at her sassiness.

"You don't have to go there, Diana! Just cause you're hanging out of your evening gown. And where is Michael?"

"Oh he's over by the apple-bobbing station." Sure enough there is Antonio replete with one glove, sequined jacket and sunglasses. I grin over at him and he waves with the one gloved hand.

"You two really went all out didn't you?" I say to Sharon.

"Girl, we had to come with it after last year's Danny & Sandy from Grease." And she snaps her fingers to emphasize her point.

"Yeah, you guys did look pretty awesome," I say thinking back on the previous Candy Fall.

The night is so fun. We had right around 145 people. They ate the snacks, they bobbed for apples, they entered the costume contest and they danced. Well, at least the parents danced. By 9 p.m. I was bopping to the beat in the corner when I saw Josh's Robin mask through the crowd. He was coming toward me so I decided to meet him halfway on our half-court dance floor.

The DJ put on "Unthinkable" by Alicia Keys and it was a kind of movie moment because while the intro was playing we were walking toward each other and then when we were face to face we fell right into a slow dance .. .well as best we could with my wings and his cape. All the wives and those with dates had rushed to the floor. It was probably the most mellow song played the whole night. Josh sang to me, which was both entertaining and sweet. He was singing close to my ear, giving me a shiver down my spine. Nothing like being serenaded by the black Robin. We were only interrupted as we passed by Antonio and Sharon. We broke into incredible laughter because Sharon was singing to him in almost full voice and throwing her fur around.

Josh was my first date at the Candy Fall, which made the night even sweeter. One year a guy named Dean Williams and I were dating at this time of the year and Sharon thought he would be my date. But he asked if Chris was going because he thought we could go to some "Halloween Ball" on the same night. I sent him to the ball alone and came to this event with my son. I'm sure Dean met some willing Cinderella. I prefer a simple life and he always had a party invite. I don't even own party clothes so we were officially over that November.

At the end of the night we cleaned up all the surface items while Harvey and his janitorial crew swept and dumped trash. The boys helped, but also fought crime, so we eventually told them to wait for us on the bleachers. Once we were finished we all hugged goodbye. I thanked Sarah, especially for looking out for my Robin while they were working the door and I told Coach Rob his DJ friend Mikey J really rocked the house. It was a bit rainy so Josh went to get the car since the four of us had come together.

Thank God for my great hearing. After he went out of the front door I heard Derek say to Chris, "My dad hasn't smiled this much in my whole life." Chris didn't quite get it, I don't think. I couldn't see his face, but it took him a minute to answer. I couldn't turn around because then they would know I could hear them. They were on the bench in the waiting area and I was by the door.

Finally, Chris said, "Well maybe he's really happy tonight."

Then Derek said the words any mother would love to overhear her man's 10-year-old son say: "He's happy *all* the time since he met your mom. It's kinda creepy, but I guess it's better than him frowning all the time." And just like that Chris changed subjects and they were talking about the new cheat website he had found for one of his XBox games.

I smiled from my head to my feet.

I make him happy. So much so that his son notices it's me.

I stood there feeling a goofy happiness. Josh honked and I called the boys, waved to Harvey and the crew and said thanks. We jumped in the car and I reached over and kissed Josh on the cheek with my big cheese grin.

"Is that for getting the car," he asks, pleasantly surprised. Dreamily, I stare over at him and sigh and say, "It's for everything."

The next couple of weeks swirled around us. We only had four more games of this season and then the boys would be on break until the end of January. Those few weeks we were crazy finalizing the after-school roster and contacting the parents to see who would be coming back for the Winter League. The annual Christmas party as well as the caroling outing would need to be worked on as soon as we returned from Thanksgiving break.

The Tuesday before we were set to drive up to Oakland, Sharon and I had lunch at Chipotle.

"So are you all ready for your big trip to see your parents and introduce your new stud?" she asked, batting her eyes.

"Yes, I really am. I'm a little concerned my dad will give him a hard time, but my mom should love him. I know my sisters do. It's a big step bringing a man to meet them, but I feel really good about our relationship."

"Ooooooh! I'm so excited for you. Both of you. I can't wait to hear every detail and I better get a text Thursday night."

"You will be busy with your grandkids, lady, but I will text you."

"You better, missy," she says, smiling. "On a different note. Is Rick still taking Chris to see his mom Thursday morning?"

"Yes, that's the plan. Chris was not happy because Derek will have to stay behind, but I told him it's only a few hours. Then I made him feel guilty when I reminded him his Grandma Lucy only gets to see him twice, and often only once, a year. That shut him right down."

"Yeah, he'll be glad once he's there cause he's a sweet kid."

"Yes, he is," I say.

We finish out the day at the office with holiday spirit in the air and Josh and I finalize our meet time of 9 a.m. in the morning. We decide to take the scenic coast route up to the Bay Area and drive the inland Grapevine route back home so we can get home quicker. Chris and I leave to go home, both excited, and pack everything by 7 p.m. Then we order a pizza and talk about our road trip. Usually, we fly, but since we have guests I agreed to the drive. About 11 p.m. we both crash out and both of us probably dreamed about our holiday adventure.

Like clockwork, Josh got to my complex about 8:58 a.m. We loaded up my car and were on the road by 9:15. I had talked to my mom about 7 this morning and told her she would see us sometime tonight. We made our way to the 405 Freeway and then to the 101 Freeway. This was after stopping at the McDonalds on Sepulveda for Egg McMuffins and chocolate milk for the boys and iced mochas for us. We chatted about what we would eat, the cable cars, going to Gamestop if the boys could talk us into it and of course the Golden Gate Bridge at sunset. We stopped in Santa Barbara for lunch and walked a bit by the beach before taking off again. We drove all the way to Monterey without stopping so the boys both fell asleep. We cranked up the Eric Benet and Kem on my iPhone and grooved, occasionally holding hands. As I sat back in the black leather passenger seat I closed my eyes and smiled because I had never been happier in my life.

I wasn't even looking for anyone and he showed up.

We flew up the highway, stopped off at Monterey. Visited a few stores, had a snack, bought some T-shirts and taffy and were back on the road in about two hours. On our final stretch it was dark, but the boys were chatty and excited. Trina texted me asking how close we were and I told her less than an hour. She said they were saving some fried chicken and potato salad mom had whipped up. I think Josh floored it then, as we were a bit hungry.

We finally got into Oakland and arrived at my parents' house about 7:30. The lights of San Francisco were so pretty as we crossed the bridge. As we were getting out of the car my mom, Trina and her son Matthew all came outside. Chris ran up to my mom and hugged her, "Grandma!"

"Chris, how's my favorite oldest grandson?" She said smiling intensely. She had not seen us since the summer and she was so happy. Then she walked over to me to hug me while Chris went to hug his Aunt Trina and his baby cousin Matthew.

"Mom, it's so good to see you," I said, happily giving her a big hug.

"How is my independent girl?" she said, stepping back to get a better look at me.

"I'm fine, Mom, doing really good." And I hug her again as Trina comes closer. I hug her hard when I greet her and then I see their attention turn to Josh. I see Trina already giving him the once-over and, even though it's dark out, I can tell she approves.

"Mom, Trina," I say as I walk over to stand next to Josh, "This is Joshua Hart, the man I told you about."

"Joshua, it is so nice to meet you. I am truly honored to have you and your son celebrate Thanksgiving with us," and before he can speak she reaches over for a hug.

"Thank you, Mrs. Johnson. My son and I are so grateful you allowed us to come down with Alicia and Chris."

Mom is smiling as Trina tips around her and waves, "Hi, I'm Trina, the favorite sister." Then she reaches over to hug Josh as well.

"I've heard a lot about you, Trina."

"All good, I'm guessing?"

"Absolutely," Josh says and we all laugh.

"Coach, Mom, you forgot Derek. He's hiding in the back seat." Chris opens the door and Derek is there being shy.

"Derek, come on out and meet my family," I say. "This is Josh's son, Derek. And, Derek, this is my mom and sister Trina and Chris's cousin Matthew."

"And he's my best friend in the world," Chris adds proudly.

They all say hi to him and he sort of stands behind my maxi dress hiding.

"You are so handsome, young man! Glad to have you at our home," Mom enthuses. And when he's quiet I hear Josh say his name low so only he can hear. You know, that dad voice where you know you better do what they say or else.

"Thank you, Mrs. Johnson. I am very happy to be here," he speaks up. And then my mom grabs his hand and pulls him from around me for a hug.

The holiday was off to a great start.

We entered into my childhood home. It's a big southern-looking house with a porch that wraps around the front and one side of the house. There's a swing and a few wicker chairs on each side of the great big front door. As mom opens the door, the smell of her delicious fried chicken invites us in. Josh has our bags and sits them down as we enter into the front foyer. There are stairs to the right or you can go directly into the dining room. It's already set with a beautiful fall arrangement that has mini pumpkins and glitter drizzled throughout. I am sure my mom spent a small fortune at Michael's buying these decorations because these little fall accent pieces are all over the living room, which is actually more like a den. There is a huge brown sectional that has three recliners, a huge 65-inch flat screen and a window seat that looks out over their quiet neighborhood.

Mom ushers us through the den and back to the kitchen. Here, we sit at one of the islands to eat while the other island is set up as a buffet with the fried chicken, potato salad, corn, rolls and salad. I see that she and Trina were really trying to impress the company. And they do because I can see it all over Josh's face. Then once he starts eating he has them both captivated.

"This is the best chicken I've had in my entire life!" Josh says between bites.

"Me too," interjects Derek. And my family is all smiles.

"It really is delicious, Mom. Thank you so much. We were gonna stop at In-n- Out."

My mom frowns.

"Not when you're a guest at the Johnsons," she replies, and Josh smiles at her. The charmer!

"Alicia, you would have been in big trouble had I not texted you," Trina says, rolling her eyes.

"Whatever, Trina, I was gonna call first, tattle-tale," and Chris cracks up at this and then Matthew follows suit. He simply loves his big cousin.

Just then my dad walks in. "Daddy," I yell running over to him.

"How's my pretty girl?"

"I'm good, Daddy," I say, overjoyed to see him.

"She's such a goody two-shoes," I hear Trina whisper to Josh. And he whispers back, "I've noticed." Trina just finds that hysterical and I go over and punch him and tell her "Am not!" while pushing her.

"Daddy, I want you to meet my guests – Joshua Hart and his son Derek."

"He's my coach for soccer grandpa and Derek is my best friend," Chris says and Derek smiles. I beam at them because they are so cute.

"Nice to meet you, Joshua. And you as well, Derek," my dad says in his deep baritone voice as he reaches to shake hands with them both.

"Nice to meet you, as well, sir. And thank you for allowing my son and me to spend the holiday with your beautiful family." Mom and Trina are completely taken by him and my dad gives him a genuine smile.

"Well, we're glad to have you. Alicia never brings friends home so it's nice to know she actually has some." And then he chuckles deeply.

"Dad, I have friends! They just weren't worth you meeting them."

"Aww," Trina says.

Josh and I exchange glances, and I know he's feeling pretty good.

First guy could mean only guy, if he plays his cards right.

Afterward, we sit in the living room talking about everything. The neighbors, when Jackie is arriving in the morning and what sights we must cover on Friday. At 10:30 mom says she is going up to bed. She explains the sleeping arrangements. Josh and Derek will have the guest room downstairs off the kitchen. I will have my old room, Trina has her own room where she and Matthew are currently staying. But for tonight Chris and Matthew will sleep in Trina's room and Trina will stay with me in my twin beds.

Chris pouts out loud. "Grandma, Derek and I were planning on sleeping in the den." But I can tell my mom is not feeling it, especially with company coming tomorrow.

"The boys can both stay in my room with me," Josh says to my mom and they start cheering, but little Matthew starts crying that no one wants to sleep with him.

"You can stay with us, too, Matthew, if it's okay with your mom." Trina has her mouth open but then shakes her head yes. Matthew starts jumping up and down and then the boys head toward the room.

She whispers, "This man is a keeper" in my ear. Funny, I keep hearing that and I think I agree.

Once mom goes up, I get a text while we are watching *The Tonight Show*.

"I'm snowed in at Lake Tahoe and I'm not going to make it to Oakland until Friday probably. Can you take Chris to see my mom in the morning?"

I show Trina the text and she is livid. So am I, actually. He was supposed to get Chris in the morning to see his mom and then have him back here for my parents' Thanksgiving dinner. I haven't seen his mom in eight or nine years and the one time I have a man for the holiday he pulls this.

"Why are you in Lake Tahoe anyway?!"

"I took vacation early and took the last flight out tonight. I didn't know there would be a snowstorm, sorry"

"You're always sorry. Why can't you take him on Friday when you fly in?"

"She is already upset I'm missing Thanksgiving. Can't you just do this one thing for me?"

This one thing! I think about how selfish and slouchy he is, but I refuse to go there with Josh here. So I'll do what I always do. Suck it up and take Chris.

"I'll take Chris. I don't want your mom disappointed twice in one day."

"You remember where my mom lives?"

"Yes. Goodbye"

"Thanks A"

I didn't even bother replying back. All I could think was how much I can't stand him. Josh must've seen who I was texting. He took my hand and held it and kept watching TV. Never nosey, just there for me. I calm down and put my head on his shoulder. I smile to myself because I'm so glad he's here.

9 Giving Thanks

After Trina and I get the boys settled in Josh's room, we say goodnight to them and quietly tip-toe up the backstairs past our parents' room to my room. We are a bit giggly, so much so that it reminds us of our childhood. We would run up the backstairs from the kitchen and dad would be in his study and yell, "Walk! No running, girls" in his deep voice. My eyes would get as wide as saucers because I did not like getting into trouble. I would put my head in the door and say, "We're sorry, Daddy," and he would nod and say, "It's okay, Alicia." I would let out a sigh of relief and Trina would already be waiting by our rooms calling me "Miss Goody two-shoes." Oh, the memories.

Attached to dad's study is my parents' master suite, which is a large room done in ocean blue and white. There's a big bay window that I always loved. It overlooks the back yard. The back yard is all grass and has a swing set, a gazebo, a garden and pond, and, of course, a basketball hoop for the grandsons.

As we get to our rooms we collapse on my twin beds. We have Jack and Jill bedrooms so we are connected by the larger upstairs bathroom. Jackie's room is across the hall because as the oldest she got the private bedroom and bathroom.

My mom left the rooms just as they were decorated when we all moved out. So we sat in my pink princess room with the pink comforters, pink recliner and white blinds. A sheer pink valance covers my windows. In Trina's room, Mom had recently gotten rid of the trundle bed with the purple and lavender spread and bought a queen-size bed, although she did keep the hideaway bed for Matthew.

"Alicia, my sista," Trina says resting on her elbow, "I really like your friend."

"Isn't he great?"

"Yes. He's so nice, just like you said. Great with the kids, the parents and he won me over. He gets mad points!" I giggle and then turn over on my back.

"You can see why I keep wondering if he's for real. Who's this great?"

"But guess what, Sis, you already went through not-so-great. As a matter of fact you're still going through that, so I think it's time you get Mr. Wonderful." And she means it genuinely.

"You're right," I say and pause. "That's why I decided I'm going to be open to whatever happens and not so guarded. Of course, I can't help but to be myself."

"Ain't that the truth!" she interjects, but then adds, "and that's a good thing."

"But I'm enjoying the ride this time, Trina, I promise," and I sit up to look at her. "I really really like him" I say with a goofy grin.

"Aww me, too! He is great, and cute, too. You were right he is h-o-t hot!" And then she puts her finger to her lips then to her arm and makes the sizzle noise and we break into high school "you gonna get in trouble cause it's after midnight" laughter.

After we get on our jammies, turn off the lights and lay in the dark she rags all over Rick, and I let her. We chat until way after 2 a.m., but it's so much fun.

In the morning I am awakened to the smell of bacon and coffee. Usually I would brush my teeth and run right downstairs as is. Instead, I take a quick shower, throw on a little bronzer and unwrap my hair and comb it straight. I throw on sweats, T-shirt, pink robe with pink slippers, to appear I sort of got out of bed looking like this, and go down the back stairs to the kitchen.

I see its only 9:30 and I'm hoping I can still help my mom in the kitchen. When I get downstairs she and Trina are in full swing. Mom is working on the scrambled eggs and bacon and Trina is cutting up potatoes for hash brown bites. I ask where I can jump in and mom directs me to get started on the waffles. She informs me that they were nice and let me sleep in after my long drive. She and Trina were up early and had already set the table for Thanksgiving dinner, as well as setting the island and nook in the kitchen for the breakfast.

Mom is in her element. She used to co-own a catering business with her sister, but when Aunt Loretta passed six years ago, she sold the business. Now she cooks for her family and loves having company so they can all make out over her delicious meals. Mom only worked because she wanted to be busy. Dad is an excellent provider. As a lawyer for more than thirty-five years he was invaluable to the DA's office, so much so that they kept him on after retirement to consult. He's not full-time, of course, but just goes in when they call him on a case. Because of this, Trina got hooked up and works in his office for one of the lawyers.

Mom asked how we slept and Trina told her we had a sister slumber party and then laid the Rick bomb on her.

"Oh, Alicia, I'm so sorry, and with your company here, too." Then shaking her head she says "poor Rick." I turned around from the waffle iron for that one.

"Mom, poor Rick? He spends his life trying to make mine more difficult!"

"I know you think that, Alicia, but he does what he does because he's miserable about messing up his life with you." I sigh loudly.

"I see what you're saying, but did he ever stop to think changing his ways might at least put us on better terms. That's all I'm saying."

"Me too," Trina says. "I don't like the way he messes over my nephew or puts pressure on my sister." My mom smiles about this.

"I know girls and that's why you have each other to build up and protect. I did such a good job raising my girls." She says this with the proudest look on her face. She is beautiful with caramel skin and hardly any wrinkles at 68 years old. My father is the same way so I literally got hooked up with great genes. She still has her girlish figure and she wears her dark brown hair, which has just the tiniest bit of grey, in a bun. She is quite stunning.

"Well, Alicia," she says, "just know you are doing it for Chris so he can know his grandmother and you're doing it for Lucy. I know it's unfair, but you'll be fine, baby."

"I know, Mom, I called Lucy already and told her we would come for noon. So you girls take care of Josh for me."

"Oh girl, I got Josh covered! We are doing all your baby photos, track meet videos and maybe your wedding video," Trina teases, breaking into hysterical laughter.

"Oh my gosh! You better not!" I say throwing the closest dishtowel at her while she is still in stitches.

"Okay, girls, it's time to eat. Alicia, go get the boys and Trina go get your dad," she orders, amused.

As Trina heads upstairs I go down to the boys' room and knock. Josh says to come in so I open the door to find all the boys on the floor. Josh, Derek, Chris and Matthew all have controllers and I smile at the sight.

"Hey guys," I say, and only Josh says good morning. So I grab my iPhone out of my pocket and snap them.

"Time for breakfast. Grandma says right now so save your game or finish it really quick." They whine a bit but start shutting it down. I get good-morning hugs from all the boys and then Josh shocks me by shutting the door behind Matthew. He takes me in his arms and greets me with a sweet kiss.

"Good morning, Beautiful," he says, looking in my eyes.

"Good morning," I say looking right back at him, more breathless than I meant too. I mean he did just take my breath away, but I'm so obvious about it.

Still holding me he asks, "Did you sleep well?"

"Yes" I say smiling, "and you and the boys?"

"Yes, we had a great night. Matthew crawled in the bed with me at 3 a.m. and stole the cover most of the night," which I laugh at, but . . . .

Matthew had the best spot in the house last night.... Whew! Keep your mind pure, Alicia!

"You are too sweet for keeping them Josh, really."

"It was no problem. I have one already so it was just two more of the same," he says and then he kisses me again. "First good-morning kiss," he says, pulling me even closer, "I could get used to this," and he kisses me a third time.

I've just about lost reality in the Josh dream world when Trina starts banging on the door.

"Let's go, lovebirds," she says and turns the knob to open the door. Of course we're leaning on the door and she says, "I'm telling mom you're doing dirty stuff in her house!"

We both laugh with our heads together.

"Here we come," Josh says, and he gives me one last peck on the lips. "Let's go," he says and opens the door.

"Morning, Trina," he says passing by her.

"Uh huh . . . . Morning Josh," she says with her eyes on me.

"Alicia, you don't have any lip gloss on!" She loudly whispers at me. So I take it out of my pocket and roll some across my lips.

"Okay, let's go," I say, and she grabs my arm.

"Making out in the guest room, you hussy!" She teases under her breath. Then she breaks out in a grin, "Get it, girl!"

I tell her to zip it while trying to wipe the blush from my face. As we go up to breakfast I still feel the tingle from his lips. Best Thanksgiving ever!

Breakfast is awesome and everyone gets their grub on. I even talk my dad into letting us watch the Macy's Day Parade on the kitchen TV. It's my favorite. I used to watch it as a little girl and act like I was the majorette of all the marching bands with my invisible baton until one Christmas when dad bought me one, it was really on. Now I enjoy the whole parade, especially the scenes from the Broadway shows.

After breakfast I hustle upstairs to put on my black jeans, black Kenneth Cole boots and my purple sweater set with the shimmery cardigan. We don't dress up for the holidays, but definitely no T-shirts or flipflops. When I told Josh no shorts for Thanksgiving dinner he told me his mom used to make him wear a tie and dress pants so wearing jeans would be easy. I was personally excited about his jeans, but I was keeping that to myself.

When I got downstairs to get Chris, he and Derek are crowded around Josh in the window seat. As I get closer I see that Josh is skyping, and I figure it must be his parents. Sure enough he says, "Here she is, Mom, Meet Alicia" and in an instant I am on screen speaking with Josh's mom, Judy. And then I meet his dad, Bill. They say they've heard so much about me, thanked me for being so kind to their son and grandson for the holiday and to please thank my mother and father for the invite. When I say goodbye to Bill, Judy says, "Alicia, you are as beautiful as Josh said. I've been praying for a nice girl for my son and I am so thrilled you make him happy." I blush, and at this point Josh moves in to get in the camera with me.

"Mom, enough already. Can we have any secrets?" We all laugh.

I say, "Judy, it was a pleasure to meet you. And thanks for sharing those secrets with me."

She chuckles before saying "Same here. Take care for now, Alicia." I stood up and he squeezed my hand and smiled up at me from the computer before finishing his conversation with his mom.

I tell Chris to grab his jacket and I give instructions for my mom and Trina to take good care of Josh. I plan to be back by 2. Unfortunately, that is not a lot of grandma time for Lucy, but this is my weekend and I need to get back. I hug everyone and I apologize to Josh again for being a lousy host. He says he understands and that he will be fine. Trina had told him she had the photo albums on standby despite my wishes and he and my dad would be watching the game by 2. I knew my grandma, aunt and uncle were coming today so I was hoping to be home before they arrived. Derek was a little sad, but my mom was going to let him and Matthew help decorate cookies, even though she had not planned on making any.

Chris and I made our way from the Trestle Glen neighborhood, where my parents live over to the Upper Laurel area, where Grandma Lucy lives. It is less than 20 minutes away, which is one of the few saving graces Rick had. We pulled up in front of her quaint little house with the diamond shaped window she always placed her Christmas tree in, and the big Elm tree that covers most of her front yard.

Lucy Parsons was always such a sweet woman to me. She was always nice and was pleased that her son was getting good grades hanging out with me in high school and not out late at night getting in trouble. Her husband, Rick and Connie's dad, left the family when the kids were very small. Rick could barely remember him and once his father left he didn't do anything for the kids, just a check here and there and sometimes a Christmas gift.

Rick said he would never forget their birthdays, though. Lucy worked two jobs to support them and keep the house. I had not asked him what was up with his father in a long time.

We parked and walked up to her front door with a basket my mother gave me from the law firm. It looked so lovely with the box of See's candy, Martinelli's Sparkling Cider, Perrier water, cheese, fancy popcorn and the like. Mom said we were so blessed that we should spread our blessings around, and as we got closer to the door I realized moms are always right. It seemed very quiet and I wondered if Lucy was even home. Chris was quiet and I understood, so I didn't bother him. If his dad had made it to town, Chris would have been over here half the day. As I thought of that, I told him lose the sad face and smile. Of course, he gave me a phony one and I poked him. As we were having our moment, Lucy Parsons opened the door. She seemed smaller than I remembered her, and her face, though still pretty, had aged more than it should have.

"Chris! Look at my grandson. I missed you so much, sweetie" and she reached for him so I pushed him a bit to get him moving and he hugged her.

"Hi Grandma."

"And, Alicia! Hello sweetheart, you look beautiful," she said as she held me at arm's length.

"Hello Lucy," I said, giving her a warm hug. "This is for you from my mom." And her face lit up.

"Oh! This is so beautiful. Just like Lois to send over something so lovely. Please give her my love."

"I certainly will," I say as she ushers us into the house.

"Sit down you two. Let's sit and catch up. I have lemonade and iced tea and Chris' favorite cookies. I made them last night, cinnamon sugar."

"Oh yes, I love those! Thank you, Grandma," he said, and then gave her a big hug. She hugged him tight and I almost felt bad for her with this empty house and no sign of family.

"Where are Connie and the grandkids," I ask, hoping to hear they would be over any minute. Lucy looked sad for a minute before composing herself.

"Well dear, I guess Rick did not mention it to you. Connie got married this summer and her husband moved her and the kids to Arizona. The Phoenix area. She looks at me and smiles sweetly, although I can still see the sadness in her eyes.

"She said they would be having this first Thanksgiving with his family."

"No Lucy, he didn't tell me. That's great news for her, but sorry you won't have them here this year for Thanksgiving."

"Yes me too, Alicia. Then when Ricardo said he was stuck in the bad weather I figured I wouldn't get to see any of my grandchildren this year," and she looks down at the floor in an effort, I believe, not to cry. All I can think is how raggedy Rick is for leaving his mother alone on the holiday.

She then looks up at me. "I just thank you so much for taking this time to stop by. I know it's inconvenient and it's taking your time away from your family so thank you so much, I am so grateful." Now she's trying to keep the tears from coming so she stops, and rubs Chris on the back.

"They are so good, Grandma," Chris says to her and that makes her happy. I have to hold it together because my eyes are almost watering.

Chris asks if he can watch TV and, of course, she says yes, so he turns on the Disney Channel. She and I sit and chat about Chris' grades, his soccer playing, how good a boy he is and about her son. She tells me that she was devastated that he did not do right by me and that she was embarrassed by his behavior as both a husband and father. Then she explained how Rick's father was the same way. He started out being loving and excited about their future as a couple and family. His parents had pretty much disowned him when he got serious about her, the Puerto Rican girl who worked at the corner diner. His family expected him to marry within his race and faith. In their eyes, he let them down so they let him go. They did not celebrate his marriage or support it in any way. Even when the couple had kids they never wanted to see their grandchildren. She did say Rick's grandmother sneaked over a few times and would send him and Connie gifts on their birthdays and Christmas, but no regular contact. She said Walter, Rick's father, then started drinking and hanging out and not being a father or husband. Eventually, he told her he could not stay married to her and he left them. Lucy spent the rest of her life raising her two kids and providing for them, just as Rick had told me before. Lucy said she did the best she could to raise Rick as a good man, and then she began sobbing. I scooted over on the couch to put my arm around her and tell her it was okay, that she had done a good job.

"Oh, Alicia, thank you for saying that, but I am so sorry for what Rick did to you and how he treats you and my grandson."

Chris turns around to look at her, but I mouth to him to turn around. It was okay. I don't know if he totally believed me, but he obeyed.

"Lucy, you did what any mother would have done and you took care of your family. Rick is a grown man now and the decisions he makes are his own and no reflection on you. You have always treated me kindly and with love."

She thanked me and told me how grateful she was again that I brought Chris to see her, as I held onto her with tears stinging my own eyes. After she sat up she went to her room to refresh and wipe her tears. It was almost 2:30 so I texted Josh to check on him.

"Hey u, what's going on at the Johnson house?"

"Me missing u." My heart skipped a happy little beat reading that.

"Aww, I miss u too. We should be leaving in the next 10 minutes though so hold on"

"I'll try. I'm sitting between Trina & Jackie looking at your baby pictures. You look exactly the same...adorable!"

"Omg! I am going to kill them! Why aren't u watching football?"

"It's on but when Jackie got here she had to question me, the twins had to interrogate me and your dad and brother-in-law said I was on my own"

"So sorry!! I'll be there to rescue you soon :)"

"I'll be waiting."

I smile widely. I think I actually miss him. I close out my phone just as Lucy walks back in. "You're smiling, dear. Is that a gentleman you were on the phone with?"

"Well, yes. It's the man I've been seeing and he's over at my mom's house." A look of horror crosses her face.

"Alicia, I have kept you from your family and *your* boyfriend! Let me pack up these cookies for Chris and I'll let you two go."

"Okay, Lucy, thank you so much. Are you going to your sisters for dinner?" I ask her, and she walks back in to tell me her sister decided to go to one of their cousins this year and she doesn't care so much for them.

"I'm just gonna stay in and relax."

"On Thanksgiving?" I'm feeling terribly for her.

"Well, I bought myself some cornish hens and some fixings and tomorrow Rick should get in town and I'll make him take me out." She went back into the kitchen and I think Rick could easily flake on her, and besides that it will be the day after Thanksgiving – totally not the same thing. I knew what had to be done. So after she and Chris came out of the kitchen I told her to get her coat because she was coming with us. She argued with me a bit, but her sad eyes turned happy as soon as she realized I was serious. How could I leave Chris' grandmother alone? Because of her I have Chris, so we piled into my car and headed to my mom's. While she got her coat I texted Trina that I was bringing Lucy for dinner and to let mom know. When she texted back: "just Lucy?" I replied "yes, she is all alone today."

Chris and Grandma Lucy talk all the way there. He told her all about Derek his best friend in the whole world and that he couldn't wait for her to meet him. I smile because although Rick tried to ruin my day I realize he couldn't because I choose whether it's good or not, and it's turning out great.

When we get to the house I open the door and I am so happy to see my big wonderful family. The smell in the air is so delicious, and I can't wait to eat. My dad, Josh, Derek, my brother-in-law John and Uncle Bobby are all watching football. I hug Uncle Bobby and John and re-introduce them to Lucy and then I hug Josh as if it's been weeks since I've seen him. I look in his eyes and all I feel is love.

Alicia, are you in love with this man? This is much sooner than I would have allowed myself to be.

I shoo the thought away and bask in his warm brown eyes.

"Alicia?" And it's Grandma Lucy tapping me on the shoulder.

Whoops! Guess we were in our own world.

"Lucy, please meet Joshua Hart, the man we spoke about earlier. Josh, this is Grandma Lucy." He gives her a hug and she shakes her head in approval.

"Nice to meet you, Joshua," she says as she continues to check him out. "I like him, Alicia." And then to Josh she says "take care of her. She's an extraordinary woman."

"Yes ma'am I will," he says. And with a pat on my cheek she follows Chris back toward the kitchen. "I'm gonna go see my, sis" I whisper to him and I head toward the kitchen as well. Right before I get to the door the twins, my nieces Jennifer and Jessica bum-rush me in a double bear hug.

"Auntie Alicia!" they both scream in unison.

"Hi girls," I yell back, hugging them both tightly.

"We love Josh!" "He is so much fun," Jenn says, "He is so cute!" Jess says. "We approve," they both say in unison and hug me again. And then I enter the kitchen and I see Jackie. She comes over for some sister hugs and Trina joins us because she's silly.

"Little sis, finally! How's my girl?" Jackie says looking like a CEO in her Misook pants set and heels, obviously purchased at Nordstrom, her favorite store. Her twins are also always dressed in the latest outfits and shoes from Brass Plum, the juniors department in Nordstrom. She got married at 21, just one year before I came out to stay with her in L.A. They say middle kids are sometimes the left out ones or the child who doesn't get a lot of attention, but I've found I have the best of both worlds being the closest with both my older and younger sister. I give her a big tight hug back.

"Jackie!" I yell. "I'm fine, Sis. How are you?"

"I'm good, doll. And I bet you're good too since you drove out here with that stud in there," she says playfully fanning herself.

"Yeah, I know. I think he's pretty cute, too," I say all smiley. And then she gets that drippy look.

"Are you in love, Alicia?" And she looks at me expectantly as if I would admit to all these women in the kitchen if I loved this man when I can't even admit it to myself.

"Well, I really really like him so let's just say I'm headed in that direction." And she claps her hands together and lets out an excited scream.

"You really are a cornball aren't you?" Trina says from across the kitchen.

"I was thinking the same thing!" I add and we crack up.

"Shut up you two," Jackie says semi-pouting.

"Enough, my darling daughters," Mom adds. "Now let's finish up these vegetables and the salad. Lucy and Aunt Tee just sit and enjoy yourselves. Tell the twins to look out for great-grandma. She should be arriving shortly."

The kitchen is the Johnson women's hub, and we talk, laugh, cook and get caught up in there for the next hour. My beautiful grandma showed up with my mom's cousin so that was a treat for us all as we had not seen her in almost eight years. At 4:30 all of the food was set out and all 17 of us sat down to eat. The dining table held 12 so we shoved in two extra chairs for the twins and had Josh bring in the fold up card table for the kids and that's where the three boys sat. My mother had outdone herself with a huge turkey, two hams, prime rib, dressing, mac and cheese, green beans, spinach soufflé, mashed potatoes, creamed corn, green salad, homemade monkey bread and corn muffins.

Dessert included apple and pumpkin pies as well as pumpkin cheesecake and peach cobbler. And, of course, the cookies she decorated with the boys earlier. As I sat and looked at the spread I thought how could I not invite Grandma Lucy. She was so happy to be there with Chris.

My dad blessed the food and we ate, shared stories, laughed and fellowshipped way into the night. The boys eventually went to play video games, but not before annoying their girl cousins first. What's Thanksgiving without kids? Somewhere in the middle of all the noise while Josh had his arm around me, he whispered in my ear, "This has got to be the best Thanksgiving ever."

I looked at him smiling my agreement and whispered back in his ear, "I was thinking the same thing."

10 Tourist Attractions

That night as I am lying in bed I think back over the great day we had. After dinner there were family games like Charades, Scattergories and Scrabble for us hard-core gamers. Grandma Lucy had so much fun she wasn't ready to go until 10:30. She hugged both my parents and thanked them from the bottom of her heart for the best Thanksgiving she had in her entire life. I think she truly meant that. Aunt Tee gave me her thumbs up on Josh and even Uncle Bobby said he was a "very nice guy for me," which says a lot since Uncle Bobby is a quiet man. As my grandma and cousin left, my grandma said it was "so nice to meet your future husband." I blushed and simply said "thank you," because you don't argue with Grandma. I figured maybe I should take it as a sign.

Josh and I drove Grandma Lucy home and she talked all the way there about how lovely my family was, that she wished she had a family like that growing up and even wished she had it now. When we arrived at her house we both walked her to the door. She gave me the absolute biggest hug and told me she was sorry about Rick again and then she whispered even lower, "He didn't even call me today." I told her I was sorry and that I was glad I could be there for her today and she smiled. She told Josh to hold onto me and never let me go. That one almost knocked me out. Her son is so bootleg she has now told another man not to let me go. Wow, I thought, that is saying a lot. Josh told her "not to worry." I raised my eyebrows to their entire exchange.

We waited for her to lock her door and then we walked hand in hand to the car and then drove back to my mom's in the same manner.

When we got back the boys were in the room playing XBox while the adults and twins were watching "Thor." We joined them and us night owls even hung out for *Iron Man 2*. We packed it in about 3 a.m., and now here I am drifting off with great memories of a wonderful holiday.

Morning comes, but I barely roll out of bed by 10 a.m. Before getting dressed I call Sharon to give her all the updates from yesterday, especially Rick's rudeness, and bringing Grandma Lucy over for dinner. She knew it was big news since I called her instead of texting her. I told her it was too much to be writing and she agreed. She spent the day with her two sisters and two brothers after doing most of the cooking. She had me cracking up telling me she made everyone wait on her hand and foot. She said it was the least they could do since all they brought were paper goods, rolls, sodas and Costco cakes. She skyped her son and found out she is expecting another grandbaby so she was celebrating.

"Did all your family love Josh?" she asked as I was about to get her off the phone. "Girl, they loved him! My grandma called him my husband and Jackie, Trina and the twins all gave me their approval. He's in with this family, so he just needs to keep it up," I said smiling into the phone. "Even my mom has been charmed by Mr. Hart," I say chuckling.

"Well, if Mrs. Johnson likes him, he's really in." We chat about the rest of the trip and I tell her today is Black Friday shopping at Union Square over in San Francisco followed by an early Chinese dinner in China Town and a drive up to Lombard Street. I told her my parents were keeping all the kids while us adults hung out. Then tomorrow we'll close out the trip with a full day of sightseeing ending with the Golden Gate Bridge. She wished me fun and romance the rest of my trip before we sent each other love and hung up.

The twins came in at that point to say good morning and let me know Josh helped my mom with breakfast this morning. They also told me they talked a lot about me and that my mom shared with him about Rick and how I am now guarded because of it.

Wow, Mom!

"So girls, how do you know all of this was said?" I ask. It is hilarious watching Jennifer and Jessica look at each other as if to say, should we tell Auntie the truth?

"Well, Auntie, we were going in to get some cereal," Jennifer said, "but when we pushed the kitchen door just a bit, there was grandma talking to Josh," Jessica added, finishing what Jennifer had started.

"Okay, so why didn't you just go in and interrupt?" I asked them with raised eyebrows.

"Because we wanted to know if Josh might tell grandma he loves you," Jennifer said.

With my puzzled expression I asked them, "Why would he say that to her?" Jessica said, "because Mom says she can see it in his eyes!" Then I knew this was all about Jackie. She probably told the girls to be on the lookout. So I bought in to it.

"Well, did he tell her that he loved me?" They both start to smile.

119

"Auntie, not exactly, but the look on his face when he's talking about you," Jennifer said dreamily, "says the love is in his heart."

Lord, these girls are 14 years old and hopeless romantics just like their mom. "You really think so?" I ask.

"Yes" they say in unison, smiling from ear to ear. We continue our discussion a bit more and then I send them to tell everyone I'll be down in a little while.

I dress comfortably in Jeans, grey sweater and grey Ugg boots.

"Okay, people, lets pull it together and get ready to hit the streets! The shoppers are going to be out and annoying." Everyone was dressed so I realized I really had slept in. Guess I needed it. After a quick bowl of Wheat Chex, Jackie, John, Trina, Josh and I loaded into the rental Expedition John picked up at the airport. We headed over the Bay Bridge into San Francisco, chatting along the way. My sisters grilled Josh all the way to Union Square.

"Alicia used to get in big trouble coming to the city on Friday nights without telling dad" Trina's big mouth said, and "Alicia got in big trouble for going to the 10th grade dance without asking permission," Jackie added.

They just laughed and kept coming up with stories.

John felt bad for me. "She's a great sister-in-law, though," he said winking at me in the rear view mirror and trying to shut the girls down.

"And I love my brother-in-law," I say back to him with a wink of my own.

He really is the coolest, most laid-back man I know. He lets Jackie do what she needs to do, and because she takes good care of him, he is okay with her big important job at the hospital. Plus he's a great father and provider himself, as owner of his own construction business, which has been located in the Riverside area for more than 10 years. His interruption didn't work, though, as they then started in on him. It was hilarious and Josh was taking it all in. I was sitting in the middle of him and Trina and he chimed in when Trina mentioned how when I thought I might get in trouble I would think of every possible scenario that could happen, totally stressing out and how she would tell me to just relax.

Josh thought that was hysterical. "I know what you mean, she over-thinks all the time!"

Trina said, "Oh Lord, even you've been exposed to her" and she joined in with him and they even high-fived each other.

"Really!" I said, "Hello, I am sitting right here." They both babied me and each gave me a kiss on the cheek trying to win me back over.

It was good times all day long. We started at Macy's moving through the massive crowds and then we walked through the actual Square making our way all the way down to Fisherman's Wharf via bus.

We looked at purses, smelled perfumes and colognes along the way, stopped to eat clam chowder at the Wharf and grabbed coffee's at Starbucks. We all ended up spending money at Kids Foot locker on outfits for our kids and tennis shoes for all three of the boys. I walked Josh through Sephora to help with Christmas gift ideas for me, in case he was wondering. In addition to the great makeup, there are train cases, makeup bags of all sizes, and gift cards, of course. By the time late afternoon hit, I had seen a great jacket I could get Josh for Christmas and I smelled several colognes that had great gift sets like gym bags that I think I might get him as well. I bought both my sisters and nieces makeup bags at Sephora and my mom a beautiful wrap I found in a great boutique near Ghirardelli Square. Josh and I rounded out our purchases with souvenirs for Sarah, Harvey, Jill and a little something for Sharon.

We next went to our favorite spot for an early dinner in Chinatown and were able to chat, with the guys talking sports while us girls caught up on all the latest. The day ended with a trip to Lombard Street. It was early evening so the lights were up even though it wasn't totally dark yet. It was beautiful! We took pictures of ourselves with the view in the background. We took silly pics and finally had a random person take a group shot of us. Trina said she was posting that one on Facebook. Even though we all have pages we are terrible at posting so I asked her to email me copies of everything she had been taking.

We made our way back to the car, and on the way Josh's close friend, Davis, from San Diego texted to tell him they hoped he had a happy Thanksgiving, to give Derek their love and to tell me hello. I was reading as he texted that it was "The best Thanksgiving he and Derek had ever had." He also went on to tell him about my sisters, mom and all my family.

His friend said, "Man, I am so happy for you and I can't wait to meet Alicia."

I said "Aww, he is so sweet!" Trina leaned right over me and asked, "Who's sweet?"

Josh told her it was his best friend Davis from San Diego. This crazy girl says "Ooh, is he single, Josh?" I looked at her with wide eyes, "Trina!" But Josh just chuckled.

"Actually, Trina he isn't. He is happily married."

She sighed, "Okay, good for him. I guess I won't hate. But keep an eye out, aight?" We all laughed at her comment and Josh told her he would. I thought about Coach Rob back home, but didn't want to bring him up since he is unhappily separated. He wants his wife back so I figured no sense getting her excited for a man still holding a candle. Josh had spoken with him yesterday and he said he was miserable on the holiday. I felt horrible for him since he's such a nice man.

When we got back to the house the kids were so excited to see us. We found out my parents had taken them to the movies and then for dinner at Round Table pizza. We sat around the living room lounging as the kids gave us the rundown on the entire day. I know how blessed our kids are to see their grandparents regularly and it warmed my heart seeing Derek take to them as if he were one of the grandkids.

Hmm . . . he could be one of them one day.

My mom goes into the kitchen to make coffee for everyone and while she's gone the phone rings. She calls me into the kitchen and when I go in to see what she wants she says "Rick is on the phone." The frown on my face says it all, but I pick up the phone on the counter anyway.

"Hey," I say, as carefree as I can.

"A, I just wanted to call and thank you for taking Chris to my Mom's. It made her whole year! She couldn't stop talking about everything." I relax a bit hearing how pleased Grandma

Lucy was about spending the day with my family, and her grandson especially.

"It was our pleasure. I enjoyed the time at her house and so did Chris. She got her grub on and then stayed late hanging out at my Mom's. Were you able to get to her house today?"

Funny, it seems at this moment I hear an airport announcement.

Is this fool in some airport?

"Well, actually, after I got snowed in. We ended up going back to my friend's house for Thanksgiving. So today you know I called her and she said she was okay if I just left to go back home."

Oh my gosh! Only the Lord knows how grateful I am that Lucy spent the day with us. She would've been all alone the entire holiday weekend.

I shudder at the thought.

To this loser, though, all I can say is, "wow." And somehow his tone changes after mine goes south.

"Thing is, I knew it was okay with her after she went on and on about your wonderful parents, family, spending the day with Chris and then her over-the-top reaction to the soccer coach," he says with more than a hint of sarcasm. Now this makes me want to laugh in the phone and I try hard to keep the pleasure out of my voice. I can just imagine Lucy going on and on about Josh.

Then he goes, "I'm trying to figure out the purpose for him to go with you to my Mom's house. He's not your family and he's not Chris' dad!" And as usual this pathetic man has gotten funky with me.

"Rick, I'm not trying to hear anything *you're* saying. I left *my* company to take Chris to *your* mom's because *you* weren't here to take *your* own son to see *your* own mom! So when I took her home it was late so my *boyfriend* drove us there cause he's a *gentleman!*" Now I had started to raise my voice, but I wasn't yelling – yet. I just felt the need to emphasize some words to this ridiculous man. Of course, my mom has come over to rub my back and Trina and Jackie obviously realize who I'm talking to and come in to lean on the island as I finish the conversation.

"Now do you want to talk to your son? Otherwise, I will see you in L.A.!" And this time I am screaming.

"Yes, I want to talk to Chris," he hisses.

"I'll get him," I hiss back. Trina heard me and went to get Chris. He bounded in to speak with his dad.

"Hi Dad. Where were you for Thanksgiving?" And that's all I had to hear before shaking my head.

Why does my child have to ask his father where he was for Thanksgiving? I hope this loser gets it together for Christmas.

Then Trina says it out loud. Mom tells us to keep our holiday spirit and help her take the coffee and cocoa into the den. Once everyone is settled with their mugs, I find a spot next to Josh on the couch. I snuggle against him and he kisses my hand and asks me if I'm okay.

"I am now," I say, kissing his hand back.

After a fun night of movies and popcorn we all hit the hay. All I can think is what a great holiday vacation this has been and wonder if Josh will come back with me next month. With him here, even when Rick is annoying I can hang up and be with

Josh and everything will be right in my world. Then I drift off to sleep.

Saturday arrives and I know I have to make our last day the best, which is hard to do since every day has been incredible! After a light breakfast of cereal, toast and fruit we hit the streets early. We pile into two cars and head back to San Francisco. We head to Bay Street with the rest of the tourists to line up for the cable cars. Every visitor to the city must ride at least once. Chris and Matthew hadn't been in years so they were as excited as Derek. And after only a 45-minute wait we were able to catch a ride. Up the hill we went and all of us had a blast, not just the kids. I don't know how we talked daddy into coming, but even he was enjoying the ride and the grandkids' excited chatter. And with twelve of us, we take over most of that particular cable car ourselves.

Trina is snapping pics of all of us with her Candy Apple red Nikon camera. As the hill gets steeper I'm forced up against Josh and I apologize.

"No need to be sorry," he says. "This is actually quite comfy." We have an intimate laugh and share moment before Trina says, "Aww! You two are so annoyingly cute."

I give her a look. And then I look at all my family and realize everyone is really here. They must like Josh and Derek as much as me because they are all doing the tourist day with us. I sneak a peek around Josh's shoulder and see Derek explaining something in detail to my dad while Chris listens intently. It's like my son really has a brother and I love that for him.

At the top of the hill where the cable cars end or begin, based on where you boarded, sits the City Centre Shopping Mall.

Inside is a fabulous Nordstrom for Jackie and the twins to browse through, being their favorite store and all. It's hilarious to have my parents out during this crazed shopping time but dad does well once he finds a bench to chill on.

John and Josh take all the boys to Game Stop, which is close by. John also mentions the Apple Store to Josh so they decide to check that out, too. Because of the guys, Trina and I get to go with Mom, Jackie and the girls to Nordstrom. On the way up the elevator Trina says, "Alicia, I love that Josh of yours. He has let my child bunk with him every night and now he takes him to the game store so I can shop with you girls. He is the one for us!"

We all laugh. "I'm not kidding, though, he seems to be as wonderful as my other brother-in-law, John. So if you hook up with him, then I know my Prince will be arriving shortly thereafter."

"Trina, he will come in time, baby. You are doing a great job with your son and your life. The right man will come," Mom says. Trina gives her a side hug. "Thanks, Mom."

"Mom is right about that, Trina. And, Alicia, I like Josh too," says Jackie. "He is down to earth, has a warm friendly personality and he makes my sister smile."

"And we like him too, Auntie," the twins chime in.

"Well, I'm glad I have approval from the most important people in my life," I say, giving them all a cheese grin.

Shopping with all the Johnson women is hilarious. Mom likes to look at the St. Johns, Jackie favors the Classique line, the twins head straight to Brass Plum and Trina heads down to shoes. As for me, I'm more of a Point of View girl. About two hours later Josh calls me to say my dad and John took the cable cars back down to get the cars and that he and the boys are sitting in the Food Court eating pretzels. I round up all the women and we head toward the main entrance where Josh and the boys are waiting.

"They should be here any minute, ladies," Josh says.

"Thank you so much for allowing Matthew to hang with you guys," Trina gushes at him.

"Are you kidding me. I wouldn't have it any other way. He is a great kid."

When we see the cars we all run out into the chilly bay breeze and jump in. It's about 2 p.m. so we go have a late lunch at the Cheesecake Factory. Everyone is starving and we have a fun, loud and rowdy family lunch. I keep looking over at Josh who is in a deep conversation with my dad. I'll have to figure out what they were discussing later. I keep everyone focused so we can finish and get across the Golden Gate Bridge. The sun will be going down by the time we leave and it is going to be really cold. So glad I told everyone to get their heavy coats.

We make it across to the north side of the bridge with the tons of other tourists and park at the Vista point scenic area that gives a perfect view of the bridge. You can take photos all day and even walk down the slope a bit to get a shot upward at its magnificence. I never tire of coming to see it because it is one of the most beautiful locations in the world, I think. I can tell by sneaking a glance at Josh that he is thoroughly impressed. My dad comes closer and puts his arm around me and slows my pace.

"Hey, Dad. So glad you and Mom came out with us today. Us girls don't get you two out together too often. So thank you, Daddy."

"Alicia, I just wanted to see you and this young man together and that's why I came."

"Really?" I say, looking at him surprised.

"Indeed. You are my little girl and I had to see who was so special you brought him home for the holiday."

I look up at him then and he is absolutely serious. "Rick has put you through a terrible time and my grandson also. I can't tell you how many times I wanted to kill him or at the least bring you back home to live with me. But I like Joshua. I know your sisters and mom do, too, but as the man in your life, I say take it slow. He is a great young man and if he is who you decide to be with then you certainly have my blessing. But make it for you, baby."

Then he kisses me on the forehead and calls my mother over to keep him warm, he says.

I stand alone for just a minute composing myself. I have tears fighting to come to the surface, but I don't allow them to. That's why my dad came, to see Josh interact with me and to speak personally with him. What else could a girl ask for? And knowing that, although he's been quiet all these years, he's wanted to hurt Rick for hurting me, now that really warmed my heart.

Trina and Jackie come over to link their arms with mine.

"Daddy talk, huh?" Trina asks.

"Yep," I say, still trying to hold it together.

"Trying to hold the tears in?" Jackie asks.

"Yep," I say as they put their heads together with mine.

"That's a great shot," Josh says. "I got it. The beautiful sisters."

"Thank you, Josh, but you don't have to include those two in your comments," Trina says. Jackie and I laugh.

"Shut up, girl! He was talking about me" I say, putting his arm around my shoulder.

"Whatever!" she says.

Then we take a hundred photos – of the kids, the kids and the grandparents, the boys, then all the men, then all the women. Josh and I take at least 20 of us together. Some with the iPhone turned toward us with the bridge behind us and some Trina took. We are most definitely freezing as the sun threatens to disappear for the day. John asks a random man if he will take a photo of the entire family. He agrees, and we all pose in a big group as he snaps us.

"Now let's get out of here everybody," John yells. "To the cars."

Josh grabs my hand to pull me back as I am on my way with the group.

"It's freezing, Mr. Hart!"

"I know, but thank you for this whole weekend, for saying yes to the miniature golf double date, for being wonderful. You have my heart, Alicia Johnson. Please don't break it," Josh says before he kisses me.

In the freezing cold, in the midst of the tourists, with John and my dad now honking the horns, I don't feel cold anymore, just warm on the inside. I have his heart and he asked me not to break it. I kiss him back.

"I won't," I whisper in his ear, and then I grab his hand as we run back to the cars.

11 Heading Home

As we roll down the I-5 toward home, I lean back and close my eyes. Being able to spend that quality time together and getting to see my whole family and having them meet Josh was priceless. It was like he came into my life at the perfect time.

After our full day of shopping and sight-seeing we come home to one more night of family movies and popcorn. We packed and made a plan to head out at 10 a.m. Pretty late for a drive home from the holiday, but we all decide to have a family breakfast.

John and Jackie have to leave at 10 as well to get to the airport on time to return their rental car. In the morning we all chow down on waffles, bacon, eggs and potatoes – one last meal from my mom to all of us. We all crowd around the island, some standing, some on stools and then all the kids were crowded into the breakfast nook making plans for the next visit. And that's when my mom asks everyone what they want to eat for Christmas.

"Traditional turkey and dressing" I yell out first. "Cornish hens" Jackie says and everyone boos her.

"No one wants hens over turkey," Trina says. Jackie sticks her tongue out at her.

"How about your green bean casserole, Mom, we haven't had that in a while," John says. And we all ooh and ahh over that suggestion.

"Peanut butter pie," Chris yells and then the twins say, "Christmas cookies." Then as we are all thinking and there is a lull, Derek says, "Chocolate cake in the shape of a Christmas tree!" Josh and I look at each other because this meant Derek had decided he wanted to be at the Johnson house on December 25th.

"I have never tried to make a cake like that before Derek, but I think it's a great idea," my mom said as everyone agreed. Derek was beaming with pride. Then she looked over at Josh. "And what about you, son? Is there anything special you would like to see on the Christmas menu?" Josh looked at me again with a sheepish grin.

"Well, Mrs. Johnson, I haven't been formally invited to come back for Christmas." I keep eating, trying not to laugh and then Trina interrupts it all.

"Well, we are inviting you. You don't have to look at Alicia for permission."

I crack up. Her boldness is hilarious.

"It's true Josh. We wouldn't have it any other way. You and Derek have to be here," Jackie adds. Derek has a smile so big I wish I had my camera out.

"Looks like you're in," I say to Josh pushing his shoulder with mine. He smiles completely and tells my mom, "I really like your corn pudding, so can we have that on Christmas, too?" She puts her hand over his from across the counter and says, "We sure can."

I feel warm and toasty all over. My family likes him as much as I do and they are all so funny showing it. The kids start talking about seeing the lights at Jack London Square next time and how we could go caroling again like we did a few Christmases ago.

When it is time to leave it's kind of hard. I hug my mom and dad and thank them for everything. They tell me they are proud of me and they will be praying for me. They tell Josh to drive safely and my dad tells him, "Take care of my little girl," to which he said "not to worry" and my dad hugs him goodbye.

Wow, he really made an impression on my whole family.

My sisters, the twins, John and especially Matthew give him big love and my sisters both whisper, "He's the one, Sis," in my ear. The twins had already decided he is their new uncle and even John said, "He's good people, Lil Sis," as well as letting me know he threatened him if he ever hurt me.

Nothing like family, I think to myself. Then I look over and Derek is hugging my parents goodbye and when he gets to my mom he says, "May I call you grandma, too?" And I can see Josh is going to say something, but I grab his sleeve because I knew my mom was okay with it.

"You would like to call me grandma, Derek?" He shook his head yes.

"I would be honored to have a new grandson," she says and hugs him big and gives him a big kiss on the cheek. He smiles a wide smile and tells Chris, "your grandma is my grandma, too." Chris is so happy for him. We drive away after that waving until we cannot see them anymore.

After burgers and fries later up the highway, the boys crash out somewhere near Bakersfield. That's when Josh tells me about Derek's other grandparents. He told me how his parents were there for him and Eleanor during the delivery and birth and how his mom had moved in to help care for the newborn. Eleanor had an aunt that lived in San Diego, but she never came to see the baby or call.

He thought that was very odd, and when he would ask Eleanor about it she would just say her aunt was busy. When he asked about sending photos via email or even hard copies to her parents, Eleanor said, "I already did," and basically told him to stop bugging her. Well, one day Eleanor's mom called and he answered the phone. He greeted her, asked her how she was doing and told her Eleanor wasn't in.

"When do you think she will be back?" Mrs. Cole asked.

"I'm really not sure," Josh replied. "But since I have you on the phone I just wanted to make sure you got the photos of Derek." Silence on the other end, he said.

"Who is Derek?" Mrs. Cole asked.

He almost fell out of the chair, he said, because obviously she had to be kidding. "Derek is our son. Didn't Eleanor tell you?"

Her mom started to chuckle softly. "Joshua, she never even told me she was pregnant. I guess she knew how badly I would talk about her. I cannot believe she set herself up like this! I certainly thought she was a lot smarter."

Josh cleared his throat, "Excuse me?" he said.

"It's just that I had her when I was 15. It was hard and a struggle and I never did in life what I had planned. I told her not to go laying up with no man and have no babies at a young age! I suspect that's why she never told me."

Then Josh was silent. "Oh, I see," he said, finally.

"No offense against you or the baby, but she probably realized her mistake and was too embarrassed to tell me. I would have killed her if she didn't graduate."

Josh was literally shaking his head at this point.

"Well, Mrs. Cole, I'll be happy to inform you that she is thrilled at being a mother. We are very happy and I plan on asking her to marry me."

He said at that point she let out a sigh and a laugh and said, "Good luck with that."

He said he was quite distraught and as they closed out the conversation he asked if she would like a photo and she said, "Sure, text me a pic of the kid." He was so angry and hurt by Eleanor not telling her mom that he said he paced and paced till she got home.

When she finally arrived he asked her one last time if her mom had gotten the photos of Derek and she said yes.

"Liar," he yelled.

"What are you talking about, Josh?" she shot back.

"I talked to your mom earlier today and she never even knew you were pregnant!" he yelled.

At this point Eleanor tried to compose herself and sat down, smoothing her skirt.

"I didn't tell my mother because she said I needed to stay focused on my life and career and not on boys. She already went through having a baby young and she knows it can hold you back from your dreams. I just didn't want to disappoint her."

Josh said he was so angry he could barely contain himself. He picked Derek up out of the playpen.

"This is a disappointment? This innocent baby that's a part of both of us! How can you even think that, regardless of what your mother told you?"

She got angry herself then.

"This is why I didn't tell you, Josh! I knew you would be mad. I had to do what was best for my life, and keeping this from my mom was best for me. You live in a fantasy world!" she said glaring at him. "I love Derek, but I need to make money and be a success and I don't know if I can do that with a kid."

Josh said he felt as if someone had taken the breath out of his body. Who was this person and how did he fall in love with her in the first place? he wondered. He knew he got caught up with her looks and charisma at first, but he could not believe she was so shallow.

"So having a career is more important than family?" he asked.

She sighed and came over to him and grabbed his hand.

"Josh, family is important and I love you and Derek. But this is not what I planned for myself and I'm having a hard time dealing with being a mother over going on to graduate school. I just don't know if I'm ready for all this!"

He could not believe it. He took his hand away.

"Well I will never give up my son for anything. I would support you and take care of him while you finish your education, but if you can't handle this or being with us then let me know." And he stormed away and slammed the door to their bedroom.

So she wasn't interested in being a mom and probably not a wife, and her mom wasn't interested in being a grandmother. So far she had not stepped up and he had been doing everything. He decided to give her more time but still distance himself. It was too late for him, though, and he did not protect his heart.

"So of course you know the rest. About a year later, after all this happened she had made an about-face, or so I thought."

He kept his eyes on the road as he went on.

"After she left before the wedding, Derek asked for her all the time and it was like she had died because it became obvious she was never coming back. When I tried to call her or her mother they wouldn't answer. Once when her mom answered she asked me to please stop calling because her life with me and with Derek was over."

I gasped at hearing that.

"I know," he said. "Who says that about their grandson?" His right hand was balled into a fist on the gear shift. I placed my hand over the top of his and intertwined my fingers with his. Obviously, talking about this was very painful, and my heart went out to him. He relaxed a bit then.

"That's why this trip was so special to Derek. He thanked me every day for bringing him. He really took to your mom just as he has to you. I guess we both are pretty taken with you."

I smiled and squeezed his hand as I leaned back in the passenger seat. Was our chance meeting a hookup for the future? Only time would tell, but it sure seemed possible.

When we got to my house and opened the garage we woke up the boys so Josh and Derek could get in their car. Josh transferred the luggage before running my suitcases up to my door, while the boys got out the car chatting about how much fun they had. While they were talking I put my arms around

Josh's neck to hug and kiss him goodbye. "Thank you for coming with us. It was truly the best Thanksgiving."

He put his head against mine.

"Are you kidding me, it was our pleasure so thank you." One last hug and then the boys came over so they could say goodbye to us grown-ups. I squatted so I could give Derek a big hug.

"I'm so glad you came with us for Thanksgiving, Derek." He gave me a big tight hug back.

"Thank you, Alicia," he said and kissed me on the cheek. I smiled at him and he hugged me again.

"I love you," he said in my ear, and before I could answer he scurried around to his dad's side to get in the back seat. He left me there with a lump in my throat. I stood up and we waved goodbye. I decided to keep his declaration to myself, but I guess the weekend really made an impact on him.

"Thanks again, Mom," Chris said, hugging me after the garage closed. "It was so much fun having my best friend there. And Coach Josh, too."

I smiled at him, "It was fun wasn't it?" As we were walking up the steps he said, "Mom?"

"Yes Chris"

"You really like Coach, don't you?" I grinned at his honest question.

"Yeah, I do like him, Chris," I replied. "How do you feel about that?"

"Well. It's kinda cool since Derek is my best friend. So," he mused, "If you marry him, Derek will be my brother and my best friend."

"Wow, you have it all figured out, huh?" I said coolly.

"I was just thinking is all. Derek was too. He said you would be a cool mom and I told him coach seems like he would be a cool dad."

Wow, here I was thinking they were talking about video games and they were having intellectual conversations about us being a family.

"We do like each other, Chris, but we're taking it slow. Marriage would definitely be a ways off, but I'm glad you like Coach and I'm glad Derek likes me," I said, hoping this was a good response for him. "We do have fun together don't we?"

"Yes, we do! I love that it's so much fun. Sometimes I wish my dad was more like Coach." I feel my heart skip a beat wishing I could protect him from having to feel that way, but I can't.

"I know baby. Dad wants to do better, he just doesn't know how."

"I guess we should pray for him then. That's what grandma said." Another wow, I think.

"Yes, she is absolutely right," I say while thinking how smart my boy is.

"I'm real tired, Mom. I'm gonna go up to bed now." And he gives me a kiss goodnight.

"Okay, babe, I'll be up in a minute to check on you." And I take a minute to sit on the couch and replay the last two conversations I just had with two 10-year-olds. Deep stuff, I think, as I get up to turn the lights out. Then I grab my bags and make my way upstairs.

12 The Phone Call

The next few days are great. It is nice to be back in our routine. Going to work, having soccer practice and then spending weekends with Josh is something I have become used to. I realize I really liked him in the equation.

When he arrives at the Center on Tuesday, we give out our souvenirs. Sarah, Harvey and Jill are so excited about the little knickknacks, but I think it is the thought that counts with them. The girls are additionally excited that we had spent the holiday together. They both pull me aside later to tell me how exciting it is that we are an item. I guess taking a family trip is kind of a big deal.

Coach Rob stopped by on Wednesday and said, "Heard your house was the place to be this Thanksgiving." At first I feel nervous like "*Oh my gosh, does everyone know my business!*" But then I realize I needed to calm down and go with the flow.

"Yes, it was. My mom is a major cook so it was truly a culinary delight," I said smiling. "That's great, Alicia. Coach shared with me what a great time he had with you and your family. He seemed pretty happy yesterday when we talked."

I couldn't help grinning and thinking how great it was that he felt comfortable talking to Coach Rob. I could always pump him for information should I ever need too.   "Oh he did?" I say, acting surprised.

"Yes, he said it was the best Thanksgiving holiday he ever had. He's a good guy so all the best to you both," Coach Rob says as he looks toward the door where his son is waiting.

"See ya at practice then," he says, walking away. I nod my head, "Yes, see you then. And thanks," I add. I'm glad to know Josh had found a good friend since moving down here.

On Thursday, Sharon and I start pulling out the decorations from the gym's storage cabinet. December has come around again and today is the first. We will spend the rest of the day and most of the next decorating our lobby and gym, as well as the beautiful trees Harvey purchased the past weekend. We will decorate the gym, entry way, meeting rooms and our office area, while Harvey will be working outside, hanging the lights and spraying snow on the trees and bushes. It truly is the most wonderful time of the year!

In addition, Sarah, Sharon and I place mini trees on our desks, spray snow and hang decals on the windows. It is loads of fun being in the office. At least once a week I bring in peppermint hot chocolates from McDonalds, but most days I can be found at Starbucks grabbing a Caramel Brûlée Holiday coffee.

Sharon and I have already discussed my whole trip, her new grandbaby that's on the way and what she cooked for Thanksgiving. Now we were talking about how my family invited Josh and Derek back for Christmas.

"Alicia, that is just too sweet," Sharon says.

"Yeah, it was pretty ingenious the way my Mom included them in the Christmas dinner menu. I know Derek was hoping to come back, but Josh seemed equally as eager."

"You can't blame him. I've had your mom's cooking, and if it wasn't for Antonio always wanting to be home for the holidays I'd be jumping in the car with you, too."

I chuckle.

"Sharon, you are too funny! You and Antonio are always invited."

"Girl, I wouldn't bring that man to your momma's house to eat and then find a couch and snore the rest of the day," she says completely serious.

"Well, my uncle does that every holiday so he would fit right in," I shoot back.

By Friday at the close of the day we have the place glistening and shimmering with lights, garlands, tinsel, snow, lighted presents and bowls of candy canes. Harvey secured a beautiful wreath and Sarah placed bulbs in it for the finishing touch on the main door. We are so proud of our work. Josh came out of his office that we had also decorated with lights and garland around the doorway. He puts his arm around me while I'm taking the whole place in.

"Great job everyone" he says. "It looks like a winter wonderland in here."

Everyone tells him thanks, and how glad they are that he likes it. Then he whispers in my ear, "My girl is so talented . . . and hot." I can't help but smile and I whisper back, "You really know how to charm a girl, don't you?"

He kisses me on the cheek and says, "Only you, love, only you," as he walks toward the gym. Sarah has obviously caught the entire exchange and walks over to show me the mistletoe.

"I'm going to place this right at your desk so he'll have to kiss you every time he asks for a file," she says, winking.

"Leave it to Sarah and you two will be married by Christmas," Sharon says.

"Got that right!" Sarah agrees. "Alicia does not need to be bothered with any more busters. Coach Josh is the real thing. Listen to your elders," she says, patting me on the arm. I tell her I will while Sharon and me exchange amused glances.

As Saturday's game rolls around a chill comes into the area. I pull out one of my heavier sweaters, my favorite black Ugg boots and an Aztecs soccer team scarf. I decide to rock Josh's coach jacket once he picks us up. It's way cooler than mine, plus it makes me feel like a grade-school girl wearing her boyfriend's jacket. With only two games left we are winding down the fall soccer session. Between now and the winter session, Josh will go into full campaign-and-recruit mode, as well as teaching the Soccer Techniques class with a smaller group of boys. Of course, most of the team has already signed up so he will remain very busy.

After the game today Rick is taking Chris for lunch, a movie and then a sleepover at his house. This would be the first time we have seen him since we spoke on the phone after Thanksgiving. I'm not really looking forward to it, but Chris is, so I act like it is going to be so fun for him. All I can think is that he better be good to my boy and show up. He was already 15 minutes late. About halfway into the game, though, I spot him coming down the bleachers. It is a small group of parents, as attendance usually dwindles as the season progresses. Rick's tardiness is definitely noticeable and the overly made up, super skinny jeans-wearing blonde on his arm is under-dressed as well as embarrassing.

Right away I know there will be a problem with their fun outing because Extra Mascara Barbie has shown up. And sure enough, as the game ends Chris bounds up to me to ask if we can we get his stuff out of the car for his dad's house. But before I can respond, Rick walks up with Blondie.

"Hey son, give me a high-five on the great game!" Chris's expression changes a bit once he realizes this woman he didn't know was with his dad. He high-fived him back as he says, "Thanks, Dad," with a question in his eyes.

"Oh yes, forgive my rudeness. Chris, Alicia, this is my friend Kristy."

She smiles a very big shiny lip gloss smile.

"So nice to meet you both."

We both say the same thing to her, even though I'm not exactly telling the truth.

"Dad?" Chris asks, "are we still having our sleepover?"

He looks at me and then back at Chris.

"Yes Chris, of course. Plans are still the same."

I look skeptical, but Chris excitedly says, "Yes!" and then runs over to gather his things.

"Excuse us, Kristy," I say as nicely as I can to Extra Mascara Barbie.

"Oh sure," she replies, staring off into space.

"Uh Rick, are plans really the same for today?" He looks around again. I'm thinking, Omg, where's the camera!?

"Well, I mean, I do have to take Kristy to an audition, but right after that we can drop her off and then go have our sleepover."

I twist up my mouth to keep from shouting or pouting like I want to. What is she, 12? I think.

Instead I say, "What about lunch, Rick? He's always hungry right after a game." He shakes his head in agreement.

"Yes, I know. I'm gonna get him some drive-thru and we can hang out in the lobby where the audition is."

I try to smile like it's a good plan but it's so hard. At least he has a plan, even if it is whack.

"Does Kristy have a car? Is there a reason you have to take her?"

He looks down at his feet, so I know he's going to say something stupid.

"She doesn't have her license yet, plus she respects my opinion of her acting."

Thankfully, Chris runs up with Derek so I don't have to respond to his ridiculous statement. Do I want to send my son with Extra Mascara Barbie? Of course not, but what can I do? I will not ruin Chris's weekend, so I deal with it. When he does hug me goodbye, though, he asks why Kristy is there and I give him a brief explanation. When he looks up at my face he looks so sad. My mommy intuition perks up and I ask him what's wrong, even though I already know.

"Why does he always ruin everything?" That's it! I tell him I'll talk with his dad to adjust the plan so they can hook up later.

"Come on, big man, let's go," Rick says until he realizes something is wrong and does a double-take.

"What's wrong?" he asks, sounding impatient. "Kristy really needs to get to that audition."

I wave him over and send Chris to sit next to Mascara girl.

"Look, Rick, Chris is unhappy about Kristy being in on your father-son time. Is it possible to go ahead with her to the audition and you pick him up after, or I can bring him to your house?" He looks frustrated now, and annoyed is not far behind. He is thinking of something smart to say when Josh walks up.

"Hey, Rick," he says, breaking the current tension.

"Yeah, hey coach, good game."

Josh thanks him and then asks if I'm ready to go.

"I'll meet you at the car in a few minutes," I say.

He says all right, but about midway up the bleachers he sits down with Derek. Chris is still waiting patiently on the front row to hear the outcome.

"I guess I understand," Rick says, "I just didn't think it would be a big deal, him seeing me with a woman." He seems genuinely perplexed. "I mean, you're dating his coach right in front of him."

I stand there thinking of a million things I could say to him but I don't with the boys, Josh and Barbie looking on.

I do, however, say, "Well, you know his time with you is very special and he doesn't like sharing. That's all. So you wanna call me later, or text me and let me know the plan."

I feel great. I have diffused the situation without telling him off like he really deserves.

"Yeah, okay, Alicia, that's cool. I'll call you."

Then he turns to Chris, "Okay, son, we will hook up later. Just you and me" and he winks at him while ushering Kristy up the bleachers.

"Okay, Dad, see you later," Chris says happily, and I know all is well with my 10-year-old.

Chris gets up and hugs me. "Thanks, Mom," he says. I hug him back, "Any time, baby. You deserve your own time with your dad. But he's excited about your sleepover, so it'll be fun later."

He agrees, "Yeah it will. And now I get to go to Shakey's with you, Derek and Coach so it's still going to be a great day!"

He runs up to where Derek and Josh are sitting. The boys start talking and head up to the car. When I get midway up the bleachers and reach for Josh's hand I realize he's on the phone. He looks up at me and tells the person on the other line, "One second." He doesn't get up.

"I just need to finish this call and I'll be right there," he says.

I say okay, but something in me wants to sit on the bench next to him and wait. Any other time I think he would have pulled me down on the bench next to him.

I decide not to over-think it as I make my way to the car.

The boys are there and I release the locks so they can put their stuff in.

"Where's coach?" Chris asks. "Oh just finishing a call," I say.

"I think he's talking to my mom," Derek says ever so casually. "He thinks I don't know it's her but he always looks mad once he says hello and realizes it's her."

I'm shocked by the information I'm hearing, but I play it off. "Did you already speak to her just now?" I ask, trying to discern if he really knew it was his mom.

Derek looks at me directly then and says, "I never speak to her. She never asks for me."

My mouth opens and I feel terrible.

Why is she calling if not to talk to her son?

I place my hand on his shoulder. "Maybe it's not her on the phone every time," I say softy.

"No, it is. But I'm okay, Alicia. I'm used to it." And with that he gets in the back seat and immediately into a totally different conversation with Chris.

I'm left trying to decide how I feel about him talking to Eleanor. I want to ask him whether he was talking to her when he comes to the car, but I have no reason to.

Besides if I ask twenty questions on her calling but not asking to speak to her son, I'll be out of order. Maybe she's having a baby with her new husband and wants Josh to tell Derek about his new sibling, or maybe she's trying to mend her relationship with Derek. I realize I have to keep the thoughts light and I push them out of my mind for the time being as I see Josh walking toward the car. Maybe she remembers how cute he is, I think, as he smiles at me when his eye catches mine.

To meddle or not to meddle, that is the question.

13 Reassurance

After Shakey's and fun hanging out, Chris and I head home. I don't know how to feel about Eleanor's call or possible calls, as Derek mentioned. I also don't know what I can say to Josh because it is really none of my business, so I'm just left with my thoughts.

Rick did text me about 5 p.m. and let me know he was on his way to get Chris. Chris is so happy, and I am, too. At least Rick kept his word and I won't have to console my son because his dad forgot him. When he picked him up I gave Chris a big hug and a kiss goodbye, and Rick said he would have him back tomorrow early evening so he could get ready for school.

After they leave, my mind started racing in terms of Josh and Eleanor.

Maybe she doesn't necessarily care about being Derek's mom but she wants Josh back because she left her husband or maybe her job didn't work out or her life plan didn't work out, so she thought she could come back to what's comfortable, or maybe she realizes after all this time she does really love him and if he's willing to take her back, she's willing to dump her husband!

The scenarios are endless, so I try to watch television to get my mind off things. I watch the last half of "Waiting to Exhale" on Oxygen. As I sit there with my popcorn I know this is a perfectly free night to hang with Josh. He and Derek might just be watching movies or at the Bridge playing miniature golf, I think. I decide to text him and find out, instead of watching

Lifetime movies all night, not that I mind watching Lifetime movies all night.

"Hey Coach, what's up tonight?"

"Hey u, not much. Just watching some tv while lil man plays xbox. Chris go to his dads?"

"Yeah. I'm just sitting here watching tv too"

"Lifetime? Lol"

"Lol! Not yet. Watching a movie on Oxygen."

"Oh big difference, Lifetime channels sister"

"Lol! Be quiet!"

"Kinda sad without the baby boy I bet. Come over."

"Well…I don't want to interrupt guy night"

"Are u kidding me, Derek will have u all to himself! I probably won't see u at all"

"Ha! Ok. I'll grab my keys & see u in 15. We need food?"

"We could order pizza"

"We always order pizza…how bout Lasagna & salad from Compari's?"

"Cool. I'll order"

"I'll pick it up on the way. See u boys soon"

"Can't wait"

I feel as if all is well after getting my invite, and after I pick up the food, get there and get welcomed with hugs and kisses, I really feel fine. We had the same fun we always do, just without Chris. Josh was right, though, Derek monopolized all my time by taking me on a tour of his room, showing me baby photo's and shots of him with his grandparents and pics of him with his play aunt and uncle in San Diego. Downstairs we watch "Race for Witch Mountain" and the "Tooth Fairy." I am never mad at an evening of Dwayne "The Rock" Johnson movies. Seeing him is always a joy.

Josh's place is small but perfect for the two of them. It's off Green Valley Circle behind the Fox Hills Mall. It's a cozy two bedroom with a den, small kitchen and one full and one-half bath. Josh really likes it because it's easy to clean and just enough space for the two of them. Their bachelor & son pad, he calls it. Big screen for Josh with a small screen for Derek to play his games sits in the den. Then another pretty big TV is in Josh's room in case he needs to watch several sports stations at once.

I feel a calm come over me as I relax in the arm he has draped around me with Derek leaning on my shoulder. At one point Sharon sends me a text to see how things were with me being kid-free tonight. Of course, I tell her I have my other son with the really cute dad. I ask her if I could go to church with her tomorrow and, of course, she says absolutely. We make a plan and I will be at her house at 9 to ride with her and Antonio to the 10 a.m. service. Because of this and the fact that Josh doesn't like me out late alone, he tells me it's time to go at 11 p.m.

"Let's go, Alicia" he whispers in my ear as we halfway watch the news. Derek is now officially asleep on my shoulder.

"I can't, Derek's asleep," I say softly.

"Don't even try it. I don't want you out late."

"I live 15, probably 10 minutes away at this hour, Dad," I whine.

"I don't care. Let's go," he says again. I snuggle deeper into the nook of his arm.

"You think you're slick," he says, kissing my hair and laughing softly.

"Okay," I say, dragging the word out, but not moving. This of course causes him to tickle me and then I really am laughing out loud.

Carefully, without waking Derek, I turn toward him on his couch, which is even smaller than mine. "You really want me to go," I say with my face right against his, nose to nose.

"Come on, Alicia, now you really gotta go," he says without moving an inch. So I kiss him and I don't move an inch either. He kisses me back, first gently, then more urgently. His arms are around me tightly. Seconds later, his hands are making their way under my shirt so that he is caressing my bare skin.

Uh oh? I should stop him.... But it's an intense make-out session and it feels good.

You can go further without anything happening, my mind says betraying me.

So I kiss him more intensely. But then his hands are everywhere it seems and I suddenly feel an internal alarm going off as I feel the temperature rising between us. Then he starts to kiss my neck. Trouble is knocking on the door and I need to get up and leave – now! And then I hear a still small voice: *Alicia, get it together!*

I don't know if it's the sound of Jesus or my mama, but it certainly wakes me up. Didn't I just tell the woman I was going to church in the morning! I had to pull back from him after I pretty much started the whole thing. If not, all the vows and promises to myself and that we made to each other, were going to be broken.

"Josh," I whisper to him between kisses, "Josh, I think I better go." He realizes it then, too, as he whispers back, or rather heavily breathed back, "Oh yeah, yeah you do." Now he is nose to nose with me. "Alicia Renee Parsons, you need to listen to me when I make a suggestion," he says kissing me again.

"Sorry" I say in the teeniest of voices. He kisses me again, "apology accepted. Now let's get you outta here. And fast."

He helps me up carefully as Derek is still crashed out completely. I take a peek at my watch and it is 11:30. Wow, guess that did get a little hot and heavy.

"I'll be watching you from the patio," he says, hugging me goodbye. "And text me when you get home. Okay?" He gives me a peck goodbye.

"I will. Thanks for the fun night, Stud," I say, laughing at my own comment.

"You're welcome, sexy," he says.

When I get to the car he was up on his balcony.

"Bye, Coach," I whisper loudly.

"Goodbye. Get in the car. And text me," he said. And I wave as I pulled out of the parking space.

When I got home I texted Josh that I was safe and sound.

"Good," he wrote back. *"Now let me go take a cold shower so I can go to sleep, u tease"*

"Lol! I am not a tease, you were just outta control!"

"Lets call it even temptress"

"Temptress, Lol! Fine, we're even :)"

"Night beautiful"

"Night Josh"

After this fun exchange I get up to find something to wear to church. It is obvious I need to not only go, I need to pray for strength, a lot of strength.

By 9 a.m. sharp the next morning, I'm pulling up in front of Sharon's. We have a great time driving over and fellowshipping at church together. The pastor was harping on staying clear of situations that would cause you to fall off from your walk with the Lord. I almost felt as if I needed to cover my face for I was sure he was talking directly to me. I was pretty sure the Lord set that message up just for me. During the invitation, I prayed my own prayer to God to let Him know I heard Him loud and clear!

I apologized for the couch make-out session and promise to keep it clean from now on.

After church, we make our way to the car and Josh and Derek are waiting for us. My mouth is open in happy shock and Derek runs up to hug me around the waist.

"You made it, good to see you both," Sharon says, walking over to hug Josh.

"Yeah, it was easy to find," he says.

"Glad, you came out," Antonio added, giving him the one-shoulder hug.

"Hey Alicia," Josh says while I'm still in surprise mode.

"Hey Josh," I say smiling with a question mark.

"Yeah, well after Sharon texted you, I went in my room and texted her that we wanted to come too," he says, winking at me. "And you gave great directions by the way," he says to Antonio.

"You two are so sneaky," I say shaking my head amused.

"Well, look little girl, if someone wants to worship the Lord, who am I to stand in the way," Sharon says, raising her hands in praise.

"Thank you, Sharon," he says giving her a little shoulder hug. "I needed to talk to God today," he says looking over at me.

Sharon raised her eyebrows and said, "Well, praise God, glad I could assist!"

"Okay, you two," I say, giving them both a look. "I'm glad you came today though and brought Derek," whose arm was still around my waist.

"I'm hungry, Alicia," Derek says, breaking up the church chatter.

"Well, what should we have then?"

He thinks for a moment, "Red Lobster."

Antonio says, "Okay then, buddy, Red Lobster it is!" It was a great afternoon of eating, talking and laughing. Chris would have loved this weekend so I figure when he talks to Derek he's gonna pout about what he missed out on. Hopefully he and his dad had an equally great time together.

After lunch, we went back to Sharon's and the guys went in the house to watch the game while she and I sat out on her sun porch overlooking her beautiful garden.

"So, what did you think of Josh's surprise," she asks, knowing I loved it.

"I thought it was really sweet," I say, "and it really was a pleasant surprise."

She pulls out her phone. "Check out his text to me, after you and I had talked." I proceed to read her phone. He talked about how he wanted to come to church as well but would meet us

159

afterwards so he wasn't completely infringing on my time with her.

"Wow," I say smiling.

"I know. Who does that? I wanna be where she is but not infringe on her completely," she says. "He is so respectful of you and your time."

I shake my head in agreement.

"I think he loves you," she says, bringing her voice to a whisper. "We know Derek does, but I think his dad does, too."

I open my eyes wide at this. "You think so, Sharon?" She shakes her head yes, "I do, Alicia. All that stuff about you having his heart was a creative way to say it as far as I'm concerned, but then his actions speak even louder."

I find myself smiling, but trying hard not to. She is quiet for a minute and then says, "You probably love him, too. I know your stubborn self won't admit it, but you do. And I bet your heart already knows this, but your head gets in the way."

I stare at her with one of my looks, "Oh, well, thanks for assessing this for me, love guru," I say chuckling softly. She laughs a bit too.

"I'm just trying to help you see the light. And I know opening up is hard for you, but if you look deep you'll see. But at the same time, you know I always want you to protect your heart and take your time with it. You don't have to tell him until you feel like it."

We sit after that for a bit and I try to decide if I should tell her about the possible Eleanor call, but I think no. This conversation gives me a whole other angle to think about. If I do love him, is it too quick? Is it still the honeymoon phase? What if he's too good to be true?

We spend the rest of the afternoon hanging out watching TV, drinking sweet tea and cheering the guys while they play dominoes. About 4 p.m. Rick texts me that he's bringing Chris home in about an hour so I hug everyone and thank Sharon and Antonio for the absolutely great day. At the car I hug Derek and then I hug Josh.

"I can't believe you came today. It was so much fun. Thank you."

He hugs me back. "It was my pleasure and Derek's. I'm just glad you were okay with us crashing your day."

I stand on my tippy-toes and place my nose against his. "You can crash my day whenever you want," I say. Then I kiss him and start to back away.

"That's all you get. I heard the pastor today and I gotta flee temptation," I say smiling.

"I heard him too! Trust me, it's the last time I let you stay over past 10," he says and we both crack up. "Call me later," he says.

"I will," I say, and then I get in my car, wave and head out to meet Rick and Chris.

Thankfully, when they arrive, Chris is super happy. He says they went to the movies, ate at Roscoes and topped the fun off today at Santa Monica pier. "We had the best time, Mom!" Then he hugged his dad real tight. "Thank you so much, Dad."

Rick looked so elated and I think if he would keep this up they would have a close relationship and he and I could have a non-volatile one.

"I'm glad, big man. So I'll see you at your last game this Saturday." He smiled big.

"Great, Dad, and then you'll come to Shakey's, too?" I looked back and forth between the two of them and really want to know the answer to this one.

"I sure will, son." Chris starts cheering. "Oh yeah! We're gonna win and then celebrate."

Rick put his overnight bag down and then says: "Okay then, you guys have a good night and do well at school this week, son."

They hug. "Bye, Dad," Chris says.

"See you, son. And see you Saturday, Alicia."

I give him a reassuring nod.

"Absolutely, see you then." I close the door and then sit down with Chris to hear even more details about his great sleepover. I smile as I listen intently to his blow-by-blow account from the time Rick picked him up until he dropped him off. If he could just act like a good dad all the time, the world would be a much better place, I think.

After calling Josh to chat a bit, I go to bed with good feelings of my own and fall asleep thinking about the last two weeks before Christmas. It is going to be busy with Chris' last game, his class party, the Center's Christmas toy giveaway, the caroling event and, of course, our staff party.

I also have a few visions of sugarplums dancing in my head . . . then sleep comes.

14 Holiday Stress

It's two weeks before school is out for Christmas break. All busy moms know we really have to keep it together during this period. You have to juggle the class party, the school Christmas play, the office party, the caroling outing, the invites to parties, the church Christmas musical, your child's gift exchange, your own office gift exchange, the teacher's gift and your own tree trimming and decorations, plus the gifts you buy for family, friends, the hairstylist, manicurist, babysitter, your kids' friends, your boyfriend, and if you live out of state from your parents, your costs if you intend to visit them.

I just have one kid, and it's sometimes overwhelming! I can't even imagine the moms that have three or four kids, each with activities to juggle. Of course, if I make the eternal hook-up with Josh I will have two kids. However, they are the same age so the teacher can just get one big gift. Plus I'll have a husband to help me out.

As I lay across my bed that first Monday I make lists of all my things to do. I am going to start making purchases that day at Starbucks. Gift cards from Starbucks are something almost everyone can use, so half of my list will be covered by those simple purchases. Additionally, I check on my orders for the hospital gift shop. My floral designer, Savannah, is hard at work every Monday, but for the next three weeks I have hired an assistant for her. Floral orders increase during the holiday season because, unfortunately, many people are in the hospital on

Christmas Day. I always believe my designs will brighten up their day, and I feel that I'm spreading Christmas cheer to those who may not have much. Additionally, it helps me with the December expenses, because I order my own arrangements for Chris' teacher, and I can bring arrangements to decorate the counter at the entry way to the Center. This year I'm going to send one a week before Christmas to my parents, as usual, but also to Grandma Lucy, so she can get some Christmas joy early.

My mom had called me earlier this morning to make orders for some of her friends. I don't do personal orders, with the exception of my mom. I told her we would be flying out two days before Christmas so I could get a little shopping in and that I would be staying through the 28th. Josh wanted us to go to San Diego with him to meet and get to know his San Diego friends who were like family. My mom thought it was nice he wanted us to meet them, but said Trina had an attitude about me leaving before New Year's. We both laugh about her selfish little sister ways.

She also said she had been praying for us, and I knew then it was her voice I heard Saturday night at Josh's house, but I kept that to myself. Plans were set and lists were made. Hopefully, if I followed everything as I'd organized it in my head, I would have little to no holiday frustration.

The next two weeks are perfectly smooth. First, I made it to the final Aztecs soccer game of the season. The boys won and everyone was going to celebrate at Shakey's, of course. Families, friends and fans, which included Jackie, John and the girls, as well as Sharon and Antonio. Before we went over we had a quick ceremony. I had sent out an email informing the parents we would be giving awards to all the boys that day. I made sure I called and sent a text to Rick to make sure he would be there. He did show up – about three quarters into the game. I was fuming! He did make it, but I know Chris saw him show up late, plus he came with Extra Mascara Barbie again.

OMG! How do you go right back to stupid in just one week?

Then when Chris got his award he over-clapped and over-yelled. My family and close friends couldn't even be heard for his over-the-top noise making, which clearly said, "I'm doing this because I miss everything else." I looked up the bleachers at him and cut my eyes, although I'm sure he didn't see me because he was looking at his phone! I had to deep-breathe so I wouldn't lose it completely.

When Derek's name was called, not only did Sharon and I yell for him, but my family did, too. His little face was beaming so proudly, and I was really happy for him. So was his dad. He looked over and winked at me, and I knew my family making a big deal warmed his heart as well. After Josh thanked Coach Rob for all his assistance, Coach Rob then asked for the mic and Josh crossed his arms wondering what was going on. Rob went on to talk about Josh for a few minutes and, of course, that's when he figured things out.

"We've had a winning season, Aztecs, so make some noise!" Everyone cheered and the team made noise on the bleachers with their feet.

"Thanks to Coach Josh Hart we have all learned to play like champions, win with class and congratulate the other team if we had to," and everyone laughed. "In honor of your first season, Coach, we are giving you this extra special award of champions."

Everyone cheered and clapped some more. Josh was smiling and proud.

"Thank you, Aztecs, for all your hard work this season. I'm so proud of each and every one of you. To Coach Rob, you have helped me from day one and I appreciate all your assistance. Let's do it again next spring! To all the parents in the stands I thank you for your support of your sons and our coaching staff." More applause, more cheers.

"And finally, to our team mom, Alicia Parsons, thank you for being the absolute best. You are the heartbeat of the office and this team," and it appeared he wanted to say more but didn't. I was sitting next to the team on the front row with a smile a mile wide. Coach Rob brought me over a team trophy as well, which I held up high in one hand. Josh and Coach Rob had really gotten me good, and I was touched. I got claps and cheers too, especially from the team.

"Now, if you can, parents, family and friends, please meet us over at Shakey's to celebrate. Thanks again for being a part of this season, and we'll hopefully see you next year."

Everyone clapped and the boys were up on their feet. Parents were coming down to say hello and thank you to the coaches, and some even to me. It looked as if everyone could make it over to the restaurant so we were going to pack the place out.

My wonderful family came to congratulate Chris, Derek and Josh. After the hellos and congratulatory hugs, the twins told Josh how great the game was and how they wish they lived closer so they could come to all the games. Jackie noted how sorry she was they couldn't come out more and John said next season they would do better. Sharon and Antonio came down with them to show their love and let us know they wouldn't be able to go over to Shakey's. I hugged her for coming and told her how much I appreciated it.

"'Oh girl, I wouldn't have missed this last game for the world! Plus I knew they were giving you a shout-out." Then she got closer to me and whispered, "He was going to buy you a gift but when I told him that would be unusual he said he would come up with something else. So if you get a negligee later tonight, don't say I didn't warn you." I laughed hard. Sharon is a mess.

"I'm just saying, Alicia," and even she had to laugh with me.

"What are you chicks laughing about," Jackie said, coming between us to hug us both.

"Aww, Sis, thank you guys so much for coming out. You really surprised me."

She smiled mischievously, saying, "that was the plan. And when I called Sharon she gave me the scoop, and here we are." The two ladies smiled at each other in victory.

"You are too much, and I love it," I said, giving them both another squeeze. Then John and the twins get closer and I hug and make over them too.

"John, thanks so much for coming out. You guys are awesome."

"No sweat, lil sis. We figured not only would you and Chris like the pleasant surprise, but Derek would too." I look over at Derek then, laughing and talking with Chris and the twins.

"Yes," I say, "he is definitely glad to have you all here. Can you guys hang for pizza or are you hitting the road?"

He put his arm around me, "Staying put. We're with you today." I am really happy.

Josh comes over and joins the conversation celebration. Then finally as everyone has departed and we decide to head out, I realized Rick never came on the field. I was hoping he at least spoke with Chris before he left. As we start up the stairs I see him and Extra Mascara talking to Chris, Derek and the Twins. Lord, I'm glad Trina isn't there. She would've asked why this woman was at her nephew's game and given him a piece of her mind.

Instead, Jackie and I stopped to grab our kids. Rick said hello to me and Jackie but hugged her as well, saying long time no-see. "Jackie, the twins are beautiful. It's really good to see you and John." John gave him the peace sign walking by. He never much cared for Rick once he started showing out.

"Thank you, Rick. How are you doing?" he shrugged.

"Oh, I'm good. Business is good, thanks for asking. By the way, this is my friend Kristy." Jackie is so sweet and greeted the girl kindly. She knows the woman looks over made-up and like she's on something. I wonder if she has an audition this week, too, so I decided to ask.

"Uh well, yeah actually she does, A." I looked crazy. I couldn't even fake the funk.

"Okay, then, well thanks for coming," I said and walked on up to the car. He stood up then and yelled something to me like he'd call later, as if I actually cared. That was some fakeness in front of all my family, I guess. Once I was in the car, I watched Chris give him a hug, Josh corralling Chris and Derek toward the car and then my girls coming over to my window.

"You okay, Alicia?"

I sighed, "I'm just over him is all. I just get tired of his drama all the time. Sorry for walking away," I say looking up at both of them. Sharon pats me on the shoulder and heads out to take care of her errands. Jackie, John and the girls follow us over to Shakey's as the celebration continues. Toward the end we gave out gift bags we made for all the kids as Christmas gifts. We filled them with candy, gift money to Baskin Robbins and gift cards to McDonalds or Burger King.

Josh and I went in together on their gifts and they all loved them. And for Coach Rob, a Best Buy gift card, for which he was both surprised and grateful. It was a wonderful afternoon for all.

As the last five days of school approached I had done well with my list of Starbucks gift cards for all the special people who do things for me in my life. And today I was making sure Grandma Lucy and my mom got their flower arrangements by the end of the week. Chris and I had taken photos by our Christmas tree that we put together with Josh and Derek on Sunday. Trimming the tree and drinking egg nog with my man was pure bliss! I could definitely see myself continuing that tradition in the future. Now I was at Target getting the photos made into Christmas cards. We took lots of shots so I am doing a collage that we can both have at our houses just for us. Of course, I'll get a few extra in case Sharon or my sisters want a copy.

Wednesday night was the boys' school Christmas program. They were both in the chorus since that's all they had time for with practice. They wore reindeer antlers standing on the back row and Josh and I were snapping and videoing the entire performance. I had to admit it was really fun having someone to do all the usual Christmas tasks with. And as Friday came around we closed out the boys activities by buying gifts and food for their class party. Josh brought pizzas and I made cookies and brownies. Additionally, I had picked up toys for the boys gift exchange, plus I grabbed two trusty gift cards out of my stack for their teacher. One from each of them. She would be hooked up until the new year!

I had sent Ms. Sanders flowers at the beginning of the week so she hugged me thank you when I arrived. I realized then that Jessica Waters, Ms. Hour Glass shape was there working the food table with me. Josh was helping with sodas and punch, but mostly horsing around with the kids.

"So how's it going with Mr. San Diego over there," Jessica says, nodding in Josh's direction.

I'm a little taken aback because she surprised me with a whole sentence since we've only said hello a few times on the field.

"It's going great actually," I said smiling tentatively.

Hmm, is she after my man and trying to see if we're happy?

"That's wonderful, Alicia. I know we don't know each other exactly but you are someone I really look up to."

Now she's really piqued my interest.

"You look up to me?"

"Yes I do. You do the single mom thing so well, and you really seem to have it altogether. When my husband left me last year I was a mess and never thought I could get out there on my own two feet," she pauses for emphasis, it seems, and she's got me. I am totally intrigued by her comments.

"But there you were everyday, making it happen with Chris. It was only this soccer season that I've seen his dad come around. Before that I thought his dad wasn't in his life."

I was shaking my head on and off as I listen intently.

"I know it seems weird that I was watching you so closely, but I needed to see someone who was doing it and making it. A lot of us do it, but you are making it."

Looking down, she starts stirring a pot of some strange looking dip, and then she says, "and now that I've seen you with Coach Josh, I thought how great for her. He's really nice and has totally helped me with some of Ryan's anger flashes. The whole divorce thing really threw him for a loop," she says as she looks over at me. "Wow, you must think I'm a little loony, so forgive me for talking so much."

At this point I let a slow smile spread across my face.

"No you are fine. I was just surprised to hear your thoughts. Thank you for saying those things to me. I just make it happen because that's what us moms do, but I'm speechless that anyone actually noticed. I appreciate you sharing," and I really meant it.

Here I was thinking she was trying to take my man and she probably doesn't even want to see one right now. She was kind of an airhead, I could tell, but genuinely sweet.

"Well, hopefully we can be friends now, Alicia. You know, like mom friends," she says with a nervous giggle. And I'm sure any other time I would have thought she was completely crazy, but she shared her heart so I understood what she meant.

"Sure, Jessica, absolutely."

After that we laughed and joked about the boys, the season, how nutty Christmastime can be while at the same time being wonderful. She also shared with me that she and Coach Rob had begun talking, and that although she enjoyed spending time with him, she wasn't exactly ready for a relationship. I encouraged her to simply take it slow.

Josh had to head out early as he had to write his rules and regulations for his new program. He hugged me goodbye. "You'll give Derek Ms. Sanders gift for me? I gotta get outta here." I kissed him on the cheek.

"Of course, Coach. I got it covered."

"So I saw the bonding going on with you and Ryan's mom. What was that all about?"

"Well, if you must know, she wanted to tell your girl how much she rocks."

"She's just finding that out?" he asks, as he walks toward the door. He throws me a kiss before telling the boys he would see them later.

I spent the rest of the afternoon as a class mom, cleaning up, letting the kids use my iPad to sing along and dance, too, and then I had the boys give Ms. Sanders her gift. She loved it of course. As I told the boys to get their stuff together I checked my purse to see if I had one lone gift card left, and I did. I buy several $5 cards for just-in-case random gifts. So I went over to tell Jessica goodbye and put one in her hand.

"Just a little Christmas coffee on me."

She looked down at it and said, "Oh my gosh, thank you, Alicia," and then she hugged me. "Oh sorry about that. You are just too sweet for doing this. But I don't have anything for you!"

"Jessica, you don't have to give me anything. I just wanted to bless you so just receive it. Merry Christmas."

She hugs me again, and it's hilarious because I wouldn't have pegged her for a hugger.

"Merry Christmas to you, too." We wave and I get the boys out to the car.

"Have a good time?" I ask them. "The best party ever," Derek says. "It was so fun, and thanks for staying, Mom," Chris says.

The parties then continued as Saturday was the Center's annual Christmas caroling outing. We all meet in the parking lot about 4 p.m. and we drive over to some local hospitals and senior citizen homes in a caravan. Sharon and I pass out the song lyrics and once checked in we proceed to walk through the wings of the Children's ward and then we head to the next location and walk the halls of the senior homes caroling. Most times the people who are there join in and it's the greatest feeling in the world to bless those who are sick or don't have their family at this time of the year. Most of the places are my floral clients so I simply make the plans with them when they order their Christmas arrangements and poinsettia's. We had a huge group of parents, kids and additional family members this year. It was wonderful to share the spirit with others and I absolutely loved the caroling outing.

Afterwards, we go back to the gym and everyone partakes of Apple cider, egg nog, hot chocolate, Christmas cookies and cakes. We employees provide most of it, but several parents bought or baked this year so it was really nice. We had the Christmas music going and Harvey even had the kids playing

Simon Sez in the corner. I figure if I had not found a job so great I probably would have moved back to Oakland by now. I really fit in here, though, and I'm doing my passion, which I think in a corny way is literally just making people happy. The coordinator who hired me really took a liking to me and she has let me come up with all these zany event ideas, but they work. We have more community interest and more parent participation. Plus, if I had left I would have never met Josh, and that would have been a travesty, I think, as I look over and blow him a kiss.

The last two weeks of the year the Center is pretty much a ghost town. We close down the last full week, but the week of Christmas we might come in to do cleaning or purging, if there is time. Since the holiday was falling on Friday, we would be leaving for Mom's on Wednesday. Most of us work Tuesday through Friday but we all decided to come in Monday, work a little and have a party for our little staff at lunch. Since Lucille's was now over at the mall we decided to order in. Josh picked everything up and he and the boys joined us at noon. We grubbed on ribs, chicken, links, potato salad, biscuits, French fires and corn. It was a huge spread and all of us – Josh, Sharon, Sarah, Jill, Harvey, myself and even Lance, who only worked at nights now – got our grub on.

Of course the boys got plates since they were out of school and hanging with their parents. We played music, chatted about our holiday plans and then did our gift exchange. Sarah had pulled my name.

"Aww, what a surprise, Sarah, my favorite! A Starbucks gift card!" I said laughing, and everyone else did, too. She wrote a super sweet message inside about being my on-site mom, wanting the best for me and that she loved me.

"Thank you, Sarah," I said giving her a tight hug.

"Did you look at the gift card, I wanted to make sure you could get several coffees, teas & bagels during the holiday," she whispered, and when I looked down it was $50 on the card.

"Sarah, you didn't have to spend this much," I said, almost gasping. "The minimum was $10!"

She shrugged, "Who cares, I get my friends what I want them to have."

I smiled shaking my head, "You are too much, girl!" She smiled back at me, "Yeah I know."

I gave Harvey a Home Depot gift card since he said he has been wanting to work on his back yard, Lance gave Sarah a beautiful scarf, Jill gave Lance an iPad case, Harvey gave Josh a gift card to Foot Locker, which we were all amused by.

Sharon gave Jill some beautiful earrings and Josh gave Sharon a gardening set from Williams-Sonoma, including basket, gloves, tools and watering can. She was ecstatic.

"Josh, I can't believe it. This set is so beautiful! Did Alicia tell you I'd been eyeing it? I cannot wait until spring. My garden is going to be even more lovely!" She gave him a hug, "Thank you so much." He smiled, impressed at his gift skills and told her she was very welcome.

"It was a great idea," I told him, pulling him to the side.

"Yes, she is even more excited than I thought. Good looking out on the store though, that made it real easy."

I shook my head, "Good, that's what I'm here for."

He put his arm around me and we surveyed the happy room. "Great party, Parsons." I agreed as everyone was talking and laughing and eating dessert as the boys had already cut the cake and opened the cookies.

The Center's phone rang. Since I was right next to Sharon's desk I yelled "I got it."

"Happy Holidays, Sunset Park Community Center. May I help you," I asked pleasantly into the phone.

"Yes, I'm looking for Joshua Hart. Is he available?" This most professional woman's voice asked.

"He certainly is. May I tell him who's calling?"

"Eleanor Dean." My heart did a somersault, a double back-flip and a high dive all in 30 seconds.

"Of course, let me transfer you, Ms. Dean," I said before placing her on hold. Josh turned around when I said her name.

"It's for you," I said, trying not to look irritated that she called during our party. She could've texted or told him whatever it was later. But then I realized he looked annoyed too.

"I'll take it in my office," he said without offering any other information. Then he turned and kinda stormed over to his office.

I transferred the call and of course couldn't stay on the line because the Christmas music was playing and they would've known I was listening.

"What's up, girlfriend?" Sharon asked, handing me a piece of cake. "Was my gift not the greatest! Girl, Josh is the one for us!" she said, smiling and laughing. I tried to change my expression, but couldn't.

"Alicia, you okay? It looks like you've seen a ghost."

"Well, I sort of just heard from one. Eleanor was the call that came in. She's on the phone with him now," I said with concern in my voice.

"Oh sweetie, don't worry about her. He loves you. She's probably just wishing him Merry Christmas."

I looked down kinda mellow.

"Nope, you are not going to let this bug you, you hear me?" So I got it together and looked back up with as best a smile I could muster up.

"Yes, ma'am, I hear you."

"Now let's get back to the party," and she grabbed me by the arm and led me over to the dessert table.

I tried to shake it, but the call stayed with me. So business-like and proper she was. But I would not let this bug me at Christmastime. I would ask him later what she said, but for now I grabbed the boys and made them both give me a kiss on the cheek under the mistletoe.

15 Home for the Holidays

On Tuesday I was home doing laundry and preparing everything I needed to pack for the trip. We would be gone through the 28th to my mom's, then fly home and drive out to San Diego either that night or the next morning. With the news he shared with me after the party was over last night, I was unsure I wanted to go to San Diego, let alone stay until the new year. I was considering returning from the Bay Area on the thirtieth since I have an open invitation to Sharon and Antonio's for gumbo.

Last night, after we all started cleaning up Josh came over to me and put his arm around me.

"I know you're wondering what that call was all about, love, and when we get out of here I'll tell you." I was hoping he didn't want me to act like it didn't matter and just say, "Oh that's okay. I don't need to know." I'm not that girl. Instead, I looked over at him and said, "Thanks, because the call did surprise me and I was wondering what was so important."

I tried to say it casually, but I was kind of saucy. I think it surprised him. I know it sure as heck surprised me.

"Not a big deal," he said, kissing me on the cheek before walking over to help Harvey put some supplies away. I remember looking at him thinking, man I'm in serious like with this guy. And I knew then I had to give him the benefit of the doubt.

On the way to my house we chitchatted about the party with the boys. They had a great time and so did we. Sharon spoiled them with early Christmas gifts so we knew we would be visiting Game Stop on the way home so they could spend their gift cards. When we finally got back to my house it was easy to talk because they boys were excited about trying out their new games.

"Eleanor has been calling and texting me for the last two weeks," he began. "She kept texting she had something very important to tell me. She called me after one of the games recently," and of course I knew because Derek was correct when he told me it was her.

I continued to listen intently. "She said she was going through a bad patch with her new husband. They had lost a baby and it made her think about Derek."

Oh my God! He should've hung up in her face! How you gonna call the baby daddy of the baby you left to sulk about the baby you lost! Is she kidding?

The disdain on my face obviously showed.

"I know, Alicia, I was pretty disgusted that she would call me as well. She wasn't calling to talk to Derek, just asking a million questions about him which she's never done except randomly on holidays and his birthday." He cleared his throat before going on. "Yesterday she called because I stopped answering her on my cell. I told her she needed to talk to her husband and that he would help her get through this. She went on to say that she really needed to see Derek and she knows that will make her feel better."

Now my mouth was open and I had a frown. Finally, I spoke, "Well, what did you say to that?" He moved uncomfortably on my couch and that's when I knew he told this sorry excuse for a mom yes.

"Okay, so I told her we had Christmas plans, of course, and New Year's plans. She went on to say she had talked to Davis' wife Skye in San Diego and she knew we would be coming there in time for New Years." More squirming. "So she said she had booked her flight to San Diego and was hoping I would allow her to spend some time with Derek."

I raised my eyebrows as if to say, "seriously." I was shaking my head in disbelief and tried to choose my words as carefully as possible. "So what did you decide, Josh? Are you going to allow her to hang out with Derek?" And then I continued on. "If so, it sounds like Chris and I need to stay home. You don't need us in the way during this delicate family time."

His breathing changed before he spoke and I think one of his hands balled into a fist.

"Alicia, I invited you to meet my friends and spend the new year with me in my hometown. Davis and Skye are expecting *all* of us. Regardless of *if* Eleanor shows up or not, I want the both of you there. I invited you and I meant it. You're not getting rid of me on our first New Year's Day. And if *we* decide to come back to Sharon's okay, but you're not staying here alone. Eleanor is manipulative and the world revolves around her in her mind, but even if she shows up she's not messing up my plans. I have to kiss my girl on New Year's Eve."

Then he turned toward me and looked me in the eye. "I won't let anything mess up our plans. You got me, Parsons?"

And he seemed unsure about what I would say, but he was so adorable and so sincere. How could I say no to that face?

"Yes, I got it." I wasn't so sure I wanted to come face to face with Derek's mom on the weekend I was meeting his best friend and family, but I figured with him by my side I could handle it.

As I packed quietly I kept rehearsing all kinds of scenario's that could go down. I still wasn't thrilled about her showing up, but I knew I needed to stop worrying about it.

The next day we caught our flight to Oakland and by early afternoon I was sitting on the sun porch drinking ice tea and catching up with my mom and Trina, while the boys were with Matthew playing video games and my dad and Josh were watching some game in the den.

"Okay, so you're telling me he is trying to let the boy's bootleg mama see him for New Year's?" Trina whispers to Mom and me loudly.

"Yes, Sis. He says nothing will come between us but that he is open to letting her see him if she doesn't show out. I am not thrilled at meeting her, and I'm not all that sure I want to go to San Diego with him anymore," I confided to them both. Trina was already shaking her head no.

"Nah, I'm not feeling it. You don't need to be down there should some drama erupt. You guys got a happy thing going on and you don't need to see a no-good mom in action. You'll be disgusted! Now, if I go you'll have backup at least." And we all laugh at her comment, although I am sure she is serious in her joking.

"Okay, girls, I hear what you're both saying, but Alicia, baby, you may need to go on and go. Not because I want to put you in a situation of possible drama, but because of Derek. What if the whole thing is really bothersome for him? You will be there for him and so will Chris. That is something you should think about before making your decision, too."

I shook my head in agreement. Mom was right; what if it's horrible for Derek? I've grown to care about him like a son, and if he were to be hurt or disappointed, I would want to be there for him. Then again, he does have his dad's best friends so somebody would be there for him. It was obvious I had two sides to think about and that's just what I intended to do.

Later that evening we ate dinner, hung out and talked with my parents, and then Trina and I made a mad dash over to the mall. It was the last night of shopping for the holiday hours and the place was packed. We had about three hours until it closed so we focused and got through with everything with 30 minutes to spare. We decided to stop at the Coffee Bean and take a load off. We had just ordered two Winter Dream lattes when her ex, Michael, came in the door to get in line. I decided to approach him.

"Hey Mike," I said hugging him. "Long time no-see." He reached to hug me back, "Hey, Alicia Keys! How's my sister-in-law doing?" I smiled at him.

So good looking, so charming, so stupid.

"I'm good. Just down here with Trina doing some last-minute shopping."

He looks around me at my mound of packages, "I see," he says, chuckling.

"Oh, Michael," Trina says walking over with our drinks.

"Hey, you," he says, quickly checking her out from head to toe. She was cute with her little tight jeans and fitted sweater. "I was just telling Alicia it was so good to see her," he said.

"Yeah, she visits on holidays when she knows she needs to move home," and we all laugh at this.

"Well, you can join us," I say and I know Trina wants to kick me so I don't look at her.

"Oh, well, thanks, ladies, but I gotta get Matthew's bike over to my mom's so he'll have it on Christmas Day."

That lit her up. "You got it, Mike? I thought you couldn't find it," she says, more than elated.

"Well, at first I couldn't so I kept calling every store till I found a Spiderman one for him."

Then she hugged him. "That's great! He is gonna be so happy! Maybe I could bring him over and stay till you give it to him."

Poor Mike. He was still stunned by the hug and here she was asking could she come over, too. But he smiled then, "Of course. That's a great idea. So see you Christmas Day about 1?"

She shakes her head yes, "Absolutely. We will see you then." They both look a little happy to me, but I'll wait till a brother leaves to ask.

"It was great to see you, Mike," I say, reaching over to hug him goodbye.

"You too, Alicia. Take care now. And see you, Trina." And she waves at him and says okay as he heads out the door with his coffee.

"Excuse me, Miss Trina. Michael is still in love with you!" I say to her in a loud whisper.

"Girl, I'm not thinking about Michael Grant! He should've been in love when we were married, instead of micro-managing me, leaving me at home with an infant and trying to decide if he wanted to be married," she says looking irritated but at the same time a little disappointed.

"You know, Sis, he was probably just too young when you got married. He didn't know who he was yet. But now seeing him with you, it appears he knows he made a mistake. I feel kinda sorry for him."

She looked up at me from her latte as if to say she did, too. But I know my little sister, and she won't admit it. "You need to feel sorry for him. He broke my heart and he's not getting it back."

I told her I understood but deep down I really don't think she's over him.

That night and in the morning we are wrapping up our gifts like crazy and taking them down to the tree. We hung out and just relaxed, chatted, and we drank lots of egg nog while my mom made Derek's Christmas Tree cake. Early evening we made our way to Jack London Square to get a bite and see the big tree and all the lights. Josh and I took all the boys and we were able to have romance time. We held hands, stole kisses and had the whole PDA thing going on. The boys were thrilled with their little outing. With Christmas being the next day they were so excited.

Josh and I had gone overboard on video games for both the XBox and the DSi and we were very excited about their reactions. I had gotten Josh the latest iPhone with the Siri feature. It was a little better than mine but since he had the first version, I had to update him. He would be pleasantly surprised, I think. Then to make sure he was totally covered, I got him a few new cases, an iTunes card to buy music and apps, and a Starbucks card since it was our favorite hangout spot. I had hooked up everyone with something brilliant that fit their personality. I love to buy presents so I absolutely adored this time of year.

On Christmas morning the sun rose over my parent's house, and although it was quiet you could smell cinnamon rolls all over the house. If everyone else was like me they were hurrying up getting dressed and downstairs to the kitchen. Tradition starts with a healthy breakfast of fruit, yogurt, cereal and obviously today these delicious cinnamon rolls and a cup of java to get us going. Then everyone heads to the den to position themselves around the Christmas tree. Mom or dad open with prayer and then Chris usually serves as elf for the day with Matthew assisting, and passing out the gifts. This year was no different, except that I had the most wonderful guy in the world to spend the day with, who greeted me with a kiss that literally took my breath away. He caught me right before we went into the kitchen.

"Well, Merry Christmas to you, too," I said kissing him back.

"Merry Christmas, Alicia. I am so happy to be spending today with you. This is my gift you know. You didn't have to buy me anything."

I look up at him with a slight smile. "I guess I could take your gifts back since you said that," and we both laugh while looking in each other's eyes.

I could have looked in them a bit longer, but Trina came by and hit me right on the butt. "Let's go, lovebirds. Jackie and the crew are here."

We follow her and go to greet Jackie, John and the twins, and Christmas morning commences. The whole morning goes just as I said. When it's time to open gifts the three boys are ecstatic! They are going crazy over every game, every gift and every gift card. It was a joy to watch them. We took videos and pictures of everything. The twins getting Hello Kitty luggage, Trina getting a Louie briefcase from my parents, Jackie giving John an iPad and me giving Josh his phone. I had wrapped it in the actual box inside of two bigger boxes and then a gift bag. When he got to the final small box, he looked over at me and said, "You didn't." It was really fun seeing the cute little-boy look on his face.

"Don't know," I said nonchalantly. He rips it open and stands up from the couch.

"Alicia, I can't believe you did this. But I'm so glad you did," he said, with a wide smile. Everyone was cracking up at his reaction of seemingly just seeing a slam dunk. I was highly amused and knew I had done the right thing. He came over to me in the recliner and gave me a huge bear hug.

"Aww thanks, Babe, you're the best!" I was still laughing and he was still being silly as everyone said "aww" and the boys frowned and said "uhhh!" All except Derek. He seemed happy at the exchange and had the cutest little grin on his face. I think the big family Christmas was just what he needed.

"Get a room!" Trina yelled and everyone laughed, except Mom, who scolded her – "Trina!" And she quieted down and said, "sorry Mom," which made us laugh even more. I had a similar reaction to his gift to me, which was the latest Coach Rainboots with matching purse and umbrella. Then the purse was stuffed with Starbucks and Chipotle cards. He got a huge hug and kiss for all that, even though I did notice the thumbs up to Mom and Trina.

It was a beautiful day from start to finish. Michael did pick up Trina and Matthew and I gave her the eye after telling her earlier to "be nice to him since it was Christmas after all."

Rick actually showed up on time to get Chris and I sent a huge Harry and David basket I had picked up yesterday to Grandma Lucy. He said she loved the flowers and sent me a thank-you note. I decided I would call her later and check on her day. We took time as well to Skype Josh's parents in Paris and they were having a lovely day as well and he thanked them for his and Derek's gifts that came in check form. He was very happy at their generosity.

That evening we were sitting on the porch freezing with my head on his shoulder. We were discussing the day and all the fun we had had. Coach Rob had texted him, as did his friends Davis and Skye. It appears Eleanor called to confirm her flight with them and asked if she could visit with them before we arrived. Again, I thought maybe I should just stay at my Mom's, but Josh saw my uncertainty.

"Don't even think about it, Parsons, I need you with me for New Year's Eve." I smiled as best I could. "Okay, I won't leave you hanging." He kissed my forehead.

"I can make it through anything with you by my side."

I snuggled closer to him and right then I believed that was true. Doubt was lurking, but for tonight I was putting it out of my mind.

16 Meeting Eleanor

Christmas was wonderful. The dinner was delicious, as usual, and we had a completely family fun time. Trina, Matthew and Chris all returned by 8 p.m., and Chris and Matthew showed us all the gifts they got from their other grandmas. Derek did really well seeing all the new things the boys got, but I know it must have been a bit hard. That's why when he was the only boy there, all the men played a game of basketball with him and then the twins had him in the kitchen helping make cupcakes. He was too cute and overall I think he had a really good time.

Later that evening as we sat and watched TV, I noticed Josh got a text from Eleanor (Elle as it was listed in his phone). I'm sure he knew I was looking. She was asking what she could get Derek for Christmas. A cell phone, A Toys r Us shopping spree, clothes. Josh wrote her back. *"Less is more."* Then he sent another one *"Game Stop is his favorite store."* She texted back *"thank you. Can't wait to see you both, xoxo."*

Did this heifa just send hugs and kisses to my man? I gave a dirty look to the phone.

"You see the whole conversation or you want me to scroll back up for you," he whispered. I pretend to be a little shocked as I said, "Oh, did you think I was reading those?"

"Um, yeah," he said and we both laughed. I noticed he did not respond to the xoxo's so I snuggled closer to him as we watched Bruce Willis get the bad guys in one of my all time favorites, *Die Hard 2*.

On our last day in Oakland, after we had packed up, us girls met in the kitchen for a proper goodbye. Coffee in the nook with a streusel coffee cake my mom had whipped up that morning. I knew I needed to leave her house or I'd be eating straight through the new year!

"Okay, so what happened with Mike? Alicia said you two ran into him at the mall and he looked like a sick puppy," Jackie asked Trina.

"First of all, Alicia is a tattletale. Second, he did not look like a sick puppy," she said as she rolled her eyes at me. "Over at his mom's he had, in fact, got the Spiderman bike with a helmet, pads and new tennis shoes. Matthew went crazy; he was so happy," she recalled smiling.

"Aww," Jackie and I said in unison. "Did he say something about his feelings, though, Sis?" I leaned in and asked wide-eyed.

"You get on my nerves, Ali!" the name she uses when she's annoyed with me. "Well?" Jackie added.

"Mom? Do something about your daughters," Trina whined.

"I can't control these two, Trina. But the way you're whining, something must have happened. Do tell."

Jackie and I cracked up.

"I can't believe y'all! Fine, nosey ones. He did pull me to the side before he brought us home and said he was sorry for all the trouble he had given me in the past after the breakup, as well as saying it was his fault we even broke up at all. Then he asked if he could call me sometime for a date," and she rolled her eyes again, but this time she was trying to hide her smile.

"I knew it!" I yelled and Jackie said, "Me, too. I knew he still loved you when you broke up. You should have separated and not divorced, but nobody listens to me." At this point Mom stepped in.

"Girls, leave your sister alone. She did what was right for her at the time, Jackie and Alicia. She now has to seriously consider what she's going to do."

Then she looked at Trina. "What are you going to do, baby girl?"

It was a funny moment because even Mom wanted to know the scoop. Michael really messed up bad, but he is a nice guy, just too young before and he made stupid mistakes, but we all liked him.

Trina listened to all our input and then said, "I might consider it. In time for Valentine's Day maybe," and we all found ourselves amused at her answer.

The Christmas visit ended in hugs and kisses. I gave my dad a huge hug and kiss before I left because he had slipped me an extra check and told me to pay myself back for the plane tickets and then to get maintenance on my car because he knows I always forget. In addition, he said to get Chris new tennis shoes, a coat and new jeans. It was just from him he said because I was his only little girl totally on her own and he still needed to take care of me a bit.

"Thank you, Daddy," I said after giving him another huge hug. "Your secret is safe with me," I whispered as I kissed him on the cheek.

"I have no idea what you're talking about," he said with a straight face and when I started to laugh he joined me. Nothing like a great dad, I thought as we drove to the airport. I, of course, had decided to accompany my man to San Diego, and I would be strong. My mom had even prayed for my strength right there in the kitchen. For all of us, actually, as we went into another new year. I would unpack tonight, re-pack tomorrow and then we would hit the freeway midday.

As we drove down to San Diego holding hands, I tried to quiet my thoughts. Maybe all the child's mother did want to do was be with him for a couple of days. Maybe losing her baby recently really did bring her to her senses. Then I looked over at Josh and wondered what he must be thinking, as well. I had never asked him but I guess he probably did have some thoughts of his own. The boys were both knocked out in the back seat as they had played video games till about 2 a.m. at my house. Josh had hung out with Coach Rob, Harvey and Lance from the office playing pool so I let the boys have a sleepover at my house. We had small talk on the way down about Christmas, the new soccer class he was starting in January and his relationship with Davis and Skye since High School. They really had been friends for years so I could see how they were like family.

When we finally got to the San Diego area Josh took the 8 Freeway toward Mission Beach, the area they live in. Their house was just a few blocks from the water, and it was a cool and beautiful winter day. Their house was two stories and pretty modern on a cul-de-sac. It had a high ceiling in the entry way and formal living room where their Christmas tree was. Then there was a huge kitchen with an island for cooking, a bar with stools, and connected was a kitchen nook that looked out to their pool. And connected to the giant nook was a large den with a big loungy-style couch that looked great for naps as well as various recliners.

Their son Devin is 14 and their daughter Destiny is 7. Additionally, there was what was called the "kid's den," which had TVs and furniture to match each kid. Josh told me there were three bedrooms upstairs as well. He also mentioned Skye got an inheritance about ten years ago and that's when they were able to move here.

I loved Davis and Skye right away. When I got inside the house they both hugged me but Skye hugged me like my sisters do – hard, like she'd missed me. The kids also hugged me and Chris.

"It is such a pleasure to meet you, Alicia! And you are just as pretty as Josh said. And Chris, even more handsome than I could have imagined." Chris blushed and said "Thank you, ma'am."

She shooed away his "ma'am," saying, "just call me Skye, sweetheart. Everyone does." They are good-looking people. Davis has a whole Idris Elba look going on, which is probably why Josh said people often mistake them for brothers. And Skye has an Egyptian princess look, kinda like Jasmine in Disney's "Aladdin." The kids were equally as beautiful. I guess you could call them the picture-perfect family.

They ushered us into the den and there we talked about their high school days, college days and when their son Devin was born. Josh is his godfather. The boys played video games while Destiny played with her new dolls from Christmas. When she showed me her room earlier I got to see all her presents. For just a few moments I imagined having a daughter of my own, but Chris was 10 so I would be starting literally from the beginning. I wondered to myself, what if Josh wants more kids? But I figured we'd cross that bridge when we got to it. On the tour we also saw the large back yard with the pool, grassy play area and barbecue deck.

Davis told us he would be grilling steaks for dinner, and I was excited about it. Something other than turkey sounded great I told him and he agreed, stating that was why he had Skye buy the ribeyes. Additionally, they showed us the pool house, which was where Chris and I would be staying the next three nights. Skye said they had just remodeled it and we would be the first to stay there. It was an adorable one bedroom, one bath with a mini living area and mini kitchen. It was like having my own hotel suite and I was thrilled. Maybe this visit would be like a mini vacation, I thought, and I was glad I had brought the latest Kimberla Lawson-Roby novel with me.

About 4 p.m. Skye and I got busy in the kitchen, working on the sides for dinner. She had everything to make a baked potato bar as well as a mini salad bar. We seasoned the steaks and took the corn out to the deck for Davis and Josh. I didn't feel like holding out anymore, and because Skye was super nice, I felt comfortable asking her anything. So as we are chopping and prepping, I said, "So Skye, when is Eleanor set to show up? At the New Year's Eve party?"

Skye kept chopping for a second and then she turned to face me. "Well, Alicia, let me clue you in on Eleanor from a woman's point of view," and for this I stopped chopping as well.

"Eleanor is supposed to come to the party a little early and spend time with Derek before the festivities begin. However, she called us last night and said she was landing on the 30th, which is tomorrow, and that she would try to sneak by in the evening. Knowing her, she will do it unexpectedly, even though we said no about 20 times. She is what you call "a piece of work," she said, making quotations in the air with her finger to make her point.

"Hmm," I said, wondering. As we both went back to chopping she went on.

"The night before the wedding we had Eleanor stay with us so we could bring her over to the church in her wedding gown. But the next morning when I went to wake her she was gone. Davis found the note, and he was so angry at her. If he could have found her and killed her, he would've."

It was even worse hearing the story from someone else's perspective.

"He took it upon himself to tell Joshua, and it broke his heart to do it. To this day whenever she calls he will not speak to her. He just passes the phone to me. We became friends because of the guys but after that I didn't have much to say to her. She hurt our family, Davis' best friend, so she's not exactly our favorite person."

I realized I didn't even have to make a comment because Skye was laying it all out. "We didn't ever want him to leave San Diego, but when he started calling Davis to rave about you, we were so happy. We heard a smile in his voice and knew you must be someone special. And you are just as lovely as he said."

Now it was my turn to speak. "Oh thank you so much for saying so. I was kinda blessed by meeting him, as well. Tough marriage before with an often absentee father. When Josh showed up at the Center we had an instant connection, but hurt people are always concerned with getting hurt again so I tried to resist him, but it didn't work." And to that comment, we both laughed.

"Well, we are thrilled to meet you and your handsome son Chris. Derek is thrilled about you, too. He told me on the phone one weekend that you were like the mom he never had."

My mouth opened slightly because I knew he was fond of me, but wow. "That is so sweet. I am quite taken with him, as well, and the boys get along so great. It's been a pretty perfect connection."

"Well, I am so excited for you both. So when Eleanor comes around just don't let her get under your skin, because she will try. She's very into things: where people shop, live, and their bank accounts. She didn't used to be like that, but once she had the baby and felt pressured it was like an alien took over," Skye said, shaking her head. "If she hurts Derek again though or disappoints him I might beat her down myself."

We go on preparing the dishes and laughing until it's time to eat.

Dinner is out on the deck and even though it's kinda chilly, they have a fireplace so it's doable. The kids do a lot of the talking, especially their daughter Destiny. She's like the twins in one body. It's constant, but she's so cute it doesn't matter. Davis gets beers for himself and Skye and offers one to Josh and me.

"Nah man, I'm good," Josh says. "Me too," I add.

"So you were serious last year when you cut out the special occasion drinking?" Davis asks.

"Yeah, it's always been recreational for me anyway, so I figure why bother. Besides, Alicia takes me to church and the pastor seems to always know what you're doing personally. I'm not trying to get busted out in the sanctuary."

I laugh out loud at Josh's comment.

"A church man, eh? This girl is the best thing that ever happened to you, brother."

Josh looks over at me, "I told you guys." I look over at Skye and she is smiling. "Amen to that," she says.

As I go to sleep I think back over the entire evening. I love his friends and I'm really glad I came to meet them and support him. He stayed with me for a little while in my private house and I got to tell him how much I liked them.

"I knew you would. And they feel the same about you," he said kissing me.

Thursday was a chill-out day. About 3 p.m., though, Skye did take me along with her and Destiny to get something for the party. The party was going to be at their house with friends from their jobs and parent friends. Skye said about twenty-five in total and that she hired a caterer to bring in all the food, along with waiters to pass trays throughout the night. It sounded really elegant. She bought Destiny a silver dress with a ballerina sheer skirt, ballerina-style silver slippers and a tiara that she begged for.

On the other side of this boutique was a ladies section. Although I had brought a beautiful dress to wear, I eyed a silver tank dress that had a sheer jacket to go along with it. It was more simple than what I brought, but it shouted "tray passed event" better. Besides Skye and Destiny thought it was beautiful and Destiny loved the idea of us matching, so I got it. After we stopped for coffee and hot chocolate at Starbucks, which were my treat, we made our way to the house. The sun was down and as we pulled into the driveway Skye said, "Oh boy," because parked in front of her house was a white Range Rover.

"What is it?" I asked. "I think we have a visitor," she said, and at that moment I figured it out.

As we walk in the door we see Davis at his desk near the kitchen. His back was facing the den and when we come into view I see Josh hanging on one of the bar chairs, and finally over in two of the lounge chairs are Derek and a woman I presume to be the infamous Eleanor Dean.

"Hey, babe," Josh says and jumps up to hug me and give me a kiss on the cheek. I feel the woman staring into my back. Skye pats Davis on the shoulder and goes over to Eleanor. She stands up to greet her.

"Skye, my friend. It's been too long," she says.

"Elle, how are you?" Skye says, giving her a half hug.

"I'm doing great. Especially now in the presence of my angel, Derek," she says patting him on the head like he's a puppy. Derek looks sick. You know like he was forced to be in the den visiting her, which he obviously was.

"Alicia," he says, running over and hugging me hard.

"Hey sweetie," I say with my arm around his back.

"Derek, why don't you introduce us," Eleanor says. He reluctantly lets me go and takes my hand to bring me closer to his mom.

"Eleanor, this is my dad's girlfriend, Alicia. Alicia, this is Eleanor."

I don't know whether to break into hysterical laughter or console her because he just gave her a huge gut punch and it definitely threw her off her game a bit. Instead, I do neither and it's okay because Davis breaks the silence by grunting.

She puts out her perfectly manicured hand and says, "Hello, Alicia. It's very nice to meet you. As you probably know, I'm Derek's mother," and she looks over at Derek and says, "I told you it was fine for you to call me mom."

He stares her down and then finally says, "Yes, I remember."

Wow, this is even worse than a cold shoulder. He is done with this woman.

I shake her hand and say, "Nice to meet you as well, Eleanor," even though deep down I wonder if it's *really* nice to meet her. She has long flowy hair down her back, and probably weighs about 125 in soaking wet clothes and shoes, and she's tall with really long legs. She is probably Creole since she has the look and is from New Orleans. She is light-skinned, not bright-skinned, with pretty hazel eyes. She looks like a super model with her 7 for Mankind jeans, Chanel jacket and purse and the latest Louboutin's, or should I say red-bottom shoes, as they are often referred to.

She is stunning on the outside, but for all her niceness I do not think her insides match.

"So how long have you and Josh been together?" And before I could speak Josh says, "A long time. Come on, Alicia, I'll walk you out to your room." I looked around and it seemed they were all there to protect me. Even Davis had stood up.

"Okay, then, Alice, I guess I'll see you at the party tomorrow night." I looked at her with an amused grin.

This troll is trying to get under my skin already!

But before any of us could correct her, Derek said, "Her name is Alicia," with authority and annoyance.

"Oh I'm sorry, son. I do apologize, Alicia." I smiled phonily at her, "No worries. Until tomorrow then."

Josh grabbed my arm and ushered me out back.

I could not wait to text Trina and Sharon. There were going to be plenty of fireworks this New Year's Eve.

17 New Year's Eve

As I stand in the kitchen with Skye I let my mind wander back to last night. She is busy laying out snacks as the caterers are everywhere getting things prepared for the party that begins in less than an hour. She is stunning in a dark purple sweater with a deep v-neck, framed with rhinestones. It was fitted and she wore a great leather pencil skirt with it and some rhinestone laced heels she said she bought five years ago on sale at Macy's.

My little silver dress turns out to be the perfect party dress. It is straight but flared just a bit at the bottom so with a nice midnight dance it should look great on the makeshift dance floor Davis and Josh pieced together in the living room. I brought strappy heels which sets the outfit off just right. Skye thought I should go without the jacket/wrap thingy but, of course, that's not me so I wear it. It is shear so that was saying a lot for me.

Last night after we went back out to the pool house, Josh said "you handled yourself great. I'm so sorry. Eleanor has always been a bit snooty, but she was so out of line." He looked so concerned and was waiting for a response from me, I could see.

"Well, I was ready, you know. Skye filled me in big time and we all know people who think a little more highly of themselves." I sit down and look up at him standing by the counter.

"Please don't be offended," I say, "but with your personality and warmth, how in the world did you two hook up?" He shook his head and said "I know."

I then add, "Well, obviously I am sure you were struck by her obvious beauty, but then after that what kept it going?" I didn't know a better way to ask. There was no way for it to come out nicely. He came to sit next to me and stared straight ahead as he went on.

"We met on the field and right off the bat we had the whole phys-ed focus thing going on. And as a person with no threat to her future she was content to date and be herself. She was a whole lot nicer in college. Now, I wonder if she was always like she is now and I just missed it, or was she truly different."

He seems genuinely perplexed.

"Well people change. Maybe because you were in love you were forgiving and maybe you're right, without the pressure, she was different." I try to smile reassuringly at him.

"I guess so," he concedes. "I know I don't appreciate the way she treated you and then there's Derek. I didn't know he was so angry."

I sat closer and put my arm around him. "I appreciate you sticking up for me, so this time I'll let her slide. Derek is the most important one so make sure to talk to him before the party." He nodded in agreement even though he still seemed bothered. He kissed me on the cheek, "Thank you Alicia." I put my head on his shoulder and told him he was welcome.

The first guest arrived around 8 p.m. and from then on it is a steady flow. I meet a few old college friends that Josh was thrilled to see, co-workers of Davis's and several parents who brought their kids for the 16 & under New Year's party in the rec room. It is a fun event with great music, delicious food and the perfect date.

I sneak away about 8:30 to call my parents and check on them. Mom says Trina was in the living room with Matthew and Michael. I tell Mom I was about to text her and mess with her.

"Hey Trina, how's Michael?" I write, starting off the texting.

"Girl, I knew it was you that just called mom! How is San Diego and how is Eleanor?"

"Don't try and change the subject fast thang!"

"Alicia Johnson Parsons, I am not fast! This man stopped by to see his son"

"Umm hmm... and the love of his life"

"Whatever missy! Just give me my update...tell me about this Eleanor chick"

"Well in a nutshell, she is kinda snooty and uppity. She has great clothes, shoes & hair but after that she's all downhill"

"Ok so are we talking Halle Berry at the end of Boomerang when Eddie Murphy comes to her new office stunning?"

"Lol, Bingo! Just imagine her with really long hair. Her attitude is like Grace Jones in Boomerang though, LOLOL!!"

"Oh lawd, you poor thing sis. Do I need to come down there for back-up? Cause you know I will"

"Haha, thx but I'll be ok. Josh has got me. If anything, she better look out for Derek. He has got her number and he is emotionless towards her"

"That's a shame, she did that baby so wrong he has animosity. Well I'll be praying for him. I'll tell mom too also"

"Thank you Treen. I guess I better go find my man before one of these San Diego single ladies hit on him"

"No worries big sis, he only wants to be with you, his Brown Sugar he's got a Love Jones for," then she adds a smiley face and red heart emoticon for emphasis.

"Well thank you. I feel much better now" I write, adding a happy face with a wink.

"Well early Happy New Year, even though I will text you back at midnight"

"To you too baby sis, and please give my love to my brother in law, lol"

"Shut up girl! Love you"

206

"Love you too, xoxo"

I shove my phone back in my purse and make my way back inside the party. Before I get to the door, though, I grab a mini pizza and a napkin and see Josh talking to an old friend inside named Bill, or was it Bob. But as I open the door to the living room I see Eleanor has arrived in grand style with a red satin cocktail dress, incredible shoes to match and her hair is in a bun. Her red lipstick matched perfectly as well and the bad girl in me thought, Hhmph, all she needs is a pitchfork, but I keep it to myself. That is until Skye shows up next to me.

"Alicia, where were you?" Skye whispers. "This cow came into my house asking for her college sweetheart. Scanned the room and then said there he is when she saw Josh. I had to hold Davis back!"

My eyes get wide as I listen to her while biting into the delicious pizza square I had picked up before I responded.

"I can't believe her. What did Josh say?"

She rolled her eyes, "He didn't know what she said because he couldn't hear her over the music. Davis came over to me and said why did I let you invite Satan to our party," and I fall out laughing. I can barely contain myself, so much to the point that she starts laughing with me.

"It wasn't that funny, Alicia," she says, even though she was still laughing, too.

"It's just when I came in I thought to myself that all she needed was a pitchfork," and then both of us are almost in tears.

The song that was playing ended and before the next one started up there was a lull and Skye and I are noticeably tickled about something. I see Eleanor look over at us, roll her eyes and look back to Bill (or Bob) and Josh. Josh excuses himself to come over and see us. He kisses me on the cheek as he puts his arm around my waist.

"You two are certainly having a good time," he says innocently.

"It's your girl here. She is hilarious," and I look over at Skye.

"Me?" says Skye. "You started it," and we dial it down a bit.

"I'm so glad you two are hitting it off," he says and he is genuinely happy.

"She is great," Skye says, and I agree with the statement in reference to her.

"Well, let me go check on the food and make sure we have enough," she says, "and I should check on those kids, too." I suggest Josh and I do it instead because I want to check on Chris.

"That's perfect, thanks a bunch," and she goes into the kitchen while Josh and I make our way through the crowd to check on the kids. He is holding my hand and leading the way and we are greeting people along the way. Red dress can barely keep her eyes off of us I can see from the corner of my eye.

We get to the kid's room and they have Beyonce on the iPod system. The boys are all crowded around two TV's playing XBox and PlayStation 3 and the girls are singing on microphones to the Beyonce songs. Chris and Derek wave us over to watch them play. We have to peek around the other kids to get a visual. Destiny runs over to twirl around so I can see her dress.

"You look beautiful, Destiny." She smiles and bats her little eyes. I smile back.

"Thank you, Alicia, and you look beautiful, too." Then she pulls Josh's jacket and when he looks down at her and says hello she asks, "Do you like Alicia's dress, Uncle Josh? I helped her pick it out. Doesn't she look beautiful," she beamed.

This girl is too much, I think, smiling at her along with Josh who is smiling as well.

"Yes, Destiny, you did a great job. Alicia looks beautiful and so do you, gorgeous," he says poking her on the nose. She giggles and blushes and says, "Thank you, Uncle Josh."

Then she twirls away. We laugh as we stand there holding hands.

"Dad, are you looking," Derek yells. "Yes, son," Josh says, giving his attention to the game. So we're standing there watching kill after kill wondering when he or Chris is going to get finished with their round and whispering about it when Eleanor enters the room and walks right up on us.

"Hey you two, what's going on in here?" She asks sweetly with her imaginary pitchfork.

"Oh we're just watching the boys kill each other in their video game Elle," Josh answers.

"Oh yes, I went to that Game Stop place like you said. And I want to give him his gift," she says.

"That was nice of you. They'll be done in a minute," Josh says. Right after this the boys win their round and start making noise and high-fiving their other obvious team members. Derek and Chris get up smiling walking over to us.

"We did great, didn't we, Dad? You saw us, right?" Derek asks.

"We annihilated everyone Mom," Chris adds.

"Yep, we sure did see you guys handling your business," Josh says.

"We sure did," I say, agreeing with Josh.

"Derek, your mom wanted to see you for a minute," Josh says with his hand on Derek's shoulder. Derek frowns but turns to look at her.

"Hi Derek, I have something special for you," Eleanor says.

"Oh, hi," he says, less than enthused.

"Let's go over here and sit down, son," she says to him. He kinda looks around hoping someone would save him, I think, and Chris did.

"This is your mom, Derek?" Chris asks eagerly.

"Yes," was all he can manage.

"Who is this, Derek?" Eleanor asks.

"This is my best friend, Chris Parsons. Alicia is his mom," Derek says, finally giving his mom a little personality.

"So nice to meet you, Chris," she says shaking his hand.

"Nice to meet you too, ma'am," he says properly like his momma taught him.

"Oh just call me, Eleanor," she says as charming as can be, and he responds with "Okay, ma'am," which I personally think is hilarious.

She finally acknowledges my presence by saying, "He is such a handsome boy, Alicia."

"Why thank you, Eleanor He is my greatest accomplishment," I say proudly.

Then she whispers: "Is his dad another nationality? You know with the wavy hair and different coloring than you, I figure he must be mixed with something."

Unbelievable! She will not break me and I count to 10 in my mind.

"No he's just black." I guess in her mind he's only handsome because he's mixed. I wouldn't even think to mention his Spanish grandmother, cause on his birth certificate he is black.

"I'm going to give Skye an update on the kids, excuse me," I say.

Josh tells me to wait and catches up with me.

"You don't need to say anything, Josh," I say before he says a word. He catches my hand and squeezes it and I slow down as my anger starts to dissipate. I can't be mad at him for her, but I want to slap her so bad I can taste it, and I'm not even violent.

We go to hang by the kitchen bar and talk with Skye and Davis. I update her on the kids and she tells me in about 30 minutes the countdown will begin. We are excited and I take note of the servers lining up the glasses for champagne and sparkling apple cider for the midnight toast.

A few minutes later we see Eleanor come back in the room and, thankfully, find some unsuspecting single man to fake-laugh with. Then after her comes the boys. Derek gave Josh an envelope, saying it was his Christmas gift from Eleanor.

"It's a Game Stop card, Dad," he said rather annoyed.

"And it's for $350," Chris whispers to me and Josh.

"Wow!" Josh exclaims as my eyebrows go up. She has a whole lot of making up to do and I guess it starts in Game Stop money.

"He told her he didn't want it," Chris says, looking more than surprised.

"Derek, I hope you said thank you," said his dad.

"I told her thank you, but I didn't need it. She insisted I keep it so I told her I would share it with Chris. Otherwise, I didn't want it," Derek replies with a complete stone face.

"I was happy," Chris says to us with a big smile. "And then I said thank you."

"Glad to hear that, Chris," Josh says looking directly at Derek. "I'm going to thank Eleanor as well but tomorrow we are having a long talk, son," and he walks over to Eleanor to obviously thank her for the gift and apologize for Derek. I was hoping he wouldn't be too hard on him because I sensed that this whole scenario was way too hard for him.

"Come here, sweeties," I say to both boys, putting my arms around them.

"Derek, are you okay? I am sure your mom just wanted to get you something really big because she's missed you so much." He looks up at me a bit sad now.

"Alicia, if she missed me she could have just said so. I can't be bought with a gift card."

My mouth opened and I had to close it quickly. So wise and smart for a little guy. Chris had a lot to deal with because of his dad, but at least he saw him every blue moon.

I squeezed his arm tighter. "It'll be okay, Derek," I say.

"You think so? My dad is so angry with me."

"I'll talk to him about how you feel so when you two talk maybe he'll take it easy on you. Okay?"

Then his bright little smile was back. "Okay," he said. Then he hugged me.

"Thank you, Alicia." And then Chris hugged me, "Love you, Mom."

"Love you guys, too. Now go beat up on those older boys and win your tournament," I said.

"Yeah let's go, Chris," and off they went toward the back of the house.

I see Eleanor watching them walk away. She probably noticed the hug, too, but I couldn't be worried about her. He had every right to have an opinion about her. Besides, she shouldn't have picked a public event to try and win him over.

Josh made his way over to me at ten minutes before midnight. "Everything okay?" I ask.

"Fine, and even better because you're here."

The waiters start passing out the drinks and we take two glasses from the cider tray. Davis turns on the TV so we can see the ball drop and do the countdown with the city of New York. Josh and me are standing near the doors leading to the backyard and he has one arm around me and holds his glass in the other. The last 10 seconds come so quickly "10-9-8-7-6-5-4-3-2-1" and everyone yells "Happy New Year!" We say "cheers," take a sip of our drink and then we kiss. It was like the first kiss, sweet and soft. There is yelling all around us, some people cheering, others singing loudly while others drunkenly sing "Auld Lang Syne." Some people head to the dance floor to dance to the Kenny G version of the same song. Josh grabs my hand and we go into the living room to sway to the music on the cool makeshift dance floor. After a few minutes he whispers my name. "Alicia," and I look up into his deep brown eyes. He kisses me and leans his forehead against mine.

"I love you, Alicia Parsons," he says and he kisses me again. I smile, completely caught up in this moment. I grin so widely and I'm giddy. He loves me. He really loves me. And maybe I have felt the same way and just didn't want to admit it, but my heart already knew while my head was trying to figure it out.

I kiss him again. "I love you back, Joshua Hart." And now he has the big grin and he stops to hug me and pick me up slightly to twirl me on the crowded little dance floor. Then he puts his arms completely around me. We have a passionate kiss, and across the room we hear Davis yell "get a room!" and we laugh again and so does everyone else. I think I see the devil in a red dress staring at us from the corner, but I close my eyes. She is so not a part of this moment.

We spend the rest of the night dancing, laughing and saying I love you a million more times. Skye hugs me when I tell her, and I text Sharon and Trina the news when I take a break from the dance floor. Girls love this kind of stuff and they are as excited as me.

I had another best night ever and it will be one I'll never forget, because he loves me!

18 A Brand New Year

One of the best nights ever ended with us sitting on the couch in the den, holding hands and telling everyone goodbye. It was probably 4 a.m. when we decided to call it a night and I went over to my room. Chris and Derek fell asleep in the game room so we got them pillows and blankets around 2 and left them there on the floor. Skye walked Eleanor to the door. She had invited herself over for New Year's Day gumbo. Skye didn't know how she was going to break the news to Davis and I was thinking of how Derek was going to feel.

By noon I had managed to get up, shower and try to look presentable with my tired eyes. Thank goodness I don't drink because I bet I would've had a hangover. I called my mom to tell her and dad happy new year. She asked about Chris, Josh and Derek, and wanted to know whether his mother had shown up at the party.

"Not only did she show up," I told her, "she showed out." I told her how she tried to win over Derek with an expensive gift and how he wasn't having it.

"So now I am just trying to be the voice of reason for both of them. Josh doesn't want him to be rude, but Derek doesn't want to be bought. I just want to be there for them both," I confided to her.

"Well, then that's what you do, Alicia. You can see both sides, and that's where you have to help Josh so he can realize

Derek is not going to embrace her so quickly after all these years. I hope he knows he is blessed to have you."

I smiled thinking about his declaration last night.

"Well Mom, I think he might know, he told me he loved me last night." I could hear the smile in her voice,

"I knew it! Were you happy, sweetheart," she asked.

"You know, Mom, I really was. I wasn't expecting it although I felt it between us."

"And what did you say to him?"

With a giddiness in my voice I said, "I told him I felt the same."

"Oh that's great! You two had a really nice night, and I'm so glad. He is a nice young man and your dad and I really like him."

"Yeah, he is kinda wonderful."

"Well, I'm happy for you, honey. Just continue to be obedient to God and He will give you the desires of your heart."

"Yes ma'am," I said, wondering if God was reminding me through her to not hang out late over his condo. But I shook it off.

After we ended the call I made my way over to the house to see what everyone was up to.

When I entered the kitchen Skye and Davis already had the house smelling good. Josh was in the back with the kids they said, so I asked if I could help with anything. They still needed to make a salad and whip up the corn muffins, so I got out the salad stuff and started chopping.

"So, Alicia, how are you feeling this morning? Still floating on air a bit?" Skye asked.

"Yeah, I definitely am," I said smiling over at her.

"Okay, so what's with all the smiley happy girl talk?" Davis asked.

"Josh told Alicia he loves her," Skye said in a loud whisper.

As I stood there blushing Davis comes over and kisses me on the cheek.

"Finally! The girl who stole my man's heart. I mean I was a bit upset when he took my godson and moved to L.A., but finding you was worth it."

I stood there still blushing and smiling as he went on.

"That evil satanic woman broke his heart and I still wanna slap her every time I see her," he said sounding disgusted. "But him finding you, now that warms my heart."

I started to giggle a bit.

"Davis, the kids might hear you!" Skye said, pleading.

"The kids don't like her either, Skye. And Alicia you don't ever have to be nice to her should you ever see her again," he said as he stirred the large pot of gumbo.

I sort of chuckled and said, "I'll remember that," and then he laughs with me.

Skye on the other hand looked horrified and I knew she had to confess.

"Davis, you might have to put up with her for a bit today. She begged me about coming by today and when I told her it probably wasn't a good idea she said she had a flight out tonight so it wouldn't be for long."

Davis had lost his smile and looked as if he might implode.

"Unbelievable," he huffed before marching out of the kitchen.

"He acts as if I invited her when he knows I wouldn't," she said sounding annoyed.

"Don't worry about it," I said, trying to comfort her, "maybe she won't show up."

She noted how that would be nice and we made more small talk before I left to go check on Josh and the kids. Of course all the boys were playing XBox, but Josh was playing the wii with Destiny. They were dancing to the Michael Jackson experience game and it was hilarious watching her boss around her Uncle Josh. Finally, I literally laughed out loud when he tried to moonwalk.

Everyone looked up. I got good mornings from the boys and Destiny, and an "are you laughing at me" from Josh. I laughed again.

"Alicia, will you play with us?" Destiny asked.

"Yeah, you come moonwalk and see how easy it is," Josh added. I agreed and while Destiny was going through the song selections he came behind me and put his arms around me, kissed my neck and whispered in my ear, "how's the love of my life this new year?"

Feeling all fluttery I replied, "Very well, especially now that I'm with you."

Oh my gosh, are we that couple? The all-the-time-gooey kind? It's just brand-new love. And it's kinda fun.

The day was going along great. Davis' parents had come over, along with his brother, his brother's wife and their three kids. Additionally, so had Skye's grandparents. It had been a nice day of food, chatting and of course football.

About 5:30 in the afternoon, Skye came over and whispered, "Maybe my prayers were answered, Elle may not show up" and I smiled and agreed with her.

Unfortunately, that desire was not to be. At about ten after six the doorbell rang and there she was in her St. John yachting outfit, replete with a St. John purse and accessories. She must have really struggled in life because everything she wore or carried had to be designer. My Ugg sequined boots were the most expensive things I had on and I wore them with my Old Navy pants and hoodie set I got for $24.99 on sale. Now, granted, I always like to carry a nice purse so I had my Michael Kors, but still, I am not label crazy nor could I be with a son, a condo, a car note and the list goes on.

I saw her sizing up my outfit as if we were in high school as she passed me by giving me a super phony hello. I responded with an equally phony "Hi." Davis did not look in her direction and when she said hello nicely to him, he said "hey" without ever looking in her direction.

Josh looked sick about her being back at the house and as she approached him sitting with Skye's grandfather, I think he literally tensed up.

"And who is this lovely lady, Joshua," the grandfather asked. And before Josh could say a word, she extended her hand and said, "I'm Eleanor Dean. So nice to meet you, sir. I'm Josh's former fiancée and we have a son Derek you may have met already."

The grandfather didn't really know what to say besides "oh," and when I looked at Josh he was so pissed. He grabbed her arm told the grandfather to excuse them and brought her into the kitchen where Skye was baking and I was on the stool keeping her company.

"Look Elle, I've been really patient with you wanting to come see Derek, but your behavior just now was out of order. You don't introduce yourself as someone's ex fiancée or as the woman I have a son with. You're simply Derek's mom and that's it." My eyebrows were raised in happy amusement. Skye was shaking her head in agreement and Davis had come to get a glass of anything to hear the conversation.

"Well, I'm sorry you feel that way. I was just trying to make it plain so he could see where I was connected. Sorry for upsetting you, Josh. You could've pulled me to the side to say all this instead of trying to embarrass me."

Before Josh could respond Davis spoke up. "Eleanor, you embarrassed yourself showing up here, speaking rudely to Alicia and disrespecting my house with your presence. I've had enough, and if you can't be more considerate you can leave." And he wasn't in the least bit kidding. Skye came over and touched him on his arm to calm him down.

Eleanor held her head up and responded calmly back to Davis.

"I will just go and see Derek, if that's all right and then I'll leave. So sorry to have disturbed your holiday party."

It almost seemed as if she was trying to fake cry, and it was very unattractive. She walked away looking wounded and Davis turned to Skye and demanded, "Never again!" She shook her head in agreement and I gave her a look of sympathy.

Josh seemed flustered and turned to both of us and said "sorry you had to see that ladies" and he left, I guessed, to go supervise Eleanor's visit with Derek.

After he was out of earshot Skye said quietly, "We're not sorry we had to hear it," and we both laughed as quietly as we could.

When Eleanor came out of the back she floated through and told everyone goodbye without stopping. She even yelled over her shoulder, "I'll text you Skye," and then she was gone.

I looked over at Josh and he looked deep in thought. When I finally caught his eye, I mouthed "you okay?" and he gave me a dull smile and shook his head yes. But something didn't seem right with him. It wasn't until our drive home the next day that I found out why he looked the way he did.

We had hugged Skye, Davis and their kids and I thanked them for an amazing weekend. Skye and I exchanged numbers and Destiny asked when I could come visit again. I really liked them all and could see why they were Josh's closest friends. Before I left, Skye said, "I'm so glad he met you, Alicia. He hasn't been this happy in years. Take care of him and he will certainly take care of you. I see the love in his eyes and I have wanted that for my brother." Then she hugged me again and said "thank you for loving him."

I felt really special as if I had brought their friend back to life. I didn't know I had it like that and I was all smiles. Funny thing was I felt the same about him in my life.

So we're headed back up the 405. Jazz is on, boys have their earphones on playing their DSi's and then he drops the bomb.

"Eleanor told me that she wants to come back to L.A. at the end of this month while her divorce is finalized. She's hoping if she's around Derek more often he'll get used to her and they can build a relationship."

My mouth is open. I would have to see this mean evil witch all the time? I was horrified because she's horrible! I looked over at him in sheer terror.

"I know, baby, but I need to allow her this time for my son. I don't want him to grow up angry at me for keeping her from him."

"But Josh" I said, "you haven't done anything wrong. She left. She created his anger and hurt feelings."

"I know, but I would feel awful not giving her a chance when she literally begged me for it."

"How long are we talking," I asked, trying not to sound as disgusted as I was.

I'm all for a child being with his mother, but there's something phony, calculating and manipulative about this woman. But what can I do? She is the boy's mother.

"She thinks staying a month should give her great time to bond with him so she's going to take a leave from her job."

A month! I might pull all my hair out or drop kick her for real in all that time.

I feel my heart beating fast because I just didn't like the sound of this.

"Oh," I said dryly. "And where does she plan on staying," I asked, clearly annoyed and not hiding it.

"It's kinda funny, she actually asked if I had room at my place."

I looked over at him crazy and said, "Excuse me."

He chuckled a bit and said "of course she can't, so she's gonna ask her company to look for temporary housing for her in the area."

I was so irritated I'm unsure of what he said after that. Just the thought of her being around day after day made my skin crawl. But I loved this man, I thought looking over at him, and I loved his son in the back seat. Who am I to stand in the way of Derek's relationship with his mom?

I took Josh's hand in mine and smiled over at him. I knew I would have to suck it up and I determined right then I would be there for him no matter what.

19 An Unpleasant Surprise

As I un-decorated our tree and took down the Christmas cards, I thought over what a great holiday season it was. I was in love with a great guy who had a wonderful son. I had a loving family and great friends and, of course, the best child in the world. This New Year was starting off well and I was excited about all the possibilities.

On Wednesday we were back at the center and, of course, the first order of business was to un-decorate. After hugs and talk of what we all did for Christmas and New Year's we jumped right in. Sarah had messages to return and her phone was as busy as ever. The New Year always reminded everyone to do something new or sign up their kid for a program to get things started off right, and this would last well into the month of January before tapering off.

Harvey was busy outside taking down the lights in front while Sharon and I were in the gym packing things away. I had called her yesterday to chat about my New Year's weekend, but she wanted to know more.

"Now explain this to me again. This woman had an attitude with you every time she showed up at the house," Sharon asked.

"Yes, she was funky every single time. I originally was nice, but then I just let it go. She is one of those people that you just don't wanna be around, I can tell you that much."

"And little Derek sees right through her, wow!"

"Yes, he seems to, more than his dad. And I get what Josh is saying about not keeping him from his mom, but good Lord, she kept herself away!"

"It seems to me that after seeing you she may have thought, shoot, I need to move to L.A. and get that little girl off his arm. I know she can't be trusted."

"I don't think so either. I'm going to be watching her like a hawk, Sharon,"

"So am I girl, so am I," she says and we both laugh.

"So tell me again about the big I-love-you moment."

I go ahead and give her a detailed account of the dance floor love moment and she of course tells me she told me so. We also talk about her New Year's gumbo fiasco and how her stove broke. Antonio had to rush around on New Year's Eve before everything closed to buy her a new one. Then to top it off, they weren't doing any deliveries so he had to borrow his friend's pickup truck. She had me laughing so hard I could barely breathe. After lunch we were able to finish everything up and the center was good to go for another twelve months.

Josh came in later that day and we immediately started preparing for his new class, which would begin the next week. We prepared the roster and the schedule and then, while I called parents, he worked on his sessions. We were very busy because in addition to that I had to work on the first quarter newsletter, close out the last soccer module and get started on the next one.

Josh and I stole time here and there over the following week. We had Chipotle one day for lunch and did movie night with the kids over the weekend. We went to church with Sharon and

Antonio and, of course, hit up Starbucks several times over the next ten days.

Finally, the third Saturday of the month was on us and Josh's first class began. We had twelve boys and he, with the assistance of Coach Rob, started them on their eight-week Soccer Mechanics class. By the time we start the next season our sons and these other boys will be pros on the field. Chris was excited and once I had my coffee I was too. Once everyone was settled and all the parents had dropped off their kids, I went back to the Center to tie up a few loose ends for today's session.

While I'm sitting there, Trina calls me on my cell.

'Hey, sis," she says.

"Treen, whats up, girl?"

"Just had a minute while I'm sitting here at Matthew's T-ball practice so I thought I would call you."

"How funny, I am at soccer class. I just got the boys settled with the coaches and I'm in my office getting some filing done."

"So wow, our lives literally consist of parks and practices," she says with a laugh.

"Yes, they do," I agree. "So how's Matthew and how's Michael?" I say.

"Alicia, you need to quit with the Michael comments. I believe he is fine, but I know for sure your adorable nephew is great," she says with a little sass in her voice.

"Okay, Miss Thang. Glad to hear my nephew is well. I was just checking since the man had the whole starry-eyed thing going on at Christmas."

"Whatever. I am being nicer to him but only because he's not acting like a jerk."

227

"Well, good to know he's acting right," I say.

The conversation goes on and she tells me about some new shoes she just got and how last week one of the partners was trying to hit on her. Once she told him who her father was, though, he stopped bothering her.

"Funny looking little guy," she said, and we crack up.

After about 20 minutes we hang up. I finish my busy work, lock my desk, say goodbye to the Saturday receptionist and make my way back over to the field. The class should be over soon and then Josh and me are supposed to take the boys tennis shoe shopping.

As I head over across the field I see some of the parents are starting to arrive. But someone stands out in the small crowd. Someone on their cell phone with their legs crossed. Someone with bright red lipstick, a gorgeous trench coat, probably Burberry, with big shades and hair like a wild lion's mane.

Oh dear God! Is that Eleanor?

As I get closer, I see that it is in fact Eleanor.

It's not even January 25th, so why is she here? Please tell me she is stopping through Los Angeles to tell Josh she got a job in Australia or China even. Please let her not have arrived early for her stay.

I slow my pace as now I am in literal fear. My whole personal life is flashing before my eyes. I thought I had at least another full week to prepare myself mentally and physically for this chick. This is horrible.

Because I don't want to be bothered speaking to her or hearing her phony voice talk back to me, I sit on the far end of the boy's bench and hunch over the note pad on my clip board.

I'm silently praying that when I turn around it won't be her I saw, just someone who looks a lot like her. But alas, I turn my head and yep, there's no mistaking. It's Eleanor Dean.

Practice wraps up and parents are calling for their kids. Chris comes over to sit next to me.

"Mom, did you see that Derek's mom is here?"

"Uh huh," I say, so I won't have an attitude in my voice.

"Derek is so mad. He saw her when we were on the field and he said, "Why is she here?""

"Oh he did?" I ask with genuine concern. I hate this for Derek, he is such a sweet boy. But with his mom around he goes sour.

"Yeah, he's over by her and Coach now. Coach seemed kinda surprised, too. You think we'll still go get our tennis shoes now?"

"I don't know, Chris, so I guess we better go find out." I get up and have him get his duffle bag.

When we approach them, Eleanor is standing up and laughing annoyingly with Coach Rob. Derek's head is down and Josh seems to have a set tight jaw. Things don't look too good.

"Hello, Alicia, Chris," Eleanor says. More tight jaw from Josh. Derek, however, comes over to put his arm around me.

"Hello Eleanor," I say, and before I can stop myself I go ahead and ask. "What brings you to Culver City today?" She does a phony laugh, throws back a piece of her lion's mane and looks me straight in the eye and says:

"Well, I'm in town indefinitely," she says. "Didn't Josh mention it to you," she states matter-of-factly. Chris grips my waist even harder now as if fear has set in. She is something else, I think.

"You know he did mention it in passing, I just didn't realize today was the day," I say back sweetly.

"Yes today is the day, and I have plans for my guys to take me to get settled in my new apartment."

Now, I want to punch her right in her evil mouth. And I am not violent, as I said before, but this broad brings it out of me.

"What guys?" I ask, not being able to help myself. She gives off a fake giggle.

"Alicia," Josh says. "Derek and I are going to take her to get settled in, that's all." This is the most chill and coolest guy I've ever known, and even he has stress lines in his face.

"What about the tennis shoes, Dad?" Derek whines.

"How 'bout we go later to pick them up, buddy?" Josh says trying to diffuse anything.

"I can go with you guys. I'll be more than happy to get them for you, Derek," Eleanor says.

This little boy glares up at her and says in an unhappy tone.

"No, thank you, Eleanor. We were going with Alicia and Chris."

Josh is sweating, and he looks at me for help and although I want to punch the mother, I feel for Derek.

"Derek," I say turning to look down at him. "We can wait on the shoes. We can get them later on today or if it ends up being too late, we can go tomorrow. How's that?"

Derek fumes and I see the sadness in his eyes, but I wink at him so it's just between us and he kinda half smiles at me.

"Okay, Alicia. As long as you wait for me." And then he looks over at Chris.

"Sorry Chris," he says in the saddest of voices.

"It's okay, Derek. I can wait as long as you can," and they both for the time being seem content.

"Elle, I need to speak with Alicia. My car is open so we'll meet you up there," Josh says to her in a slightly irritated voice. It doesn't put her off, though.

"Okay, great," she says. "Nice seeing you again, Alicia."

"'Charmed," I say in a monotone voice back to her.

He reaches out to me and hugs me. "Hug me back" he says after I stand there emotionless. I want to be mean, but I go ahead and hug him back.

"Baby, I am so sorry," he says into my ear. Then he looks at me. "I'll make it up to both you and Chris. I did not know she was coming to town this early."

"Whatever, Josh. I am not thrilled and hope she won't make these unannounced visits so often. I think my skin was crawling while she was talking."

"I don't know why she acts like she does around you. I guess she could be jealous of your intense beauty," he says, giving me a peck on the lips.

"She is quite annoying, so you better be glad I love you or I wouldn't put up with it." He hugs me tightly again.

"I don't deserve you," he says, and I reply "you probably don't," and we laugh. "And Josh, don't be too hard on Derek, I know he's showing out, but this is a lot for him."

"I know it is," he says, kissing me on the forehead. "It's a lot for me, too."

We gather up our junk after this and make our way up to the cars. Derek lags behind with Chris and I am sure my boy is doing his best to cheer him up. When we get by our cars we see Eleanor with the window down chatting it up with Coach Rob.

"Here they are," she says, as we all get closer. Derek mopes over to the trunk and puts his stuff away and then he gives Chris a high-five and me a hug goodbye. Josh starts up his car and rolls down the window.

"Call you later, okay?" he says winking at me and I shake my head and say yes.

Eleanor says out the window to no one in particular "goodbye everyone" so the three of us say goodbye and I add "and good riddance" under my breath. Coach Rob laughs a bit at my statement.

"I know what you mean," he says.

"You do?" I ask, shocked.

"Alicia, she went on and on while you guys were down there talking about how in love they were and how they *were* going to get married. She said he was the true love of her life and she is hoping to get Derek *and* Josh back."

I looked at Coach Rob sideways.

"Please say you're kidding."

"I wish I could but she was rambling and I let her so I could tell you guys about it. You're gonna need to watch out for that one."

I shook my head in disbelief and took a deep breath to calm my fast heartbeat.

"Thank you for telling me. I met her on New Year's weekend and I knew she was trouble, but I see she actually has plans."

"Yes, and she sounds determined. I was telling her you guys are an item and inseparable, but she says it's probably more of a fling. That's when I knew there was no talking to her."

"Wow," I commented.

"Yeah, scary. I'll help you keep an eye on her and I'm here if she gets out of hand." I smiled up at the 6'2 Coach Rob. He's got a taller Tom Cruise kinda vibe going on.

"Thanks Coach," I say.

"Well, guess I'll get out of here. See ya next week then," he says.

"Yes, next week. Take care," I say before getting into the car.

I sit there for a minute before starting up the car.

"Mom?" I look in the rear view mirror to see Chris a bit sulky.

"Yes Chris. You okay, son?" I say turning around.

"Just sad we couldn't hang out with Coach and Derek. Plus Derek is so sad his mom is here. He told me he wishes you were his mom, too."

"My goodness," I say to Chris, and my heart softens at the thought that Derek is that distressed.

I guess she really might need to step up as a mom, and quick, or she will lose her son altogether. Of course it's her own fault, I think, but I'll try and support Josh. However, if she thinks they're a package deal she's got another thing coming.

20 So Annoyed

After that talk with Coach Rob I watch Eleanor very closely. She has been herself for about two weeks now. I have put up with her smart mouth, nasty attitude and foul personality all in the name of love. But seriously my patience is running thin. Thing is I can take a lot. I will let bad behavior in a person go on for a long time and then I either blow up or walk away and never have to see them again. Of course, in this situation I didn't have a lot of choice but to put up with her if I wanted my time with Josh.

To deal with this I had to constantly talk to Jesus. I asked him to help me have a good attitude, not a sarcastic mouth and sometimes I just said "Jesus take the wheel" before I smack this witch off her broomstick!

Trina and I have talked over these few weeks and she is on edge to come down here and size her up for herself. She said since she's not Josh's woman she can show out, cuss the girl out and fight her, which I found very amusing. She called her an unroyal princess. A wannabe Cinderella, but phony and fake.

"Fakarella, sis, that's my new name for Eleanor."

I hollered. And when I told Sharon she laughed, too, but tended to agree with Trina.

As we sat at the table on the first Saturday morning in a long time that Derek has been allowed over our house, they reflect on their sleepover. The boys were finishing up their cereal before we headed over to the field for soccer class. Derek looked up and asked if he could come back over after their class. I understood his desire to be away from home since Eleanor has arrived for her visit. For him, it has been super annoying.

Josh had made plans with me and broken them because she had gotten tickets to plays or concerts. And Josh has been in a different place, too, because he's probably frustrated, which, let's face it, he should be. Josh has repeatedly asked if Chris could tag along with Derek and his mom, but I only let him go twice. She may think because Chris is nice to her that Derek will eventually come around, but I figure she needs to earn that kind of respect on her own. I realize I have to answer his questions and be sensitive to what he's going through, so I try.

"Well, don't you have plans to hang out with your mom later?" I look over at Chris and he shrugs with his head down.

"Yes ma'am, and that's why if I come over here, I can tell her I already have plans." I smile over at him.

"Can he, Mom?" asks Chris.

"Well, Derek that would strictly be up to your dad. With your mom in town, especially to be with you, I can't infringe on her time."

"You can't?" he asks, looking up at me in desperation.

"No, Derek, I can't. I'm sorry."

"But, Alicia, she takes Dad's time away from you, too, and that's not fair either."

Wow, if only this kid knew he just hit a sensitive spot in me.

I had to fix my face and take a breath before I responded.

"Well, although I do miss your dad when he is with you and your mom I know it's for you, so it's worth it to me. You are worth it to me. Do you understand?"

He nods his head that he does.

His face starts to distort. "I just wish someone would have asked me what I wanted," and he starts to cry.

I feel horrible and want to cry because no child should feel this bad about being with their mother, the one who carried them for nine months!

"It's going to be okay, sweetheart," I say leaning down to put my arm around his shoulder. Chris agrees with me that it will be okay and Derek shakes his head as if to say he knows.

"I love you, Alicia," he says.

"Aww, come here," and he turns in his chair to hug me.

"I love you too," I say, fighting tears the whole time myself.

As I do the dishes after the boys go upstairs I think about how hard this whole thing still is on Derek. I kinda wanna slap Josh because I'm starting to find myself a bit angry at him. This child should not still be upset by his mother's reappearance in his life. By now she should have won him over a bit, I think. When I ask Josh about it, he seems to think Derek will eventually come around. I personally don't see it and find myself upset that I can't get Josh to face up to it. I'm trying to keep my distance and be this wonderful girlfriend who's quiet, but this is really starting to get to me. I decide I will try to approach him with it. She has made their son miserable and made me want to shake Josh several times to show him this is not working for Derek, or me for that matter.

After the boys and I were ready we make our way over to the field. Josh told me he would be in his office getting some paperwork done before class, so I pulled around to the Center to check on him. We park and I see Josh's car and Eleanor's rental. I am feeling kinda pissed and really don't think I'll be able to hide it.

"Looks like your mom is here," Chris says to Derek. Derek grunts, and from the rear view mirror I can see that Derek sinks down in his seat.

This poor kid.

"You guys wanna run in here with me and then I'll drive us around to the field?" I ask them looking into the back seat, even though I already know the answer.

"No, that's okay," Derek says.

"We'll run across the back to the field and see you over there, Mom," Chris says, having his boy's back.

"Okay, guys, I'll see you over there in a few minutes."

They say goodbye and I get out of the car trying to work on my attitude. I want Josh to know I care this broad is here, but I don't want Eleanor thinking I'm jealous or upset, so I breathe in and exhale.

You can handle this, Alicia.

I open the door and wave to the weekend receptionist. I immediately can hear her fake laughing before I get around the corner to the offices. As I near his, she is standing in the doorway laughing at his every word. I'm feeling nauseated, but I keep a straight face. And then she spots me. Phony laugh turns into phony face.

"Oh, we have company. Hello, Alicia," this fake plastic evil Barbie says.

"Hello," I say calmly. I hear Josh shuffle to get up from his desk and push past Eleanor to come see me.

"Hey you," he says looking sheepish. He knows her being here would annoy me so he's trying to be cool, but I'm irritated.

"I just came to see if you needed me to pull anything for you before the class," I say real laid-back. Just keeping the peace is all I wanna do.

Eleanor speaks up before Josh can respond.

"Oh I'm sure if Josh needed you, he would've called you," she says tartly.

I swear I wanna pop her right in the face. No, this cow did not just say this to me.

"Well, that goes to show, you don't know what you're talking about, Eleanor. He doesn't have to call me because I know he needs me. I stopped by because this is what *I* do for *every* class and *every* game. It's *our* system," I say rather smartly.

And then we do the stare-down.

Let her say something else.

The phony smile curls at the corners of her mouth and I know she must be thinking she better shut up or she's gonna get slapped back to the bayou in no time flat.

"Okay," Josh says, and he looks distraught. He needs to, though, because this drama is because of him.

"Come in, Alicia, I wanted to ask you about the paperwork you left for me." Then he turns to Eleanor.

"Gotta go, Elle. I need to meet with Alicia so I'll just bring Derek over after class. Then I'll meet you guys later for dinner."

My eyebrows lift in confusion because we have plans for dinner. As a matter of fact this whole "before Valentine's weekend" was about us. We were set to do a fancy dinner tonight and then we planned to go out with the boys Sunday afternoon for miniature golf. It was a flashback to our first date, our double-date with the boys. But with this new revelation I can see he is scrapping the start of our plans. For all I know she has candlelight dinner plans for herself and Josh on Tuesday, which is actually Valentine's Day. I am fuming!

"Okay," she says and I see her through the mini blinds try to reach in and hug him. He pulls back, though, which I applaud internally and then I hear her stiletto's walk across the lobby to the door.

Good riddance!

Before he can even ask about the paperwork I light right into him about the dinner plans I heard them speak of.

"Josh, I thought we were going to Rock Sugar for dinner tonight. I can't believe you forgot this was the start of our Valentine's weekend of fun. Chris is going over to Sharon's to hang with her and Antonio since you told me Derek was going to be with his mom." I sound a bit hurt and I am. Did he really forget so quickly?

"Alicia, I am so sorry," and he sits down in his chair with his head hanging. Like father like son, I see, and I'm feeling more pissed by the second that she is doing this to two of my guys.

"Elle is having such a hard time reaching Derek," he goes on, "that I told her I would start going on more of their outings so I could be a buffer for her. He's still not warming up to her."

If he only knew.

"I was just trying to help out so she can strengthen their relationship. Since this is such an issue for Derek I was hoping you wouldn't mind. Coach Rob and Jessica already volunteered to keep a bunch of the team kids so we could have Valentine's Day all to ourselves. It can still be romantic, Alicia."

I see he is trying to search my eyes for my agreement, but instead I fold my arms and take a seat in one of his chairs. I stay quiet and just stare at him. He cannot be this stupid about Eleanor.

"Josh. Derek did tell me today that he did not want to go out with her tonight and asked me if he could stay overnight at my house. He seems very upset at the way things are going. He told me this morning that he wishes someone would ask him what he wants. And I'm not trying to be pushy or give you an opinion about your son's relationship with his mom, but he's so upset about it."

Josh listened and shook his head as if in agreement with me. But when he looked up to speak to me he seemed annoyed.

"Look, I am sorry about tonight. I was wrong for not telling you first before making the arrangements but when Elle showed up here this morning that's what she wanted to talk to me about. And you just said it yourself. She is in fact Derek's mom. It is my responsibility to make sure she has a 100 percent chance of connecting with him. So if that means I have to help him along by going with him to see her, then I will. He was out of order asking to stay at your house tonight and for whining to you about our family problems, and I apologize for that, but I can't apologize for wanting him to have this opportunity with his mom."

His face is stern. I'm trying to read him to see if he is seriously telling me off. I'm in shock for a few minutes and my mouth is open in disbelief. I quickly recover and respond.

"You know what? You are absolutely right. If you want the two of them to have that awesome mother/son relationship you are going to have to make it happen. Your son is hurt, he's crying even, because, sorry to tell you, he is not bonding with her! And I am hurt because you just apologized to me about him confiding in me. I don't know if you knew this but we" – and I point to him and then myself – "are in a relationship. If your son comes to me about anything I am going to be there for him, just as I would hope you would with Chris!" I feel my chest tighten and my blood is boiling. Josh looks offended but I don't care and keep going like a wild woman out of control. It's like I can't help myself.

"She is not a very nice person. We all just put up with her and you, you act like just because she's Derek's mother her behavior does not need to be checked. But it does!" And I say those last few words in that shrill high voice we ladies use when we are really mad. Shoot, men sometimes use it, too.

He stares at me in disbelief.

"Alicia, I know how she can be. She left me with my son as a baby. I know she's tough to take, but I have to believe," and he pounds his fist on the desk for emphasis, "that she really wants to be Derek's mom now."

I sort of jump, but he doesn't look at me. He fiddles with the papers on his desk, and leans back in his chair a bit.

"I'm sorry if this is hard on you, but I have to do it," he says almost yelling at me.

I'm quiet and staring at him. A million things are running through my mind and I know not only is Derek tired of her, I am too. She's shown up at the office on an almost daily basis.

Our dates start or end with her texting or calling to interrupt, and her rudeness to acknowledge me as Josh's girlfriend. Well, that makes me want to physically hurt the girl or have someone do it for me.

"Well, I guess I don't have a choice then, do I." I say pretty much glaring at him.

"I just need to step back and give you some space. Not so much for you but for myself. I don't want to be disappointed anymore."

He looks up then. "I disappoint you?" And he looks kinda hurt about this but I don't care because he just smashed my feelings ten different ways.

"No, *you* don't disappoint me," I say. "I just find my feelings getting hurt on a daily basis and I'm being pushed out of your life. That's disappointing, and I don't like it. And rather than feel the pain, I'll just give you some space."

Now *I* look sad, because I am. I'm trying to fight the tears because I know I need to be stern.

He looks hurt and exhausted, but again he needs to see how serious this mess is with Eleanor. He gets up and comes over to me. He pulls me up from the chair and takes me in his arms and I try not to, but I find myself holding on tight.

"I promise, things will get better," he says into my ear.

I am calmed, but I don't lose sight of why I was so heated in the first place. "I just need to help Derek out, but I don't want there to be any space between us."

Then he releases me a bit to look in my eyes.

"Like right now, how there is no space between us, that's how close I want you to stay," and I look up at him and into those warm caring eyes and I'm a sucker, completely and totally.

"Okay, Parsons?"

"Okay" I sigh with my arms around his neck. And then out come the tears. I wanted to march out of there mad and angry and turn on my heels. I wanted him to know how angry I was but really I'm just overwhelmed like Derek. I'm miserable and feel like I'm losing the relationship we have had such a great time building. I have the mad tears where you almost can't get a grip on your breathing. I am literally sobbing.

"I'm so sorry," he says in my ear and he kicks his door shut with his foot.

He holds me until we have to go over to the field. We don't say another word and I'm not completely sure of how he is going to move forward changing things up a bit with Eleanor.

I know one thing, though. He knows how I feel about that phony Fakarella and how miserable Derek and I both are. Let's hope a change is on the horizon.

21 Changes

After the day's session Chris and I run some errands and then about 4:30 p.m., head over to Sharon's. I figure I may as well give her the news in person that I didn't need her and Antonio's help that night. She told me Antonio had bought barbecue ribs, corn and beans last night especially for Chris and I felt bad I was messing up the plan. Besides I was feeling a bit dejected after my talk with Josh. It had been hard the last few weeks and I had been trying to keep my feelings to myself. But between Sharon, my sisters and my mom asking me constantly if everything was okay with Eleanor around, I was about to burst. Hopefully, with information and not in tears but only time would tell.

Sharon answered the door in her jean capris, yellow tee and sun hat. I knew she must have been working in her garden today.

"Hey sweetie," she says giving me a hug and welcoming us in. "Hey Chris, ready for a night of food and fun?"

"Yes, Auntie Sharon."

"Well go on out with your uncle Tony, he's on the deck working on dinner."

As Chris walks away, she turns to look at me.

"What's up girl? I thought you were coming for 6." And I can't speak. At that moment all of the drama, all the smart remarks, mean comments and ugly actions of Eleanor Dean weigh on me like a ton of bricks. And although I had no intention of telling Sharon about it in tears, it unfortunately comes out that way. I put my head down and try to compose myself as I feel the tears stinging my eyes.

"Alicia pie," she says. Her name for me when I'm sad or frustrated. "What's wrong, love? Is it Josh – Eleanor?" She asks this with an attitude, her hand on her hip.

"Well," I sputter.

"Oh wait" she says, "come sit down on the couch, and tell me everything."

She knew a lot of the drama of her showing up and texting and interrupting our plans, but she was shocked to learn how disrespectful and mean this woman was. Then when I told her about Josh she was done.

"So you're saying he is still trying to come with the whole this-is-my-son's-mother angle?" I nod yes.

"Well, I don't know if I'm feeling that, Alicia. He can't keep using that as an excuse for her funky attitude toward you."

"I know, it's really not okay," I say, much more calmly than when I arrived. "Today I told him it was obvious I needed to give him space because the closer I am to the situation the more input I feel almost led to give!"

"Well, that's understandable," she comments.

"And that's how I felt. He seems to think as long as I stay close we will be able to get through all of this, but if he doesn't think my input is valid I think I need to step back."

"You are absolutely right. He has got to value your opinion. Otherwise, you're not operating as a couple. Oh my goodness,

Josh. I could never imagine being mad at him, but if he's making my girl this miserable, then I am mad at him."

I smile weakly.

"Thanks, girl."

"Of course, I got you. I just hope I don't run into Eleanor, or she's toast!"

We both crack up.

"On a serious note, what do you think is going to happen on Valentine's Day?"

I shrug my shoulders. "I have no idea, Sharon. Your guess is as good as mine. I sure hope he doesn't mess it up or this could be the beginning of the end for us."

She shakes her head in understanding. "I totally feel you. Well, come on," she say's getting up. "Let's go see how the guys are. I think they might've eaten without us." Then we head outside.

That evening she asked me if I wanted to go to church the next day and I said okay. I had been going pretty regularly before the New Year, but since Eleanor showed up I had been moping and watching Sunday services online mostly. We had such a great evening eating barbecue, chatting about everything and then watching "The Game Plan" and "The Rundown," two movies they had rented on Apple TV, which The Rock starred in. In my current state a little eye candy on screen was just what I needed.

Sharon gave me a big hug and said "no worries" about Josh. I hugged her back tight before Chris got his hugs and then we were on our way. "Mom?" Chris asked on the way home.

"Yes, son."

"Are you sad that Josh couldn't keep your date tonight?"

Wow! Did I not hide my feelings good enough from my 10–year-old?

"Well, I was a little disappointed, but I had such a good time tonight that I am perfectly okay," I said, hoping that would suffice.

"Well, I miss Derek. And not just when I don't see him, but the old Derek. He's so mad or sad all the time now."

It was more of a statement than a question, but I felt bad for my boy.

"Are you concerned about him?"

"Yeah, Mom, I am. His mom is trying to force him to love her and he and I think if she just acted like a real mom, like you, then he would, without all the presents and outings."

I sigh as I pull in our garage.

Again, such big thoughts in such little boys' heads.

They shouldn't have to deal with such adult problems and I find myself mad at Eleanor again for barging in Derek's and all of our lives. If she was sincere and sweet and apologetic then maybe it would be different. But she's so phony and mean.

"I know, sweetie, and I am so sorry Derek has to go through all this. Maybe his mom thinks that's the best way to reach him. We just have to hope she comes around. And you just continue to be a good friend to Derek and that will help him while he goes through all this. Okay, Chris?"

"Okay, Mom," he says, a bit melancholy. "I'm going to pray for Derek at church tomorrow and his mom." I smile at my baby boy.

"That's very sweet and I know it will help." I hug him and send him up to his room.

I decide to get my clothes together for church the next day so there would be no rushing. I would never make Antonio late to church, he hates to be late. As I was digging through my shoe box I get a text from Josh. It was about 10 p.m., so I was surprised to hear from him since the entire night had passed with no communication.

"Hey Parsons, how was your night"

"It was great Josh. Thx for asking. And yours?"

"It was ok I guess. I missed u all night"

"You did, that's so sweet :)" I'm not really sure I'm feeling him but I'm trying to be nice!

"I hope you're not still mad at me babe. I think things went way better since I went along."

"I'm sure they did...and I'm not mad." A few minutes pass by as if he's thinking of something to say.

"Well can we hang out all day tomorrow?" How badly do I want to say *"you sure Elle won't need u to go buy groceries or get a manicure with her, but I skip the sarcasm this time.*

"Maybe". Then I wait a few minutes for effect. *"I'm going to church in the morning with Antonio and Sharon and then we'll probably go eat, but we still have our afternoon plans with the boys"*

"Oh." And I know I have hurt his feelings but I had to. He needs to feel my pain.

"Derek has been wanting to go back to church too". Ahh! He used the Derek card. He knows I can't resist that kid.

"He has, eh? Well if you guys get to us by 9 we can ride over together to Sharon's. We plan to leave there by 9:25."

"Yes we would love to come, thx baby. We'll see u then."

"Ok, see u then." And I *know I'm doing the right thing because it's church. Everyone needs to be in the presence of God*

"I love u" he writes finally, and my heart melts. *Aww, how can I ever be mad at him?*

"I love u 2".

I finish getting everything ready for church and go to sleep happy and content. I get to see Josh tomorrow and hang out all day with him and Derek. Chris is going to be happy and Sharon will be thrilled that he is coming as well. Life is great at this very moment and I close my eyes and sleep well.

The next morning we are on schedule and downstairs eating breakfast by 8:30. Chris has on his new sweater vest I got him with his button-down polo shirt, jeans and loafers and I was wearing new houndstooth slacks with a black INC sweater set and hot new Kenneth Cole boots I got on sale at Macy's. Actually, the whole outfit was from Macy's. I was looking church-chic as I gulped down my coffee and toast while Chris finished his cereal.

At 8:55 we went down to get in the car. There was no call Josh had arrived, no cell phone call as of yet and no text. I was starting to wonder if something was wrong. So before I got in the car I texted him. Besides being concerned, Chris was anxious to see Derek and get to spend most of today with his best friend.

"Hey, where are u guys? We're waiting in the garage and just wondering if you're ok."

I go ahead and start up the car and open the garage. Chris is whining for me not to leave. And since I can get to Sharon's in 17 minutes we can easily wait another five or so minutes for them, so we do. A few minutes later my cell rings. *Uh oh* I think as I get that kinda sick feeling in my stomach.

"Alicia, hey. We're running really really late this morning," he says a bit out of breath.

"Is everything okay?" I reply, still concerned at this point.

"Well, we were on schedule when Elle called me to say her car wouldn't start. I drove over to give her car a jump but the battery is literally dead."

No, you're dead!

"Umm hmm," I say annoyed.

"Alicia, I am so sorry. I don't think we can even make it to Antonio's on time to ride to church with you guys."

Internally I count down from 10, I try to breathe, but I'm so mad I can't even get even breaths out. Finally, I speak and it's not good.

"Josh, there is a company called AAA. They will come to your house, bring you a battery and install it. All at your front door. I can't believe you got roped into her trap. This is all about seeing you and having you at her beck and call!"

Chris' eyes open wide because my voice is way high. He looks kind of scared because I rarely have the need to raise my voice in front of him.

"Is that what this is all about, Alicia? You're jealous? I would have never thought jealousy was your style."

Oh no he didn't!

"It's not!" Now my voice is high and shaky. I can't believe this is playing out in front of my son. Josh sounds downright angry so either Elle is standing there thrilled because he's upset or Derek is petrified like Chris. Either way this is terrible and right before church, mind you.

"In no way could I ever be jealous of that mean, evil, conniving sorry excuse for a mother!"

I could no longer control myself as everything inside was rising to the surface.

"Derek doesn't deserve everything he's being put through. You tried, Josh, you tried, but it's not working. She is NEVER going to be the mother you wished for your son. Talk to him! He's told my own son he's completely miserable."

Very low Josh says, "Are you through?"

"No, actually I'm not. To let her ruin this one day we were going to have together is just beyond me. It's so not worth it, and now Chris is crying so his day is officially ruined as well."

Silence. I'm driving over to Sharon's with mascara tear stains and I'm shaking. Chris is crying and I reach back to pat his leg because I can't believe he had to hear all that. Finally, he speaks very calmly.

"Alicia, I'm sorry to have ruined your day but the reason Elle called me was because she needed to get to the airport. Her mother is very sick and she is taking a flight out this morning. She didn't have anyone else to turn to. I'm shocked because this isn't even like you," he says, having the nerve to sound disappointed.

"And this is not like you. She could have taken a cab or a Super Shuttle and been on time."

'Unbelievable," he says with what I'm sure is a clenched jaw.

"It sure is," I say in my most sarcastic voice.

"I guess I'll just talk to you later then," he says sounding highly irritated.

"Or not," I reply, knowing it is an ugly thing to say but he needs to feel me on this.

"As a matter of fact," I go on unable to control my sarcasm, "if you're too busy later we can just cancel our miniature golf plans with the boys." I hear Chris sigh in the background but right now this is for effect and I know I'll have to deal with him later.

"It's like that?"

I don't reply and he sighs heavily, "I'll call you later."

"Okay," I answer. And then I hang up without saying bye. That's the ultimate kiss-off, and I hate it when someone does it to me.

We're in front of Sharon's and I'm trying to fix my face before Sharon and Antonio see our car from the window and come outside. And as much as I now don't feel like going to church I probably really need to be there. I wasn't very nice to Josh but he was being so stupid, has been so stupid. And then Chris touches me on the shoulder.

"You okay, Mom?" And he looks bewildered as if he's wondering who I am.

"Yes, Baby, Mommy is okay. I just got very angry at Coach. He was saying some things I didn't like, so I told him. But I apologize for being so mad and yelling in front of you." I look at him and he seems to warm up to my regular voice.

"It's okay, Mom. I think a lot of the things you said were true, especially about Derek's mom."

Wow, even my child can now see the devil when he's masquerading in a dress!

"I did get a bit carried away in my anger, but she does need to be nicer," I say smiling at him.

"Yeah, she can be kinda rude to other adults, especially you, so I'm glad you told Coach. Maybe he'll ask her to stop now."

"You know what, maybe he will, Chris."

"Mom, are the plans with Coach and Derek really canceled for tonight?" he asks with deep concern.

"I don't know, Chris. I said it out of anger. So we'll just have to wait and see."

"Okay, Mom," he says, sitting back looking sad. I do feel bad for him and I even feel bad for Derek. But mostly I feel sad for me.

Just then we see Sharon waving from across the street. We get our Bibles, or in my case my iPad with my Bible app and make our way over to their car.

We give hugs all around but before we get in the car Sharon pulls me to the side.

"You okay, girl? It almost looks like you've been crying."

"Well yeah, just a bit. I had a falling out on the way over with Josh, and Chris heard the whole thing. Josh and Derek we're coming to church, too, until something came up this morning," and I give her a look and she instantly knows why.

"Eleanor" she whispers and hisses at the same time. I nod my head yes.

"I'll tell you all about it at lunch. For now I need to go ask for forgiveness for telling my man off."

Church is awesome as always and I enjoy praise and worship immensely. The pastor brought the Word and managed to read my mail again when he lightly touched upon forgiveness. He said that even if the other person has done something wrong and we feel hurt or betrayed, we still need to forgive so we can be free. I knew then I had already forgiven Josh, even though he is not in his right mind, and I knew I was going to tell him I was sorry as well. Not for what I said, but for how I said it. I'll figure out how to make it come out right, but I really was sorry we fell out and that the guys missed church.

Afterwards we went to lunch at the Cheesecake Factory in Marina del Rey. It was bustling with church folk as usual, so we found some seats over in the bar area to wait. I decided to text Josh before getting into my morning details with Sharon.

"Hey Josh, just checking on u. Church was great and I wish you had been there. I wanted to apologize for my outburst this morning. I hate fighting ☹" A few seconds later he responds.

"I hate fighting too Alicia so thank u for saying that. I apologize too because I could have handled things differently" I smile.

"I got you a cd of the message, it was on Unforgiveness :)"

"Nice"

"We're at Cheesecake Factory now so I just wanted to see if we were still on for later." A few minutes pass…

"Yes of course. Elle missed her flight so we did brunch at Knotts, but we are good for this afternoon." Were my eyes deceiving me or did he just say he and spawn of Satan are at Knotts having a fun day with Derek, after eating biscuits and chicken at Mrs. Knotts restaurant? *"I'll call u as soon as we get back to town."*

I don't even know if I can respond. Anger builds and I try to push it back. I will not be mad. I can't allow myself to go there again. I realize right then on Sunday afternoon. Right at that moment at the Marina del Rey Cheesecake Factory, right here in Los Angeles County that my man doesn't get it. I realize at that moment in time that actions speak louder than words. I vow right then to myself that I will from this day forward, *show* him how I feel. I decided right then that I would not worry about what happens tonight or on Valentine's Day or any other day. If we were meant to be it would just have to work itself out.

"*K*" I text.

"Okay, Alicia, now tell me what happened this morning," Sharon leans over to ask.

"I sure will. I've got a lot to tell you, girlfriend."

22 On Good Terms

Once we get home from lunch we change clothes and I sit down for a little Lifetime TV. I DVR "Army Wives," then go over to CBS to record "The Good Wife" and "The Mentalist." I am not going to stress over Joshua Hart. If this is the way things are going to go then I will just live my life quietly with my son and move on. This emotional roller-coaster is for the birds, and I'm tired of it.

Chris comes down about 4:30 to ask me if we are still going miniature golfing with Josh and Derek. Honestly, I don't know and I tell him that. He is crestfallen and looks like he literally just lost his best friend.

"Sweetie, I'm sorry I just don't know what's going on with the plans, but as soon as I do I'll let you know." He shakes his head okay and I ask if he wants to watch some "Good Luck Charlie" with me, and since it's one of his favorite shows he agrees to join me. We laugh through two episodes and then I ask him if he's hungry. He says yes but he wants to wait just in case we end up going to eat. This is when I know it's time to at least text Josh. I am so mad at him I can't see straight. It's one thing to let me down, but now you're messing with my kid. I have an issue with that.

"Hey Josh, it's almost 6 pm. Plans were for 5 & Chris is asking"
I press send and wait.
About 6:15 he calls me.

"Alicia, hey. We were back on this side of town about 4 but Elle locked her keys in her apartment and it's taken forever to get a locksmith to come out. She was hoping we could break in ourselves but it was virtually impossible."

I cannot believe he's telling me this like I care. I grunt in response.

"He's just about to leave, though, so we could swing through to get you guys and be over there no later than 6:45." I want to kick him to the curb so bad, but my son's face is in great anticipation of my response. And then I think about Derek and know he probably looks the exact same. I quickly decide what I can do to make the boys happy.

"That's a waste of time. We'll meet you at Johnny Rockets. With it being a school night and all why don't we just eat and then figure out another day to golf."

I see Chris frown so I place my hand over the receiver and whisper to him, "We can just stay here and order pizza. I don't even want to go anymore."

My jaw is set and he knows I mean business. "I wanna go," he pleads, and I shake my head once to say okay.

"Oh wow, okay. Derek's going to be disappointed, but you're right. It has gotten late. Dinner it is. We can still come and get you guys, though," he says almost begging me.

"No, it's okay. We'll see you there in 15." He knows I am not happy now, but says okay and hangs up.

I look at my son. He is not happy but he doesn't say a word, just goes to get his jacket. I slide on my silver sparkle Tom's that look great with my jeans and grab my grey hoodie. We head over to the Bridge and meet them at Johnny Rockets. The boys are immediately happy and start talking like crazy. As for me I can barely look Josh in the eye. He tries small talk, asking me about church and our afternoon. I give him one word answers and forced smiles. After burgers and fries he moves his chair over by mine and leans in towards me.

"I know you're mad, but will you please just talk to me."

"I am talking to you, Josh." I look at him and give him a fake smile.

"Alicia, I'm sorry things worked out so badly today – and tonight," he adds after I look at him sideways. "I didn't mean for the day to get so out of hand and you have every right to be angry at me. I'm sorry, babe. Can you forgive me?"

I stare at him for several minutes. His good looks and charm won't be winning me over that quickly this time. But finally I speak.

"Of course I can forgive you. Pastor just spoke today on it, as I told you. I would never hold this against you. But, Josh, this relationship with Eleanor inside of our newly blossomed one, is not working for me. I'm always frustrated and it's just not that fun anymore," I say honestly to him.

He looks down at the floor and he knows I'm right.

"I know this is hard, but please give me another chance."

He's sincere. A little stupid about his baby's momma, but sincere. I shake my head yes and he leans in closer and I turn my cheek to him so he can give me a kiss.

"That's all I get?" he asks, looking surprised.

"That's the best I can do right now, stud."

He grins his Colgate smile and says "that's fair."

I hear Chris tell Derek, "Maybe now things will get back to normal" to which Derek agrees, and that makes me smile.

They walk us to the car and once there Josh hugs me and it feels like an apology. I believe him, even though he's totally annoyed me and I hug him back. He releases me while his arms are still around my waist.

"As for Valentine's Day, it's going to be our day. No matter what it's just gonna be you and me. You got it, Parsons?" he promises, looking deep into my eyes.

"Yes, I got it, Coach," and I give him a genuine smile and then a genuine kiss.

We say our goodbyes and we make our way home. Chris and I are both happy and I trust this week will be better for us. I am sure hoping so as I pull into my garage.

**

Once I dropped Chris at school, I have plenty of time to oversee the final details on the Valentine's Day deliveries. I had hired extra staff to help Savannah work this past weekend because Valentine's Day is big business. The hospital had doubled their order from last year so I was very excited that they were relying on me so greatly during holidays.

At the warehouse I was grateful to find that deliveries were already being made. In addition to my formal orders, I always send my parents and sisters Valentine flowers. This year I even include Grandma Lucy. Since we bonded over the holidays I intend to keep in close contact with her so she can have a strong relationship with Christopher. I'm also sending friendship flowers to Skye and even a little something for Destiny. It's a big day of love so I go all out.

Trina, called just then to check on the flowers she had ordered through her assistant, and I told her they had gone out early this morning. Of course there are florists in San Francisco, but Trina will always order from her big sister. Then she asked me what we were doing for Valentine's Day tomorrow. I then proceeded to tell her about the crazy Sunday we had yesterday and that at this point I would just be happy to see him tomorrow.

"That is so annoying, Sis. I want you guys to get back to your happy place, like you were over the holidays." I wholeheartedly agreed.

"Since you can't get a room" – I crack up at this statement – "you should plan a simple yet exciting evening of dinner and walking on the pier. Somewhere with water since you love the beach so much." I agreed.

"He says the whole day is full of surprises, though, Treen so I guess I have to wait and see."

She loved the mystery, and then I told her I was surprising him by giving him flowers as well as a huge box of See's candy, since they are not the norm. Plus I had managed to score some courtside Lakers tickets for next month. I was feeling pretty excited and she loved all my plans. After teasing her about the dinner date she agreed to go on with Michael, I let her go.

When I pick up Chris later I give both the boys a box of Avenger Valentines to fill out. Although they said valentines were for girls they thanked me because they had decided they would pass some out the next day. I already knew this so I simply patted myself on the back. At home I made a vase of flowers for their teacher using supplies I keep around in cases like this. Josh texted me, thanking me for the valentine's for Derek. He reminded me that tomorrow was our day and that even though we would be at work he had some surprises up his sleeve at the office. That made me happy and I went to sleep after laying out my black straight skirt with the red camisole and black shrug. I had to be in the color of the day of course. I even pulled out my red heels. And I rarely wear heels to my community center job.

The next day I dropped Chris off with his valentines and candy bags. I also dropped in to give the flowers to their teacher. On the way out I ran into Jessica.

"Happy Valentine's Day," I say. "Thanks, and you, too, Alicia." Then she said, "Hold on a sec. I have something for you." She runs across to her car and comes back with a Starbucks card.

"Oh my gosh, thank you," I say smiling brightly.

She grins, "Yeah, I've been waiting for a chance to get you something for all you do." I give her a quick hug before saying goodbye and getting in the car.

Before I drive away I have a few texts. One is a group text from Trina and Jackie. Trina says *"sis, my flowers are so beautiful and I am so surprised,"* and she adds a smiley face winking because she knew good and well those flowers were coming. *"Happy Valentine's Day"* she adds with a red heart. Jackie says *"ditto…you never forget me and I love you so much, xoxo!*

I write them back a note and press send.

The second one is from Rick and I almost pass out when I see his name. *"Happy Valentines Day A. My mom got the flowers from u last night and literally flipped. That was great of u."* My eyes are open extra wide because Rick said something nice to me. I text him back to thank him.

My last text is from Josh. *"Happy Valentine's Day to my girl. I love u."*

Electric shockwaves radiate throughout my body and my heart is full. Even with the drama we are going through I can't help but love him, and I text back the same to him.

Now I put the car in drive because I must get to the Center before him. I pull up and am glad to see I beat him and it looks like I beat Sharon, too. As promised, Savannah has delivered all the flowers to the Center. Josh's are huge so I take his to his office first, then I get Sharon's and everyone else's in the office. Sarah comes around her station to give me a big hug and Harvey says, "You never forget, Alicia, thank you so much."

I've been doing this since I started working at the Center and don't intend to stop anytime soon. I place a basket on Sharon's desk with a little See's candy box and a Starbucks gift card and then on Josh's desk I place the two-pound box of See's next to the roses. I am too jazzed and rush back to my desk to turn on my computer and act like I am working.

My cell rings and its Skye. She says, "Who sends friendship flowers! Alicia, you are too sweet. Thank you so much, doll. Destiny is going to be so excited when she gets home from school."

I tell her how welcome she is and thank her for being such a great new friend to me. "Are you kidding, you are a keeper. I'm going to text Josh and make sure he knows it."

We laugh and then she asks about our plans for tonight. After chatting a bit we hang up, and just as we do, Sharon comes in the door. She has balloons and a gift for me.

"You're not the only one who can do surprises, missy."

"Aww, I love them. Thanks, Sharon." And I get up to hug her.

As she opens her candy and decides on which piece to eat, Josh comes through the door. He's got on his signature coach shorts and a hoodie even though it's only 61 degree's today. He tells everyone good morning and Happy Valentine's Day and delivers all of us our favorite drinks from Starbucks. He kisses me on the cheek and says he'll be right back. He comes back inside with cookie baskets from Mrs. Fields for all of us. It's like pig out day for sure but I decide not to worry about the calories.

"I brought breakfast sandwiches too," he says, and we all sigh at his kindness.

"I knew I was going to like him the first time I did my pre-investigation on him," Sharon says, smiling at the thought. I smile too remembering how she had already decided he was single and needed to mingle with me before he ever came to work on his first day.

"Yeah, I guess you did call it, didn't you." She shakes her head. "Sure did. You have me to thank for Mr. Hot Stuff."

I nod and say, "Thank you, Sharon," and we giggle like school girls.

The day is great. Josh could not believe I got him that many flowers and said he had never been given any before. I was really impressed with myself for that one. He had a huge grin when he opened the door and saw them. We barely worked as we stopped to chat with each other throughout the morning. Savannah reported midday that all orders went out for delivery and we had another successful February 14th.

At lunchtime Josh came to my desk, orders me to get my purse and my flats and tells me it's time to go. I am totally caught off guard because I'm halfway full from all the junk we have eaten thus far. He taps Sharon on the shoulder when we leave and she gives him the thumbs up. Man, these two are sneaky I think and when I look at her with suspicious eyes, she just winks at me.

He doesn't say much on the drive to the beach, which is obviously where he's going. He's got on a jazz mix CD that he's made for me and it has some of my favorite artists on it. We are grooving to some David Sanborn when he parks in the lot at Playa del Rey. He gets me out of the car after going to the trunk and getting a picnic basket and blanket. I smile realizing we are having a beach picnic in the 61-degree weather. It's definitely cool and breezy but the sun is out at least.

After settling down with our blanket, he produces Martinelli's cider with clear plastic cups, he's got a sandwich platter, fruit, chocolate-covered strawberries, the works.

"I feel so special that you did all this for me, Josh." And I reach over and kiss him on the lips.

"Score for the coach" he says, and I giggle. "I just wanted to do something special for the most incredible woman I know. I hope it makes up for some of the things I have been putting you through lately." But before he goes on I place my finger on his mouth to ssh him.

"Let's not think about anything today except you and me. Sound good, Coach?" He shakes his head in agreement.

After eating, he lays back on the blanket and I lay back against him. We close our eyes and soak in the afternoon sun and the joy of being together.

I poke him in the side after a while and ask, "Isn't it time we get back to work, sir?" He opens one eye, looks down at me and says, "always the boss, eh Parsons?"

I stick out my tongue at him. "Somebody has to be," I say, and with that a tickle-fest ensues followed by a passionate "From Here to Eternity" kiss on the beach, minus the tide.

Finally, we get up and it's after 2 p.m. so I hurry him to the car. On the way back we hold hands and continue listening to the awesome CD he made. As we park at the Center he gets out to come around to my door and he gets a text on his cell, which he left in the cup holder.

It's from Eleanor and it says in the preview line, *"I need your help! Where are u?"*

23 Sweet Surprises

The bad girl in me wanted to pick up the phone and throw it out of the window or accidentally smash it on the ground while passing it to him. But when he got to my car door I say, "You left your phone. Looks like you got a text."

He took the phone, said thanks and put it in his pocket, never looking at it. He then reached for my hand to help me out of the car.

"Thanks for a great time, Alicia."

"No, thank you. That was the most awesome Valentine's date ever."

He smiles. "Just wait til you see what I have planned for tonight."

I smile back. "I can't wait." Then I look over at the office windows. "For now I think we better go inside before the staff comes out to greet us."

He keeps his eyes on me. "Everyone looking out the window at us?" he asks.

"Every single one," I say, and we burst into laughter. Then we make our way back inside and never let them know we saw them watching us. As the day winds down I am still smiling. Since returning I had gotten an e-card from Josh and every time I went to make a copy, go to the restroom or check on something, there would be a gift card or a small gift waiting for me at my desk. About 3:30 Savannah even delivered roses to me from Josh, to which I literally was at a loss of words. He must have peeked into my contacts for the number.

"So what do you think of your romantic day at the office with lunch at the beach?" Sharon asks, sitting down at the chair next to my desk.

"Well, sneaky lady, I think it has all been beyond wonderful."

"I think he has really made up a lot of ground today, girl, don't you think?" she asks.

"Yeah he has," I say, still smiling. "As a matter of fact he has gone way beyond good boyfriend territory. He's gone into super hero boyfriend status."

She shakes her head in agreement just as he comes out of his office.

"How's my favorite girl doing?" I still can't get the huge grin off my face and before I can answer Sharon says, "She is doing great because she had a fabulous day!"

In agreement I shake my head and say, "What she said."

We all laugh.

"Looks like you two were pretty sneaky working together behind my back," I say, eyeing them both. Sharon leans back in her chair, crosses her legs and says, "so true. I am a great partner in crime, wouldn't you say so, Josh?"

Laughing he comes over and places his hands on her shoulders. "You absolutely are, Sharon. I couldn't have done all this sneaky stuff without you."

She pats his right hand. "You weren't so bad yourself, Coach."

Of course I'm too happy to be anything but amused at their exchange. "So you have a romantic evening planned with Antonio?" He asks her.

She smiles seductively. "I sure do. He's taking me to dinner, salsa dancing and then sky's the limit when we get back home."

Josh and I exchange glances, "TMI, Sharon," I say laughing, "TMI."

Josh laughs, too.

"So sorry little single people. But it's not like I gave you details or anything," she says rolling her eyes. Then she breaks out laughing too.

"And what about us, what are we doing?" I look expectantly at them both. "You're not getting a word out of me, missy," Sharon says.

"Yep, sorry, Parsons, you just gotta wait."

After pouting, I ask what I should wear. "She's really pushing it isn't she?" Josh says to Sharon.

She shakes her head in agreement with Josh. "She sure is. Well girl I will tell you this. Wear your cute little red number with the shear jacket."

I blush. "Okay, I can do that." They eye each other before she gets up.

"Well, on that note I'm gone, lovebirds," Sharon says, excusing herself. "I'm gonna close down and get outta here. Have fun you two," she says hugging us both.

"You rocked it, Coach."

He tells her she did, too, then sits down in the chair, takes my hands in his and looks deep into my eyes – into my soul even. Thankfully, the office was virtually empty as he spoke.

"I hope today has made up a bit for all you've been through recently. Trust me, I know it's because of me and I'm going to do better. I promise."

I squeeze his hands, put my forehead against his and say, "Thank you for saying that. It has, Josh, I feel really special, like it's Christmastime again." I smile and he smiles and then Sarah comes around the corner to tell us she's leaving.

"Oh, sorry, kids. Didn't mean to interrupt."

"No worries, we say, and for a minute I feel like we are inappropriate, but then I remember it's Valentine's Day, so I gave myself a break for once.

"Enjoy your evening, Sarah," we yell after her.

Then I kiss him and say, "Let's get outta here, too, Coach," before grabbing his hand and pulling him up.

After closing, I make my way home to change. Josh had planned to pick up the boys and take them over to Coach Rob's house. I took my time and laid out my clothes, took a bubble bath and listened to some Boney James.

While applying my Pink Chiffon body cream from Bath & Body Works, Jessica calls to tell me Eleanor was telling the other moms outside of the after-school program that she was hoping to woo Derek's father into taking her for a romantic Valentine's dinner tonight.

According to Tina, Brian's mom, Josh showed up, asked Eleanor what she was doing there and when she asked what the plan was for the night he looked at her crazy, told her he was taking out Alicia, of course, and walked away. But then he turned back and told her to go home. My mouth was open. So she didn't need help from him like she said on that text, she just needed psychiatric help.

"Don't say anything, okay?" pleaded, Jess. "Robert told me not to tell you because it might upset you, but I thought you should know, mostly because it was weird."

My heart was beating fast, but I was relieved to know. "Jess, thank you so much. I do appreciate it."

All kinds of thoughts were running through my mind about this chick as I got dressed but I vowed I would not give her one thought during this evening. I put my hair up, but left some cascading curls out in the front. My red dress screamed Valentine's Day and so did the strappy sandals I wore with it. I calmed down and waited on the couch for my man.

He showed up at 7 on the dot looking dapper in his slacks, white shirt and sports coat. It was the most clothes he'd ever worn since I'd known him and it just proved he looks great in anything.

"You are stunning," he says coming in my entryway to help me in my coat.

"Thank you, Mr. Hart. You're not looking too bad yourself." He turned me toward him after my coat was on. "Happy Valentine's Day, Alicia."

I look up into his eyes. "Same to you." And with that he leaned down and gave me another sweet kiss on the lips.

"We should go," I say, knowing I could ditch the reservations completely and just go with what we have now. After a long look back at me, possibly even feeling the same way, he agreed and grabbed my hand to go.

We drive the 405 holding hands and being quiet as the music from 94.7-FM the Wave fills the background. After transitioning to the Santa Monica Freeway I knew he must be taking me out to eat somewhere on Ocean Avenue. I was thrilled at the possibility. Ocean Avenue Seafood and Boa Steakhouse were two restaurants I am totally fond of, but I like a good surprise so I ride along in great expectation. When Josh turned off before Ocean, though, I wasn't sure where he was going. As we headed up Second Avenue I had a flashback of my teen years and remembered a Mexican restaurant at the top of a hotel. Was that where we were going, I thought, starting to get excited. The view was exceptional there.

Sure enough he pulled up to the Huntley Hotel and it all came back. This was the hotel. Looking over at him excitedly, I said, "I haven't been here in years, but I love this place."

He smiled back. "I know, Jackie told me you used to love it." I looked at him astonished because Josh pulled out all the stops asking my friends and family their advice. We get out and once inside the lobby I realize this is not the same hotel. It's the same name, but it's much swankier now. The elevator swoops us up to the penthouse and when the doors open I realize more than the lobby has changed. The restaurant is fresh, beautiful and modern and that same fantastic view overlooking the ocean is staring back at me. I'm giddy. It's dark out and you can see the moonlight on the ocean and the lights of the city. As we wait to get seated I turn and give him a quick hug.

"Thank you, I love my surprise." He kisses me on the cheek and says, "You're welcome, Babe, and just seeing you smiling and happy is worth it."

We enjoy three courses of continental cuisine. The filet mignon is delicious and so are Josh's braised short ribs. Over dessert we discuss the view and the great day we've had.

"I just want you to know this is the single best Valentine's Day and date I've ever had," I enthuse, grabbing his hand across the table. "No one has ever treated me like this and I just want to thank you for spoiling me today."

I'm so happy telling him this that my shoulders rise and fall because I don't want to say anything else for fear of a tear or two falling.

"Well you deserve every good thing, Alicia. You are an incredible woman and I am so blessed I found you." And he squeezes my hand.

Then his phone buzzes, as it had been all night. I knew it was ringing on vibrate and he looked at it and turned it off each time. When it buzzed this time I told him it was okay if he had an important call to take. But he told me it wasn't that important after all.

"Alicia, it's Elle calling and that's why I'm not picking up."

"This time it's her, or all night the calls have been her?" I ask.

He shrugs and says, "All night." He looks me square in the eye, "That's why I'm not answering. She wanted Derek to spend the evening with her and I told her no. She got angry so I guess she's taking it out on our date. I would turn it off, but I gave Derek a prepaid phone I bought him for emergencies when we're not out together. I'm so sorry."

I smile faintly, "No worries. He should definitely be able to call you." I decide I will not let this jealous delusional woman mess up our amazing date. As we eat dessert we wonder aloud if

Harvey took his wife Evelyn to the Heart to Heart Dance the ballroom and salsa teacher Sandy held tonight at the Center. I stopped in earlier in the day and the multipurpose room was decorated beautifully. Jill did the majority of decorating and Sharon helped her. I knew the couples would enjoy themselves.

Josh's phone started vibrating that a text had come in, then another, then another. "That's probably the boys I bet," I said smiling, and hoping it wasn't what's her name.

He studies the texts for a minute before his face falls flat. If he was trying to play it off, he couldn't.

"What is it?" I ask softly. He looks up at me and shakes his head in disgust.

"It's Elle. She is saying Derek didn't want to go to Coach Rob's. She could tell and she's thinking about going to pick him up."

Now I look disgusted, "What?!" I say a bit louder than is necessary.

"She's just trying to get me to react, Alicia. That's her MO." I take several deep breaths.

"She's a liar you know," I half whisper, half yell to him across the table.

"Yeah I know," he says. "The boys are fine and I know this. But I cannot allow her to show up at Coach's house and start trouble. I'm going to call coach and warn him and then call her and threaten her. That's probably all she wants anyway. Attention."

I am pissed. I am steaming and he knows it. He reaches across to grab my hand.

"I know, babe, but I'll take care of it. Enjoy your view. Think about me and you walking along that beach and I'll be right back." He gives me a kiss on the forehead and I nod in agreement.

He's taking me for a late-night stroll on the beach. I can get with that I decide and I relax a bit. After 15 minutes, however, I'm worked up again and ask the waiter if he has seen my date. A few minutes later he shows up.

"I paid, so we can go now. Sorry I took so long." I frown a bit while he's not looking at me. "What happened and why did it take so long?"

As we ride down the elevator, he tells me that Elle whined and yelled about him not letting her see Derek and how it wasn't fair because she had a gift for him. He told her she should have made plans with him to get it to Derek. He told her she was disturbing his evening and to stop calling and then he hung up in her face. To this I could barely contain my glee.

"Gee, I can see how torn up you are about this," he says chuckling lightly.

I try to look serious, but I can't. "Well it's not my fault she lied, and you telling her off is just downright refreshing." He turns to me at the valet with a half smile and says, "Well I'm glad you're amused. If she keeps this up, though, I'll cut her off completely from my son."

As he goes to pay I rejoice on the inside. Little does he realize she does this all the time. It's the way she normally operates. He's just been blind.

We pull away from the curb and I'm happy thinking about our romantic walk on the beach. Then my phone rings. I look down and it's Jessica. My heart sinks because right away I know Eleanor is the reason.

24 Finding My Way

I answer the phone, even though I don't want to.

"Alicia, you guys better get over here right away. Robert is outside talking to Eleanor. She just showed up here screaming about what Josh promised her.

"Apparently," she went on, "she's ranting that Josh told her she could pick up Derek and we're telling her she cannot. Robert will not let her in and has told her she needs to leave, but she won't." I sigh heavily and looked over at Josh.

"Jessica, we are so sorry about this. We are on our way now." And then just to make myself feel better because this cow is messing up my walk on the beach, I say before hanging up, "Tell her to stop screaming and leave or you guys will be forced to call the police."

Josh looks horrified, but I don't care. "See you in a few," I say before hanging up.

Looking defeated, he asks: "Elle showed up at the house?" I shake my head yes.

"She worked hard to ruin our evening but you know what, Josh, I'm not going to let her. This has still been a wonderful day with my awesome, sexy, wonderful boyfriend. You will just owe me one romantic walk on the beach."

At the light before we get on the freeway he reaches over to give me a quick kiss and says, "You got it. I'm sorry about this, but thank you for being so understanding. Today was all about you because I wanted you to know how important you are to me."

I squeeze his hand and although I loved my day I still had to deal with my feelings about this pyscho interrupting our date and scaring the kids at the house. Coach Rob and Jessica had about eight of the boys with them.

When we arrive at Coach Rob's house off Sawtelle Boulevard, there was Eleanor's rental and she was sitting on the porch. This troll was waiting for us to arrive so she could show me how she messed up our evening. I wasn't having it and she was going to see our date was just fine.

Josh got out, came to my side to let me out and we walked toward the front door holding hands. As we approached she got up. Her hair had that lion's mane unkept look. She had on a Michael Kors grey velour sweat suit. I could tell from the MK logo on the zipper. Her shoes matched her purse, as if she needed a purse to terrorize kids.

"Finally, Josh, I had to do all this just so you would hear me! I told you I wanted to give Derek a gift today and that's all I wanted to do. If you had just returned my calls. I don't understand how you could be so rude to me."

I stared at her in disbelief. She called him rude when she had constantly interrupted him all night long. I imagined myself slapping her as I stood there and had an out-of-body experience while Josh let go of my hand to step to her.

"Are you kidding me, Elle? You tried to ruin my first Valentine's Day with Alicia over something so trivial. You could have given him his gift yesterday. You're acting ridiculous and I wish Coach Rob had called the police on you and pressed charges!"

What? I could barely believe my ears and wished I had voice-recorded it on my iPhone. To see her face crumble when he said that was worth the drive over here. Now if she could just take this moment and get mad enough to leave town, my life would be back to butterflies and pixie dust.

I watch her change from mad to embarrassed to a phony whine thing.

"Josh, I am just so sorry. I didn't mean to make you so mad. I just have never been around for a holiday with Derek and I wanted to show him how special he really is to me. I didn't want him to think I forgot him."

And then this buster starts to weep. No water is coming out of her eyes, of course, but she is phony-crying unconvincingly. She deserves an award for trying to get over on Josh, that's for sure. He has her sit back down on the steps and I stare at both of them with a sickening, twisted mouth frown that I can feel from my head to my feet. And then she looks up at me with her three tons of phony eyelashes and says sweetly, "Alicia, I am so sorry I ruined your date night," and then added in some sniffs as if I was the Academy Awards nomination committee.

I say sweetly back to her, "Well that is a very nice thing to say, Eleanor," and then I turn sour, "except I don't believe you." Josh looks over at me with a surprised yet impressed face.

"Just so you know, though, you could never have messed up my night. He spoiled me rotten all day long. He is the best boyfriend ever," I say sweetly once again.

Josh is shocked at my display of phoniness, but maybe he'll realize I'm just acting like Eleanor! I give him a kiss on the cheek and tell them I'll get the boys. To this Josh smiles realizing Eleanor did need to know her stunt did not diminish the excitement of our day. And I know she thought she broke me because Josh seemed confused at her ridiculous performance, but I didn't, and for once he wasn't.

After collecting the boys, apologizing to Coach and Jessica and saying goodbye to them all, we made our way down the steps. Jessica grabbed my arm for a moment to tell me I looked gorgeous and she was glad that despite this interruption that my night was good. I assured her it was.

"Oh, Derek, I'm so sorry if I made you feel uncomfortable. I have a gift for you though," Eleanor said when we got down to the cars.

Derek kept moving closer to me in what almost seemed an act of fear. He did not respond to her.

"Here you go, son," she said, as she handed him a balloon with a stuffed bear who was holding what else, a Gamestop gift card. Derek just stared at her until Josh finally told him to say thank you so we could leave.

"Thank you, Eleanor," he said with what seemed a concerned frown. He was probably wondering what the heck she was doing there.

"Okay, that's it, Elle. You gave him the gift. Goodbye," Josh told her.

In that weird phony whiny voice she told him okay and thanked him for allowing her to give Derek the gift. He shrugged and unlocked the car doors for us. He waved toward the house at Coach Rob who was watching it all from the window.

"I guess I'll go then," she said. The whiny voice now gone. We locked eyes and she rolled hers at mine before saying, "Goodnight."

I wanted to rush her and throw her to the ground, but instead I let her fake self jog over to her rental Taurus.

Once in the car, the boys, specifically Chris, went into a blow-by-blow account of when she showed up. How Derek was annoyed and how the other boys were wondering why she came over in the first place. I finally had to tell him we got the drift because Derek was feeling badly about it.

At my house they parked and walked us inside. Chris asked if they could have a glass of Sunny D, and when they went in the kitchen to get it, Josh wrapped his arms around me.

"That was not the way our evening was supposed to end, beautiful."

I told him I knew it wasn't and to stop apologizing. "I have something for you," I said smiling. "I was going to give it to you at the restaurant, but things got a bit out of hand."

He sighed, "I know and I," and before he could finish, I kissed him and told him no more apologies. I opened my purse and pulled out the Lakers tickets.

"Oh my gosh! I can't believe you did this! Thank you so much," and then he twirled me around while I giggled.

"You're welcome, sports junkie," I said after he put me down. He kissed me again as the boys came back into the living room.

"Should we go back in the kitchen," Chris asked in that kid-like disgusted way.

"No you don't have to, guys," Josh said. "Besides, you can witness me giving your beautiful mother this bracelet set."

I looked at him and half shouted, "No way! You got me a million gifts today." He smiled slyly as he pulled it from his jacket pocket, "Yeah, well not any jewelry, and I wanted you to have something personal."

It was a beautiful white gold bracelet and anklet set.

"You're tooooo much," I gushed, and gave him one more big kiss on the lips.

Chris said, "Oh enough already," but Derek just laughed at him. I see that Derek is not bothered by our affection, just glad his dad is happy.

They left on that note and after my exciting day I could barely go to sleep. I ended up joint emailing Jackie, Trina and Sharon. I figured I could update all of them in one fell swoop. I didn't leave out any of the high points, including Eleanor's reign of terror and especially my beautiful jewelry to close out the day. I love that Josh told Eleanor off and if he could do that more often, life with her around would be way more bearable.

The next day it was hard to have a regular work day after all the excitement of Valentine's Day. Before Sharon had ever got in the office, my sisters had already started emailing me. They were both happy Josh handled his business by treating me special for the day. Jackie was thrilled about how excited I was about the Huntley Hotel and Trina was happy he put Eleanor in her place, but was really mad she messed up our moonlit walk on the beach.

Once Sharon got there and asked about our date I told her to check her email for a full review. She laughed but once online she was oohing, awwing and saying "what" to the screen.

"Alicia, I cannot believe she can be so ridiculous. Interrupting the evening for nothing," she said, sounding as irritated as I was. "I'm glad he told her off, but he should have sent her home before letting her see him. You really need to watch that one. Coach Rob was right. She is after both the son and the dad."

I shook my head in agreement. I would continue keeping my eye on her.

By 10 a.m. that morning, Josh had not shown up to work. I texted him and almost 30 minutes later he texted back that he would be in shortly. Elle had a flat tire and called him.

He couldn't be serious. Just when I thought he had gotten it. Just when I thought he saw her for what she really was, I realized he didn't. Since he's a smart person he realized you don't mess up a woman's Valentine's Day, especially when you're trying to impress her and apologize for the recent past drama you've caused her. But getting right back to dumb after last night's stunt pissed me off.

When he finally gets to work I have an attitude. I go in his office and he tries to explain why he needed to help her. As usual, it was lame. I complained to him again that she was playing him, but he of course defended his actions as just wanting to keep the peace for his son by helping his mother. For the next two weeks things were pleasant between us, but definitely not steamy like our Valentine's date.

The first weekend in March was too much for me to bear. We had plans to go to Magic Mountain with the majority of the boys and their parents after class. But when Elle showed up looking disheveled and crying at his car before we drove off, he asked the entire caravan to wait. I saw her talking animatedly through the window and I thought I might be sick.

"Why is he talking to her this long?" Derek asked. "Everyone wants to go." Again the child was embarrassed. I consoled him for the 20 minutes it took for Josh to counsel her or calm her phony drama down. After 10 minutes the caravan left because I insisted. I told Jessica we would catch up and just to keep her phone on.

As I sat there staring at them out of the window I thought back to last month and him asking me if I was jealous of her.

Jealous? Of all things . . . .

So I sat there and contemplated what it was I could be feeling.

I knew I was irritated and annoyed, but what else did I feel? Was it jealousy? No, I didn't slight her for being Derek's mom. I'm a mom and she delivered him. She left him but she did, in fact, go through labor. Her talking with Josh now or even when she makes her ridiculous calls didn't make me jealous. It just makes me want to slap her. Was it sadness? Yes, I was sad. Sad we were dealing with this. Sad Derek was miserable. Sad Josh couldn't see her for who she really is – a nightmare. Was it anger? Yes, I felt some. I think annoyance and irritation stems from anger so, yeah, I was a bit angry at her interrupting our life. How would I deal with this? I needed to back up for real. I have to show him how I feel. I said I would the last time she pulled that her-mom-was-sick crap. But this time I have to be strong.

Me talking to him about it doesn't seem to work, but me showing him just might be the ticket.

After he got back in the car I didn't say a word. We caught up to the caravan at a gas station up the freeway and I was myself again, happy and talking. But I had made a decision in my own mind and heart. I would protect myself and show him how I felt from now on.

25 Protecting My Heart

Monday comes and I make no contact. Tuesday comes and I make no contact although I know today, he is coming in the office. I get no Starbucks, I buy no muffins, no donuts or oatmeal. I show up at my regular time, make tea at my desk and chew on my granola bar. Today he sent me a text early to say he would be in at noon. I texted back "okay." I did not ask why, inquire about his morning or evening or make any extra comments. Since I had the time I printed out his schedule for the week, gathered pending applications for the next soccer module and printed out a copy of the newsletter that was published and e-emailed to the parents and placed each item on his desk.

Usually I sat in his office with him and we went over anything in case he had questions. But this way he could look on his own and I can sit at my desk.

About 11:45 I go over to Sharon's desk to let her know I am leaving for lunch.

"So you're taking off right before Josh gets here, I see."

"Yes I am. Will you cover me when he gets in and let him know I'll be back in an hour?" I say to her with a sad smile.

"I certainly will," she says winking at me. I wave goodbye and head out to my car. I'm not even hungry yet, but I wanna be unavailable when he gets to work. This way I don't have to hear what happened this morning and he can think whatever he wants about me. As far as I'm concerned, he needs to miss me with all his drama. After we got back from Magic Mountain yesterday I had given Sharon all the scoop and she was totally with me on my plan to just back up and let this thing play out. Whether good or bad it takes me out of the drama and gives me some time to de-stress.

I called Trina this morning and finally updated her on what had been up since Valentine's Day. She had a few choice words about Josh and Eleanor. I had to calm her down because she had gone into full potty-mouth mode. All I could do was laugh. She decided she would come down this weekend. In her estimation she really missed me and needed some sister bonding time. I knew that meant she was coming to place herself in the mix and probably get in Josh's face. Since childhood she was always my protector. Even though she is my baby sister she lets nobody mess with me. I will turn the other cheek in most situations that are negative, but Trina, has no problem setting anybody straight. She already made a plan for how everything would go down. I laughed as she stated she would fly in Friday night and we would go to a light dinner. Saturday it was on as she would attend soccer class with us in hopes of running into Eleanor.

Sunday we would drive out to Jackie's and go to church with the family and we would stay late into the night so Josh could miss me. On Monday she would hang with me until her flight at 2 p.m. She wanted me to totally live my life without including him. I had to explain to her how hard that would be since he is my boss. She told me it was possible I just had to be strong and maybe a bit heartless, things I'm not so good at. But she said she would train me. And to this I truly laughed out loud.

I decide to just grab something from the food court at the Fox Hills Mall. The point was to be out of the office when Josh got in. After finishing up a Panda Express Bowl I made my way back toward the car, but seeing I had a good 20 to 30 minutes left I stopped into Forever 21. Looking at their cute jewelry was always fun and for $25 you could have a whole bag of items. While browsing I get a text.

"Hey, Sharon said u took off for lunch. I was hoping u would work through today." He was hoping I would work through lunch so we could order in something together about 1:30. I knew he would want to but I've got to switch some things up to protect myself.

"I did run out, I missed breakfast today but I can order u something when I get back"

"Cool. I've gotta few questions for u on some of this paperwork so just come on in when u get back"

"Yes sir," I replied back formally.

He must not have noticed my short answers yet because I did not receive a text back asking me if something was wrong. I collected my earrings, bracelet and necklace, paid and then went to my car. Sharon called.

"Hey Sharon."

"Girl, you are not going to believe this. Eleanor dropped him off in *his* car about 40 minutes ago. Sarah caught him getting out of his own car and I had to keep from slapping him when he walked in talking about good afternoon," she said, clearly annoyed.

"Well, that just lets me know I'm doing the right thing. I've got to separate myself from this madness! I am too old and this is so ridiculous!" I basically yell. "See you in a minute" I say before we hang up.

I pull into the parking lot and sure enough his car is not there. For some reason he is letting her use it and I'm not asking why. I sit for a minute wondering if I can do this. It's hard to ignore anyone but even harder to ignore him. I put on my game face and get out of my car.

Once inside I go to his office after leaving my purse at my desk. I knock and sort of wave to let him know I'm back in the office and he tells me to wait while he finishes up the call he's on.

"Hey, Parsons," he says smiling at me after hanging up.

"Hi Coach," I say coolly.

"I appreciate you preparing all my reports for me and leaving them on my desk. You have a good lunch?"

"Yes, I did. Just ran over to the mall."

"Everything okay?"

"Yeah everything is fine," I say with a weak smile. He stares at me and I know he doesn't believe me, but he moves on. I ask if he has any questions about the files I left for him, and he does so I get my note pad and we sit down for a run-through.

When we're done I go back to my desk.

Sharon catches my eye on the way out and I give her a thumbs-up. She smiles and I know she's proud of me.

I'm cool from that day forward throughout the end of the week. We meet several times and I'm as cool as the other side of the pillow every time. I bring in Starbucks Thursday for him and everyone so I don't stray too far off my regular routine. We grab dinner with the boys that night and its only after he calls and says he and Derek were wondering what we were doing. I told him we had gone to Fridays in the Ladera Center. He made a hint that they were hungry too and when I was assured it was just the two of them I asked if they wanted to join us. The boys were thrilled and Josh and I talked about the fact that Trina would be in town this weekend. He said he looked forward to seeing her and asked about getting together. I told him we were open. Little did he know, if things didn't go down smoothly this weekend, he would not be so happy to see her.

I did find out from Chris that Derek was furious that his dad was letting Eleanor car-share with them. Somehow she made up a story that her rental car agreement was up and it would be another week before she could get a voucher from her company. It shocked me to believe Josh could be that dumb, but I kept it pushing and acted like I wasn't the wiser.

On Friday, I worked quietly at my desk biding my time until work was over. Coach Rob came in and he and Josh had a strategy meeting and lunch. They called asking for paperwork a couple of times, but overall I worked straight through the day. About 4 p.m. I got a call, and it's Eleanor.

"Eleanor Dean for Joshua Hart, please," I rolled my eyes before drily stating, "Hold while I see if he's available." She was about to make a comment, but I put her on hold so quick she didn't get it out.

"Eleanor on line one," I call into his office to say.

"Thanks, Alicia."

I say "no problem" before hanging up. I start closing down since my lunch was only a half hour. By 4:15 I'll be prepared to blow this joint.

I chat with Sharon about Trina coming in tonight and all our plans. She tells me she's going to stop by the soccer class tomorrow to say hello and I give her a hug goodbye. I stop by Josh's office to let him know I'm leaving and he asks me to come in for a second and close the door. He gets up and comes to hug me. I hug him back but, it's not loving. I realize I have started closing myself off from him and because I'm on "hurt alert" I haven't allowed myself to feel the comfort of our relationship. And it's his fault! He has made me a bit cold, and I hate it. This means I'm losing my trust in him and sometimes for me, there's no coming back from that.

"What's wrong, babe? You haven't been yourself this week," he says with his mouth right next to my ear. I do still get an electric shock from the nearness of him, but my defenses are up.

"Nothing, Josh, I'm okay. Just a busy week," I say in the most authentic voice I can muster.

"You just seem faraway to me. I hope it wasn't about that call with Elle. She is trying to get herself a new rental car today so I can have my car back." I shake my head like, okay, whatever. He goes on, "you've been scooting in and out of here so fast we haven't had much time to talk, or kiss," and he puts me at arm's length to look at me. He's so handsome and his face is so full of concern I feel like locking the door and pulling his shades but I can't allow myself to.

"I'm sorry" I say putting my arms around his neck, "I didn't mean to make you feel neglected," and then I kiss him. He kisses me back. And he has the softest lips and I can easily get lost in his kiss. He's so good and is the number one all-time best kisser of my life. I almost get tripped up so I back away.

"Whew, I better go before it gets too heated in here," I say as I turn the door knob to leave.

"You just gonna leave me like that?" He says stepping closer.

Man, I gotta get outta here. My knees are getting weak.

He leans in and kisses me again. "You and Trina call me later, okay?"

"Okay," I say pretty much breathless and off my game. I never intended to confront him about her having his car nor did I inquire about her phone call. Of course now I know, but the reason for her to car-share was so dumb and that still bothered me. I couldn't let it, though, so I just needed to walk away. But kissing him almost messed me up.

We say our goodbyes and I'm off to get Chris and pickup Trina. All the way to his school and then the airport I'm thinking maybe it's me that has overreacted about Eleanor. Maybe she hasn't been that horrible . . . and I realize I'm still feeling the effects of that kiss and my mind is all messed up. Yes she's been horrible and yes he's been stupid. While I'm working on not being hurt I need to stay out of close spaces with him because kissing him is like a good dessert. You keep remembering how tasty it was and when's the next time you can go back for more. I must resist!

Chris is in the back seat going on and on about Joey Parker's new pet snake and asking can he get one. I let him know that will never happen and he can probably forget ever going over to Joey's. Who has a pet snake, for goodness sake?

When we get to the Southwest arrival terminal, Trina is standing near the curb with her rolling suitcase, big Coach bag and she's either texting or doing an email on her phone. I honk and she waves and then Chris and I get out for hugs and to help her get everything in the car.

"Licia boo! Finally, I get to L.A.! And how is my favorite nephew?" She exclaims, looking at him before giving him a second hug.

"Hey, Auntie Trina," he says smiling, as he knows he is her only nephew.

"Why couldn't Matthew come?" She looks over at me as we get in the car because I knew he was going to ask her.

"Well baby, he has t-ball practice on Saturdays and I didn't want him to miss it because they are going to start having games soon."

He knows about practicing so he shakes his head in understanding and says okay.

"So what's the plan tonight, guys?"

"Well, we're open, Little Sis. Any particular food you wanna eat?" She thinks for a minute and then says, "Pizza, of course. It's the ultimate Friday night food. You guys wanna get Compari's or is that boring since you always get to eat it?"

I look back at Chris and he's okay with it so I say, "Compari's it is." We decide we will go home, get changed and freshen up and then I will run pick it up while she and Chris catch up. Right before we get home, Chris says, "Hey Mom, maybe Derek and Coach might want to come over. They haven't seen Aunt Trina since Christmas." I'm not sure how Trina will feel about it but she joins right in.

"That sounds fun, Chris," and then she turns to me, "what do you think?"

"Well, it would be fun. We haven't hung out with the two of them in a while on a Friday night. They might already have plans, but I can call and check."

Chris sort of cheers in the back seat, "Oh yeah! I hope Derek's mom isn't making him go somewhere because it will be so fun!"

Trina raises her eyebrows and looks back at Chris.

"Derek's mom is in town and makes him go places he doesn't wanna go?" Trina asks Chris with wide innocent eyes.

"Yes she does, Aunt Trina, and Derek gets so mad about it. Sometimes he even cries because he wants to hang out with us and he hardly ever gets to anymore. And he just wishes his mom were like my mom. He's even said he wishes mom could be his mom."

"Oh really?" She says with the wide-eyed innocence again. "Well you can't blame him. You do have a super mom," she adds and winks at me. I smile and chuckle internally.

"Well, you two, I will call them when I get home. Coach already said he could not wait to see Trina."

Once we're settled in the house and Chris goes upstairs Trina lights right in.

"So this poor child is not just upset, he's in tears sometimes?! And it's spilling over into my nephew's life, too? Yeah, this chick must be stopped," She states with her hands on her hips.

"Yes girl. She is running them or rather running Josh around. He appears to have no interest whatsoever in her but can I really trust that? She has the looks and the figure and I guess that might've been appealing to him and blinding him even now, but once she opens her mouth most men would run. I can't even explain this broad you just gotta see her for yourself."

I call Josh, he is thrilled and they come over about an hour later with the pizzas, some spaghetti and sodas. Trina is really happy to see him and he is equally thrilled to see her.

"So how's it been going?" He asks her after we are all sitting down and getting our eat on.

"Everything is good. Work is fine, Matthew is fine and the parents are fine. And you?"

Josh looks over at me. "Things are pretty good. I don't know if Alicia told you but Derek's mom is staying in town now so we have arranged our schedules so he can see her regularly." Then Josh looks over at Derek because the child lets out a groan.

"Are you excited about seeing your mom all the time, Derek?" She sweetly asks. He lowers his eyes

"It's okay, Auntie," he says shrugging, and although I feel bad for him, I smile because he has truly made my family his own.

We finish eating and have small talk about the boy's soccer class, Matthew's t-ball and mom's latest cheesecake invention, to which Josh was already making plans to go and taste-test.

After we eat, the boys go upstairs to play video games. We sit in the den and shoot the breeze. We are having the best time talking about nothing. Trina and Josh are making fun of my over-thinking things once again and we discuss Netflix movie options for the evening.

Trina then goes out on a limb and asks about doing dinner tomorrow night. She's thinking we could take the boys to downtown Disney and she would get to see it because she has never been.

"You know that could work. I just need to make sure Elle's not planning anything. Usually after soccer class she likes to take Derek somewhere to eat," Josh says.

"Oh, I see. Well maybe this one time she could trade out for Sunday. I never get to run down to L.A. and I love getting to spend this time with all of you," she says smiling brightly. This girl is an actress.

"You know, you're right, Trina. I'll let her know Sunday is much better." He goes into the kitchen to call Eleanor.

She looks over at me. "See Big Sis, that's how it's done."

"You think so?" I say. And before I can get another word out, he is already raising his voice with the infamous Ms. Dean.

26 Trina's Two Cents

When Josh gets off his phone call he comes back in the den with an interesting look on his face. We sit quietly for a few minutes before Trina finally says, "Everything okay?" And Josh, looking defeated says, "Well, she made plans for us to leave directly after the class tomorrow. She wants to go to Catalina for the entire day. I was going to cancel her plans, but she said she had already gotten the tickets."

He really looked stumped, but I just want to pop him in the back of the head. That is why I can't deal with this. That is why I have to walk away because I can't hear this stupid talk and then not be able to tell him how stupid it is. But I refuse to get in any fights because that's where this will go. He doesn't need to be upset, he needs to tell her the idea might be nice but for another day. But if I say this it will cause drama so I say nothing and go into the kitchen leaving him with Trina who I can see from the corner of my eye is gearing up to let him have it.

"Well, Josh, I don't really see a problem. She can do one of two things. She can move your trip to Sunday or she can just be upset about you changing your plans. If you didn't know about her plans when I suggested the Downtown Disney plan then whose fault is that? She should have checked with you before she bought the tickets. I'm just saying."

Trina sits there waiting for him to respond like she has just solved everything. Josh's head was kind of hanging and he looked up at Trina and kinda stifled a laugh.

"Trina, you don't know Eleanor. Everything turns into an issue. So I just figured I would allow her to make her plans so she could see Derek whenever she wanted and we would make it happen. She's leaving soon anyway, so do you see what I'm saying, I'm just trying to keep the peace," and he looks at her shaking her head in agreement, but then she says "No, I do not understand. She still needs to respect your time even if she is just here for a short time. You had a life before she got here and she should be asking permission every time. Well, I certainly hope you change your mind because the boys would have a great time, Alicia, tells me they have a ball whenever they get to go."

He shifts uncomfortably in his seat. If it was me I would be labeled selfish, but I guess he can't go saying that to my sister so he is cool.

"Maybe," he says clearing his throat, "I can tell her we can go out for a little while and then meet you guys out there for dinner." Trina smiles.

"That could work, couldn't it, Alicia?" She says to me while I continue to stir the same cup of hot tea I had been stirring their entire conversation.

"Sure" I say. "Oh and Josh, how long will Eleanor be in town?" Trina asks innocently.

"Well, it was supposed to be until March but she's working on an extension until April," Josh answers her. And I drop my cup. Right into the sink and it makes a loud thud and cracks in three places. There is no way I or this relationship can survive for almost two more months. Then to top it off she's probably trying to get transferred here indefinitely.

"You okay, Babe?" he asks coming into the kitchen with Trina trailing him.

"Yeah Sis, you all right?" And she knows I'm not, but her eyes tell me no worries. I tell them I'm okay and we go back and talk some more about nothing in particular. I'm in and out of the conversation because all I can think about is Eleanor here two more months getting on my nerves, driving Derek to the edge and most of all, her ultimate plan to never leave Los Angeles! That would mean calling it quits with Josh because there is no way I can deal with that woman.

The night was nice and we ended up hanging out and eating ice cream and the boys enjoyed their time together. After they left and Chris was in his room Trina re-capped the evening.

"Okay, so I can see Josh is letting her run the show and I see how he is stressing over it. What I don't understand is why he's not listening to his woman about this nightmare." She lets a few minutes pass as she lies across my bed. "I guess one reason is because what man wants to think their child's mother is a terrible, busy, annoying, insensitive glitch."

I turn around from the mirror to look at her and laugh. "Glitch, Trina?"

"Yes glitch. I'm trying to come up with unique words so I don't use bad ones."

I fall on the bed with her, laughing because she is hilarious and she laughs too. We talk more about Josh, Derek and the glitch. Additionally, I get the scoop on Michael and put in my two cents that I still hope she will consider giving him a little chance. She told me to back off because he's best to be happy she's allowing him to be her friend. We drift off to sleep and in the morning she is pulled into my Saturday mayhem.

Chris and I are rushing around getting dressed, toasting bagels and eating cereal. She yawns drinking her coffee and wondering why I have to get there at 9 if the class starts at 10. I tell her because I help run the show and besides it's only 30 minutes earlier than the other parents would need to leave. She is not feeling it, but drags herself into the car with her black "Pink" warm-up set and Ugg boots with my commuter mug. She has never been much of a morning person.

We get over to the field and park. Josh and Coach Rob are already there. We go down the steps and I find Trina a seat a few rows up from the field. It's a good spot for any action that might go down. She is hilarious with the commuter mug and my purple Tinkerbell travel blanket. Josh yells hello to her and she waves. He cracks up because she's got on sunglasses with her ensemble and her newly purchased hair, although beautiful and wavy, is a wild mess this morning. I take Coach Rob over and introduce him. He seems to like the Simba hair and sits and chats with her. Josh and I cover details about these last few classes and then at 10 they get started. Everything is going fine. I check on Trina who is doing better now that the sun has come out a bit. Then things start to heat up.

At 10:50 I look up the bleachers and I think I see Rick take a seat up high.

What the heck is he doing here?

He said he was on vacation for two weeks out of the country but would be in touch. He didn't call, text, skype or send my son a postcard. The sight of him makes me sick and all I can think is geez, he would be perfect for Eleanor and I laugh at that thought. Unfortunately, I can't even hook them up because this fool has brought Bad Weave Barbie. I think I can see her tracks from the field! I turn back to my paperwork shaking my head because I can't believe I gotta deal with him today. He would get back in his car and drive away if he knew Trina was here. I laugh again thinking of his face when he sees her. I just told her last night about his bootleg trip.

Things change again when at 11:15 the infamous Eleanor, shows up.

Wow, is it really about to be on like this!

Trina texts me: *Is there a glitch I should know about, lol*

Yes, there is, lol! But not only is IT here, Ricks dumb self is behind u too!

What! I'm getting a two for one special?! I'm about to meditate so I can be ready

Haha! You are so crazy. But I am scared...for them

You should be. It's about to be on!

And I know she means it.

At 11:35 the class is over. Out of the corner of my eye I see Eleanor march right down the steps past Trina and onto the field. Rick and Bad Weave Barbie stay seated thankfully. She comes right over to the bench where the team and I am.

"Great game, son," she says syrupy sweet to Derek.

"It's not a game, Eleanor. It's just a class," he says emotionless.

"Oh, well great class, then," he just looks at her and I really want to laugh but it's almost sad.

"Hello Christopher, Alicia."

I nod and say hello, and Chris says hello very nicely to her. Still such great manners my kid has with this woman.

"So are you all ready for our trip to Catalina today?"

"Not really," Derek says.

"Oh, I think it will be fun," She oozes, "the boat ride, lunch, then we'll tour the island and then have dinner."

Now we both know Josh asked her last night about changing the day or at least them leaving early, but she lays out their plan right in front of all of us. Josh interjects, though, which I do appreciate.

"Elle, I told you we can do the tour and lunch but then we are heading back at 4. Alicia's sister is in town," he says looking flustered.

"Oh, well you said she would be in town until Monday Josh, so I figured the *original plan* was okay." And this broad is trying to turn on the waterworks or something because she literally looks wounded, in a bad acting kind of way. Josh sighs and Derek looks miserable.

"Well, actually I am staying until Monday but tomorrow we have plans to see our other sister, and so tonight I just wanted a few hours of Josh and Derek's time. Trina Johnson, you must be Eleanor," and Trina puts out her hand to shake Fakarella's. She brushed down her curls, put on some lip gloss and nicely folded

Tinkerbell up. Eleanor is taken aback for a minute, I think, but then she shakes Trina's hand.

"Well, I can understand you are visiting, but it's only from up north I heard. I'm here from New Orleans for a limited time so that's why the urgency in this Catalina trip." We all look nauseated. Who is she kidding? Trina wants to slap her I can tell but she must have been praying while she waited.

"The city doesn't really matter now does it? Distance is what it is and I haven't been up to L.A. in a while. I'm an attorney and don't have much time for travel right now. I'm on a fast track to partnership so I'm very busy. That means my trip is pretty urgent to me as well. I suggested to Josh," and she turns to point to him, "that you guys get together tomorrow. You could easily change your tickets because the boats that take you over, go all day. This way you get your day tomorrow, and we get ours now. I mean that would only be fair."

Is it possible to hear a pin drop on an outside playing field? Well, it was today. Josh put his hand up to say something but I grabbed it and put it back down and gave him a look. Coach Rob was engrossed and fascinated with my sister. I could see Rick and Bad Weave had descended the stairs and we're listening a ways off. Rick knows Trina so he knows better. Eleanor's mouth was open and I wanted to tell her to close it before something flew in, but I was quiet. And then there was Derek. He was looking up at Trina as if she was his hero.

Eleanor composed herself and readjusted her Louie tote.

"Trina, I don't know if they will take back my tickets or not, but that's not the issue here. Josh said I could see my son whenever I wanted and there's been no problem until today.

I have a problem with you making your time here equal when clearly I as his mother take precedence over *you,*" and she makes the mistake of waving Trina off as if she's nothing with her superiority fakarella way.

"Wait a minute, ladies," Josh says then trying to save the day, but it's too late. Trina steps to her.

"Look here. I'm basically Derek's aunt. And Josh over here is just about my brother-in-law," and Eleanor sighs loudly and even laughs a bit to that.

"You can laugh if you want, honey. He loves my sister and she loves him and other than you coming and butting in their lives they were doing just fine. So I am important in their lives and I'm demanding my time, today!"

They are almost eye to eye, nose to nose. I know it's time so I grab Trina and tell her we should let Josh work this out and Josh steps in front of us and gives me a look like *"Get the boys outta here."*

I have the boys get their stuff and I grab Trina's arm again, because she is still staring Fakarella the glitch down. Coach Rob follows us and we have to walk right by Rick.

"Hey Dad," Chris says. "I didn't know you were coming. You're back in town?"

"Yeah, big guy, I made it in yesterday and I just had to see you." And he hugs his dad. I'm disgusted but say nothing. He greets me, Coach Rob and says hey to Trina. All she says back is "hey," in a deadpan voice.

"This is Cassie, everyone," and we all say hello to Bad Weave Barbie with her green contacts, gum smacking, too-tight jeans and halter top wearing in the winter under her raggedy wool coat self. On second thought she's more like Crackhead Barbie.

"Well, I just wanted to come see my boy. I thought he had a game today and then we were going to take him out to lunch." I do a double-take on her outfit first and then look at Rick. He is a hot mess, too, and I wish he and Eleanor would hit it off and both of them could leave me alone.

"Game season isn't back in yet, Rick. This is a focused soccer course. And as for today we have plans with Trina in town," I report to him. All without calling him stupid.

"Ohhh okay," he says, actually sounding stupid. "My bad. Well how about tomorrow?"

"We're going out to Aunt Jackie's, Dad," and now Chris sounds annoyed. Lord knows we need to get out of here.

"Alicia, didn't I say when I got back I wanted to spend time with Chris!" I roll my eyes at him and start up the stairs. "We haven't heard from you in over two weeks," I half yell at him. I must be in the twilight zone.

"Well, I wasn't where I could use a phone," he half yells back. OMG! What is this, nightmare day at the park?

"Then if you couldn't use a phone that means you didn't call Alicia, which means she didn't know you were coming today. Come on, Rick, give it a rest. I can't remember the last time I was in L.A. I need to spend time with my nephew," she says with an impatient voice. And now Crackhead Barbie is looking up the steps at her sideways and I'm thinking *I gotta get Trina out of here too.*

"Same smart mouth, eh Trina?"

"Yep," she says and keeps walking up the stairs toward me.

"I guess I'll just call you next week, Alicia. But don't say I didn't stop by to see my son," he yells up towards me. Trina's presence did help. At least he didn't follow us up the stairs.

"Ooh girl," she says when we reach the cars, "you got way too much drama going on. You need to come back to Oakland!"

"I know, right," I agree with her chuckling, even though I feel high stress.

Derek swoops in at this point and hugs Trina.

"I'm glad you're here, Aunt Trina." She hugs him back and we all know why.

Trina then gets in the passenger seat and next thing I know, Coach Rob is at the window talking to her. I widen my eyes looking at Coach Rob with the moves. I think he might have Jungle Fever so Michael better look out. I stand there taking in all his compliments to her and she's shooing him off. Then they start to talk about his job and her job so I get in the driver's side and randomly text Skye to let her know about the Eleanor drama at the park. She lets me know she's happy my sister was there for back-up and that I should stay strong. She also said Josh hadn't been returning Davis' calls because they had a small fall-out. Davis told him to send Eleanor home because she is a lousy mother and he should face it. I was surprised to learn that, and I realized Eleanor has programmed him to obey her only, while the rest of us just want them apart. He still hasn't come to terms with the fact that she can never be the mother his son needs and he obviously thinks that maybe if he forces Derek's relationship with her she will change. But she won't because she's herself.

The boys are in my back seat on their DSi's when Eleanor and Josh finally emerge. Josh looks like he's been in a battle, and I think Fakarella won. She comes right over to the window where Derek is and he groans as he lets down his window.

"Okay, son, I made the changes to the tickets so we're going to spend all day tomorrow at Catalina. So I'll see you then, okay?" He simply nods his head in agreement. Eleanor model-strides away like everything is wonderful. Josh looks beat but says, "Okay, let's get out of here so we can go have some fun!" The boys cheer but it looks to me like his heart isn't in it.

I text Skye that Josh is going with us, but he looks defeated. I told her to tell Davis to keep calling, he needs him and hopefully he eventually will listen.

27 Sister Bonding

Josh didn't talk much on the ride to Downtown Disney. We had dropped my car at home and all piled into his Audi. Trina fit perfectly in his backseat with the boys. I grabbed his hand to let him know I was sorry he had gone through dealing with Eleanor, but I felt nothing about her getting straight crushed by my Little Sis. I felt like maybe change was on the horizon since he really saw how funky his son's mom could be to total strangers.

Her rudeness was obvious and he knows it. Additionally, Trina told him point blank to stop letting her run the show and now I know even Davis had tried to reach out to him. I've definitely got everyone feeling my pain where he has no one agreeing with him to let her try to run his life.

He shared a bit with us about how she ranted and raved about the tickets and changing them being so ridiculous. He had finally told her it wasn't fair to Trina since she was only here for the weekend.

"Aww thanks for sticking up for me, Josh," she said. He smiled at her, but it was a weak smile and I was under the impression something else went down.

"Anything else happen. Josh? You seem a bit miffed since we left the field," I whispered to him at one time. But he assured me, with a tense look on his face, he was fine. All I could do was try not to worry about it.

Once at Downtown Disney, though, he was better and Trina and the boys were thrilled. We ate at the Rainforest Café, bought the boys several Avenger sets at the Lego Store, stopped into Sephora while the boys had ice cream at Haagen-Dazs and then watched as the boys built their own cars for almost $100 each. Josh really enjoyed doing this and built one for himself as well. We finished out the day with a movie and then dinner and video games at ESPN Zone. I was pooped in the end and the boys both nodded off on the way home. When we got to my house Derek gave Trina and myself the biggest hugs.

"This is my favorite day ever," he exclaimed to both of us and he told me he loved me before getting back in the car. I kissed Josh on the cheek and told him I loved him and he said it back and gave me a peck on the lips. He hugged Trina and told her she was something else but that he had a ball with her and looked forward to the next time she came to visit.

"And bring my little buddy Matthew next time" he added before driving away. "I will," she said, "bye brother-in-law" she yelled as he drove off and he waved back at us as he pulled out of the complex.

"Aunt Trina, I think it will be great when they get married too," Chris says, looking over at me. "It's going to be great because we love Josh, don't we?" she says, putting her arm around Chris as they walk up the stairs.

"Yes we do," he says, and then I smile because I'm happy he loves Josh. I just hope we can weather Hurricane Eleanor.

The next day we drive out to Jackie's for church. I personally like Sharon's church better but I don't say anything. Maybe I will join this year I think to myself while their choir is ministering.

Afterwards we go to Macaroni Grill and have a great time catching up, laughing and enjoying our sister time with the kids and John. Then once at her house John wants to know where Josh is and did something happen he needs to know about.

"Josh is dealing with Derek's psychopathic mother and that is why he's not here today," Trina immediately offers.

John shakes his head in understanding and says, "poor guy."

"I was hoping he would come and bring Derek. Sorry to hear he's gotten caught up with her. Nothing like a crazy baby mama," Jackie adds.

"Yeah, well we've all been suffering through," I say. "Really, Sis, so sorry to hear that," Jackie says, really meaning it.

"Ya'll don't know what's been going on?" Trina asks. "Well, let me give you a re-cap and bring you up to speed."

Even John stays put to get the scoop on the frightening and jaw-dropping shenanigans of Eleanor Dean. We are sitting in their living room overlooking their view of the mountains. It is a lovely tri-level home but this drive out here I cannot do. Of course with them both being thriving professionals in Riverside I know they are not coming back to Los Angeles to live. Times like these I treasure because we don't seem to get together enough. I vow right then to do better with my visits.

They both sit taking turns with their mouths either open, twisted or with their faces just in pure disgust.

"So sorry, Alicia. This Eleanor sounds terrible. You holding up okay, hon?" Jackie asks with sincere concern.

"It's been hard, Jacks, but I've been pushing through. Lately like Trina said, I just had to start stepping back because I was getting too angry."

"Well, you're doing the right thing. You know how we men are, if we can't see things right in our face sometimes, we do need to be confronted with it. Have Josh call me. We need to do some men things and I'll let him know, too," John says, completely in my corner.

He gets up and I get up to hug him and thank him.

"Anything for you," he says and kisses me on the forehead. "Now I'm outta here so you can have girl talk now." We laugh and go on talking.

We spend the entire day until late in the evening at Jackie's. Chris has fun with the twins making them play his video games and even taking them out back to shoot hoops. About 8:30 I text Josh to check on him.

"Hey coach, how was your day? John & Jackie were hoping u were coming. So just know u are missed."

After about 25 minutes he texts back.

"Please tell everyone hello and sorry I missed seeing them. The day was alright. Derek was not happy, again" and I read it feeling so sorry for Derek. Then he shoots me another right after.

"This morning he asked to go with u and when I said we couldn't he threw stuff and cried forever. I talked to Elle this evening about some changes. Plus I don't think I like boats"

"Lol, hope u didn't get sea sick. Sorry about Derek but hope she took things well."

"She didn't. There's stuff I have to tell u but we'll talk later."

My heart starts beating. *What kind of stuff? Stuff like I was right or stuff like he fell into Eleanor's cobweb of evil?* I think my breathing changes, but I stay cool because I'm not ready to share this news with anyone yet.

"Ok"

"It's not major. I just want u to know"

I kind of feel better, but not completely.

It's not major, she tried to sway me to the dark side, but I said no? Or it's not major she finally revealed her true reasons for coming to California?

My mind was swirling but I know I gotta stop over-thinking this.

Oh yeah, like that's easy.

I say okay, we do happy kissy face emoticons and close out the texting. I keep my mind straight as we close out our time at Jackie's with hamburgers on the grill.

"So Trina, how was the Valentine's date with Michael?" Jackie asks as we are sitting on her deck as the twins and Chris play three on one basketball with John. They are giggling and having so much fun.

"Yes girl! Tell us. I didn't ask you all weekend just so I could find out with Big Sis here," I add. Jackie catches my eye as we know Trina loves to dish it out, but can't really take it.

"What you guys! Dang, it was just dinner!" She says, obviously overreacting.

"Umm hmm, I bet," Jackie teases.

"It was. But since you nosey heifas need details I'll throw you a bone," she says being sassy.

"Why we gotta be heifa's, Miss Smart Mouth?" I ask laughing.

"Okay fine, women. If you must know he took me to Scott's. I had King Crab and he had Lobster. Then we shared the special Valentine's Day dessert. He bought me a dozen red roses and he got me the hoop earrings I have on right now. Ya'll satisfied now?" she states with an attitude.

"Aww, you shared dessert," Jackie says.

"And he bought you roses? And those earrings are beautiful," I say in an equally gooey voice.

She rolls her eyes. "Really, you two?"

"Yes really!" We exclaim together, and then we all start laughing.

"Okay, I agree it was a nice evening, but I don't trust him," she says a little more seriously.

"But Sis, what if this is the start of him really trying to get back with you? Are you even open to the possibility?" Jackie asks.

Trina shrugs. "I don't know. But we had a good time and didn't fight so I was just happy about that," she declares honestly.

"Well then I'm happy, too," I say and Jackie agrees.

"Was there any lip-locking involved in this date?" Jackie then asks.

"See, that's why I can't tell you heifas nothing," Trina says, shaking her head.

Jackie and I erupt in more laughter.

At this point John comes over and begs us to join the conversation. The kids have worn him out.

About 9:30 we drag ourselves out of the house after a full day of fun and promises to do it more often.

Trina and I chat on the way home and I do give her a little info about what Josh said. She thinks Eleanor made a pass and that was the deal-breaker for Josh.

"He may be sending that Cajun crazy right on back to Bourbon Street, girl," she says and I laugh because she's so hilarious. We think up all kinds of possibilities until we are back home and going to sleep. I drift off wondering . . . .

In the morning, I get Chris up, have him kiss his aunt goodbye and take him to school. I come back with Starbucks Chai teas and Everything bagels, and Trina is very happy. We talk while she packs up and then she gets ready to go. We take our time because we don't have to leave until 12:30.

I take her to the airport and on the way she gives me some sisterly advice.

"Listen to me, Sis, Josh loves you and even though he is tripping over this chick, he does not want to lose you. Be careful because she is stone-cold crazy and calmly tell him about himself if you need to but he's a good guy."

"Wow, you must really like him. After seeing him in action with Eleanor I know you would kick him to the curb if he was any other guy," I say in awe of her comments.

"Yeah, I really do. And if he was to hurt you, especially over this hag, he would be catching a huge beat-down from me," she says as I laugh. "We could keep Derek though, cause I love that kid," she adds.

"So do I. They are both very special to me. I will withstand the drama and push through. It's just tough sometimes," I say as I pull up to the departure terminal.

I get out and we say our goodbyes at the curb.

"Take care of you, Big Sis," she says giving me a big hug.

"You too, Lil Sis," I say back.

"Once you talk to Josh I expect a call, missy." I smile and wave. "Yes ma'am" I yell after her as I watch her walk into the terminal. I am so glad she came down, it was a great sister visit. Then my thoughts turn to Josh and what he has to tell me.

28 Eleanor Revealed

Before I drive away I call Josh. I was thinking if he could meet today I could find out what's going on with him now. I know it's gym day for him but there's more than three hours before I pick up Chris. He doesn't answer so I text him quick before the Airport police try to write me a ticket. I'm about to press send when he calls me back.

"'Hey Alicia." And I note it's very quiet and does not sound like the gym at 24-Hour Fitness or Equinox.

"Hey, Josh, I just dropped Trina and wanted to know if you had a few minutes for coffee before the boys get out of school."

"Yeah, actually I do. Wanna meet at the Marina now? It's close to where you are."

"Yes, sounds perfect," I say as I hang up. But I wonder why he isn't at the gym. What kind of news does he have to tell me? I'm nervous and I don't even know why. I try to breathe and relax so I put on my Mary J. Blige "Share My World" CD, one of my favs so I can sing along. Music always calms me.

I reach the Starbucks in the Marina off Admiralty Way and when I get inside he's already there at the counter. He's ordered my White Chocolate Mocha and my Madeline's. "Hi" I say as I lean in to give him a quick kiss.

"Hey you. Grab a seat." I find us a table near one of the windows and wait. I have a view of him waiting for our drinks and he really is hot. If I was sitting here and didn't know him I would definitely take a second look. It's cold today so he actually has sweat pants on, but he looks good in those too. He's cute and sweet and funny. I would hate for us not to work out, especially because of something stupid like Eleanor.

He comes over to the table.

"What are you smiling about pretty girl?" For this I blush. "I was looking at you and it was making me smile," and then he blushes.

And this is how it should be. We didn't even get to experience the full gooiness of being in love because as soon as we started looking like this at each other that horrible woman on a broom showed up. I am hoping he is going to tell me she has already left. He told her off and now she's gone forever.

He starts out slowly telling me how miserable Derek was Sunday. He said he had never seen him so sad. When Eleanor joined them he still couldn't recover so when she asked what was wrong Josh told her they needed to make some changes to her schedule of seeing Derek. She said she didn't understand and that whatever Josh was suggesting sounded unfair. They only stayed at Catalina for a little while because Derek wasn't talking and Eleanor was pouting. He said all he could think of was being with me and how much fun they would've had with us at John and Jackie's. I am listening intently and hanging onto every word. Is my dream about to come true? I wonder. Is the wicked witch leaving?

He says they get back late afternoon and she comes to his place to talk. Derek goes to the room and he tries to break down to Eleanor that letting Derek pick some of the places or giving him the option of saying yes or no to her plans would make him feel better. That this weekend may have been better spent with me, Trina and Chris. Then Derek could see the give and take and not just that she controls everything. But Eleanor told Josh he was out of line, that he was trying to stop her relationship with Derek because of me and it wasn't fair. She got hysterical, started crying and almost hyperventilating.

I was intently listening until he said this. This must have been when her Academy Award-winning acting kicked in because it sounded so fake to me. But this brother said he felt sorry for her and put his arm around her to console her. My eyes cut into him like two sharp razors. She took that as a sign and turned her head to kiss him.

"On the lips!" I screamed out in the mainly quiet Starbucks. He shook his head yes.

"What?! How did you allow that? How did you walk right into that one, Josh? Are you kidding me?" I say this in a harsh whisper that can still be heard by all those sitting close to us.

"She had it all planned out. I told you she planned on going after you, too. Coach Rob told me, for crying out loud! She should have never even been allowed in your house!" I am furious and I can't hide it. He grabs my hand across the table.

"Alicia, I know you're mad, but nothing happened. I don't want Elle. I was trying to tell her now might just be the time to move back home and that we should plan out some visits. That's it."

I'm angry but trying to calm down. This brazen hussy thought she could just come into my town and get my man. I was heated and looking around trying to get a grip.

"I only want you," he whispered across the table still holding my hand. "That's what I wanted to tell you. That even though I wanted this relationship for my son, that I needed to start listening to you. You told me the truth from the beginning, but I was too stubborn to listen. I hope you can find it in your heart to forgive me, baby."

I squeeze his hand because I'm still thinking about the Glitch and the kiss. In a last chance desperate act she tried to go for my man. Not that I can blame her. I shake my head yes at him and finally a little smile erupts on my face.

"This morning I wasn't at the gym because I called Davis. I was kind of angry at him for coming so hard at me about Elle being here, but ultimately he was right, too. My head was just in a bad place."

Finally, I can speak. "I'm really glad you told me everything. I've been angry so many times, but I'm glad that you finally can see that I only had you and Derek's best interest at heart."

We go outside together hand in hand. Life is pretty darn great right now and I smile.

Josh's phone rings and he answers. "What are you talking about, Elle?" So of course I stop in my tracks.

"I don't know about any texts," he goes on.

"Sorry you feel that way," he finishes and then he hangs up.

"What's up?" I asked concerned. "Elle says check my phone for texts," he says as he disconnects from the call and turns his iPhone back on. "She said she hates me and I will be sorry for not doing as she says."

I have a look of serious concern now. Crazy people say that kind of stuff!

When he clicks his phone back on he has six texts from Eleanor.

I hate you!

Why don't you want me!

How could you treat me so bad when I love you!

That tramp Alicia doesn't deserve you!

I'm not leaving and I'll see my son whenever I want!

You're gonna be sorry for what you've done to me!

"I don't take well to threats," he says out loud, but really in response to her.

"Oh my gosh, these are kind of twisted, Josh," I say, while thinking to myself that a call to the police would be in order. Next thing I know he is talking again.

"Don't ever threaten me, Eleanor. And you will only see Derek if I say you can. You keep this up and you never will."

Now my mouth is open. She is yelling at him and I can hear her.

"This conversation is over," he says and hangs up in her face. He looks over at me with my look of horror and he puts his arm around me.

"It's okay, Babe, you know she's melodramatic. Everything is going to be fine."

I shake my head okay, but deep down I'm not so sure.

The rest of the week is very busy as we prepare to close out the first successful soccer module. The boys would then have a month-long break before the next season starts at the end of April. We were going to branch out during this time, as Josh was going to start assisting Coach Rob with the Soccer Tots course. Sharon would be doing their roster and assisting Coach Rob with the details so I would be providing her support. One of our coaches recently left and Coach Rob volunteered to take it on. I like the busyness of the office, so it's fine by me.

I talked to Trina and Sharon both on Monday night and gave them the entire scoop on Eleanor's pass at Josh and her subsequent pyscho texts. I confided to them both that they concerned me and so did the way Josh was acting.

"I will fly back out there, beat her down and then pack her up myself," Trina told me, while Sharon noted: "She sounds delusional and you both need to pay attention to any more signs."

I was inclined to listen to both of them. They were both happy that he had finally seen the light and were so happy for me that things would get back to normal in our relationship. I had to chat early with Trina and late with Sharon because I didn't want Chris to hear any of it. Trina asked what the plan was for Spring Break. She even suggested we fly up north to see her. I told her that the weekend before was the last soccer class and then Eleanor would be moving back to New Orleans.

"Any place we decide to go will be celebration time for me," I told her. "I'll have Josh all to myself again and Derek will be doing cartwheels."

She chuckled at that, saying, "With you guys getting back to your happy place, you need to do something exciting," and I agreed.

"Well I will definitely consider the Bay Area, Sis," I told her as we finished up our call.

As Thursday afternoon came around I was making some copies and heard our receptionist, Sarah, fussing about a caller. She doesn't typically get annoyed since people always have a ton of questions when calling. I went over and asked her if everything was all right. She told me someone had been playing on the phone and she'd had enough.

"Like calling and breathing?" I asked.

"No," she said, "like hang-ups."

I asked her how out of the ordinary it seemed to her.

"Honey, I logged 25 yesterday and 60 hang-ups so far today. Usually I don't get 25 in a week. Most people will say 'sorry wrong number,' but this lunatic just keeps waiting for me to say Sunset Park Community Center and then hangs up."

I have the funniest feeling in my stomach when she says it because immediately Eleanor's name comes to my mind.

"That is annoying Sarah, why don't you take a break, dear. Let the machine pick up."

She's grateful and makes her way toward the break room.

I make my way right then to Josh's office. I walk in and close the door.

"Josh, have you spoken to Eleanor recently?"

"Uh yeah. She texted me this morning asking if it's possible that she hang out with Derek after the class Saturday. I told her I would ask him about seeing her this weekend but that after the game everyone would be going to Shakey's to celebrate."

"So how did she take it?" He looks at me with a knowing glance.

"Not well, but at least she didn't go off like she did last weekend."

"Hmm," I muse as I fidget with the paperclips on his desk.

"Something wrong?"

I figure he's going to think I'm overreacting to the hang-ups, but I tell him anyway.

"It's just that Sarah said she's gotten a ton of hang-ups within the last two days and it made me wonder. . . ." Sure enough he chuckles a bit.

"Alicia, I know Elle is over the top, but that is waaay over the top even for her."

"Well, I would have thought so, too, but her texts concerned me the other day, and the way she acted about changing your Catalina tickets and showing up before we left for Magic Mountain. Maybe something is going on with her, you know like from her going through this separation divorce thing. Now her not being in control of seeing Derek could have pushed her closer to the edge."

He looks like maybe he's considering my thoughts.

"All of that is true, but it's hard for me to believe she would do something so ridiculous."

"It's been like 85 hang-ups in the last two days. Sarah is really bothered by it."

He sits back in his chair.

"Well, I definitely don't think I should confront her with it because I'm doubtful it's her. Not really her style. But if someone is playing on the phone and it keeps up throughout the week, we can look into getting the service to reverse the numbers for us."

I shake my head, not fully convinced but at least he didn't say with confidence that it wasn't her.

"Okay, that sounds good. I'll let Sarah know." And I stand at the door about to leave but decide to ask one more question. "She didn't text you anymore crazy stuff after I left that night, did she?"

"No, but she called that night and I told her to calm down and stop talking nonsense or she wouldn't be able to see Derek again."

"And did that go over well?"

"Not really. She tried to over-talk me, but I told her she had no legal rights since she signed him over to me when he was five. So you see, she's at my mercy."

I again nod my head, but I'm just not convinced.

"No worries. Okay, love?"

I smile and say okay. I still feel kinda weird about the whole thing, but I go ahead and leave his office. Sarah is not thrilled about having to answer the phone again so I tell her to leave the machine on the last 30 minutes and pack up to go home.

I tell Josh goodnight right at 5 so I can get Chris home to go have dinner with his dad by 6. I'm not big on the weeknight outings because Rick never sticks to the rules. Always getting him back late when he has school the next day, but he begged me. And since he can't come out Saturday to the last class and Shakey's celebration, I was sort of happy. I wouldn't have to deal with him and Cassie the Crackhead Barbie so I agreed to this weeknight outing.

When I get over to the after-school program I'm shocked to see Eleanor's rental car in the almost empty parking lot.

29 Something Wicked This Way Came

I pull into one of the spots and turn the engine off. Why is she here lurking at the school, I wonder.

Waiting for me? Waiting for Josh? Should I get out of the car? This maniac may try to drive up on me or try to hit me. I know I watch a lot of movies, but still, I don't put anything past anybody in this crazy world we live in. After all this time of dealing with her I wouldn't be surprised if she's on meds and has recently stopped. I mean her actions are questionable.

I'm contemplating what to do when Jessica drives up and parks. I am happy that someone else is in the parking lot, so I get out and when Jessica emerges from her car I wave hello. In the corner of my eye I hear Eleanor's car start up and she floors it into reverse, then does a crazy turn and drives out of the lot like a drunken bat.

"They really need to get security out here. Who skids out of a school parking lot," Jessica says clearly annoyed.

"Jess, that was Derek's mom," I say. "I saw her when I pulled in and wasn't sure I wanted to get out of the car. I was so happy when you pulled up."

Her eyes get wide like saucers, "What! As a mom she should know better than to be so careless."

I decide to give her a little background on what's been up since Valentine's Day. Her mouth is open nearly the entire time. "Oh my," she says. "Robert told me she intended to stay in her son's life and work her way back into Josh's heart. I thought that stunt she pulled on Valentine's Day was definitely a bit disturbing. But now today's parking lot scenario, too. That's close to the line of stalking. You really need to be careful, Alicia, all of you do."

And I agree with her. I knew once I got Chris out of the house with his dad, I would surely be calling Josh.

After picking Chris up I asked him if everything was okay with Derek, and he said he seemed happier since his dad made his mom back off. They were excited about the celebration at Shakey's and were making plans to watch movies and play video games afterwards at our house. I was glad to know in their innocent minds that nothing weird was going on.

After getting home and rushing Chris to get a shower and change, his dad was actually on time. I told Rick to have him home by 10 since it was a school night. As soon as they shut the front door I called Josh.

"Hey babe," he said answering on the first ring.

"Josh, I need to tell you something. I saw Eleanor at the school."

"You mean at the boy's school?"

"Yes, when I went to pick up Chris she was parked off to the side in her car. I found it really strange so I waited a minute to get out of the car. Then Jessica showed up and when we started talking she turned on her engine, backed-up really fast and skid out of the parking lot!"

"Wait, what? You're saying she was in the lot just sitting?"

"Yes, and it was disturbing to Jessica, too. Especially when she flew out of the parking lot."

"Yeah, I can see how that could be disturbing. So she didn't say anything at all?"

"No. But she must have wanted to be seen because she wasn't exactly hiding."

"Okay. I'm gonna talk to her about it. We're meeting her for dinner now. She said she had a schedule worked out for seeing Derek."

"I don't like you guys seeing her. She could be the one doing the hang-ups. You need to pay close attention to her behavior!"

He chuckles a bit. "Okay, conspiracy theorist, I will pay very close attention," he says, seemingly amused by my drama.

"I'm just saying. Don't sleep on the bizarre actions of others."

"You are absolutely right, and so cute when you're serious like this." I can hear the smile in his voice, but this is serious stuff to me.

"Whatever, man. Just pay attention and text me later so I know you're okay." This he finds really funny and laughs out loud.

"Yes ma'am, I will. So protective. This is why I love you," he says all gooey now.

"Yeah, love you too. Just do what I say," and he laughs again, which makes me chuckle a bit, although he realizes I'm serious and says he will be on alert.

We hang up and I feel a bit better that he's going to talk to her. I still think she's weird, though.

At 10:15 p.m. I call Rick as he is late bringing Chris home. He says he took him to Santa Monica. They ate at the Lobster on Ocean Avenue, and then they went down to the pier to play a few video games since the restaurant overlooked it. I lit into him right there on the phone and all he had to say was, "Sorry, Alicia. I just missed him so much and making him happy was all I could think about doing." He says this as if it's going to make me change my mind about being annoyed at him.

"That's all fine and well, but a young man needs his sleep for school. You guys could've gone to Round Table pizza. They have video games, too."

I complain, but I know it's my fault because I agreed to a weeknight dinner when I know better. So I let it go at that point, even though he should have had enough sense not to have our son out so late on a school night.

"We'll see you in a minute, A."

I reply, "fine," but I was too through. While I'm waiting downstairs and playing solitaire I get a text from Josh.

"All is well my beautiful girl"

"Really Josh, you think so?"

"Yes babe. She said she was at the school in hopes of seeing me"

"Well then why would she skid away upon seeing me?"

"She said she was embarrassed, and apologized for everything"

"Wow, that's different."

"I know. She's going to go back to New Orleans Monday and then work out a schedule for regular visits"

"I'm really happy for u and Derek"

"Me too, and Derek actually gave her a real smile"

"Well thx for letting me know...see u tomorrow then handsome"

"Can't wait gorgeous"

We text our I-love-yous and shortly thereafter Chris gets home. I wanna slap Rick, but I wave goodbye from the steps as Chris gets out of his car. I was at least happy to know my boy had a good time. Once I got him off to bed, I lay in mine thinking. It was hard not to imagine that Eleanor's change came too easily. Her being parked in front of the school still bothered me and something about her being so sweet all of a sudden seemed unnatural. All that phony acting just turning into an understanding sweetheart wasn't working for me. I'm just going to trust her as far as I can see her. And Josh, well, I would be keeping my eyes open for him too.

When I get into the office the next day Sarah is waiting at the door.

"Alicia, you're not gonna believe this," she blurts out after saying a quick good morning. She follows me over to my desk.

"What's up, Sarah?"

"Remember those hang-ups from yesterday? Well, the culprit worked overtime.

There's so many hang-ups on the machine it's all filled up and our phones wouldn't even take voicemails. I just deleted about 25 of them, though."

"Oh wow, you've already deleted 25? How many messages were received overnight?" I ask, in sort of a panic mode.

"There were 80 new messages. Within the 25 I deleted, about three people had legitimate questions." She is not a happy camper.

"Wow Sarah. That's crazy. This is what we'll do. You go ahead and start answering the regular calls. I'll go through and delete the rest of the hang-ups."

"Okay, you're the boss. And if I get anymore I'm calling the police so they can trace them," she says completely serious.

"I agree. This is ridiculous. Get some coffee, sweetie, and I'll get started clearing the message line in a few minutes." She nods her head and makes her way over to the coffee station near the front entrance. I am stunned and hurry to get my own coffee so I can get started. The times of these calls may tell a story.

About 10 minutes later Sharon walks in and I update her on the entire hang-up call situation. Eleanor's new-found niceness and her strange parking lot skid-out.

"I think you're right. She stopped taking some kind of medication," Sharon says in shock.

"I know. And that's why I'm about to listen to these voicemails from last night. If there are no calls between 7 and 10 p.m. it will be because she was at dinner with Josh and Derek."

"And if the calls start and go throughout the night I want you to get a restraining order. Don't know if she wants to get rid of you because you represent the place in Josh's life she wants or if she wants Josh out so she can have Derek all to herself. I can't tell what that chick wants anymore," Sharon says completely concerned.

"I know right? It will be scary if it is her."

After I'm all settled with my coffee I sit at my desk and call in the voicemail code to hear the Center's messages. And just as I suspected there is a lapse in time. From 6:30 to 10:45 there are no hang-ups, but from then on there are hang-ups every 15 to 20 minutes. She must've dozed off for about two hours, but she started right back about 5 a.m. Sometimes she breathed into the phone longer and other times she hung up as soon as the message ended.

I caught Sharon's eye over at her desk and I shook my head yes. She put her hand over her mouth in disbelief. I knew it was going to be hard for Josh to hear this, but something had to be done. She needed to get on a plane home today as far as I was concerned, and I was going to do everything I could to get Josh to understand this.

This particular Friday Josh was coming in late. When he got in I was waiting with the list of hang-ups and the back-to-back times they had come in. He came in grinning about 11 a.m. with donuts and Coach Rob trailing him. They had gone to the kindergarten class at the boy's school to talk with the parents as they arrived. Coach Rob had gotten the kindergarten teacher to allow them to come in and pass out flyers about the new Soccer Tots program.

Sarah stopped him straightaway to get her jelly and old fashioned donut and then Harvey needed the bear claw. Offices were always a place of temptation for snacks, treats and sweets. I was gonna pass because my waistline needed me to, but mostly because I was about to burst with this information. After Josh personally delivered Sharon's glazed to her, he finally got to me.

"Hey you?" he said, so I can eye the sprinkles he bought for me. I smile.

"Not right now, calorie-pusher. We've got bigger things to deal with."

"We do?"

"Yes, we do. Let's go to your office."

"I'm not a pusher. Donuts are happiness," he says going into his office ahead of me. I laugh.

"Yeah, they are happiness when you eat them, but torture to lose. Anyway, sit down. I need to update you on the infamous prank caller."

"You mean the caller from yesterday has already been doing hang-ups this morning?" he asks, sitting down and getting settled.

"Actually," I say, leaning into his desk for emphasis, "they called overnight and hung up on the machine all night!"

"Really? Wow, we may actually have to look into getting the Center's calls traced."

"We may not. I made a report of the times of the calls and the only hours they stopped coming in were during your dinner meeting with Eleanor last night."

I let that settle in before finishing. "Before you met with her they came in and then after your dinner they continued. I think you may have to consider the fact that she is the mystery prank caller."

Josh stares at me in disbelief, trying to process this revelation. He sits back in his chair to ponder some more. Finally, he speaks.

"But why? I could see if I wasn't open to meeting with her last night and told her she was never going to see Derek again, but we made a plan."

He is really deep in thought, and I do feel a tiny bit bad for him, but she needs to go away, so I suggest it.

"I know you said she's leaving Monday but maybe she could leave early, like today. Or even tomorrow morning. Something is up with her and I'm concerned."

"Ahh Alicia, that's just starting a fight. She asked to come to the last class tomorrow and then Shakeys. On Sunday I told her we would take her to a goodbye dinner and then Monday she's really outta here. The calls do sound like they could be her doing, but what would be the point."

"But, Josh, she has shown erratic behavior and for that there is no point. It just happens," I say, putting my hands up in an I-don't-know-what-else-to-say manner.

"Well, look, can we give her the benefit of the doubt on this? I just want her to go home Monday and for Derek to be himself again. Then I can get some real time with you. If the calls start again today I will investigate her myself, but can we just leave it alone for now," he says. And he really seems worn out. But that's what this woman does, wear a person out. I know; I'm worn out.

"Okay. I will let it go for right now. But I'm watching her. She better be on her best behavior tomorrow or I will have her removed from the team's activities!"

"I agree, Nancy Drew" he says making fun of me. "While you're watching her, I'll be watching you," he says winking. I give him a half smile.

"Whatever, man. Nancy Drew is serious, Coach," I say with deep concern.

"So am I," he says in a flirty way.

"You're impossible," I say, finally smiling. "I'm going to work now."

"I'll be watching you," he says amused.

I give him a look before heading back to my desk. I share the details with Sharon and although she understands where he was coming from, as well, she still agrees with me.

"Watch her every move. Something about her change of heart is weird. Now maybe her man wants to get back together so she's rushing home, but if that's not it, I don't trust her," Sharon says shaking her head.

"Me either," I agree.

30 Exposed

The rest of the day goes by pretty smoothly. No more hang-ups and that evening we decide to take the boys to Islands over at the Bridge. It's like old times as we have fun eating our burgers, talking about having a break from soccer and getting back to Friday-night movies. We also discuss the possibilities for Spring Break. Maybe driving up north, maybe San Diego and maybe staying in town to go to Disneyland and the beach. Derek is like his old self laughing and having fun with Chris while Josh and I are stealing glances across the table. At one point he even texts, "I missed this," to which I respond "me too" when I catch his eye across the table.

We walk back to his car hand in hand and he asks who will dress up as the Easter Bunny for the annual egg hunt at the Center. Jill spearheads it and we all assist her. Usually Jill's husband dresses up in the costume, but I told him he was more than welcome to start a new tradition.

"Oh no, Parsons, I was only asking. I'm going to be watching you pass out Easter baskets on the sidelines."

I grin. "Oh really? We'll have to find you something to do then. We can't allow you to be that lazy."

The boys were ahead of us and as they approached the car, Chris says, "Hey Mom, there's a note for you on the window."

In the background I could hear the Jason music from the Friday the 13th series of movies. It was evil and creepy and that's how I felt about this mysterious note. I look around as Josh takes it off the window.

"You boys go ahead and get in," he says to them.

I peek around his shoulder to read it with him:

ALICIA, GIVE IT UP. JOSH DOESN'T LOVE YOU. HE COULD NEVER LOVE YOU BECAUSE HE'S STILL IN LOVE WITH ME! JUST GIVE UP BECAUSE WE ARE GOING TO BE TOGETHER NO MATTER WHAT! WE HAVE A SON TOGETHER! YOU'RE JUST A DISTRACTION BI

And before I could finish reading it he balled it up, threw it and pounded his hand on top of the car. Derek asked him was he okay through the open front door and through clenched teeth he said he was. My heart was beating really fast. She had followed us to dinner, taken the time to write the note and place it on the car, and could have been watching us right then. While he was trying to get it together I went to grab that note because this troll appeared to have called me the "B" word. But the other reason I got the note was for the police. This is evidence for when they pick her up after I report her.

"Get in the car, Alicia," Josh says firmly.

"What are you gonna do, Josh? We should just report her to the police."

"The police can't do anything with one note. Get in the car and turn on the radio," he says.

Josh is so angry I go ahead and do it, but I don't turn up the music real loud. I need to be able to hear a bit.

Eleanor must have picked up because immediately he starts yelling. I can't hear every word because of the radio and the windows being up. I know I have to protect the boys so I just have to do my best to hear by straining. In between Derek asks if he's yelling at Eleanor, and Chris keeps asking who the note was from and why coach is so mad, to which I had to come up with creative answers. I told them to put their ear phones on.

From what I could hear, he demanded, "Are you crazy? What's wrong with you? ...and you must be out of your mind." Additionally, he told her to "keep Alicia out of your mess and stay away from her." At one point he yelled: "Are you on medication? You will never see my boy again" and "try me" before hanging up.

When he got in the car, he was quiet. He started the car while still fuming. I didn't say a word and we drove home in silence. Well, except for his phone, which kept vibrating. He didn't answer it, and I just sat there with my heart still racing.

When we got to my house he came in with us and told the boys they could have some play time in Chris' room. They were excited and ran up the stairs. Then he turned to me and said, "Something is definitely wrong with her. I know jokes have been made about her being on meds, but I'm starting to wonder whether she is or not. She ranted and raved about you being the reason we can't be together and the reason Derek doesn't want her for a mom. I told her that even if you weren't in my life we still wouldn't be together. She went crazy on me yelling that wasn't true and if I just gave her a chance I could love her again."

He sits down on my couch then with his head in his hands.

"I told her she needed to leave town and we could discuss any future with her and Derek from long distance. That's when she started crying uncontrollably and said she would see him no matter what. I told her to try me and then hung up."

I had my hand over my mouth and eventually sat down on the couch next to him.

"I wanted this so bad for my son. I felt like it was my fault she left him in the first place and this was a second chance for him to know her. But right from the start it's been a disaster and I put everyone through this nightmare, especially Derek and especially you." He looked as if he was about to cry so I put my arms around him. He leaned over into me and said "I am so sorry. Alicia," and I sshed him.

Obviously this whole thing with her was about him feeling guilty about Derek not having a mom. But I have learned through many situations I know and have read about, that sometimes kids are better off without a reckless parent. It's precisely the reason Rick doesn't need to have Chris even part-time. Until he stops acting immaturely our arrangement is just fine. We sat there for hours and Eleanor must have called him 50 times over the course of the evening. About 2 a.m. he carried Derek to the car so they could go home.

In the morning, we are both sleepy at the field. Josh and I talked until almost 3:30 in the morning after he got home. Eleanor finally stopped calling about 1 a.m. and he was exhausted. I told him we should file a report but, he said she just needs to get on that plane on Monday morning and then he will get all her contact info. He is hoping her mother or aunt can give him some information on her current status. Something is definitely up, though, and he plans on getting to the bottom of it.

On the sidelines I'm just hoping she doesn't lose it and show up. Every time I see someone out of the corner of my eye I look up, but so far Eleanor hasn't appeared. Sharon and Antonio show up near the end of the class to surprise us and I wave happily, just glad to see familiar faces. The class finishes up, the boys high-five each other and the parents clap. Josh thanks everyone and reminds them to meet over at Shakey's for pizza. The certificates of completion will be given out, so we get the kids together and make our way up the steps. I link arms with Sharon and give her a quick update on last night. She is livid and cannot believe it. I tell her that I'm still in shock, too, and had been on the lookout for Eleanor. We both agreed we were glad she did not show up.

At Shakey's, the team had fun, ate pizza, and we passed out the certificates and did some networking with the parents. We wanted those kids who didn't play on the team last season to consider us for this season. I got lots of contacts and then was able to sit and visit with Sharon and Antonio. Out of nowhere while we are laughing and talking, Eleanor appears by the party area. She has a huge gift and she's overdressed for a pizza joint. She has on a suit, high heels and a face full of makeup. Her hair has been professionally done and she's smiling and looking around. Sharon and I are in shock and then she spots Derek and starts walking toward him. Antonio yells, "Hey, Coach," because he see's both of us girls can't seem to speak at all. Josh looks up from speaking with a parent, see's her and literally runs over to her just as she reaches Derek. He snatches her by the arm and she almost drops the present.

"Hey, what are you doing here, Elle?" he demands. "Get outta here now or I'm gonna call the police."

"The police?" she asks loudly so people take notice.

"Yes, the police. You're stalking my place of work, my house, my girlfriend and now my son," and he is steaming mad.

"Alicia, this isn't good," Sharon says.

"I know. I gotta do something," I say.

"No. I'll go over there," Antonio says, but before he gets up we see Coach Rob appear at Josh's side. We both sigh in relief.

"What are you, Josh's security?" she yells at Coach Rob. Now everyone is looking and Derek stands there horrified with Chris right next to him looking downright scared.

"Derek, I have a gift for you, honey," she says to him, but because he knows something is wrong he doesn't reach for it and just stands there like a statue.

"Elle, leave him alone and get out of here. This is a private party and you're not invited," Josh says loudly and very angrily. And now all of the parents are looking.

"Let's go outside and talk about this, okay?" Coach Rob says to her quietly.

"NO!" she yells and pushes him away, dropping the gift on the floor.

"That's enough, let's go. Now." Josh says, and he starts pulling her arm to drag her out of the party area.

"You're hurting me, Josh. Let go," she yells. Everyone is in shock.

"Where is Alicia?! She did this," she yells. And then she sees me and tries to come toward me but Josh grabs her tighter and Coach Rob gets her other arm and they try to drag her out.

"He doesn't love you! Tell her you don't love her, Josh," she screams even louder. But they get her out of the front door. We can still hear her yelling as the door closes.

"I hate you, Josh," she screams but alternates that with, "I love you, Josh."

I realize I need to go say something to the kids, and Sharon tells me I should while she and Jessica let the parents know what was going on. Antonio feels it best he go out to see if the guys need backup.

The boys are confused and both of them are on the verge of tears.

"Why does she hate you, Mom?" Chris asks.

"'Yeah, you didn't do anything wrong. She's the one who's done all the mean stuff," Derek adds.

I try my best to explain what's going on with his mom, in the nicest possible way. I ask them both when I'm done if they understand and they shake their heads yes.

"Alicia, I don't want to see her again," Derek says, hugging me. I hug him back, "Oh, sweetie. It's going to be okay. Your dad is taking care of it."

Then Chris needs a tight hug.

"I thought something bad was going to happen," Chris says, "so I prayed like we learned in Sunday School."

I hug him and tell him how proud of him I am. "That's why nothing happened, baby, because you prayed." I stay for a while to watch them play video games and then I go back to sit down when I feel like they are okay.

When I join Sharon it appears things have calmed down and the parents have gone back to chatting and visiting. Jessica got rid of the gift somehow so the kids wouldn't be reminded of her visit. Sharon had gotten a text from Antonio that she read to me.

"Tony says Shakey's called the police and they are waiting with her outside in the parking lot. He says please keep the boys inside."

"Oh my gosh," I say, "this is madness."

"And you are to stay inside, too. She is saying you are trying to be Derek's mother and Josh's wife and this is why they don't want her."

I want to cry myself, but I hold it together and Sharon puts her arm around me to keep me calm.

I am emotionally exhausted, but I try to keep it together as the parents slowly start to leave and we tell them goodbye.

Josh, Rob and Antonio came in at this point and I run to hug Josh.

"Baby, are you okay?" I ask.

"I'll be fine. I'm just irritated and angry. I can't believe she showed up on Derek's special day acting a fool. It must be medication!"

"So what happened?"

"She kicked, screamed and cussed us out. Obviously, Shakey's must've called the police. They took her because she cursed at them too. I told the cop I thought something was wrong and she was set to leave town Monday. And I told him all the latest stuff she had done. He said they would detain her at the station but would have to let her go, but before that they would contact her next of kin. Since I had none of her personal information other than her cell phone number, he gave me his card. Said he would call me to update me on what happened."

The boys came over and we sat together and tried to act as normal as possible. It was not the kind of way to end the season, but I know we're going to be okay. I tell Sharon that I have to believe the police will contact her family and maybe they will send for her tomorrow. She agrees that would be best.

"Anyone up for church tomorrow?" Antonio asks. Josh and I look at each other and don't have to ask each other.

"Absolutely," we say in unison.

31 Loose Ends

After a somewhat sleepless night, it was great to be at church. I think we were all so grateful to God to be free of yesterday's drama and stress. As usual, the pastor brought the perfect sermon to fit our situation. He spoke on peace and how the peace of God that surpasses all understanding would guard our hearts and minds. It was right on time, because lately I had been having a hard time sleeping at night.

We went over to Sharon and Antonio's for barbecue and fellowshipped afterwards. It was a very nice day. In the late afternoon Josh showed me a text from Eleanor saying she was sorry for everything and would contact him from New Orleans once she was back home and settled. He didn't want to say anything back to her but just to keep the peace he texted "ok," in response. We were just happy to be through it and moving on with our lives. We stayed pretty late at Sharon's and after dropping Chris and me off at home, I had time to plan my tomorrow.

Once I dropped Chris at school I would stop by to see Savannah. She was working on next Sunday's Easter orders, which were pretty mellow in comparison to Valentine's Day. We also needed to discuss the orders we were already getting in from the hospital for Mother's Day. This was another big business day for me and I would be bringing in the extra staff to assist Savannah. With a little over a month to go we had to be on top of these things. In between these two holidays I even did a little business for Administrative Assistants Day. It's definitely a lucrative side hustle for me.

About 9:30 I decided to call my mom. We had talked briefly on several occasions, but I thought I would give her the great news that things were back to normal between Josh and me. My dad answered the phone.

"Is this my baby girl?"

"Yes it is, Daddy."

"Everything okay with you and Chris?"

"Yes it is. We are fine. And how are you, Dad?"

"I'm better than I was yesterday, and every day above ground is a good day," my dad said as he always does and chuckles.

"Dad, you're too much," I said laughing.

"You and Josh doing okay?"

"Yes we are. All is well."

"Glad to hear that. Please tell him and Derek I said hello." I smiled into the phone.

"I sure will."

"Well here's your mom. Take care, baby girl. I love you."

"Love you too, Dad." Then my mom got on the phone.

"Alicia, so glad to hear your voice. How is everything going, sweetie?"

"Mom, things are going just fine."

I go on to tell her that Eleanor did try to act up a bit the last two weeks but that she is scheduled to leave tomorrow and things should be getting back to normal. I left out the crazy scenarios like the skidding car in the parking lot and the Shakey's drama. I think the note on the car and the hang-ups were more than enough for her to hear about. I'm personally skeptical she even has a flight tomorrow, even though that's what she told Josh and the police. She probably never booked one in the first place, but I can have hope. Surely she wouldn't want to get arrested, again.

"Well I am so happy she is leaving. You have been miserable, according to your sister and so has Derek. Thank goodness Josh finally saw the truth."

"Yes, it's been a terrible time but we came through."

"Well, I've been praying for you and I'm just glad to know you are doing so much better."

"I am, Mom, and speaking of praying, I have been regularly attending Sharon's church and I am seriously considering joining. Chris likes it too," I add just to make her extra happy.

She is thrilled and raving about how prayer works and how good friends make the world go round or something like that. Before we get off Trina shows up so, of course, I want to talk to her, too.

"I'm so proud of you, Alicia. Keep God first and He will take care of everything. I love you, honey," she says, syrupy sweet.

"I love you, too, Mom."

Then she puts Trina on and we chitchat about work. I ask what's up with Michael and then I share the fall of Eleanor.

"Her reign is over, Treen!"

"I am so happy because I thought I was going to have to fly back down there. I cannot believe this maniac made calls to the Center, then followed ya'll to dinner, left a note on the car and then showed out at the pizza place."

I tell her to keep it quiet because mom doesn't need to know everything.

"Girl, she went up to bed. Are you okay? I know you *say* you are but that was a lot, Sis. I hate this had to happen to you and that Chris had to see it. And let's not even talk about poor Derek," she says sighing loudly at the thought of it. "That's a doggone shame."

"I agree, but I'm okay, Trina. With time we will all get back to normal and we will probably join Sharon's church together."

"Whaaat! That's great. After that, wedding bells should start chiming and I can plan your bachelorette party." To this I crack up.

"Sure, I'll keep you posted on that date," I say.

Giggling she says, "Love you. Take care of you," kissing into the phone.

"You too, Lil Sis" and I kiss back at her.

Monday morning comes and once I open my eyes I realize the princess of darkness is leaving Los Angeles today. I get up smiling widely and find myself humming all morning long. Chris thinks I'm a bit strange, but my happiness cannot be stifled. It is going to be a great day.

After dropping him at school, I make my way over to the warehouse space we use to make our floral arrangements. Today I come in extra happy with coffee and donuts and meet with Savannah to go over everything. As usual we are right on schedule and on Wednesday she will start the deliveries of the Easter flowers to the hospital.

About noon I check on Josh. He said after dropping Derek at school he drove by Eleanor's condo to see if her car was gone and it was. Now he's about to hit the gym. He offers to bring something for dinner so we can celebrate our once again drama-free life. And for that I'm definitely in.

I'm busy going over receipts when Skye calls me. She tells me Eleanor had sent her a text this morning telling her goodbye and thanks for her friendship over the years. She said she was going back to New Orleans, possibly for good.

"Wow," I said. "Sounds like good news to me. Maybe she can Skype Derek in the future," and we both chuckle.

"Thing is, Alicia, she mentioned wrapping up a few loose ends before she left town. I asked her what kind of loose ends, and she said I will know soon enough. I thought it was kind of strange, and just wanted to make sure everything was okay with you and Josh."

"Yes, we are good. He said her car was gone from the condo and the policeman he spoke with called yesterday and said they drove her home and told her to get out of town as planned, and she said with pleasure. I was rejoicing!"

"That is good to know. I just wanted to be sure all was well. Okay, hon, it was great talking to you. And so glad to know you guys can get back to that New Year's Eve love."

"Me too, Skye. I appreciate the call and I'll talk to you soon, bye."

We hang up and although "wrapping up loose ends" does sound suspect in regard to Eleanor I felt confident that she would listen to the police and leave town. Part of me did want confirmation she got on that plane so I decided that when Josh comes over later he should call somebody in Louisiana to make sure she left town for real.

Later that evening when we're eating dinner I tell him about everything Skye said to me on the phone.

"Really, that's interesting considering she appears to be gone. I haven't heard a word from her."

"Well, I guess we shouldn't worry about it," I state unsurely, "but it was kind of weird that she called Skye just to say that." Josh is quiet for a minute taking it all in.

"You know what, I'm going to call the officer to see if he can check with Eleanor's aunt. That way my girl can be at peace," he says genuinely concerned. "Okay?"

I nod my head in agreement.

After the boys go upstairs for a little playtime Josh calls the station to speak to Officer Marshall. After we had watched a bit of TV he calls back. He tells Josh that they took Eleanor at her word that she would leave town. If he wanted us to confirm it, he would dig a bit tomorrow and find out if she moved out of her apartment. Additionally he would check to see if her aunt had heard she *actually* took her flight.

"Thank you so much, Officer Marshall," Josh said. "Eleanor has surprised us more times than I would like to admit since she's been here. I don't think my girlfriend or my son can deal with anything else from her."

They finish the call and hang up. He settles back on the couch with me and puts his arm around my shoulder.

"Okay, Babe, he's going to check out everything tomorrow and then there will be no more worries about Elle or her loose-end comments. She knows she can get to Skye so that's the angle she worked." I leaned into him more.

"I do feel better that the law is looking out for us.

Good," he says kissing my hair.

We hung out until about 9. With just four more days of school we were on countdown to Spring Break.

Tuesday came and we were very busy. With the new Soccer Tot program coming up there was much paperwork to be done. Plus I was busy working on the mailers to the soccer parents. It was a long day because I had to get everything done. Josh and I were both taking next week off so we had to get it all done by Friday. That evening after settling in at home and making dinner Josh called. It appeared Eleanor's aunt that lived in San Diego could not reach her family in New Orleans and could not confirm she arrived. She told the officer she would continue to reach out to them but she was sure her niece had left town. She had not been able to reach her either.

"So basically you're saying you cannot confirm wacky Eleanor is out of the city?" I sort of shrieked rather than asked.

"Well, no news could be considered good news," Josh added with hope in his voice.

"Or no news means bad news and she's on the loose somewhere and we could run into her! This is not what I wanted to hear."

"I know, Babe," he said trying to console me. "I'm sure there will be good news tomorrow. Now that her aunt is involved I'm sure she'll get to the bottom of it."

"Yeah, okay," I said sighing. "She can just be so sneaky, Josh, and the thought of her showing up at the Easter Egg Hunt on Saturday with a basket, candy and a costume on is chilling my bones," I confess to him in my dramatic way.

He chuckles. "Really, Parsons? You ever consider acting?"

"Hey, I'm just saying. You know I'm right." He agrees and we chitchat a bit more before hanging up.

On Wednesday I work straight through lunch and then floor it over to the warehouse about 4 p.m. I just want to check in with Savannah and confirm that the orders have started to go out for Easter. I also want to put together a few small arrangements, especially one for my dining table and for my co-workers Jill and Sarah and, of course, my girl Sharon. About 5 p.m. I pack up and tell Savannah I'm heading out. Things are well under control and I tell her I'll call her Friday to check in. She is a great manager and now that all orders are under way I can focus on what I will wear to the Easter Egg Hunt. I'm so thankful I don't have to head it up and I can just hang out with the boys and Josh. I'm on standby to work one of the candy stations, but that would be easy. I had told Josh I was making the boys baskets for Sunday and he said they would make fun of me, but I know they won't. My baskets will be filled with their favorite candies, points for their Playstations and gift cards to Johnny Rockets. We had a long day but had gotten all of our mailings complete and phone calls made. Thursday and Friday would be a breeze and then Spring Break we could relax. I was looking forward to it. Plus Officer Marshall called Josh at noon to say he would have a confirmation by the evening about Eleanor being back home. That was good news I couldn't wait to hear.

I head over to the school to pick up Chris and Derek while listening to some old school Brownstone and feeling happy about life. Josh and Coach Rob had a meeting with the private Christian school parents so I was picking up Derek, and we had planned to hook up later.

When I arrive at the school I go to the sign-in sheet as always and I sign out Chris, but when I attempt to sign out Derek I see *E. Hart* in the signature column next to his name. I start breathing fast, my head starts spinning and I feel sick.

Eleanor has signed him out. Eleanor did not leave town. Eleanor has Derek.

32 Unbelievable

Chris sees me now and runs right up to me in a panic. He has complete fear in his eyes.

"Mom, Derek's mom picked him up a little while ago. He told her she was supposed to be gone and that he was not leaving with her. She grabbed his arm and snatched him and told him to shut up! Then when I came over to say something she told me to mind my own business." Then he starts to cry. "He was scared mom, so scared."

I hug him tightly. "Oh baby, I'm so sorry. But we're going to find him."

Just then one of the after-school counselors comes over.

"Chris told us what happened. We were outside on the playground and it must have been one second our backs were turned. We have been trying to reach Mr. Hart, but so far no luck. He called earlier to say you were getting Derek."

Now the counselor is starting to freak out, but I don't feel sorry for her, I want to smack her. Through heaving gasps she tells me they did call the Culver City police and they should be there any minute.

"So how long would you say they've been gone?" I ask in an annoyed voice.

"Like 15, 20 minutes max," she answers.

Then I look at Chris and bend down and hold him by both shoulders.

"Chris, this is very important. Did you hear Eleanor say anything about where they were going?"

He thinks for only ten seconds and says to me, "She said we don't have time for this. We have to get you home."

So I stare at him, thinking really hard, and I realize this nut case, this pyscho broad, this freak of nature must be trying to take this child to the airport. But there is no way she can get away with doing this. The police could catch her at the airport if we tell them.

But she wouldn't try to drive across country would she?

"Come on Chris, we gotta go," I say. Then I look over at the counselor I'm disgusted with and tell her to have the police call me on my cell if they have any other questions.

We run out to the car and drive away. I'm trying to keep calm and think of where she might go with Derek. I call Josh and he doesn't pick up. I text him 911 and I pray. I look in my rearview mirror and Chris looks terrified, so I tell him everything's going to be fine. And I believe that, because it has to be okay. About 30 minutes pass and I have been by Eleanor's condo, Josh's house, back to the Center and now I'm on Centinela, coming up on Sepulveda.

Finally Josh calls me. He has spoken to the school but he has also spoken to Eleanor. She did take Derek with her and she told Josh to meet her right now or he may never see Derek again. He is surprisingly calm considering the circumstances.

"Well where are you going," I ask frantically.

"She told me to meet her at Chace Park in the Marina."

"Oh my gosh, what is she up to Josh... I just keep thinking about Derek."

"It's all I can think about, too," he says back. "I did call Officer Marshall at the station and Elle had given him a bogus number for her aunt, but today he tracked her down and learned Elle had not left Monday. Her aunt said she told her she was leaving tonight and not to worry, that she stayed to take care of some loose ends."

"Oh my gosh. This is so crazy! How could she take Derek?" I'm trying to hold back the sobs that are trying to escape.

"I'm on my way to the park now," I tell him.

"Alicia, I don't know if that's such a good idea. I don't think you need to see Elle and honestly I don't know what she's capable of."

"I appreciate your concern but I'm almost to Lincoln now. I'll hang back, babe, I promise."

"I guess," he says unconvinced. "I'm getting out of my car now. Officer Marshall is coming, too, so just tell him who you are. I'll feel better if you're with him."

"Okay," I say in a small voice.

"I'm gonna hang up, Babe. I think I see some figures way out by the railing. See you soon."

I say okay and hang up. I'm internally freaking out. What if she's done something to Derek? Of course the fact that she kidnapped him, period, probably has him completely frightened. I look back to check on Chris before I turn into the parking lot and he's crying silent tears.

"It's going to be okay, son," I say in a wobbly voice. I can't believe he has to go through this, but I drive on in. I see a few police cars parked near Josh's so I drive over and pull in nearby.

"Ma'am, we're dealing with a serious situation in the park and we need to keep this area clear," the officer says to me after I roll down my window.

"I know officer, I'm with Joshua Hart and I know his son's mother Eleanor has kidnapped their son and she's brought him here," I reply slightly out of breath.

I can tell they still don't want me to stay, but he speaks to the other officer who says I can pull in but not go into the park. In obedience, I park my car and go stand near one of the police cars. Officer Marshall, who has been working the case from the start, comes over to give me an update. He said two officers had been sent in to assess the situation. A third one would get very close and report back on radio what was going on. Additionally, he said that Eleanor's Aunt Irene had been contacted and was horrified to learn her niece had moved here to harass Josh and his son. Apparently, Eleanor had gotten divorced following two miscarriages and was told she could no longer have children. That was when she left New Orleans and the family had not seen her since Christmas.

"Did she say if she was on medication?" I asked the officer.

"No ma'am. Just that she never dealt with any of her losses by grieving or speaking with anyone. Around Thanksgiving she started telling her mother about Derek, and her aunt noted that she even mentioned to her that she never should have left Mr. Hart."

"Oh my gosh! She needs some serious help," I say to him.

"Indeed. That's why our counselor will be here shortly. Once we get the child we will take her to the station and she will be placed in observation. Her aunt has agreed to pick her up and take her back to Louisiana. This will all be over very soon, ma'am."

"Thank you so much, officer. I'm Alicia Parsons, so nice to meet you," I say reaching out to shake his hand.

"You're quite welcome, Ms. Parsons," he says, shaking my hand.

He asks another officer to talk to Chris while he lets me listen in on the update from the officer in the park.

I feel a lot better knowing Josh has a backup with weapons, but I'm concerned about Derek and I can't get my heart to stop beating fast. An Officer Martin checks in to let Officer Marshall know that he has assessed the situation and the woman suspect described as Eleanor Dean does not appear to have any weapons. She has a very tight grip on the boy, said to be Derek Hart. He is upset and crying and keeps telling her she's hurting his arm, but otherwise appears to be in good condition.

I put my hand over my mouth in relief, but I'm tearing up again. According to Officer Martin, the father, Joshua Hart, is conversing from a distance with Ms. Dean. He is calm and telling her he will do whatever it takes for them to be a family if she just lets his son go. He further reports that Ms. Dean does not believe him and is yelling obscenities and calling him a liar. He is steadily making his way toward them. The other officers are in place to move in on command.

Officer Martin then mentions that there is a nearby boat slip she appears to be inching to. He's unsure, but she could be planning a getaway, he says over the radio. Officer Marshall instructs them to move in.

Several minutes pass and we hear someone yelling, "STOP WHERE YOU ARE!" Officer Marshall calls on the radio for an update. Several tense minutes go by. Finally, Officer Martin is heard again over the radio. He reports that as Josh got closer she told him to back up because he was a liar and that she was going to take Derek with her.

Josh continued to approach her and could see that the suspect did, in fact, have a knife jammed under Derek's arm. I gasped at the news and tried not to break into an all-out sob, knowing Officer Marshall would likely make me leave if I did. I fought it off. The officers closed in on her yelling for her to stop and not take another step. One of the officers stayed a distance back with his gun drawn. As she tried to flee with Derek, Josh ran toward her with the officers following close behind.

Then it seemed the radio went dead, and as we waited almost breathless, I did start to cry soundlessly. I looked over and was happy to see the officer talking to Chris and showing him all of the gadgets in the police car and keeping him oblivious to the drama.

Finally, Officer Martin came back on air, saying they were on their way to the cars with the suspect in custody. Josh had rushed Eleanor and knocked her to the ground. He covered Derek with his body while another officer got the knife out of Eleanor's hand, pushed her to the ground and cuffed her.

Officer Marshall got me out of sight as they got closer. Eleanor was met by the counselor, who calmly told her they were going to take a ride and talk. She was crying loudly and dramatically. She had some blood on her blouse and her hair was wild and all over her head. She had on a sweat suit, which is so unlike her, and she kept saying between sobs that she just wanted a family, and how she would never hurt Derek and that she loved Josh so much. They placed her in the back seat of a patrol car and drove off and out of the parking lot.

"Ms. Parsons, here they come," Officer Marshall said. By now, Chris had gotten out of the police car. I grabbed his hand and we ran toward Josh and Derek. Chris hugged Josh and I wrapped my arms around Derek, who, like me, was still crying.

"I'm so sorry, Derek. I love you so much," I cried.

"I love you, too, Alicia." Josh and Chris joined us in a big group hug right there in the parking lot with all of the officers.

"Officer Marshall, thank you so much for taking care of my family," I said giving him an impromptu hug.

"Well, you're very welcome, Ms. Parsons," he stated, giving me a little half smile.

Josh shook his hand and thanked him for everything as well. They asked us if we needed a ride home, which we didn't with two cars in the lot.

Josh called Coach Rob and asked him if he could get my car after giving him a brief rundown of the evening. Of course he agreed.

Then we piled into Josh's car and drove home together. We were all quiet and I held onto Josh's hand all the way home. I knew he needed to be strong for his boy, and mine, but the tears ran down his cheeks as we drove up Jefferson toward home. So I just held on tighter.

33 Getting to the Heart of It

After trying to get the boys to eat a bit last night, and after a very bad night of sleep, we kept them home from school. I called the office to let Sharon know why we both wouldn't be in.

"Alicia, please tell me that was a movie you were watching and not real life," she pleaded.

"Nope, Sharon, it was real life. I almost can't believe we just lived through it but I was there. When Chris isn't around, I'll give you all the details, my friend."

"Whenever you're ready, Alicia-pie. I'm just in shock. And everyone is okay?"

"Yes, we are going to be fine. Josh has errands so he's going to drop Derek here in a few minutes. He's going to the police station to give a statement and confirm Eleanor's aunt is picking her up today."

We chatted a few more minutes and then Josh arrived with Derek and McDonalds for breakfast. We had both decided the boys needed to chill out after what happened. We were also planning to call the church and see if the boys could talk to a pastor about the ordeal that Derek and Chris had been through. We decided this on the phone at 3 a.m. when neither of us could sleep. We also decided to join the church this month.

"Hey guys," I say, opening the door.

I get hugs all around and then call Chris down to join us for breakfast. We talk to them to see where they are with all that had happened.

"I slept well," Derek said. "I was upset when Eleanor made me go with her, but I knew my dad would come to get me. He's my hero."

Josh and I catch eyes across the table. I can see how proud he is of his son.

Then Derek says, "And then Alicia, you and Chris being there just helped make it all right. I know one day we will be a real family because we already act like one."

Before either of us can say anything, Chris pipes up and says, "And I cannot wait!" Then we all laugh at his enthusiasm. Small talk ensues as the boys finish up their hash browns.

After the boys go upstairs to play and catch up on homework, we talk about how well Derek has dealt with such a harrowing situation. I tell Josh I will call the church just the same and get us an appointment for them. His plans are to swing by the office and then the police station to fill out reports. He hugs me and then kisses me very gently on the lips.

"I can't even express to you how much I love you," he whispers to me. And with that he turns and bounds down my front steps.

"See you soon," he says, turning back before getting to his car. I wave and say okay, still reeling from his kiss.

While he is gone I call Trina and then Skye. They both are in total and complete shock and cannot believe what we had been through. While Trina would be updating Jackie and Mom on the scenario, Skye says she is going to wait a few months to tell Davis.

"He might fly down to the bayou and kill her," she says without conveying even a hint of humor. Skye felt guilty and kept saying how sorry she was and thinking that if she had reached out more to Elle maybe none of this would have happened. I tell her that nothing was stopping that hurricane. I tell her to have a great Easter and Spring Break, and she tells me to do the same and then adds: "And our door is open if you guys want to escape down to San Diego."

Trina was concerned about Derek, but then said Josh handled his business rescuing his boy.

"He's a keeper, Sis. He went through that stupid zone almost pushing you away with Eleanor, but he loves you. And when he finally saw what you saw, he turned on a dime. That's a good man, girl. And he's my future brother-in-law, holla!"

We both laugh. The humor is much needed and very therapeutic after what me and my three men have gone through.

"The boys have us getting married, as well," I say. "I'm so glad you can all see into the future for me."

Leave it to Trina to say smartly back: "Well, we needed to. You know how slow you can be." We talk a few seconds more before saying our goodbyes and I-love-yous.

As the boys play I spend the afternoon checking my laptop for work emails and answering parents, as well as updating Savannah on my dramatic life and checking on her and the staff. She said she had everything under control and to please just take care of the boys and enjoy my break. I also email the school about the after-care program. I explain to them about Eleanor skidding out of the parking lot after hanging around in it and then about last night's mishap with the sign-out sheet and subsequent kidnapping. I suggest considering some kind of patrol and/or security until the last worker leaves. Earlier I had called to let them know the boys would be out the final two days before break, and based on what had happened the principal said that was to be understood. She was very understanding and wished us a happy and quiet break.

About 4 p.m. Josh returned and gave me the complete rundown. He got to the station, met with Officer Marshall and gave his statement. The officer told Josh that according to their on-site counselor Eleanor was dealing with some type of post-traumatic stress disorder. Paperwork would be generated and placed in the system saying as such, along with Josh's statement. In addition, she would always have the kidnapping on her record. Based on that, she was not to come to Los Angeles without Josh's knowledge.

The Culver City Police Department had placed her in the system and their counselor would be conversing with whatever therapist she would be seeing in New Orleans. The nightmare was truly over. Josh said Eleanor's Aunt Irene was there and had asked if she could speak to him if he showed up before she left.

"Did you see her?" I ask.

"Yes, I did. She wanted to shake my hand and apologize on behalf of their family. She always knew I would do a great job taking care of Derek, but back then she had no say over her sister and was told to be quiet. I told her I forgive all of them, but that I never need to see any of them again. I said that Derek needs time to heal and if he should ever ask for his mom again I would find her. So unless that day comes they won't be hearing from me."

"Wow," I said. "All that had to happen before she realized she had made a mistake."

"Exactly," Josh said, shaking his head in the affirmative. "She had to go through all of that trauma and then she realized she missed her son."

He puts his head down before he went on. "I can't believe I got sucked in. And I can't believe you didn't walk away for real. I put you through a lot, Alicia. Guess I've got a lot of making up to do."

I link my arm in his and say, "You certainly do, Coach. You certainly do." Then we just hung out watching TV with his arm around me being completely silent. We were together, but alone with our thoughts. The boys interrupted us for dinner and afterwards asked if Derek could sleep over. Of course we said yes, knowing it might keep the incident off of their minds.

The Saturday Easter Egg Hunt was really nice. Jill had outdone herself with the decorations with the assistance of Sharon. The word had definitely spread about the kidnapping and the moms kept stopping me to chat and tell me how frightening it must have been, or that the after-school program always needed some kind of security check.

Jessica gave me a huge hug. "You know you were already someone I looked up too, but now you're my idol." I told her that Josh had been the hero, but she said the way I held it altogether was what she admired about me.

"I just don't know if I could be here today all calm and collected," she said. I thanked her and told her I had my moments. And to think I thought she was pushing up on Josh when she truly wanted a friend.

The boys had fun laughing and giggling with the girls and boys of the Center and even hunted for eggs. At the end of the day I gave all my girls their Easter flowers.

"Alicia Parsons, in the midst of this storm I know you did not stop to make us arrangements," Sharon said, fussing at me. "Sharon, I had already made them, my dear. Just delivering today." And I reached over and hugged her.

"Oh, all right then. I was about to let you have it, missy," she said, linking arms with me.

"I could see that," I replied, smiling.

On Sunday, Josh picked us up for church. He told me Eleanor's Aunt Irene had called him while he was getting ready. She wanted to let him know they had returned to New Orleans and Eleanor was going into a facility to get the help she needed. I was happy to hear it. Happy to be with Josh, happy to be with the boys, just happy about life.

Church was great and I truly praised the Lord with a grateful heart. It was super crowded since it was Easter Sunday but it was good to be there in the midst of the congregation. Sharon's grandkids would be in town so she was really excited. We went to brunch in Marina del Rey at the Marriott and she told me all about her plans for the week. She was working half the week and would be off Thursday and Friday. After lunch we gave her and Antonio goodbye hugs and then the boys hugged us, too. I laughed about this and said, "Thanks for the hugs, guys, but you're going with us."

Derek, with a huge grin said, "Nope. We're not."

I'm puzzled. "What are you guys talking about?"

"Yeah, Mom, we're going with Auntie Sharon and Uncle Tony," Chris says. "You're going with Coach."

I look at all of them. I see Josh is trying to keep from laughing and so is Sharon.

"Antonio, what's going on here? I can see these two must be up to something?"

He shakes his head yes. "Alicia, they got you again. The boys are coming to our house the rest of the evening. You and Josh have some unfinished plans to attend to."

Now I'm smiling at the sneaky duo.

"Really, guys? What are we doing?" I ask.

"Mom, just go along for the ride and stop trying to figure things out," Chris says patting me on the back. This made everyone laugh.

"Fine. Then let's get outta here, Coach," I say grabbing his hand.

Sharon laughs and says, "Guess she likes our plan, Josh."

"Looks like it," he says, holding my hand. "Guess we'll see you guys this evening then."

We say goodbye and after getting in the car, he says, "Not a word. This is my Valentine's make-up date."

I reach over and kiss him sweetly.

"Got it. Not one word."

We drive away and he heads to the movies. There we take in two movies at the new dine-in AMC theaters. We laugh and eat popcorn at the comedy and I snuggle with him at the romantic flick I talked him into seeing. Holding hands on the way to the car I thank him for the great afternoon and I tell him I'm thrilled to have some one-on-one time with him.

He heads north on Lincoln and I look over at him while he's driving.

"We're going somewhere else?" I ask, elated that we have more time together.

"Yes, one more stop," he says.

The sun has almost set and he heads up Venice toward the ocean and I start to get excited.

He tells me I look beautiful today and I return the compliment to which he smiles and kisses my hand. We continued to the Santa Monica Pier making small talk and re-capping the fun of the day. I confess that they really got me, and I was elated about it.

We park and walk up the pier. It is really busy and crowded so we make our way down to the sand. I carry my sandals in my hand, flip-flops Chris snuck out of my closet and had given to Josh that morning. It was right after the sun had set and the sky was a dark blue with just a hint of dark gold streaks way out over the ocean.

"It's so beautiful," I say, stopping him by pulling him closer to me with our clasped hands.

"So are you," he whispers into my ear leaving a kiss there which tickles me and makes me smile.

"Thank you, Josh, not just for the compliment," and I turn to face him and put my arms around his neck, "but for today, for right now. I love you. Didn't think I would ever let go again but you made me a believer."

I'm looking in his eyes and he smiles. So handsome, beautiful smile, great teeth which I noticed when I first met him, and he stares back. We sway to some music in our heads.

He backs away a bit, still looking intently at me.

"Alicia Parsons, you are, without a doubt, the best thing that has happened to me in a long time. I had closed my heart off to love or relationships because I felt I owed my son all of my time. But you, you make me and my son happy."

I feel happy all over.

"I do plan," he goes on, "to marry you someday in the not-too-distant future so I hope you feel the same. Thank you for waiting me out these last few months."

I beam, taking it all in.

"I want to be with you only and I plan on making you as happy as you have made me since I first laid eyes on you." Then I hug him again really tight. I release him a bit to look back in his eyes again.

"I promise to be with you only, too. I wasn't sure I trusted men or trusted love or even myself, but I do love you, Mr. Hart." And then we kiss for real. Hands in hair, needing a room but knowing we're not gonna get one. It was an old school Hollywood kiss with the cued music, the fade-out scene and then the credits rolling.

I don't know exactly how the rest of my life will go, but I'm loving this moment and looking forward to what lies ahead with Josh Hart and our boys.

About the Author

Stephanie Price Buchanan is an author of short stories, poems and songs. Since childhood, she has pursued an interest in writing. Her love of storytelling has found its culmination in her first book, Getting to the Hart of It. Buchanan currently lives in California with her husband and three children